OVER THE YAZOO

EARL N. M. GOODING

ISBN-13: 978-1717367532

ISBN-10: 1717367534

ACKNOWLEDGEMENTS

Warm Winds over the Yazoo was written several years ago. Finally it is in print, and for this, a few special people deserve my gratitude. My wife Lela typed the hand-written manuscript and later Elaine Pope (now deceased) put the typescript on a computer. Lela and Elaine's enthusiasm for the narrative was gratifying and helped keep the work from total neglect while other issues dominated my "front page." More recently, Jean Hall Dwyer extended considerable editorial and organizational effort to prepare the book for publication, while Lela read it at various stages and did the final editing. Shalanda Edwards-White of SEW Multimedia Design Services did the graphics for the cover and saw the book through the final steps to printing and circulation.

TABLE OF CONTENTS

FOREWORD

The end of the decade (circa 1866-1876) officially called Reconstruction in the United States of America was the beginning, in the South, of a period almost a century long in which segregation and racial hatred perpetuated the worst evils of slavery. *Warm Winds Over the Yazoo* is a historical novel set in the early years of this dark period. The primary story thread unfolds unhurriedly, beginning in a white community and moving to a segregated community where blacks and whites co-exist quietly in conditions that they consider much safer and pleasanter than other areas of Mississippi. But the peace is ephemeral; as the work progresses, even major characters are dwarfed by the massive forces that engulf them.

Beyond the plot that traces events in human lives, *Warm Winds* is a saga of early post-Reconstruction South. The author's careful research has resulted in a work that presents verifiable historical and social issues, and his education in the behavioral sciences is evident in sound psychological commentary and social criticism. Prejudice, suspicion, and distrust exist among people of the same ethnic background as well as between different races, while affection, respect, and generosity surface among and between all sorts of people. As he airs racial tensions, the author gives people on both sides of the fence opportunities to defend their positions, tenable and untenable. Moral and ethical issues that play out in the novel are timeless and universal: hostility generated by cultural and geographical differences; conflict between personal conviction and the need to observe society's mores; the dangerous line between ingenuity and deception in the silent resistance to unfair laws; lies told to avert violence, bloodshed, and heart-crushing anguish; political manipulation and deception; the creation of the pack; ignorance that plays into the hands of greed and injustice; a corrupt criminal justice system.

Vivid details of topography and geography, along with routes and landmarks, create a countryside that quickly becomes familiar to the reader. Nature serves also as a source of symbolism and analogy: the majestic Yazoo and the evolution of the seasons, the fierce thunderstorm and the tornado that destroys everything in its path, forests of tall pines and fields of maturing cotton, meadows of wild flowers, the clouds, the moon—all carry metaphysical meaning.

The author's interest in people and their stories results in a large number and variety of characters, and in many life stories that while not directly connected to the story thread are vitally connected to the unfolding saga. And the reader gets to the end of the novel with the sense that this is not the end. Once more has been vividly brought to life a slice of American history that reminds us, in the popular words of William Shakespeare that the "past is prologue" . . . "to the swelling act" (*The Tempest* and *Macbeth*).

Lela Gooding, Ph.D.

ONE:

THE BURIAL

They wrapped the stiff, emaciated body in the soiled white cotton sheet on which it had lain in sickness and for the past two days in death. Rolling the body first to one side and then on the other, they enfolded it in the old gray blanket that usually hung over the foot of the wooden bed. With great exertion and clumsy care, they removed the body from the bed to the floor, and partly carrying, partly dragging, got it to the front door of the little cottage. Billy carried the upper part of the body, making supreme effort to keep it from touching the floor. "Be careful. Hold her up," he directed his sister, Sandy, but in spite of their valiant effort they could not keep the blanket from dragging along the floor.

Billy backed the old horse-drawn wagon up against the step of the front porch. The wagon was slightly higher than the porch on which the body now lay, and it was thus with great difficulty and struggle that the two children succeeded in pulling the corpse onto the wagon's floor. Having accomplished this adult task, they seemed for a moment perplexed, not sure what further course to follow. Then, simultaneously, they carefully tucked the blanket around the body, which during the arduous trip from the bedroom only a few yards away, had become partly unwrapped.

Holding the placid old mare by the bridle, Billy led the little funeral train to the place of burial some two hundred feet to the south of the house not more than thirty feet away from a grove of pine trees. In the center of the grove the trees were large, probably forty-five feet high, with smaller ones towards the border of the yard. Between the patch of trees and the barn was a grass-covered area. Part of the morning it lay in the shadow of the pines, and in the evening under the shade of the barn. There in the soft, sandy soil, a shallow grave had already been dug that morning. Using a hoe, a pail, and a small fork the children had picked and scraped away at the sandy surface. With difficulty they had inched their way into the soil, which became more defiant and resistant as they intruded further beneath its surface. Now scraping with the hoe, now digging with the fork, now removing the soil with the pail, now resting, the two children gradually had made a cavity in the ground.

The wagon stopped at the burial site and Billy turned the wagon around so that its back faced the side of the empty grave. Using as much care and strength as they could muster, the children pulled the corpse from the wagon. It struck the ground with a soft thud. "We're hurt'n' her!" Sandy began to cry.

A feeling of profound bewilderment swept over Billy. He too felt like crying, but he remembered the words of his mother. He could still hear her voice: *You are the man of the house, Billy, until your daddy comes back.*

How many times over the past had his mother reminded him of this fact? Billy bit his lips. He looked at his sister in desperation. "Stop crying, you hear me!" he said, partly pleading and partly demanding. "I done told you, Ma's dead, she's gone to heaven." He paused for a moment, looking at his sister. "We's got to bury her the way they buried ol' Grandpa Vanderver when he died. They dug a hole, they put him in it, and they covered it up. That's how they bury dead people and Ma's dead." Billy placed his hands consolingly on the shoulders of his sister who, wiping her tears, was desperately trying to understand the reasoning of her brother. "We can't leave her in the house while she's dead and go to New York to find Pa. We got to bury her first."

They shifted the body so that now it lay parallel to the hole. Billy pondered the task before them. The body would be placed into the grave by using the same method they had used in getting it down from the bed and off the wagon. He would hold the upper part, let Sandy hold the other end and together they would lower the corpse into the hole. It was as he mentally reviewed the mechanism of interment that he realized the grave they had dug was not long enough to accommodate the body. "The hole ain't long enough," he informed his sister. "If we put Ma in the way it is, her foot will stick out after we cover her body up." With these words, Billy took the hoe lying beside the grave, lowered himself into the hole and proceeded to hack away at one end.

"Go pick some flowers while I finish this," he directed his sister.

"I want to stay here with you," she pleaded.

"All right. You can help me with the bucket to clear the dirt from the hole."

The shallow grave needed at least another foot added to its length to accommodate the body. Resting at intervals, with beads of perspiration gathering around his nose and across his forehead, Billy continued to hack away at the sandy soil at one end of the hole. Slowly and painfully the extra length was added and after what appeared to be hours the job was completed. The hole, though an average of three feet deep, was shallower at the two ends so that it appeared to curve from the two ends down towards the center.

Billy explained to his sister how the body would be placed in the grave. She would stand at the foot of the grave, he would stand at the head. Working together they would pull the body over the side and into the hole. The plan worked and the body was lowered, or more accurately, dropped into the hole. As it lay, it was slightly on its side, with the head somewhat lower than the feet.

The children stood looking in silence at the wrapped form within the grave. It seemed almost incredible that the frail figure enfolded in the blanket before them was actually the body of their mother. Yet there she was, as Billy had explained to his sister, "Gone home to heaven." What seemed so puzzling to the mind of Sandy was the path her mother had taken to heaven.

"Why do we have to cover her up in the ground, when heaven is in the sky where the clouds is?"

"I don't reckon I know," Billy responded. "But that's how people go to heaven. Remember that's how old Grandpa Vanderver went to heaven? After he died, they buried him in the ground." While still finding the logic of her brother incomprehensible, the girl accepted the explanation and sighed.

Billy recalled that flowers had been placed on Grandpa Vanderver's grave and that several weeks later, the dry flowers were still there. "Let's go gather some flowers," he directed his sister. "You pick some by the barn, I'll get some over there." He pointed towards the house. Near the front of the house was a rose bush, a few red buds yet remaining from the spring bloom. These he picked along with some yellow marigolds, a branch of lavender crepe myrtle, and a few wildflowers that blossomed nearby. Having gathered the flowers they laid them on the loose soil piled up beside the grave.

It was now time for the burial ceremony. "Let's kneel and say the Lord's Prayer as Ma taught us," Billy directed. They knelt on the loose earth, and together they repeated the Lord's Prayer. "Our Father which art in heaven, hallow' be thy name, thy kingdom come, thy will be done on earth as in heaven. Give us this day our daily bread, and forgive us our trespasses as we forgive them that trespass 'gainst us. An' lead us not into temptation, but deliver us from evil, for thine is the kingdom and the power and the glory forever and ever. Amen." As they ended the prayer, tears were streaming down the faces of both children. Billy stood up, and brushed the soil from his knees.

"We's got to cover Ma up now," he said. "Help me push the dirt back on the grave." Slowly the earth was pushed into the hole, Billy using the hoe, and Sandy a piece of board. Stones were carefully removed from the loose earth and thrown aside. When all the earth was raked over the body, the tired children rested for a moment in the shade of the pine grove before rounding off the little mound and making a border of stones around it. They then took the flowers and placed them over the grave.

"We's got to pray once more," Billy informed his sister. Sandy started to kneel, but recalling that in the final prayer at Mr. Vanderver's burial, the preacher, along with others at the gravesite, remained standing, Billy explained: "We don't kneel this time. We's got to stand up and bow our heads." He watched his sister as she bowed her head and closed her eyes then he began to pray.

As he prayed, Billy stood, his feet slightly apart, his hands clasped together, his tear reddened eyes open and gazing skywards as into the face of God. His childish, quivering voice was raised to an unusual pitch by the emotions, the frustration, the anxiety, the utter despair of the occasion, and the uncertainty that lay before them. "Oh Lawd," Billy began his prayer, "You done called Ma away to heaven, you done took her away from us. With Pa up in New York, you done left me an' my sister Sandy all alone. We don't have no one here to take care of us now, no relatives, nobody!" There were elements of both complaint and accusation in his voice. Sandy, her head bowed and her eyes closed, was mildly startled by her brother as his voice rose higher. She opened her eyes, looked at Billy, then towards the sky in which direction Billy gazed as he spoke. It was as if she suddenly realized the Billy was being rude to God. She looked part in fear and part in amazement, as she would have done had Billy spoken in this manner to their father, a man who was loving but also of stern discipline.

But Billy's words were more like the puzzled query that a confused child directs to his father. He stood at the foot of the grave gazing steadfastly into the sky. He could imagine the face of God like that of a big father looking down at him, listening sternly, with understanding, yet with some disquiet over the element of defiance in his voice. He hoped that God would understand that it was not defiance, or a desire to be rude; it was simply that he, not by choice of his own, had been placed into a situation over which he had no control, and little experience to deal with. What was being said was more like a conversation between father and son.

"We don't know why you done it," Billy continued his prayer, "but you musta wanted Ma awful bad in heaven to take her way from us like this. What is we goin' to do now? Who will take care of me an' Sandy?" he demanded. Tears brimmed his eyes and flowed down both sides of his face. "What d'ya expect us to do now?"

Billy paused as if waiting for an answer, and in the transient moment of silence, the children could hear the mysterious fitful voices of wind in the pine trees nearby. It blew softly from the southeast, and as it whispered among the needles of the branches, there was a low, plaintive sound, as of a choir weeping in the distance. The grove of trees, their tops like green inverted cones, slowly swayed back and forth in the wind. On the chimney of the little cottage, a lonely mockingbird, whose nest lay in the pine grove, was singing a long, melancholy dirge. To the east and south, low hills enshrouded in a bluish haze looked on in stiff silence, and above, within the infinite dome, white, fleecy clouds piled high like massive heaps of cotton stood almost motionless against the hazy blue.

There was no response to Billy's question, at least not in a form that the children could understand. Yet, the closing words of the child's prayer reflected conciliation. "We don't know why You done this to us, but before Ma died she told me and Sandy that You always have a reason for what You done. Me an' my sister want to be with Ma again, so we's goin' try to be good so we can go to heaven where she is."

Having completed his prayer, Billy took his sister by the hand. "Let's go now. We's got to get to New York so we can find Pa." With the other hand he held the rein of the horse as they walked back to the house. On the porch they stood and looked back at the grave. Billy shifted his eyes from the grave to his sister, then to the silent house. His heart pounded rapidly as a nimbus of uncertainty swept over him. "If only Pa was here," he thought. "If only there was some older person to tell us what to do now. But there ain't none in Rocky Bottom." He remembered his mother saying, "We got no friends here in Rocky Bottom. They don't like us because I come from up north, I'm a Yankee. We got to live by ourselves and be independent. Them few people from Rocky Bottom we used to be friendly with are all gone, so we only have ourselves to rely on now."

"It's goin' to be all right once we find Pa," Billy assured Sandy as they walked into the house. "Let's pack some things to take with us, some clothes and some food to eat along the way." Billy pulled the dusty leather suitcase from under the bed and placed in it a few pieces of clothing for himself and Sandy. From the kitchen shelf he took two jars of homemade jam which he placed in a pillowcase along with a few apples from the tree at the side of the house, the last remaining loaf of bread that his mother had baked more than a week before, a small jar of homemade butter, and a knife.

It was now time to leave. Billy closed all the windows of the house, making sure the latch of each was secure. Then calmly turning to

Sandy he said, "Let's go and find Pa." When he reached the door, Billy paused and surveyed the house. There was the quiet bedroom in which his mother had died, there was the parlor, the kitchen with the oak table around which he and Sandy had dined so often, and there was the crude fireplace. Above the fireplace was a photograph of the family taken some two years earlier, at a fair in Bolton. The picture showed Sandy seated on her mother's lap, and Billy standing by his father. Walking over to the fireplace, Billy took the picture and placed it in the suitcase. "No use taking anything else," he assured his sister. "Once we find Pa we'll be back." They walked out the front door onto the porch. Billy was about to close the door when he paused and re-entered the house, to return in seconds with a pillow and a blanket. Now closing the door he took a large stone from near the step and placed it in front of the door. He would have preferred to lock the door, but neither he nor Sandy had been able to find the key. Carefully placing the suitcase and other items into the back of the wagon, the two children climbed onto the wagon seat. Billy took the reins, and Sandy sat at his side.

"Come on," Billy said, "let's go." The mare, long accustomed to responding to commands from the young voice, raised her head, still chewing on a mouthful of grass, unmindful of the drama evolving about her. The muscles of her shoulders tensed as she pressed her body forward and slowly the wheels of the wagon began to turn, moving across the grass-encumbered yard up towards the path leading to the narrow dirt road. As they turned onto the path, the two children looked back. For a fleeting moment they caught glimpse of the grave where their mother lay. Last to be hidden from their vision was the house, then all was lost behind the trees. Now, only the open path of uncertainty lay before them.

TWO:
A PLACE CALLED ROCKY BOTTOM

It was a strange fate that had brought Billy, a child of seven, and his 6-year-old sister to this moment of tragedy and utter bewilderment. At so tender an age, when they needed most the strength and confidence of adult care, they were all alone. Yet it was the tenderness of youth that kept from them the realization of the depth of the tragedy they faced, not only in the loss of their mother, but in the simple belief that by traveling north, they would somehow arrive in New York and find their father.

To the truly superstitious mind, the tragedy that befell the McBrides could well be seen as fulfillment of the prophecy made years earlier by the children's grandmother whose daughter now lay dead and buried in a shallow, unmarked grave outside Rocky Bottom, Mississippi. Years earlier in the spring of 1874, Rebecca, the children's mother, then a girl of eighteen years, had written to her mother in Massachusetts informing her that she was about to marry a Southerner, Billy McBride. The year before, the girl had run away from home or, more accurately, walked away in an effort to escape the severe and rigid Calvinism of her father. A preacher of many years, Reverend Charles Williams was determined to raise his family as a Christian model for the small New England community which he pastored. Of the four children, Rebecca was the third to leave home to escape the iron discipline of the old man. Only the elder sister, Esther, had remained unmarried, and apparently totally committed to the religious ideals of their father. For Rebecca, her home was a prison. The last whipping she had received at the hand of her father was just before she left home at the age of seventeen. The Reverend was determined to succeed with Rebecca, his youngest child, where he had failed with the other two.

With a friend also seeking to escape the rigid life of the small town, Rebecca had traveled to New York City where she found employment in a restaurant and where she met and fell in love with Billy McBride.

The mother's response to Rebecca's letter informing her that she was about to marry Billy McBride, a young man from Mississippi, was immediate and scathing. It embodied a stern denunciation which Rebecca thought more reflected the judgment of her father. She was informed that when she left home without her father's permission her future was placed within her own hands. "You brought shame and disgrace to your father and turned your back upon the dictates of God, that 'children should obey their parents in the Lord.' As far as your father is concerned, you are on your own. Marry whomever you wish"— her mother's warning was ominous—"but mark my words, it will come to naught. You will have to pay for the shame you brought upon your father. Marry if you want, even to a heathen from the South; it will have no blessings in the eyes of the Almighty."

Rebecca's father, Charles Williams, could trace his lineage back to the Mayflower. Among his forebears were teachers, preachers of three generations, and one member of the Massachusetts Assembly. Williams had hoped that his son would follow in his footsteps and his daughters would, by marriage, maintain the lofty traditions of the family. But such was not to be. Paul, his only son, named after the apostle of Jesus, had chosen in the words of his father "to follow Beelzebub rather than Christ," and was somewhere in California, though no one knew for sure whether he was dead or alive. Ruth, now married, lived in Rhode Island with her husband, who though showing great promise as a businessman, had fallen into bad times. Only Esther had remained faithful, though far from fulfilling the great ideals of Reverend Williams.

The background of Billy McBride was one of complete contrast. He had spent much of his early life in the small towns and rural places of Georgia and Mississippi. Billy's father was the single son of Charles McBride, who was the only son of Charles McBride, Senior, to grow to adulthood. The old man had been dumped onto the shores of North America, along with several other Irish prisoners taken from British jails. After seven years he had obtained his freedom from servitude in Georgia on a farm outside Macon, and married a wife who bore him three sons. Two died from malaria; only Charles, the frailest of the three, survived. Charles married a wife of Mississippi heritage; she bore him a single son whom they called Billy. But these were hard times in the South. During the Civil War Charles joined the Confederate Army and marched under the rebel flag behind General Lee. After fighting in the battles of Fredericksburg and Chancellorville, Charles was wounded and died a few weeks later without seeing his wife and son. Billy was only eighteen months old when his father went to war; thus much of what he knew of his father came from stories told to him as a child by his mother Isabella. After Charles' death, Isabella took Billy to Mississippi to live with her parents, for she had no means of support. It was well that she moved to Mississippi, for less than a month later, Sherman's army, like a massive tornado, swept across Georgia, leaving death and destruction in its path. Among the towns completely destroyed was the one which Isabella had just left.

For five years Billy lived with his mother and grandparents on a small farm outside the town of Wescott, Mississippi. Then during the winter of the sixth year, tragedy struck: both grandparents died within the space of two months. The grandparents owned two pieces of property, the one near Wescott where Billy then lived, and a small farm of twenty acres in southwest Mississippi in a place called Rocky Bottom. In the grandfather's will, the piece of property in Rocky Bottom was left to Isabella. For two years Billy and his mother Isabella lived with her sister Miriam in Wescott. Then, seeking a life of her own, Isabella visited her property in Rocky Bottom.

It was love at first sight. The land was poor, sandy soil with an unusual amount of rocks. But it was beautiful, covered by pine, spruce, redbud, a few oaks, and sassafras trees. A creek with crystal clear water flowed at the back of the land. There was a well and a barn and an old house which, though now empty, had recently been rented. Isabella knew she could make it by planting her own food and selling eggs in the town of Bolton not far away.

The neighbors showed great cordiality, happy to have a new addition to their small isolated community, and promised to aid her in cleaning up the place. They cleaned and scrubbed the old house, replaced the broken door of the barn and repaired the outhouse. Isabella was overwhelmed by the friendliness of the people, and the open arms with which they had greeted her. "It's a mighty big step for a woman and boy to take alone," they told her, "but if you want to live here in Rocky Bottom, we all goin' to help you get started. The land ain't rich, but if you can grow 'nough food to feed yourself, with a cow and some chickens you can make it."

Isabella returned to her sister's place, and with a few dollars she had saved from sewing clothes for a store in town and the few articles she possessed, moved with her young son to Rocky Bottom. Yes, she planned to grow vegetables and chickens, but she also hoped to be able to sew articles of clothing for sale in Rocky Bottom and the nearby town of Bolton as she had done in Wescott.

Isabella cast from her mind any thought of a second marriage. She would live for her son Billy and with the memory of Charles, whom she had dearly loved.

In Rocky Bottom Isabella turned strongly to religion. She spent much time reading the Bible, she attended the old Baptist church four miles up the valley where all the saints from Rocky Bottom gathered on Sundays, and helped the sick in the valley through the use of fomentations and other methods. Thus Billy grew up in Rocky Bottom alone with his mother. Her love for the land, the trees, and the natural things of the valley she transmitted to her son. Thus they lived in close harmony, and were soon fully integrated into the local community.

Exactly ten years and one month from the day Billy McBride and his mother came to Rocky Bottom, Isabella died and was buried behind the church across the valley. Billy stayed on and worked the land for another year but at the age of nineteen, a spirit of restlessness came over him. He had never left Mississippi since his mother brought him from Georgia as a child, and he had seen Rocky Bottom change over the years. Many of the families residing there when Billy arrived had moved from the valley. Of the twenty families that had inhabited the Bottom, only seven now remained, scattered across the valley.

Billy decided to go and take a look at the world. He gave his dog away to a neighbor, sold the chickens, the five cows, and the furniture and left the valley, assuring his neighbors that he would return one day. Driven by the desire to explore the land which his neighbors in the Bottom viewed as "enemy territory," Billy crossed the Mason-Dixon line, and traveling by train arrived in New York City. He was fortunate to get a job at the waterfront within two days of his arrival, and a place to sleep in a cheap boarding house. But within weeks of his arrival in New York, Billy began to long for the place in Rocky Bottom, Mississippi that had been his home. Scenes from the Bottom would flash before his mind, the hole in the creek where he had fished and played as a boy, the pleasant little house. Billy promised himself to return one day to the Bottom and settle down and raise a family.

In the month of May winds blowing from the south across the Hudson excited a spirit of expectation and renewal. Billy McBride and Rebecca Williams were married. They lived in New York another year, then with the few dollars they had saved, clothing and other domestic artifacts they boarded the train for the long journey to Rocky Bottom, Mississippi. Neither of them had been truly enamored with the city and now they were married and looking forward to raising a family, both were equally anxious to leave the city for a quiet rural home.

⌢ ⌢ ⌢

It was towards the end of July when they arrived at Rocky Bottom. They had traveled by train up to the town of Bolton fifteen miles away. There they had purchased a horse and an old wagon into which they had loaded their belongings and thus traveled to the Bottom. The heat wave which had parched much of Mississippi during June and early July had lifted two weeks earlier, and was succeeded by heavy rains, leaving the valley in lush green. A string of tornadoes had passed over the area bringing damage to farms across the Delta, but Rocky Bottom had remained unscathed. In the more than two years of Billy's absence, much of the farm including the yard around the house had grown into bush. The Bentons, who lived a half mile up the road, had kept an eye on the place and had left a few cows on the land "to keep the grass down," but this effort was only a partial success. The house showed little deterioration from disuse; the most serious challenge of the moment was removing wasps' nests from under the eaves of the roof and the porch.

Rebecca immediately fell in love with the place. It was just as Billy had described it. The peace and quiet was overwhelming. The house with three rooms was not as spacious or comfortable as her Massachusetts home, but it was livable, it was their own place, and with some repair could be made into a lovely home. They climbed from the wagon and stood looking at the place in silence, Rebecca's hand clasped in her husband's. As they contemplated their new home, a sweet peace seeped into Rebecca's soul. She squeezed Billy's hand. "It's as if far back, somewhere in my childhood, I saw this place," she whispered. "This will be our home, we will raise our family here." They embraced and kissed tenderly.

In spite of the preponderance of rocks and limestone and the effete nature of the soil, conditions which had reduced its inhabitants from twenty to seven families, Rocky Bottom had many pleasant features and a personal charm of its own. It was almost completely surrounded by hills. Beyond it lay the plains of the Mississippi Delta. The Bottom had its own peculiar eco-system, with shrubs and flowers that Bottomites claimed, though it was never authenticated or exposed to scientific verification, existed in no other part of Mississippi. The creek and fishing holes of the valley were said to be the home of the most succulent catfish to be found anywhere in the Southland. Its hills, called mountains by the local folk, seemed to literally pull the clouds from the sky, so that in the spring and even during the heat of the summer, white clouds like massive doves would nest upon the hills in the evening, enfolding the valley under their wings. Rare was the night when Rocky Bottom was not enshawled in mist, and as the first rays of sun pierced through to the Bottom in the morning, the mist would retreat as to some secret hiding place. This was the place that Billy and Rebecca McBride had chosen for their home.

By the time the contents of the wagon were unloaded and deposited in the house, the sun had moved well towards the west. The young couple explored the area, looked into the barn, and appraised the outhouse, joking lightly about it. Billy commented on the repairs he would make to accommodate the children they planned to have. He wondered how many of the families he had left in Rocky bottom two years earlier were still around. About two hours before sunset, Billy and his bride set off on foot for the home of Leroy and Cora Benton some half a mile away. They would have ridden the wagon, but so pleasant was the evening, the couple decided to walk.

The Bentons were home. Billy could see them in the garden as he turned onto the path leading down to the farmhouse. Leroy Benton looked up from his work, attracted by the barking of their dog, Jereby. Jereby was barking fiercely, yet ambivalently wagging his tail, tempered by a vague recognition of at least one of the persons walking into the yard. "Shut up your noise, Jereby, you old flea bag," Leroy called as he saw the couple coming down the path. Leroy paused from his hoeing in the vegetable patch, leaning the hoe against a nearby fence on which grew pole beans. When he recognized Billy he called to his wife who was at the chicken house on the other side of the yard. "Cora! Billy McBride's here." Wiping his hands on the backside of his pants he walked towards the approaching couple, a smile breaking over his leathery face. "Well!" he said. "It's Billy McBride sure nuf. I don't believe my eyes." He shook his head laughingly.

Billy was delighted to see his old neighbors, a childless couple who had been close to him and his mother in times past. As Cora Benton emerged from the opposite side of the yard Billy called to her, "Hi there, Mrs. Benton. I told ya'll I'd be back!"

Cora Benton had broad pleasant features, a square matronly look, and dark brown hair that fell on both sides of her face. "You sure did. You sure did, Billy. You sure did," she answered Billy's greetings. There was a broad smile on her ruddy face as she wiped her hands on the dirty apron tied about her waist. As she spoke she drew nearer to Leroy, who now stood at the side of the front porch studying the approaching couple. Cora had responded to Billy's remarks but it was on Rebecca that her eyes were fixed. As she smiled, she exposed her brown teeth stained by tobacco which she and Leroy regularly chewed.

"It's sure nice to see you back in Rocky Bottom, Billy boy." Leroy had broken a piece of twig as he left the garden to greet Billy and he now chewed on it as he spoke. "Jus' the other day, me and the missus was sayin' we wonder whar is Billy, how he's doin' and if he's comin' back." He looked over at Cora, as if for verification.

"Yes," interjected Cora. "We sure bin wonderin' 'bout you. Just last week it was." As she spoke to Billy, Cora, with a cautious smile on her face, was scrutinizing the woman next to him from head to toe. Leroy was just as curious about the girl standing beside Billy. As he talked to Billy his eyes would dart over to her, and as if not desirous of being caught looking at her, he would immediately shift his gaze back to Billy.

Billy placed his hands on Rebecca's shoulders, slightly urging her forward as he spoke. "This here is my wife, Rebecca."

Rebecca, who had perceived the cautious behavior of the couple, extended the smile already on her face. "It's a real pleasure to meet you all. Billy has told me so much about you wonderful people of Rocky Bottom."

The change of expression on the faces of the Bentons was instantaneous. The words coming from Rebecca's lips were like the first shots of the Civil War all over again—a crisp, clear, northern, Massachusetts, Yankee accent. Leroy stopped in the mid motion of a chew on the twig he had in his mouth, and Cora, who was still holding on to the lower part of her apron, let it drop. As if in search of security from some impending danger, she edged nearer to her husband.

The welcoming smiles on both faces were replaced by an incredulous look of uncertainty. "Well, what d'ya know," Leroy exclaimed, allowing a shallow smile to flicker on the right side of his face. He took the twig from his mouth with two fingers, dropped it to the ground, and looked at it as it fell. "Honey, you hear that?" He looked at Cora.

She responded as if cued by years of acting together, "I sho did! Ain't it strange—he jus' a little boy the other day." She was still looking at Rebecca, a discernible frown on her forehead, now appearing, now disappearing. "Congratulations to ya both."

"Well, I'll be! Are ya both fixin' t' stay in the Bottom?" Leroy asked.

"Yes," Billy replied, smiling broadly, though somewhat discomforted by the change he had perceived in the expressions of the Bentons. "Ever since I left the place, I have been looking forward to this day. My wife loves it already. It is so peaceful as compared with where we just come from."

"Oh, yes," Rebecca added, "I never thought there was any place in the South so beautiful."

As Rebecca spoke, Leroy and his wife were staring at her in amazement. "I don't b'lieve my ears," Leroy was thinking to himself. "A Yankee woman done come to live in Rocky Bottom!" The Bentons had never before heard the voice of a Yankee woman; nevertheless, they had recognized it from all the descriptions of Northerners they had heard over the years. "Dem folk up the creek will sure be plumb happy to know you is back, Billy Boy. Yes, sirree! Few people come into these parts, and them is usually passin' through. But as I said, them what is left in Rocky Bottom gonna be real pleased to know that you is back."

"An' that you brung a missus from up North," Cora added, nodding in agreement with her husband.

"The McMillans is still on their place," Leroy informed him.

"Yeah," Cora added, "Bogg and Maggie McMillan and their girl Billie Jean. They sho' nuf is gonna be glad to know that you is back with y'r new bride. The Wilsons, the Wrights, the Vandervers, all is still in the Bottom. Seven of us families, now yours gonna make the eight'. I reckon by tomorrow noon they all will know you is back to stay. Come to think 'bout it, Billie Jean's folks was askin' fer you less than a month ago. 'Wonder what become of Billy,' they said." Cora looked at her husband for verification.

"Yeah," he agreed, partly closing his right eye. "It was Billie Jean's birthday, they was all talking 'bout old times and teasing Billie."

Billy observed that the sun was rapidly falling. It had already dipped behind the trees, casting long shadows across the yard. He wished the Bentons a good evening, saying once again how happy he was to be back. "So long," he said, "We'll be seeing you."

"Sure, Billy, sure," the couple waved back.

The Bentons stood and watched the newcomers as they walked across the yard and headed toward the Rocky Bottom road. Not a word was spoken for several seconds as the Bentons stood gazing at the point where Billy and Rebecca had just vanished behind the trees. It was Leroy who broke the silence. "Well, I'll be a cotton pickin' nigger," he murmured. Cora looked at him and back at the spot on the path where the couple had just disappeared. "Well, what d'ya know," he said, shaking his head in disbelief. "I kin hardly b'lieve it."

Cora was still silent, but a malicious smirk was gathering on her face. Her eyes were still on the path, as exciting thoughts flowed through her simple mind. "Imagine what Billie Jean, Bogg, an' Maggie gonna say when they hears that Billy Boy done took hisself a wife, an' a Yankee woman at dat!" She laughed. It was a sort of fiendish giggle, which she tried to suppress. Suddenly the spell seemed to be broken. It must have been Cora's fiendish laugh that did it.

Leroy spat on the ground beside him—a dark brown salivary substance, which landed at the base of the post of the porch where it was aimed. "Well I'll be a green-eyed monkey," he said, looking towards the direction where the couple had disappeared. "Dat boy done sold us down the river. After all we done fer him here in Rocky Bottom. Done gone up North"—as he spoke his voice was rising in indignation—"an' marry a no-good Yankee woman."

Cora still gazed at the spot on the path where the couple was last seen. It was as if they had just witnessed a case of sinning against God, and it was only a matter of moments before lightning or some other natural phenomenon would consume the guilty. "Billy Boy," Cora murmured, "What you done, ther ain't no forgiving fer it."

"The only worser thing you could'a done," Leroy added, ferociously slashing the air beside him with his hand, as if it held a knife, "was marrying a Jew or a nigger." Leroy, holding his wife by the arm as if to protect her from some perceived danger, entered their home, closing the door behind them.

Billy and Rebecca walked quickly along a path already shaded by the lengthening shadows of the evening. As soon as they left the Bentons' farm Billy assured his wife that the response she had observed from the people who were to be their neighbors was a typical response of folks from the Bottom to strangers. "Once they become accustomed to you, they are usually very friendly and open," he assured her. "They usually don't take to strangers readily, but once you are accepted you become one of them."

Billy was trying to convince not only Rebecca but himself, that all would be well. Rebecca responded that her people who too were from a small town took rather cautiously to strangers. So she clearly understood. But whether the people of Rocky Bottom took to her or not, it would make little difference. All she cared for was Billy's love and attention.

For a while they walked in deep silence. They could hear their own footsteps on the dark stony sod. Along the primitive road, lavender, pink, and white phlox bloomed, pipe worms raised their soft heads, and wild petunias and black-eyed Susans with their dark purple blooms blushed in silent tolerance as honey bees stole their pollen. A lonely dove called plaintively from the evening shade somewhere in the pines nearby. Its call was answered by another across a small creek partly hidden by dense foliage. A startled squirrel dashed across their path and scurried up the trunk of an old oak tree, angrily chattering from the hidden side of the trunk.

Billy saw and heard it all, although abstractedly absorbed in reviewing what had transpired at the Bentons' place. After all, he should have expected that marrying a Northerner—a Yankee—would not be taken lightly by so conservative a group as the inhabitants of Rocky Bottom. Every family along the Bottom, as far as Billy could recall, had some reason to dislike Northerners. After all, even he, Billy, had lost his father to a northern shell during the Civil War. Everyone he had known in the valley had some story, some legend or myth, of a relative killed or maimed by Sherman and his troops, or some battlefront tale of Northern atrocity, either real or imagined but so often retold that it had come to be part of a broad reality. Now he could understand the significance of Cora's mention of Billie Jean. After all, before he left Rocky Bottom, folks in the Bottom including the Bentons had been pressing him to marry Billie Jean. The girl was still single, and here was he, with a northern woman as wife. Now he understood the cynicism of the Bentons in their expression of how happy the people in the valley would be to know of his return and marriage.

⌃ ⌃ ⌃

Leroy and Cora Benton had retreated into their house reeling from the shock of meeting Billy and his Northern wife. They closed the door behind them as they continued their expressions of horror and predictions of how the community would respond to the bad news. Beyond all this there was a feeling of excitement that had suddenly entered their otherwise humdrum and boring lives. Excitement about what had just transpired, the information which they had acquired, and which, as it would be recorded in the annals of the Bottom, they alone would be responsible for passing on to others. There was a feeling of importance, a feeling of self worth, that fate had bestowed upon them this part to play. This was added to the anticipation of the horror, disgust, and anger that would emerge and would set the tone for valley talk for months to come, through the winter and perhaps into the next year.

Cora could scarcely contain herself as she pondered how her neighbors the McMillans would react on learning that Billy, who might have married their daughter Billie Jean, had married a Yankee instead. "Poor Billie Jean. Dat child done waited two years secretly hoping that Billy would come back and marry her, and now he return sho nuf but with a Yankee woman. I can jus' amagin' how dat po' chile heart gonna break when she hear what Billy done. I reckon," Cora thought aloud, "this valley goin' be talkin' 'bout this still come next spring. I kin hardly wait till tomorra" she looked at Leroy with a devious smile, "to tell that poor girl an' Bogg an' Maggie what Billy done."

Leroy walked towards the door; partly opening it he spat outside and closed it again. He began pacing back and forth across the room in the center of which stood the dining table with utensils left over from the earlier meal. He moved over to the window that was half opened, and glanced outside. "Till tomorra? Till tomorra? This can't wait till tomorra!"

"Same thing I bin thinkin'." Cora's response was quick and eager.

There was a spontaneous rush of action. Leroy hastened outside to the horse which was tied near the barn. By the time he had hitched it to the wagon, Cora, a shawl over her shoulders, was waiting to climb on.

Urging the horse they raced over the bumpy road, covering in a few minutes the half mile which stood between them and their neighbors the McMillans. "It's gonna be dark soon," Leroy said as they raced along. Cora remained silent, accepting the discomfort of the rugged ride, unpadded by the cotton cushions which lay in the wagon but had been ignored in the haste.

When Leroy and Cora Benton pulled into the McMillans' place, the horse was breathing heavily and frothing at the mouth. Bogg and Maggie were seated on the front step of their small farmhouse; Billie Jean sat in the swing attached to the roof of the porch by two chains. As the wagon pulled into the yard, they all rose. In fact, they had heard the wagon before it turned into their yard, and could tell that whoever was driving it was in a hurry. It was coming from the south, so it was most likely the Bentons. As the wagon came to a halt, the McMillans could tell by the sober expressions on the faces of Leroy and his wife that they carried urgent news. Leroy climbed down from the wagon and greeted the McMillans as he moved to help Cora alight. "Hi ya'll." But he was unsmiling and did not look at his neighbors, instead showing an exaggerated solicitude towards Cora, an unusual phenomenon which told the McMillans in no uncertain terms that something was amiss. "Somebody musta died," they thought.

Bogg walked up to his neighbors, his wife Maggie standing in the background with Billie Jean. "What's up, Leroy?" he inquired.

Before Leroy could open his mouth to reply, Cora blurted out, "It's Billy McBride." Her voice was low as if intending to keep the message it bore from the two women standing not far away, yet loud enough to assure that they heard what was said. They heard and came forward quickly.

"Billy! What happen' to him, he ain't dead, is he?" Maggie asked anxiously.

"No, he ain't dead, but it sho nuf better if he bin dead and buried 'side Isabella McBride—God bless her soul—after what he done gone an' done," Leroy responded.

Bogg, not particularly a quick speaker, was parting his lips to ask what the boy had done. "But what—"

Cora, anticipating the question, blurted, "That no good rascal done gone an' married a Yankee woman." She paused momentarily for the news to sink in. She looked curiously at Billie Jean to audit her response. "He ain't only hitched to a Yankee—a right purty one at that—

but he brung her here to Rocky Bottom, as bold as a nigger." Leroy was trying to add certain information but Cora would have none of that. "He brung her over to our place and says they's come here to stay in the Bottom."

There was a brief moment of silence, Maggie sympathetically looking at her daughter and Cora taking it all in. "Fancy Billy McBride doin' a thing like that," Leroy lumbered. "As me an' Cora said," he added, "it's just as if he'd gone and married a Jew or a nigger."

Billie Jean, who had stood uncomfortably in the gaze of Cora, threw back her head, and her large hazel eyes flashed as she responded, "Fer as I is concerned, Billy McBride can marry who he want. He ain't beholden to me or nobody I knows. Could a married someone other than a Yankee, but it ain't my concern."

The Bentons had tried to create as ominous an air of disaster as possible. But Billie Jean had not swooned nor given any overt expression of pain or agony suffered by the news. Rather she displayed an air of haughty indifference.

There was an element of disappointment shared by the Bentons as they rode back to their farm. The response of the McMillans, especially Billie Jean, had not been as dramatic as anticipated. "That chile tried to hide her feelin's but you can tell she is burning up inside." Leroy did not reply. His mind was absorbed in reviewing the occurrences of the evening.

By lunchtime the next day, when the sun stood slightly to the south overhead, every family in the Bottom was talking about Billy McBride. The Vandervers who lived not far from the church at the other end of the Bottom, never close friends of the McMillans, were not particularly concerned that the boy had not come back for Billie Jean; rather it was his Northern wife that bothered them. "It's a pity Billy went an' done a thing like that," old man Vanderver commented.

^ ^ ^

For a young woman nurtured in the New England climate, Rebecca proved to be amazingly adaptive to rural life in the South. She spent the first few days in the Bottom cleaning, sweeping, removing cobwebs, and tried her hand with a hammer and nails to stabilize loose boards on the floor. There was apparently a leak in the roof of the house, for watermarks had stained an area on the floor, rotting away the wood. This was replaced by Billy and the area on the roof with the leak was sealed. By the end of the first week the house had taken on the appearance of a small but lovely home.

Though it was now August and late summer, Billy turned over the soil beside the house and planted a vegetable garden. Apple and peach trees planted by Billy and his mother years earlier were in full fruit. Billy showed Rebecca how to can peaches and wild cherries that grew in exuberance in the area. There was a romantic innocence in the excitement and happiness displayed by Rebecca in her new home. Never once did the possibility of suffering, of pain or agony, of challenging human problems come to her mind during these early days in Rocky Bottom. Billy was amazed by all of this, but if there were troublesome questions in his mind, he did not reveal them to his wife.

Yet Billy was concerned at the possibility of having to live in a friendless community. It was this concern that caused him one day to tell his wife that if ever she desired to leave, if ever she lost her love for the place, he would gladly move to wherever she preferred to live. He was amazed that Rebecca shared some of his concern. "So what if the people around here do not want to be friendly to us?" she asked. "We have our own life to live. As much as we would welcome neighborliness, our happiness should not depend on it. This is our place, and so long as we have each other's love we can make it here."

Days gave way to weeks in the month of August. None of the people from the Bottom visited the McBrides. It was as though no one else lived in the Bottom save Billy and Rebecca. Billy for his part had discreetly decided to lie low, rather than possibly exposing his bride to further embarrassment by trying to force himself on the community.

On the third Sunday evening in August, just after a mild shower, Charles Vanderver rode on his speckled brown horse into the McBrides' yard. Rebecca saw the stranger coming towards the house and called to Billy, whom she followed onto the porch. Vanderver dismounted and exchanged greetings with the couple. He was pleasant but formal. He apologized for not having come before. He thought Billy himself would have called or attended church, but since Billy had not and since he Vanderver was passing on his way to Bolton, he had dropped in to say "hello."

Billy related to Charles his experience at the Bentons' place and the conclusions he had drawn there from. "Perhaps its good you acted like you did—I mean not going to see nobody," Vanderver replied. "You reckon correctly, Billy. They is all saying you shouldn't a brung back a Yankee," he paused, "a Northern wife. No offense, ma'am." He looked over at Rebecca, touching the tip of an imaginary hat on his head. "You's got to realize that there is still in these parts mighty hard feelings 'gainst Northerners. Most people including my family lost somebody in the war. I don't even like to talk 'bout what dem soldiers of Sherman done to my uncle's farm in Georgia." Billy was about to respond, but Charles continued to speak. "I wouldn't tell you no lie, Billy, me and the missus was not happy when we heard what you done. My boy Sam don't care one way or another, and Elizabeth and Jillian are both married and livin' in Jacksonville.

"I ain't saying we are happy," he glanced in deference at Rebecca, allowing for the first time a brief smile to escape his face, "but we is all white people, we is all Christian people, and sooner or later we all got to work together as part of the same nation. So I come to welcome you and your wife to Rocky Bottom. Whenever ya'll want to come visitin' ya'll is welcome to do so. When we're finished with the fall work, me, Sam and the wife will come over."

Billy thanked Vanderver for his kindness, expressing an understanding of the position he had presented. Rebecca also responded. She pointed out to the man that she was no more responsible for being a Northerner than he was for being a Southerner. Her feeling towards people from the South was just as positive as to people from the North—in fact she had married a man, not because of where he was from but because she loved him. By the time the conversation ended they were all laughing. Vanderver waved goodbye as his horse cantered out of the yard on to the dirt road leading to the town of Bolton.

⌒ ⌒ ⌒

Much of the fall was spent cleaning up the farm. By the time the winds began to blow for increasingly long periods from the North, ushering in the months of winter, the house and barn had been repaired. Billy had been good with his hands even as a boy. Living alone with his mother, the responsibility of being the only male in the house had forced him to be a jack-of-all-trades. Now he built a bench for the porch, and with white paint purchased in Bolton he and Rebecca gave the house its first painting. He rebuilt the outhouse, adding a new seat and a door with a bolt inside. Water for the house had to be brought from a spring some two hundred yards behind the house, but Billy determined in himself to dig a well a few feet away from the house come spring.

Before returning to Rocky Bottom with his bride, Billy had made meticulous plans as to how he would survive economically on the farm. They would build up a small herd of cattle, raise chickens, grow their own food, and with money from the sale of the cows and chickens they would be able to purchase clothes and other necessities.

In September Billy purchased two milking cows from a farmer on the road from Bolton. He also bought some hens that were already producing eggs. By the time the cold weather arrived, the McBrides were well settled in to the routine of their farm. November was a pleasant month; the wind varied its direction, now from the north, now from the south or northwest, each bringing to the valley its peculiar tone of warmth or chill. There were a few frosty nights in December, but these were mild when compared with what Rebecca was accustomed to in New York or Massachusetts at that time of the year.

The change in the weather was matched by a visible change among some families in the valley towards Billy and his wife. During the mild winter with its decreased demand of outdoor chores, Charles Vanderver kept his word that he and his family would come to visit; and as word of Billy and Rebecca's industriousness spread, the Knights and Cummings followed suit. Their visits were reciprocated and neighborly relationships ensued. In the Bottom, a typical early spring set in, with promise of another pleasant year in the Bottom.

One early March morning, while the wind still slumbered and the trees stood placid, silent, motionless, heavy with the morning dew which clung to the leaves and needles like myriad of crystal diamonds, Billy milked the cows and hurriedly returned to the house, leaving his damp, dark-green footprints marking his path to and from the barn. A heavy mist which all night long had engulfed the quiet valley hung low over the land, like a white cotton shawl enfolding the delicate shoulders of dawn. On the side of the farmhouse and across the yard, spring flowers smiled in the early morn. Yellow dew-encumbered daffodils and wild crocuses clustered in delicate patches of white, lavender, and pink bloomed here and there across the yard. All night long there had been activities in the house, Mary Vanderver and Anita Cummings were there, and Billy had kept a vigil with them. Occasionally he would rush to the bedroom drawn by the painful cries of Rebecca, only to be assured by the women that everything was "all right."

Recharged by a cup of black coffee, Billy sat, red-eyed and disheveled, on the porch on the cedar bench which he had made, and vacantly watched the coming of the day. He sat with his two hands pressed between his thighs as much to keep them steady as to keep them warm. Off to the right over the creek in the bottom of the valley and along the side of the hill, the mist was beginning to rise and scatter like a flock of silent geese whose nesting place had been disturbed by some unwelcome intruder. The mist moved in silent streams upward along the hillside and across the vale.

Suddenly, the first golden ray of the morning sun broke through the mist, but it was soon gone only to return in greater splendor, covering sections of the valley in its warmth, and causing the dewdrops to sparkle. And just as Billy became aware of the beauty of the moment, the stillness of the dawn was broken by a sudden startled cry; it was the cry of a newborn baby.

The child was named Billy after his father. Just over one year later, early the following summer, Rebecca gave birth to a second child, a girl whom they named Sandy. With the two children, the small world of the McBrides was complete.

In a short period of time Billy evolved from a young man with a wanderlust to a husband and father. Rebecca who had left her own home to escape the heavy hand of her father, herself settled down as a devoted wife and mother, reflecting in her own relationship with and training of her children, elements of the discipline and piety she had received from her father. Within five years of Billy's return to Rocky Bottom, the young couple were well on the way towards achieving the model of development they had set for themselves. Life was not sumptuous, nor was money overflowing, but life was happy. The two children became the center of joy for the family. Among their neighbors, only the McMillans and the Bentons remained in cold hostility. Never had Rebecca been happier in her life than she was now. With her family, life seemed complete and rewarding. The herd of cows grew to fifteen, and the number of chickens to thirty-nine. The McBrides also acquired a horse and a mule. Billy sold the young bulls, keeping them for one year before dispensing with them so that they could grow to good market size. Twice a year, in the fall and again in the spring, a buyer from Bolton, ten miles away, would come down into the Bottom and negotiate purchase of cattle.

As the children grew, Billy sought to expose them to some of the experiences which he as a child had had in Rocky Bottom, exploring the mysteries and wonder of the creek, fishing at the same waterholes he had frequented as a boy, and playing some of the same games which his mother had taught him. He would walk with the children into the woods and let them sit and listen to the silence then describe for him what they had heard. He taught them to listen to the excited sounds of the water playing over the stone pebbles in the creek. This he called "the talking of the creek." When they heard the murmur of the wind among the trees, Billy described it to his children as "the wind talking to the leaves." In the night under the pale silver moon, Billy would sit with his children on the step of the front porch and experience with them the enchanting fragrance of the honeysuckle across the yard. In the vegetable garden young Billy at the age of three was planting his own little patch, with Sandy watching closely and trying to do likewise. When the children planted corn only to dig up the seeds a few days later to see if they were growing, Billy patiently took the opportunity to teach them valuable lessons of nature and life.

As the children grew older, they were given more serious chores—collecting eggs, picking peas and beans in the garden—many of which were done with the care and delight of children at play. By the age of five, young Billy already had an air of maturity beyond his years. He asked a thousand questions about the world around him, each of which his parents tried to answer with patience and to the best of their knowledge. Billy followed his father to the field, observing his every action and lending a hand whenever he was permitted. By the age of six and a half years, Billy was well versed in the secrets of farm life. He knew where things were to be planted and how, why furrows in the field ran along the slope rather than towards the creek, and the names of shrubs, trees, and edible plants.

Rebecca played the dominant part in the formal education and the religious training of the children. She read to them from the Bible and told them moral stories she had heard as a child from her parents. She taught the children about God and Jesus his Son, who had come to save people from sin but was put to death, and arose and went to heaven. The children learned that when a person died, if he had been good during life he went to heaven, but if he had been bad he went to live with the devil.

When Grandpa Vanderver, the father of Charles, died at the age of ninety, young Billy and Sandy attended the funeral, where they heard the preacher declare that the old man had gone "to the arms of Jesus." They saw how he was placed in a box, into a hole that was covered up, and how flowers were placed on the grave in the churchyard. When old Eva Knight died, they once again observed the same process of interment with the assurances both from the preacher and their mother that the old lady had "gone to heaven." Mother Knight, as the Bottomites called her, rather than being buried in the churchyard was laid to rest in a family grave plot behind the farmhouse where the Knight family lived. One lesson the children clearly learned from these two experiences, was that the dead were really asleep—God had "called them to heaven." Thus while the children observed relatives and friends of the deceased grieving at the graveside, they were assured it was like saying goodbye to someone going away on a long journey.

⌒⌒⌒

The depletion of the population of Rocky Bottom which had begun several years earlier neither was halted nor reversed by the coming of the McBrides. Several factors had influenced the outflow of population. The land though beautiful was not conducive to farming as on the delta, due to the poor quality and effete character of the soil. The church had been through the years the main center for social and other activities in the Bottom, but with the passing of time and as the population dwindled it had lost much of its earlier zeal. Now the pastor often found himself preaching to six or seven persons on Sundays. Also ministering to a larger congregation in Bolton, he now came to preach in the Bottom only twice each month, and sometimes in winter, the church remained closed for weeks at a time.. The youth who once filled the Sunday School had grown to adulthood and moved to points of greater excitement in Jackson, Meridian and other cities of the state, leaving only a few older folks in the valley. Soon after the McBrides arrived, Billie Jean McMillan moved to Jackson, and, it was rumored, was living with a man out of wedlock. This unfortunate development the McMillans blamed on Billy McBride.

The old folk of Rocky Bottom faced the choice of living and dying alone or moving closer to their children. Several families had moved away during Billy's growing-up years, and the exodus continued even while he and his family sought to put down secure roots in the valley. The Knights were the first to move. The son had married after serving a few years in the army and had moved to Nashville, Tennessee. The daughter, facing the option of being an old maid in Rocky Bottom, moved to Tennessee where her brother lived. The parents growing old soon left the valley to live with their son on a farm which he had purchased between Nashville and Madison. The Cummings were the next to leave. After their three children left home, things seemed to go from bad to worse. The old man Henry Cummings was experiencing more severe problems with his health. He would catch a cold in the early spring and it would stay with him well into the middle of summer. He tried a variety of medicines and local cures to control an asthmatic condition to no avail, while his ability to work constantly decreased so that now he could work in the field only a few hours daily, and even this was a discomfort. At the urging of his children he and his wife moved to Jacksonville where two of their married daughters lived.

⌃ ⌃ ⌃

Many farmers in the area including those in Rocky Bottom usually sold what cattle they had for market in the spring. The main buyer was a short, swarthy, red-faced middleman, with stout neck and prominent cheekbones giving him somewhat the appearance of an oriental. In fact, Jack Higgins was a full bred Anglo-Saxon, at least so he claimed, though some folks in the Bottom insisted that he had some Indian on his mother's side. Each spring and again in the fall, Jack would visit the valley and surrounding area, discover who had what for sale, negotiate a purchase, and soon afterwards return to the valley to pay for the cattle and drive his herd to Bolton. Higgins was not only a buyer of cattle, he was his own butcher and operated out of Bolton, though he also provided beef for several other towns.

Billy, taking a few moments from his April chores, sat on the step of the front porch to watch his children at play. They were at the side of the house, chasing butterflies. Some multi-colored, some yellow, the butterflies seemed to enjoy the chase, staying always just beyond the reach of the two children. Smaller whitish-yellow moths fluttered over the vegetable garden, landing occasionally on a leaf to deposit their patches of white eggs, soon to become small green worms and devour the succulent vegetable leaves. A blue jay from its position on a fence post at the edge of the garden made occasional swoops over the ground, returning to its resting place with a yellow moth in its beak. In the air surveying the entire scene, its dark shadow crossing and re-crossing the field, a hawk with almost motionless wings glided back and forth. Billy, intending to do some evening work in the field, was about to rise from where he sat on the porch step when Jack Higgins rode into the yard on his speckled horse. He greeted Billy as he dismounted, tied his horse to a nearby post and sat down on the step beside Billy. He took a red flowered kerchief from his pocket and wiped the sweat from his face and massive neck. "Sure hot for a spring day," he commented.

"Sure is," Billy agreed, "and it came very early this year. If it's this hot in April you can imagine what summer will be like."

Higgins looked at the children playing in the yard. "Lord! How the young'uns growin' up fast. Seems to me they is twice as big as when I seen them last October."

Billy chuckled. "It's something, ain't it? They already making me feel like an old man. I been thinking that I'm going to have to expand the house. The place is just not big enough." He scratched his head thoughtfully. "We can do with another bedroom. I think I'll expand in the back of the house, maybe add two rooms. I reckon as they grow older they will want their own rooms." He looked at the children proudly.

When it came to selling and buying cattle, Higgins was an artist. Over the years he had developed to a fine point the art of negotiation. His modus operandi involved always seeking to pay a price for cattle that would insure for him a minimum financial output and a reasonable profit. Yet no one really considered him stingy. He simply never paid out more than was absolutely necessary. Higgins usually initiated the process of negotiations even before the prospective seller realized the process had begun.

Higgins wiped his face once more to remove the perspiration still effusing from his body and rolling down his shirt collar. "Seems things is getting worse in Mississippi every year," he commented ruefully. "Everybody holding on to whatever money they got. Use' to be a time you couldn't supply Bolton with enough beef. Now lots of people eatin' chicken grown in their own backyard. Farmers all up and down the plain tryin' to sell their cattle, can't get nobody to buy. Why, just this mornin', a farmer up the road 'bout ten miles from here offered me a whole herd of twenty cows. He says to me, 'I'm getting rid of the whole keputle.' It was mighty tempting, the price he was ready to settle fer, but I says to him, 'I only buys from my old customers.'" Higgins looked at Billy out of the corner of his eye. Billy was listening, but observing some ants that were laboring at moving a crumb of bread.

"When times is hard," Higgins continued, "if there is a penny to be made, I make sure it goes to people I knows and done business with befo'. I don't know how farmers can make money when the damn price is down so low. Far as I'm concerned matter not how low the price fall I'm paying the same price I paid last year to my customers, profit or no profit."

Having made his pitch Higgins artfully changed the conversation. He inquired about the health and welfare of Billy's wife "the missus," about conditions in the Bottom, who had left, who had remained. Billy had three cows for sale and Higgins took them all, at the price he had paid the previous year.

As they talked, Billy and Jack Higgins rose from the step where they had been seated. They walked beside the house near the vegetable plot, from where they could look across the land at most of Billy's twenty acres. "It's a sure nice place you got here, Mr. McBride."

"It's beautiful all right, lots of water and beautiful vegetation, but the soil is poor. I use cow manure on these vegetables to get them as they are. A good part of this land is not good for much more than cow grazing." Their attention turned to the house. Billy pointed. "There is where I plan to add the new rooms. They should give us all the extra space we need for the next ten years."

"Or until you enlarge your family," Higgins added with a laugh.

"I can do much of the work, but I'll have to hire someone to help with the technical aspects."

"Everything cost money these days," Higgins said ruefully. "Seems there's so little cash in these parts and so much of it up North way. I was just reading in the papers this morning, they advertising for help in New York and Philadelphia. There's so much money for the makin' up there I fancy in a single winter you can make all the cash you'll need to add to the house."

"New York," Billy said smiling, remembering that it was there a few years earlier he had met Rebecca. Scenes of the city flashed across the screen of his memory, the broad Hudson River, the busy, smelly side streets, Rubenstein's café. "It's a right crazy place, but you're right when you say there's lots of money to be made there."

That night after Higgins left Billy ruminated upon the conversation they had had, especially the comments Higgins had made about the opportunities that a single winter in New York could bring. "Wouldn't this solve a lot of problems?" he thought. He could be up there during the winter, and back in Rocky Bottom in the early spring. He could even buy up North a few beautiful things for the house, things that could not be found in the stores in Bolton or surrounding areas. A bedroom dresser, for example, with a large mirror.

Aside from the house there were some other long-range objectives in Billy's mind. Directly east of his farm were one hundred acres of land that reached all the way down to the creek. Owned by an old man now living in Bolton, it had not been farmed for years, and now it stood mostly in pine. Billy had rented a section of it to graze his cattle, and the old man had promised by word of mouth that Billy could buy the place by making a good down payment and paying the rest over a specified period of time. The suggestion made by Higgins could, if pursued, enable him to work on the house in a short period of time so that he could concentrate on expanding his acreage. These thoughts flowed through Billy's mind, and the more he thought on them, the more they made sense to him.

The next evening, Billy raised the issue with Rebecca, casually, simply to determine her response. "The money part is good," he commented, "and what it would do for us, but I can't see myself being away from the family for a full winter."

When the issue was raised again, it was brought up by Rebecca at the dinner table one evening, after they had eaten and the children had retreated to the yard to play. The idea of Billy being away from home for any length of time was at the least unpleasant because Rebecca felt that she and the children needed him each day. Yet she recognized how many problems could be solved if the sacrifice were made. "It will be like killing several birds with one stone." If such a sacrifice could really enable them to add to the house the needed space, and bring nearer the expansion of their acreage, and if it were possible to get someone, a friend, maybe an older person or a relative to stay with them while Billy would be away for the three months of winter, the farm would be easily manageable. It would be for the long-range good of the family. "After all, what is three months as compared with a total lifetime?" Rebecca philosophized.

The more Billy thought of the matter during the succeeding days, the more the idea seemed attractive to him. Now he found himself thinking regularly about New York. Scenes of past experiences and familiar places passed slowly and vividly before his mind. How nice it would be to stand and look at the old Hudson flow once more, perhaps at the very place where he and Rebecca often stood, or to sit and order a meal at Rubenstein's where he had met Rebecca—to sit on the same seat, and even, perhaps, recognize some old faces! He wondered whether the place had changed any, and as he ruminated a nostalgia rose in his heart.

After church service the following Sunday, Billy discussed the tentative plans he had in mind with Charles Vanderver, now a close family friend whom Billy's children called Uncle Vanderver. "It may be necessary for me to have to go up North this winter. My greatest problem and worry is h aving to leave my family alone. If only it were possible to get someone, a relative or a close friend, who could be close by until I get back."

"Why not ask Millicent," Vanderver suggested. "If she consents I for one would be delighted to be able to help you out." Millicent was Charles' younger sister who lived with her brother's family. She had assisted in raising her brother's three children, and now, still unmarried at the age of fifty-nine, she helped in the house and spent her time writing poetry and working on a manuscript for a novel on the Bottom which for several years she claimed to have been writing.

Millicent loved the idea of "staying close" to Rebecca and the kids during Billy's absence, should he actually go up North as he suggested he was desirous of doing. The close association with Rebecca with all her vitality, and with the children, would be good for her. "It may even stimulate and inspire me to finish that novel I have been working on."

With the tentative explorations completed Billy wrote the company whose address he had got from a newspaper clipping given him by Mr. Higgins. The letter was to Bloom and Bloom Sales Incorporated, a company that peddled a variety of new household products. The reply came four weeks later. It assured him that a job would be awaiting him, and was accompanied by a statement of guarantee that he would be signed on upon his arrival in Manhattan. With the arrival of the letter, plans which formerly had been tentative became concrete and were finalized for his departure.

As the date of departure approached, Billy was plagued by doubts as to whether he was actually embarking upon the right course. Was it right to leave Rebecca and the children alone for three or four months? Was the trip really worth the cost? Did the advantages justify the pain of separation and the insecurity and possible problems that could arise during his absence? These and several other questions troubled his mind. Finally he comforted himself that the four months would pass quicker than he could then imagine.

During the first week of November when the leaves from deciduous trees in the valley had already yellowed and fallen, while the squirrels in the pine trees nearby were yet filling their abode with nuts, when the mockingbird no longer sang from the house roof, and the first deep frost had touched the valley, burning the leaves of the vegetables in the garden, Billy McBride, having taken leave of his family and friends in the valley, boarded the train at the town of Bolton for the trip to New York City. His journey to New York, though undertaken in the sadness of parting from loved ones, was to be a medium through which greater happiness would be brought to himself and family. It was to be a brief interlude of sadness for longer periods of joy.

⌒ ⌒ ⌒

New York had changed little during Billy's absence of six years. A few new buildings had been constructed but by and large the place was the same. The houses, stores, and other buildings, and their scents, mingled with the hubbub of activities along Broadway.

The office of Bloom and Bloom occupied the second floor of an aging building on a side street running off Broadway. Bloom and Bloom was operated by two brothers. It entailed door-to-door selling of selected products, mostly local, but some from abroad. The products— pots, pans, other utensils and household articles—were finding a market among lower socio-economic groups and immigrants in the Boroughs. Billy pitched enthusiastically into the task and from the very first day, notched up an impressive number of sales, a good indicator of what possibilities the winter would hold for him. By the end of the first week Billy McBride had established himself as a seasoned salesman. Beginning in the frost of the early November morning, he worked into the darkness of the late evening, imbued by the sole purpose of his presence in the city.

Bloom and Bloom were delighted by the performance of their only salesman with so Southern an accent. Billy soon had outstripped all the other salesmen by his long hours and enthusiasm. Aside from what he needed for basic necessities and paying rent for the room where he stayed, all the money he made was deposited in a bank, and once each month transferred to the bank of Bolton where he and Rebecca had started an account.

The weeks flew fast. Bloom and Bloom offered Billy a permanent position which he respectfully declined. December gave way to January, and by the end of February, signs of spring appeared tantalizing on the horizon. One more month, Billy thought, and he would go home to his loving wife and children. During the few weeks away from Rocky Bottom, Billy's love for his family, so it seemed to him, had grown a thousand-fold. "Oh how wonderful it will be to be back home again," the thought constantly replayed itself. "Only a few more weeks, with the money I have saved, I will be able to transform our little house, and bring happiness to Rebecca, little Billy and Sandy. Never again will I leave them for such a long period of time," Billy promised himself. "I don't know how I could have done it in the first place. If I had to face the decision again, I could never tear myself away."

As the days of March passed in rapid succession, Billy's yearning for his wife and children increased. Even as he had seen scenes of New York on the screen of his mind when first he had thought of the plan, so now visions of the place and loved ones he had left behind, flashed daily on his mind, tearing at his heart.

The fourth week of the month of March, Billy McBride had before him only a few days before he would board the train for his long journey back to Rocky Bottom. The Hudson was high from the waters of melting snow along its basin, and from the rains brought on by early spring weather. Massive chunks of melting ice were piling up along the banks. During the days the temperatures rose into the fifties, but as evening fell, the cold winds returning from the sea, blowing up along the banks of the mighty river brought to the inhabitants of the city the stark reality that winter though in retreat still ruled over the island.

Since mid-March, social tension had been rising in areas of the city occupied by poorer members of the community. The source of the tension was efforts of workers in a number of factories in the city to form a union for the purpose of negotiating wages and improvement of the inhuman conditions in some of the factories. Management had refused to negotiate or give any recognition to such organizations, choosing rather to dismiss any worker who was found to have signed up for union membership. As tension rose around the industries, the city's government had sent in the police to support the politically powerful owners of the industries. Violence directed against workers by the police triggered rioting in some areas of the city.

On his way to deliver some merchandise ordered earlier during the day Billy McBride crossed Broadway at a point where rowdy workers and their supporters, angry at the brutal attacks they had experienced at the hand of city police, were seeking to force the closure of businesses along the street. Billy was caught in the middle of things when platoons of police approached the crowds from both directions, swinging their clubs as they came. In the fray, Billy, an innocent bystander, was arrested and jailed. Like others arrested, Billy was charged with rioting and brought before the court. In spite of evidence by Mr. Bloom that Billy had not been a participant in the disturbance, the judge, accepting the evidence of the police, ruled that Billy was one who had taken part in a riot "against the good and decent citizens of the City of New York." Billy was given eighteen months in jail. The judge had listened to Billy's testimony under questions from his lawyer with impatience, irritated more by the southern drawl of the defendant than by the facts of the case. In sentencing Billy McBride, the caustic judge commented that most of the trouble of the city was being caused "by foreigners, niggers, and poor white trash from the South."

Rebecca was numb with disbelief when the letter arrived from Billy. Her husband, himself overwhelmed by the sudden turn of events, sought to console his wife. "I wish more than anything else in the world to be with you and the children. I never should have left you all alone in Rocky Bottom." He sought to bring what comfort he could with the assurance that the time would fly quickly. Fortunately, she was not alone with the children. She was to explain the situation to the Vandervers, and hopefully Millicent would remain with her till he returned.

It seemed to Rebecca, for a time, that life had simply ceased. All the joy, the anticipation of her husband's return in a few days, had vanished. Profound despair and depression set in, and for a time threatened to engulf her. She resisted, and by the arrival of the second letter from her husband a few days later, Rebecca settled down to a cold, levelheaded analysis of her situation. Once more Billy sought to encourage her. With luck he could even be released before his time was up. In the meantime, Rebecca's best course of action was to remain in the Bottom, and the money he had sent home should be used to support the family till his return. It would be difficult, he knew, but with God's help they would make it. Should Rebecca not desire to stay in Rocky Bottom until his return, she should take the children to her sister in Rhode Island. She should sell the chickens and leave the cows on the place; they would take care of themselves until he got back. Finally he suggested that Rebecca consult with Charles Vanderver, and see what suggestions he would give.

This Rebecca did, and the suggestions she received from Vanderver were in line with the conclusions at which she had arrived. Her best course of action would be to stay where she was until Billy returned rather than taking herself and her children away from the security of their own place to a situation of uncertainty. She could imagine how her mother and father would respond to the news that her husband was in jail, and that she was seeking shelter at her sister's home. "No," she thought, "the only possible course is to remain here with my children, and pray that Billy will be back as soon as possible." Millicent Vanderver assured Rebecca that she would be glad to stay by until Billy's return. Her stay with them had added joy and new vigor to her life. She had grown to love Rebecca and the children who called her Aunt Millicent.

In the spring Vanderver helped Rebecca prepare the vegetable garden. Rebecca did the planting herself with the aid of young Billy and Millicent. Life settled down to an uneasy period of waiting; letters continued to come from Billy, and Rebecca faithfully responded.

Jack Higgins came in April, on his routine round in quest of cattle. He had known from his last visit during the fall that Billy intended to go to New York for the winter, and expressed deep sorrow upon learning what had befallen the young man. "I know of several southern white folk," he informed Rebecca, "who bin plumb taken advantage of up North by Irish and Jewish police. A friend of mine just returned to Bolton from Chicago. Says up there in some parts of the city they treats you as if you is a nigger, if you got a Southern accent. Is there anything I can do to help?"

Rebecca informed him that she was receiving aid from Vanderver. There were, however, some things that the old man could not be asked to help with due to his age. The roof of the barn had been damaged by the spring rains in March and needed fixing. A number of fence posts needed to be changed in order to keep the cattle in. If any section of the land aside from the vegetable garden was to be planted, with corn for example, it would have to be plowed and with this she would need help.

Mr. Higgins suggested that Rebecca use the help of a colored family who lived some five miles north, outside the valley. Higgins knew the family well. The man was a good and reliable worker, and Higgins was sure that his service could be acquired at not too great a cost. He could make the arrangements, if Rebecca so desired. Rebecca accepted Higgins' offer.

That evening on his return journey to Bolton, Higgins stopped at the small farmhouse where Jim Williams, the black farmer, lived on his few acres. Jim was reluctant to go to Rocky Bottom for any purpose, including the opportunity to make a few extra dollars. Rocky Bottom in times past had developed a nasty name to black people in the county. The notoriety had originated some thirty years earlier, when a number of escaping slaves, heading northward, were caught by their pursuers in the valley and there hanged by a lynch mob. This incident became the basis for myth and legends, which projected Rocky Bottom as the last place on earth where black folk would want to go. Aside from the lynching of the escaping slaves, how much of the other stories of savagery against black people carried out during the past by the people of Rocky Bottom, was truth or fiction, was difficult to determine. What was sure, however, was that among black folk in the area, the name "Rocky Bottom," was notorious and hated. Thus, one could imagine the response of Jim Williams when his white friend of several years suggested that he go down to Rocky Bottom to help out on the McBride place.

"You think I'm out of my mind?" he inquired. "You knows how colored folk think 'bout that place, after what dey done only few years back down there. Ain't no tellin' how many innocent colored folk, who didn't know the history of the place, bin down there and ain't never return."

Jack Higgins assured Williams that whatever was the history of the place it indeed had changed. "Only a few old folk left there, and they won't harm a fly."

"Did you say that there ain't no men folk by this here McBride place?" Williams asked.

"That's right."

"And you seriously "spec' me to go an' work there? Ain't no way. I's got my wife and chillen to think 'bout," Williams said, shaking his head.

"Take my word fer it," Higgins urged him, "there won't be no trouble. I will go down with you myself, to show you that place. It's the first house you meet once you enter the Bottom. The work will only take a couple of days, and you can take your missus with you."

After much coaxing, and the assurance that the McBrides were really "nice folk" in need of help, Williams decided to go, as a "Christian service helpin' someone in need."

Monday morning Higgins came by and together they traveled to the McBride place, taking one of the Williams boys with them. After his successful introduction to the Bottom that day, Williams made a number of trips. He repaired the barn roof, fixed the fence at the back of the property, planted a piece of land, and helped with a number of other tasks that required masculine strength. After the first day, Williams brought his wife with him, explaining to Rebecca McBride that "we always works together, an' stays close together as the Good Book says." This indeed was true. The Williams family was very close and religious. They attended every service at the Primitive Baptist Church in Bolton. But there was another variable motivating Williams to take his wife Melda along. "I'll be sure nuf stupid an' beggin' fo' trouble," he reasoned to himself, "to have people start talkin' that I is on that place alone with two white women. With Melda there, there ain't nothin' nobody can say." Melda would be an insurance "'gainst anybody getting any crazy idea that I am in something down there."

The arrangement worked well. Williams took his two children, Louis and Enoch, with him on occasion. The first time they met Sandy and Billy, the children scrutinized one another from a distance. Soon they were talking and playing together. After several weeks of occasional visits to the McBrides' place, Williams lost some of his apprehension about the valley. "This place sure nuf changed lately," he mused. Having completed the last job for which he was contracted, he informed Mrs. McBride, "If there is anything else need doin', jus send the message to me up the road where I lives." The following spring, Williams returned on call from Rebecca, to perform some of the tasks he had done the year before. These having been accomplished once more he withdrew to his own work, assuring the woman as he had done the previous spring, that he would be available should he be needed on the place.

⌒ ⌒ ⌒

It was in the month of December that Rebecca noticed them. Small painless lumps on the right side of her neck. Her first awareness of their presence was one morning as she combed her hair before the mirror. Just small risings, but she could not recall seeing them before on her otherwise smooth, flawless neck that her husband had often complimented, as something carved by the hands of a skilled sculptor. As weeks passed the lumps grew larger and others appeared on the other side. Rebecca began to be aware of an occasional twinge of pain emanating from the larger lumps. Upon Millicent's advice she paid a visit to the general practitioner in Bolton, Dr. John Bune. Bune had studied medicine in New York and had returned to his native town where his services were critically needed due to the shortage of doctors in the region.

Bune examined closely the lumps on Rebecca's neck, peered into her throat, and diagnosed the mysterious swelling as the *possible* result of a cold caught in the neck--"just as people can catch a cold in the head, chest, or joints of the body, so it is possible in the neck." He gave her a prescription for some pills and some liniment for rubbing on the affected areas.

As the months of spring wore on, Rebecca began to lose weight. She realized it when she saw herself in the mirror, and her clothing no longer fit. In the meantime the swellings on her neck had become more articulate. She refilled the prescriptions from Dr. Bune and continued to apply the specified treatment. With Millicent's advice she also added to the repertoire of treatment hot fomentations on the neck.

One day in the middle of May as Rebecca gathered eggs in the chicken house, a crushing headache descended upon her. It was to be the first of a series of headaches that grew progressively worse. But in spite of her illness, Rebecca took her children to church each Sunday, making the trip in the wagon with Millicent Vanderver.

The nearest neighbors, the Bentons and the McMillans, having selected from the time of Billy's return with Rebecca as his wife years earlier, to maintain a relationship of enmity, gossiped intently about the situation at Billy McBride's place down the valley. One story was that Billy McBride had run out on his family, "left them high and dry" and gone back up North to some woman. Cora Benton had been most vocal in her assault, "There ain't nothin' happen in the Bottom like this as far back as I ken remember, and I growed up in this place. I can see that boy's poor mammy's bones turning in her grave. First he brung that Northern woman here in the Bottom, then run out on she and the chillen, leaving the woman to wither and die."

Leroy hoped that with Billy out of the way, Rebecca and the children would leave and put the place up for sale. "I knowed all along that no good boy won't a stayed here. That boy gets the devil in him. I seen it in his eyes from the time he return. If I was that woman, I'd sell that place and take the chillen up North, where she come from."

"I hear say he'll be a comin' back soon," Mrs. McMillan informed them. "Say he got in some kinda trouble up North or he would a been back already."

"Dat ain't what I heard. I hear say he is workin' up North makin' money to come back and fix up the place."

"Them is all rumor, I tell you," Leroy insisted. "That no good rascal ain't comin' back. He ain't got no decency in him. I ain't a bettin' man, but I'm ready to bet anyone that you won't see hide or hair of him in the Bottom no more."

"You notice how she is dryin' up?" Cora observed. "Just witherin' away. Next to pure skin an' bone. She takin' all this sufferin' real hard, ain't she? It beat me how she ain't left the place as yet. If it was me, I'd be outa there so fast you won't see ma shadow."

There was no meeting of the Bentons and McMillans during this period at which Rebecca's plight was not the center of interest.

⌒ ⌒ ⌒

Charles Vanderver, now sixty-five, had a heart attack during the late spring. It happened on a Sunday while he picked greens from the garden for the Sunday table. The Bentons, never a friend of the

Vandervers, saw the attack as "judgment from God, punishment that came down on him for working on the Lord's Day."

Whatever the cause of the attack, supernatural or mundane, the old man was restricted to bed by Dr. Bune. At the urging of one of his sons, Vanderver and his wife temporarily moved with his son to the town of Meridian. As soon as he recovered, he would return to the Bottom. Millicent kept her eyes on the house while they were gone and a white sharecropper who lived west of Rocky Bottom was employed to care for the few cows left in the field and watch the place during the expected brief period of absence of Vanderver and his wife.

Towards the middle of June, Millicent received a letter from her sister-in-law in Meridian. Charles had taken a turn for the worse. Millicent was alarmed by the information regarding her brother, and immediately departed for Meridian, promising to return to Rocky Bottom as soon as possible.

The month of June crawled on. Billy was to be released at the end of the first week in August. Letters from him had arrived an average of once every two weeks and were always replied to. But not wishing to add to her husband's woes, Rebecca did not inform him of her poor health. She was attacked by daily spells of headaches, which Millicent had earlier diagnosed as migraine associated with the tension she felt due to Billy's absence.

During the past year, young Billy had become an important hand on the farm. Rebecca had said to him on several occasions, "With your Dad away you are the man around here." Billy took this definition of his status seriously. As a boy only seven years old he displayed a remarkable degree of maturity as he helped with the various chores in the home and on the farm, within the confines of his strength. Now with Rebecca struck with headache and dizziness, and Millicent gone to visit her brother in Meridian, Billy's role became even more meaningful. As the tormenting headaches increased, Rebecca spent more of her time in bed, getting up only long enough to prepare food and essentials for the children. She had been reduced almost to half her normal weight.

One morning Rebecca did not leave the bed. She lay there groaning all day, occasionally calling for her husband. "Why don't he hurry up and come?" she asked again and again. The children spent much of their time sitting by Rebecca's bedside, holding her hands to comfort her. Looking at his mother lying in bed, Billy knew that something was seriously wrong. He prayed silently that the days would go swiftly so his father could return, or Millicent come back from Meridian. He had heard Millicent say that his mother's headaches were related to her worry over his father; thus in his childish mind he perceived that his mother would be well again, once his dad returned. This return was to be within a few weeks. Thus he prayed, as he looked at his mother suffer, that the weeks would pass swiftly. That night before Billy and Sandy went to bed, both knelt at the side of their mother's bed and prayed that God would "stop Ma's headaches and bring Pa home again very soon."

Sandy fell asleep beside her mother, but Billy lay awake on the other side for a long time, listening to the restless groaning of his mother. Towards midnight the groaning ceased and Rebecca fell into a deep sleep. Billy heard the sound of his heartbeats on the pillow. He could hear Sandy snoring, and the deep breathing of his mother. For a while he listened to them; then he too fell into a troubled slumber.

Next morning Billy was awakened by the sun. It had climbed over the hills and was sending its warm rays across the valley and through the window onto the bed. As he got out of bed, he could hear a rooster crowing at the back of the house. He looked out the side window and saw the rooster perched on a fence post from whence it issued the challenge to those in the hen house. Billy dressed quickly. He would milk the cow and collect eggs from the chicken house before his mother and Sandy awoke. Outside a clear morning sky greeted him. The wind was blowing from the south, warm and dry.

The horse cropped the grass at the side of the barn, switching his tail back and forth to disperse flies that hovered around. As Billy walked towards the barn he recalled how often he had accompanied his father and mother on this very mission. Now it was his responsibility. The thought made him feel like a man. He had done the milking before. The cow Millie, accustomed to being milked, usually waited patiently at the back of the barn, behind a fenced enclosure.

Billy finished his milking with the bucket less than half full. "That cow is holding back on me," he said, an expression he had heard his father use on occasion. The cow slowly walked from the barn, imperturbably chewing her cud.

As Billy turned toward the house, Sandy was approaching, barefoot and still in her nightdress. "Go back in the house," Billy directed her with a voice of authority. "Put on your dress. You know you ain't suppose' to be out here dat way."

Sandy turned and walked with her brother back to the house. "I tried to wake Ma," she said, "to ask her how she's feelin' but she wouldn't wake up. Her face is very, very cold."

Billy was annoyed with his sister. "Why you done gone and bother her fer. Don't you know Ma ain't well? Leave her alone and let her sleep. She had so much pain last night, she didn't sleep till late."

He was the man of the house. With his mother sick it was his job to keep things moving and in order. "Perhaps," he thought, "Ma will feel better this morning and will be able to get up an' fix breakfast for us." Otherwise he would do it; there was bread their mother had baked a few days before; there were plenty of eggs, butter, and milk.

Billy entered the house, his sister at his side. He placed the pail of milk on the table and tiptoed softly into the bedroom. He looked at his mother. She lay very still, her lips slightly parted, her eyes deep sunken behind closed eyelids. She lay on her back, her face towards the ceiling. Billy moved beside the bed. He looked at his mother closely. He held her hands. Her fingers were cold. Billy placed his hand tenderly on her face. He gently tried to move her head from side to side. "Ma? Ma?" His mother's head resisted his efforts, and when he raised his hands the indentations of his fingers remained on her face. Sandy was standing beside him.

"I told you so, Billy. She real quiet, ain't she?"

"Ma?" Billy called again, leaning his head close to her face. He tried to raise her left hand. It resisted his effort. He tried to open her eyes with his fingers. The eye remained partly open, the lid strangely twisted. Billy gazed at his mother silently for a long moment. "She ain't breathin'," he said. Then he turned and looked at his sister. "Ma's dead."

"Ma's dead?" his sister asked, looking at her mother intently.

"Yes," Billy replied. "Ma is dead, just like Grandpa Vanderver was dead, when they buried him by the church. She's gone to heaven."

It was fortunate that the children were not old enough to comprehend the finality of death, the permanent distance it imposes between loved ones. In their childlike perspective death was viewed more as a silent rest. It was "going to heaven." When someone died it was because God had "called them to Him." Thus they had been taught by their parents and thus believed. As they looked on the body of their mother lying in the stillness of death, the children knew not that never more would they be able to hear her voice, or feel the warmth of her embrace or bask under the reassuring gaze of her eyes. God had called her away and at some gray distant time and place they would see her again. So they believed.

But in spite of such belief, there was an instinctive feeling of bewilderment, of gloom, which soon crept over the children. For they knew not what to do or where to turn. "We is in a pickle an' a fix," Billy informed his sister. All day long they waited. Perhaps Millicent

Vanderver would be back, or Mr. Higgins from Bolton would come by. Much of the day they sat on the front porch waiting. There was none in the valley to whom they could call for help. Billy knew that the McMillans and the Bentons, the only neighbors in the vicinity, were not friends of theirs. He had heard his parents talk about it on more than one occasion, thus the idea of seeking aid from them did not enter his mind.

The following morning Billy awoke his sister and told her calmly, "We're goin' to New York to find Pa."

Sandy rubbed the sleepiness from her eyes and looked across at the body of her mother on the bed. "Are we going to leave Ma here by herself?"

"No," Billy replied. "We can't leave her here. We got to bury her the way they buried Grandpa Cummins. They made a hole in the ground, then they put him in it and they covered it up. That is what we got to do to Ma before we go to New York to find Pa."

"How come Mama is gone to heaven and we got to put her in a hole in the ground and cover her up? Ain't heaven up in the sky?"

"I don't reckon I know, but this is how people go to heaven," Billy answered. "They die, then you bury them, then God take them to heaven. We got to bury Ma, then we'll take the wagon and go to New York and find Pa."

Billy selected a spot for the grave. It was less than one hundred yards from the spot where Rebecca and her husband, on the first day of their arrival in the Bottom some eight years earlier, stood and surveyed the place that was to be their home. It was there that Rebecca, overwhelmed by the exquisite peace, the quiet, the cottage, the beauty, had declared, "This will be our home; we will raise our children here." The pine trees then eight years younger, were part of the landscape of beauty that had reach and touched her heart. Now they would stand as sentinels beside her grave.

The body was interred. The two children with a few articles they considered necessary had embarked upon the journey which they expected would take them to New York and their father.

They headed the horse-drawn wagon east along the dirt road which would lead them out of Rocky Bottom. To their right, intermittently they glimpsed through the trees the hill which rose majestically over the Bottom, a few raw spots of limestone marking its otherwise verdant side. To the left, oak trees interspersed with red bud and dogwood stretched north towards Bolton. A few hundred feet away from their farm the road curved northward and then continued east.

One mile further it would split in two, one going north to Bolton, the other continuing in an eastward direction. Billy intended to lead the mare on to the Bolton road and from there further up north where he knew New York would be.

They had already covered some three-quarters of a mile from the farm, the old mare taking her time in measured paces on the dirt road. The wind had slightly shifted and now blew directly into their faces. It sent chills of expectation through the mare. She restlessly tossed her head and on her own initiative hastened her pace. "Don't you start runnin' now. We got far to go." Billy pulled slightly on the reins, slowing the pace of the wagon. **A** mother skunk led a troop of four, black coats striped white, in single file across the road.

Sandy pressed close to her brother, her mind absorbed with complex thoughts. She knew not how they would get where they were going. But she knew that at the end of the journey her father would be there, and that thought brought a sigh of anticipation.

So absorbed had Billy been in his own thoughts that he did not observe the rider approaching in the distance. It was Sandy who first saw the man as he appeared around a bend in the road. "There's a man a comin'."

Billy focused his gaze and saw the rider approaching. He was dressed in a dark suit, his steed trotting rhythmically, closing the distance between them. Billy looked intently at the rider, narrowing his eyes, but he did not recognize him. "I wonder who he might be?"

"Maybe is Mr. Higgins or the colored man what worked fer us in the Spring," Sandy suggested.

"He ain't colored, and it ain't Mr. Higgins. Is a stranger." The children scrutinized the stranger without fear. It was a rare experience to see a stranger on the Rocky Bottom road. Further up the valley, the road crossed the creek at three places. There were no bridges; thus, the road was at times impassable when it rained in the valley or further up the basin of the creek. Seldom was the road used as a throughway.

As the stranger drew nearer, the children got a better look at him. He wore a dark gray suit and the dark felt hat on his head was slightly drawn forward to shield his eyes from the sun. His long, sunburnt face bore a cold expression, but as he drew near to the children he smiled. When he spoke his voice was reassuring as that of a preacher, and his smile engendered warmth.

"Good day to you, my little ones—lady and gentleman. And where are we off to today?" Billy pulled the reins, bringing the horse to a stop. The stranger had also stopped his steed beside the wagon. The steed eyed the mare as he cantered and capered restlessly.

Billy was about to reply to the stranger, but Sandy spoke first. "Our ma is gone to heaven and left us alone, so we is goin' to New York to find our daddy."

The man widened his usually narrow brown eyes. "Oh! Your Mammy is gone to heaven and you both are off to New York?"

Sandy was about to continue her dispersion of information to the stranger, but Billy looked at her with a scolding frown. "Keep quiet, and let me explain," he commanded. Turning to the stranger he added, "Our mother died yesterday morning and we buried her today. Our Pa is up in New York and we have no one else 'round here, so we on our way to New York to find our father."

"I see!" the stranger said. "You say your mother is dead and buried only today?"

"Yes, sir."

"And where did you bury her?"

"We buried her in our yard. There is some people living up the valley but they ain't no friends of ours, so we had to do it ourselves."

"Did you church her and everything?"

"Yes, sir, we did."

"This is obviously one of those childish, imaginative games that children play," the man thought to himself. His voice was fatherly when he spoke. "I used to play games with my sister. We used to hunt lions and elephants in our backyard, but burying our Mammy!" He lowered his voice and his smile faded. "We never played any game like that."

"We ain't playin', mister, we ain't lyin' either. Our Ma's dead. She was sufferin' from lots of pain for a long time. Then she died. We dug a grave and buried her this mornin'."

"And where did you say you buried her?"

"'Side the barn."

"And where is the barn?"

"Just a ways back up the road on our farm."

The stranger leaned slightly over towards the children. "Take me to the place where you buried your Ma." The tone was of a mild request, but beneath was an element of command. Billy paused for a moment then pulling on the reins turned the placid mare around and headed back towards the farm, the stranger's horse trotting alongside.

"How far did you say it was, children?"

"Just a ways up this road. We'll be there soon." Shortly they came to where a path led down to their farm and the mare without urging turned on to the trail. At the entrance was a piece of board nailed to a post with the name Billy McBride on it. The stranger studied the name carefully as he passed. Soon the yard, the house, and the barn came into view. Sparrows darted in and out from under the eaves. The wagon stopped before the house and Billy jumped off while Sandy climbed down on her own. "Over there is where we buried Ma," Billy pointed to the area near the barn.

From his vantage point on the horse, the man could see the upturned soil and the flowers. The children were already walking towards the gravesite.

"Wait a minute, let us look into the house," the stranger suggested. Billy went to the front door and removed the stone he had placed to keep it closed. The stranger cautiously opened the door. A moldy scent of death greeted his nostrils from the inner silence of the house. The interior of the house was dark save for the light now entering from the door, and a narrow shaft of sunlight piercing through the crevice below a window across the room. The stranger entered the house followed by the two children. To the right in the shadow a fly buzzed.

"Where was your mother when she died," he looked at Billy.

"In the bedroom." He opened the door slowly, and bending forward, looked in. The bed was partly hidden in the darkened shadow of the room. Beside the bed was a dresser, reaching up to the low ceiling. In silence the stranger surveyed the scene, the two children standing close to the door.

"We didn't have no box to bury her in so we wrapped her up in a sheet and a blanket," Billy informed in a soft voice as if unwilling to disturb the silence.

"How did you get her outside?"

"We backed the wagon up to the porch." The stranger looked down on the children in disbelief, yet knowing that they were indeed telling the truth.

As they walked to the gravesite, the stranger questioned them closely and Billy answered with eagerness. The stranger learned how the children's mother had been sick, had earlier been to the doctor in Bolton, how Millicent Vanderver had been with them but had left weeks earlier, how their father had gone to New York over one year ago and had not yet returned. He learned about the McMillans and the Bentons who lived further up the valley but had been their enemies. The children knew of no relatives, except an aunt whom they were told lived somewhere up North, and their mother's folk up in Massachusetts.

The stranger pondered all that he had learned as he surveyed the grave. "How deep is it?"

"About so deep," Billy raised his hands over the ground to estimate the depth of the hole. The man wanted to uncover the grave, but for reasons unknown he decided against it. Taking the hoe which the children had returned to the barn, he scraped more earth on the grave, carefully rounding it off and replacing the flowers. Getting some stones larger than those used by the children he made a border around the grave. In the barn he got two pieces of board which he nailed together as a cross and placed in the earth at the head of the grave. With a pocket knife he carved the name "Rebecca McBride."

With the children following, the stranger walked back towards the house and sat down on the porch. From his pocket he pulled a pouch of tobacco, rolled a cigarette, and lit it. Sitting in silent thought he sucked on the cigarette, drawing in both cheeks. The smoke emerged from his nostrils in a curling bluish stream. It rose slowly towards the ceiling of the porch.

The appearance of this man on Rocky Bottom road had been no accident. He had traveled some sixty miles from the northeast, partly through the state forest and partly through a sparsely settled farm area. He had not been on this particular road before, but he was quite familiar with similar areas of Mississippi and further north in Alabama. In spite of his clean, impeccable appearance, he had actually slept under the stars the previous night. He went by the name of Enoch Drude, and was on his way to the southwestern corner of Mississippi. Some people claimed that the name Drude was an alias. It was said that in the Birmingham area of Alabama he was known as Sam Blair and as the Reverend William Josiah further north in Huntsville. According to the best information available, Drude was supposed to have been the son of a preacher in Ohio. As a teenager he had fallen in with bad company, had participated in debauchery and robbery, and had served a term in Ohio State prison. Having "paid his debt to society," Drude sought a new life in a new environment and had thus moved into the South where he was known in different areas as the preacher, a seller of medicines and aphrodisiacs, and a businessman involved in the selling and buying of sundry merchandise.

After Drude had worked the eastern Mississippi area for a number of months, a sheriff began asking questions about him. Informed by a friend that a telegram had been sent to Birmingham by the sheriff, Drude suddenly got a mysterious "call from the Lord" to leave the area and head west. Thus he was in the process of responding to the call, using back roads when possible, simultaneously plying his trade, when he ran into Billy and Sandy McBride on their way to New York. From his seat on their porch Drude studied the children in amazement and wonder. The story they had told him was incredible, but true. As he looked at them, from somewhere within him an element of pity, like a bubble of air released from the muddy bottom of a creek by some marine life form, floated to the surface of his consciousness.

"These are indeed hard times for Mississippi and the South on a whole," he ruminated. "Wherever I have traveled in Alabama and Mississippi for the past two years, I have seen evidence of suffering among the poor, both white and black alike. I have seen countless cases of fathers deserting their families; I have seen cases of children deserted by both parents. Only last year outside Birmingham, a mother left her seven children one day to go to the market and never returned. Yet I know of others, families who are childless and would do almost anything to have at least one child around the house. The way I see the South, it is every man for himself. Some people make it through politics, some make it by working their fingers off, some have money through inheritance, and some like me make it by cunning. But these children, what do they have? No parents or relatives, alone in a big world, on their way to New York two thousand miles away, in a wagon, in search of a father who perhaps no longer exists or who right now may be living with some other woman."

Drude finished the cigarette he was smoking. He held the stub between his lips using his right thumb and index finger. Taking one last draw on the stub, Drude carefully removed it from his lips, studied it furtively, and flicked it on the grass. Rising from where he had been seated, he addressed the children. "Let's go and find your father." He walked over to the cigarette stub still smoldering and extinguished it by crushing it under his boot.

The children, responding to the piquant remark, scrambled to their feet and climbed on to the wagon. Drude mounted his horse, and now leading, departed from the yard. On the Rocky Bottom road they turned east. When they reached the point where the road forked, they kept the eastern road. Presently Drude stopped and dismounted. He tied his horse to the side of the wagon and climbed on to the crossboard on which the children sat. Taking the rein from Billy, he urged the mare onward. The summer days are long in Mississippi and it was yet a few hours before sunset. Drude let the horse take its time as it pulled the wagon slowly along the winding country dirt road.

As they drove along together Drude formally introduced himself to the children. "My name is Enoch Drude," he informed them, "but I would like you to call me Uncle Enoch."

Drude stopped the wagon for a few minutes to tighten a strap that was loose under the belly of the horse. "Have you ever been along this road?" he inquired, pointing east as they proceeded on the journey..

"No, sir."

"Uncle Enoch," the man said, smiling.

"No, Uncle Enoch," Billy replied, "we've been on the road to Bolton many times, but not on this road. Pa used to say that it doesn't go anywhere."

"It does," he assured them. "It can take you to New York or anywhere else you may want to go. Do you know anyone in Bolton?"

"We know Mr. Higgins, he buys cattle from us; there is the man in the bank that my Pa knows, and the man in the shop where we buy things in Bolton."

"We will travel until tomorrow on this road, then we will head North," Drude informed them.

The children were more relaxed now. It was as if an enormous load had been lifted from their youthful shoulders. Here at last was an adult, one who had assumed the responsibility of getting them to their father. Presently their minds drifted from the harrowing experiences of the past two days, to the anticipation that not too long hence, they would be safely with their father again.

⌒ ⌒ ⌒

Billy and Sandy traveled with the man they had been invited to address as "Uncle Enoch" late into the evening, along the road leading east out of Rocky Bottom. About ten miles out of the Bottom the road entered a forest reserve—a stretch of land some twenty miles long—mostly pines and oak trees bordered by swampland. The place was known to be infested with copperheads and water moccasins. The day was by now in its final stage of decline. The sun had fallen behind the trees and gray shadows of evening quietly emerged from the forest to envelop the road. As the dusk deepened, the travelers crossed a creek which ran toward the road. White lilies bloomed along the edges of the waters. On the other side of the creek was a clearing among the trees and to the far side of the clearing a log cabin. Drude was aware of the existence of this cabin for he had slept there the previous night. He guided the wagon off the road on to the clearing and came to a stop in front of the cabin. "We'll stay here for the night and move on early in the morning," he informed the children.

Descending from the wagon, Drude tried the cabin door. A large padlock held it firmly—the way he had left it that morning. He unsaddled his steed, placing the saddle on the porch of the cabin. He then unhitched the wagon and tied each horse to a tree where it could feed on the grass in the clearing. Drude lit a fire beside the cabin, and using the small pot he drew from his equipage and water from the creek nearby, he made a pot of tea for himself and the children. This they drank and ate bread, homemade butter, and jelly. Each child was allotted an apple.

By the time they finished eating, darkness had deepened to the point where the road was but a gray ribbon. Drude made a bed for the children on the wagon—"It is safer for you to sleep here," he informed them. "There's a lot of snakes in these here parts." For himself he selected the porch of the cabin where he had slept the night before. He rolled a cigarette and smoked it in the growing darkness. The two children lay close together in the wagon, their minds filled with the events of the day, and the hope that the morrow would see them closer to their father.

Voices of the forest rose on every hand, as a carol to the deepening shadows. The song of the cicada in the trees beyond the clearing joined with other creatures of the forest to fill the air with mystic music. The croaking of frogs along the stream, their voices indicating the course of the water through the forest, added to the chorus. Then, as if by some imperious command, silence pervaded the forest. Silence, save the small creek which continued its incessant murmur as its waters eddied and danced among the stones in the creek bed. And onto the stage of the night climbed an almost full silver moon whose beams floated down and bathed the faces of the children as they slept. Finishing his cigarette, for several minutes Drude observed the moon in its heavenly course. Then he fell into a light sleep. Several times during the night he awoke and surveyed the darkness, before falling again into slumber.

The following morning the children were awakened by the sun. Drude was already up and had started a fire, and prepared a simple breakfast, identical to the meal they had eaten the night before. After breakfast he hitched the horse to the wagon, saddled his steed and seated himself beside the children. Patches of morning glory, their white and purple flowers glistening with the morning dew, greeted the travelers as they continued their journey. They emerged from the forest reserve into an area of sparse population, marked by an occasional path leading off the road to a small farmhouse. Occasionally they would see the outline of a house among the trees, and hear the voices of children or the barking of dogs.

After noon, as the sun tilted westward, Drude guided the wagon off the road down a path leading into a farmyard. In a clearing at the end of the path stood a small, unpainted farmhouse, about the size of the children's home in Rocky Bottom. Drude greeted the man and woman who emerged from the house in a friendly manner. It was clear that they had met each other before.

"Imagine seein' you here," the man James Appleby commented. "I reckoned by now you'd be far aways from these parts."

"It's the work of the Lawd," Drude assured him, as he climbed from the wagon. "He moves in mysterious ways, as the Good Book says."

Drude had visited the Appleby place on two occasions before, and it was his former communication with them and his knowledge of the area which had brought him back to the region. James and Annie Appleby were a childless couple. They had tried unsuccessfully, on one occasion, to adopt a boy. The twelve-year-old boy, according to the assessment of one of the few neighbors who attended the same rural church as the Applebys, "had devil's blood in him." Not only was he the embodiment of laziness, but rowdy, irascible, with a vocabulary of choice expletives. After being with the Applebys for a few weeks, the boy ran away, taking with him Appleby's gold pocket watch and the contents of their moneybox.

This experience had not dampened but rather increased the desire of the couple to adopt a son, and his previous contact with them Drude was aware of this desire. He introduced the children to the couple as his niece and nephew. As the children waited outside by the wagon, Drude having entered the house informed the couple that his brother had died and left the children to his care. The mother had also recently died and he could no longer care for them due to the nature of his work: "Having to do so much traveling. So I said to myself," he told them, "I said, 'Who could be more capable of carin' for these children as their very own, but God fearin' folk like James and Annie Appleby?"

Drude's face was serious and somber, as one experiencing inward pain. "Little children like Billy and Sandy need love and care. I can give them love but I can't care for them since I'm on the road all the time. I have traveled all the way back here to bring them to you, 'cause I know how much you want to have children in your home."

The farmer and his wife looked at Drude with incredulity. "You mean you is askin' us to take them there two chillen as our very own?"

"It's either I give them to you or to another family in Rocky Bottom, who wanted the two children so much they offered to give me $500. But I said to myself, I said, No, I can't do that. My brother would want his children to be brung up in a Christian home like that of Mr. and Mrs. Appleby."

They called the children in for lunch which Mrs. Appleby had prepared. They had buttered potatoes, greens, with some fried chicken that had been left over from the previous day. As the children ate, Appleby and his wife scrutinized them carefully, asking them questions which the children respectfully answered. "This is sure nuf an answer to prayer," Mrs. Appleby thought. The children ate and went back outside to wait by the wagon

"I'll say they is right respectful and well brung up."

"My brother and his wife were God fearing people," Drude assured them. Drude now turned to a skillful presentation of his case. Since the death of his brother and wife, the children had been cared for by a farmer who had charged $250 for the service. This Drude had to pay before retrieving the children. The money offered him by the couple in Rocky Bottom would have paid the bill, with an extra $250 but he had paid the farmer with the last of his own savings, leaving him completely broke. If only it were possible for James and his wife to let him have $250 it would solve his problem. It was not a matter of paying for the children, for he, Drude, would not accept under any circumstances payment for his brother's offspring. It was simply a matter of paying the family who had taken care of the children since his brother's death.

James eyed Drude carefully. For years he had wanted to adopt a boy who would be able to help on the farm and Billy seemed just the right age for training, but they had never planned to have two children. He turned to Drude. "Me and the missus talk fer years 'bout adoptin' a boy who could grow up on the farm and maybe one day even own it. That boy out there seems just right, but I don't see how we can manage with two chillen." He looked at his wife. "What do ya think, Anna?" Anna agreed with her husband.

James had a suggestion. "Why not let us sign fer the boy, and give the girl to dem folk in Rocky Bottom?"

Drude appeared mortally grieved by the suggestion. "Part them two children? Tear a brother from the side of his sister?" he asked piously. "I couldn't live with myself if I done a thing like that. Whoever get my brother's children, I want to know that whenever I think 'bout them I can rest happy that they is together." Looking upward and holding his hands together as if in prayer, Drude continued, "After all the sorrow them children done experienced, it would be downright criminal for me to separate them."

James and his wife rose and went to the window from which they could see the children. He was particularly interested in the boy. "He looks like a tough one," he thought to himself. "How old did you say the boy is?"

"Seven years going on eight."

James wanted to talk with the children. Followed by his wife and Drude, he went outside to where the children stood by the wagon. "You is mighty quiet, ain't you, son?" James inquired, an air of kindness in his voice.

"Yes, sir," Billy said, smiling, "My dad is a farmer."

"You said is?"

Drude interrupted, "These two chillen have had a real terrible experience as you know. I ain't 'gainst them none for not wanting to do too much talking now." Putting his hands on James' shoulder, Drude led the delegation back into the house. Once inside, the question of the $250 became the center of discussion.

Sandy was closely observing the mare as it gleaned the verdure from the moist earth at the side of the farmhouse. Billy had walked away from the wagon and sat at the side of the front porch almost below the open window. From where he sat, he could hear every word of the conversation taking place inside the house.

"We really wants the boy," James was saying. "We really didn't want the girl, but if we's got to take her to have the boy, maybe we can try it out fer a while and see what happen. What do you think, Anna?"

"Is all right with me. It don't take much more to feed one mouth than two, and what's more, it would be kinda cruel as Mr. Drude says to separate them. But I don't see how we can raise the $250 to give you for them."

Drude's voice was low but persuasive. "Ah, come on, Mrs. Appleby, $250 and you have two children as your own! I'm sure y'all got more money than that hidden round the house."

A chill of fear ran through Billy as he realized that he and Sandy were the ones being bargained for by Drude and the couple. That man who had asked them to call him Uncle Enoch, was negotiating their sale. He sprang from the porch, numb with fear, as he suddenly realized the danger in which he and Sandy were. Billy ran over to where his sister stood at the side of the wagon. "Get on the wagon. Quick! Quick!" He pushed her towards the side of the wagon.

"Why must I get in? What's wrong?"

"Just do as I say," he insisted.

"What's wrong?" she asked again.

"Shh! Don't raise your voice. Get on!" Billy helped her on to the wagon, glancing fearfully over his shoulder in the direction of the house. He held the bridle close to the mouth of the horse, and led it out of the yard towards the road, keeping it on the grass to cushion the noise of the wheels.

"Where are we goin', Billy?"

"Keep quiet, I said. Don't say nothin' or we'll be in trouble." By now the wagon had climbed onto the road, and was hidden from the house by the trees. Billy led the horse a bit further from the house. Then running to the side he climbed on to the wagon, and took the bridle in his hands. "Come on, Maggie." The mare increased her pace.

"Come on, girl, come on now, quick." He tugged at the bridle. The obedient mare began to trot, then broke into a full run. The road swerved to the left and right, and left again. By now they were a full half-mile from the farm. Billy knew that Drude would come after them once he discovered their departure. He was mortified by the thought of meeting the man who had deceived them after acquiring their trust.

Looking frantically on both sides of the road, he found a spot where the trees parted. Here he guided the wagon off the road. He took the wagon about two hundred feet behind the trees, where it was totally hidden from view of the road. Jumping from the wagon he ran back over the path it had crossed from the road. He saw no telltale marks. Quickly returning Billy helped his sister to the ground. As they raced over the road, Sandy had kept up a barrage of questions to her brother. "Why are we running from Uncle Enoch? He said he is taking us to New York to Pa. Billy, where're we goin'?"

Only now behind the safety of the trees did Billy respond. "He ain't no uncle. He ain't even no friend. He was fixin' to sell you an' me to them farmers for two hundred and fifty dollars."

"Sell us?"

"Yea, just like they used to sell niggers. He was goin' to sell us as slaves to them people."

"But Uncle Enoch is a good man," Sandy insisted. "He said he is takin' us to Pa."

"He was lyin'. He brought us here to sell us. Drude is a bad man, a very, very bad man. We can't let him find us or we'll never see Pa again."

⌒ ⌒ ⌒

Drude, cogent and persuasive, negotiated with Mr. Appleby and his wife. He convinced them that even with $250 he was sacrificing the loss of another $250 so that they could have the children. "Within three years," he pointed out to them, "the boy will be old enough to do almost anything on the farm, and the girl will be a great help and blessing in the home."

James was sold on the idea. "Maybe if we looks around the house we can scrape up that much, what do you think?" he was addressing his wife.

"Maybe," she assured him, still tantalized by mellifluous visions Drude had painted on her mind. "You said we'll get a paper fer the children?"

"Oh yes," Drude assured Mr. Appleby. "I always believe in doin' things right and legal. We can make the adoption paper right here and now. Drude pulled a piece of white paper from his pocket, and with his pen proceeded to write the articles of the contract. James Appleby rose from the table to go into the bedroom to get $250 from savings he had hidden in the mattress. As he walked towards the bedroom, he glanced through the window. "I say, whar is them chillen. They ain't in front the house and the wagon ain't thar neither."

The three rushed out on to the porch and into the yard. "Oh, they is somewheres around playin," Drude assured the couple. He looked to one side of the house, then the other. "Children? Billy! Sandy! Them children they just love to ride that old wagon. I'll find them. They must be out on the road." As he mounted his steed and spurred it to a trot towards the road, he wondered in which direction they had headed. How close he had come to closing the deal. Just another five minutes and he would have had the $250 in his hands. He had to find the children and return before the Applebys backed out of the deal.

"Surely they would not travel back in the direction from which they came; after all they were fixed on going north to New York." Drude galloped east on the dirt road. "Children! Billy! Sandy! Where are you?" He went more than half of a mile. There were several wheel marks on the road, which gave no indication as to which were the ones of the wagon he sought. Surely they could not have traveled this far in such a short period of time," he thought. "Children, come out from where you are. Don't hide from Uncle Enoch. It's gettin' late, we got to head for New York."

Billy stood holding the bridle of the mare, his sister pressing against his side. They could hear the voice of Drude as he passed on the road. "Billy and Sandy. This is Uncle Enoch. Come on out, let's go to New York. Your pa's a waitin'! You can't go no wheres hiding in them there bushes."

"Come on, children, cut out your playin', an' let's go. There is wolves and black bears and rattlesnakes in these here woods." Billy pulled his sister closer to him. He could hear his own heart pounding. The horse and rider passed. Minutes later he heard the horse coming back at full gallop. It was heading back in the direction of the Appleby's farm. Drude reasoned that the children could not have traveled that far in so short a period of time. This led him to conclude that they had gone in the opposite direction, over the territory with which they were more familiar. Back in the yard the Applebys were on the porch waiting. "Seems as if they was playin' on the wagon and the horse bolted. They went west on the road. I'll be back in ten minutes," he assured them, racing out of the yard.

⌒ ⌒ ⌒

Billy and his sister waited where they had been hiding for what appeared to be an eternity. Then Billy walked out to the road. He looked in both directions. The road was empty. He led the horse back on to the road, and heading east, urged it to a gallop. About two miles further up, they came to a crossroad running north and south. Billy reasoned that should Drude come back along that road to search for them, he surely would head north, since the man knew that their destination was New York. He decided to continue east for a while, and then turn north at a later point. Shortly, even the eastern road which they had taken turned in a northerly direction. Billy was satisfied that he had made the right decision. The children did not realize that by continuing along that road, they were heading into a backwoods even more remote than that which they had traversed from Rocky Bottom--a long stretch of undeveloped territory running some thirty miles into the muddy basin of the Yazoo River.

⌒ ⌒ ⌒

For several days the conversation in the house of Leroy and Cora Benton had centered on the McBrides. They with the McMillans had almost exhausted the topic of Rebecca. How thin she had become, "reduced to skin an' bone." Gossip had been particularly intense when Rebecca would take the children to church. But for the past four weeks a sort of mystery had descended over the valley with regards to Rebecca McBride and her brood. Rebecca had ceased to attend Sunday meeting. In fact, neither the Bentons nor the McMillans had even a glimpse of her or her children. A book salesman passing through the area two weeks earlier had mentioned, upon being questioned by Leroy, that he had visited the McBrides and sold them a religious book—a children's story of Jesus, one of the several he had for sale. This had been the only information available on the family for the past four weeks.

"Wonder what's goin' on down the creek," Leroy asked Bogg McMillan as they exchanged ideas after Church service on Sunday. "Ain't seen a thing of them McBrides in fo' weeks."

"Same here," Bogg informed him. "Passed there four times in the last two weeks on ma way to Bolton, ain't seen no sign of life. Maybe they done left and gone."

"They's sure nuf there," Leroy assured him. "That book salesman says he seen the woman and the two chillen. Says he sell them a book." Leroy frowned, rubbing his chin with his left hand. Below his chin his Adam's apple stuck out like the beak of a parrot. "I'd sure like to know what is goin' on down there."

As the days wore on, the curiosity of Leroy and Cora became almost uncontrollable. On one occasion as they passed the McBride place on their way to Bolton they slowed down their wagon, carefully scrutinizing the path leading to the McBrides for signs of life. Going up the road a ways, they turned the wagon around, and once more passing the McBrides' place, they looked down the path leading to the house, hoping to garner some information on the family.

"It's real eerie like and quiet down there, ain't it," Cora observed.

"I'd say it is."

"Maybe Bogg McMillan is right," Cora said, "Maybe dey all done lef' the place."

"Nah," Leroy scoffed, sending a ball of black tobacco spittle flying to the road. "Dey' gone no ways. Dey is there just playin' possum."

Leroy and Cora Benton talked of the McBrides as they worked, as they ate, as they lay in bed at night before falling asleep, and any other time the opportunity presented itself. In fact, in an otherwise drab existence, the situation created by the McBrides, and all the rumors and speculation it engendered, had become a source of real excitement. So continuous had been their absorption with the McBrides, that Cora Benton had a dream. The following morning as Cora climbed out of bed, she told her husband, "Dreamed about them McBrides last night. I sure did. I dreamed they had a big shindig down by their place. Seemed like a weddin' to me. Lotsa peoples standin' and talkin' in small groups front the house, and nigger servants servin' them with food from silver trays. Billy was there and he was all happy like, and laughin' with everybody." With an element of surprise in her voice, she added, "Can't imagine why I'd go and dream a dream like that."

Leroy was putting on his boots as he listened to his wife. "Woman, you eats too much, that's how come you have them kinda dreams. You goes to bed at night with all that there food on your stomek. What d'yer 'spect t' dream about?"

That morning as Leroy worked in the garden plot behind the house, weeding between the rows of sweet peppers and squash, he could not expel from his mind thoughts about the McBrides. He performed his chores mechanically, and did not hear when Cora called to him from the window that lunch was ready.

"Leroy Benton, I done call you twice an' I ain't gonna call you no mo."

"You musta called in a whisper," he replied, "cause this is the fus time I's hearin' your voice."

Cora was in no mood for arguing. "I says your vittles is on the table, come 'n get it."

After lunch Leroy sat for a while on the step of the porch cleaning his teeth with a piece of twig, his eyes studying the clouds drifting overhead. It had rained lightly the night before, just a few passing clouds, but now the sky was clear. Patches of grotesquely shaped white clouds were moving in a southwesterly direction over the valley. Leroy's eyes were focused on the sky but his thoughts were elsewhere.

He rose from where he sat, and in the same motion took the pouch of tobacco from his pocket, broke off a piece of tobacco and stuffed it into his mouth. He walked over to the barn and when he reappeared a few moments later he was leading a fully saddled horse. Cora who was still working around the pot bellied stove in the kitchen, looked through the window and saw her husband with the horse.

Leaving her work she came onto the porch. "Whar's you goin wid that hoss? I thought you said that there was lotsa work left to do today."

Leroy did not answer immediately. He went around the horse, adjusting a strap on the stirrup. Surprisingly nimble he climbed on to the saddle and without looking at his wife said "I'm goin' by Bogg McMillan. I'll be back shortly. I'm fixin' to borrow his ax."

Leroy had never been able to lie to Cora and look her in the eye at the same time. He had a way of looking at the ground or glancing at her sideways when there was not complete veracity in his expressions. Cora, after having lived with the man both in common law and in church marriage for thirty years, knew her husband like a favorite book. As the horse trotted towards the bush lined path leading out of the yard, she stood, one arm holding up the porch post next to the step, the other resting on the side of her ample waist. She frowned and smiled simultaneously, her eyes narrowing as she watched her husband leave the yard. "That redneck is lyin'," she said, pleased at her capacity for reading her husband's responses. "I wonder just what he's up to now?"

⌒⌒⌒

Leroy rode out onto the creek road. He pulled his horse to a stop and glanced over his shoulder before heading in an easterly direction. Half a mile on the dirt road brought him to where the path led down to the McBrides' place. He slowed the horse and curiously scrutinized the opening that led to the house. A mother skunk foraging in the area with her brood crossed his path as a catbird called challengingly from a tree nearby. Leroy increased the pace of the horse to a slow trot, until he was some two hundred feet beyond the path that led to the McBrides. After scanning the creek road in both directions, he hurriedly turned the horse off the road into the woods that bordered the McBrides' place. He was tense and nervous as he dismounted, and tied the horse to a tree. Glancing around, he examined the bush around him for signs of human life. Cautiously, noiselessly as an old seasoned fox, he made his way in the direction of the McBrides' place, clearing the branches before his face with his hands. Soon Leroy could see the outlines of the McBrides's barn through the thicket. His heart pounded within him, the sound reverberating in his head. Leroy wanted to spit, but he held it back. Now near to the opening, he could see the small white cottage, the smoke stack protruding from the roof. "Didn't realize the house was painted," he thought.

"Wonder if he painted it or his woman? Wouldn't be surprised if she done it." Still among the trees, Leroy moved to the right so that as he got to where the yard bordered the wooded area, he was behind the barn.

From where he stood Leroy could see the chicken house and a few hens diligently scratching the earth in search of food. He could see a vegetable plot further to the right, and behind it, an outhouse with its door blown open by the wind.

Moving back toward the front of the barn, but still in the protection of the trees, Leroy carefully examined the silent cottage. The windows were shut. The front door was closed and a large stone rested up against it. "Why would a stone be jammed outside the door if anyone is inside?" he reasoned, frowning. Behind the barn once more, Leroy peeked through a one-inch crevice across the board on the side of the barn. Inside was dark, except for a ray of light entering through the hayloft. He could see that the wagon was not in the barn. Leroy decided to examine more closely the barn's interior. He moved towards the front, and with his back pressed against the wall of the barn, sidled towards the door. The door was closed but unbolted. Quietly, his heart pounding, Leroy tried the door. It creaked as it gave slightly, opening wide enough for him to enter. Part of his body was already through the barn door as he anxiously surveyed the yard to be sure that no one was watching. He ran his eyes along the border of the yard. There was the path leading into the yard from the creek road. Further to the right was a patch of pine trees. Leroy's eyes fell on a clump of flowers on the ground, and what appeared to be a small wooden cross standing beside the flowers. He focused his eyes, and for a moment seemed transfixed, his eyes riveted unblinking on the spot. His hands began to tremble, his legs grew weak, beads of sweat suddenly appeared on his face, his hair stood on end. Leroy grew dizzy and thought that he would pass out. There before his eyes was a newly dug grave and a crude cross standing guard over a bunch of wilted flowers. Leroy eased away from the door back into the thicket. Once among the trees he headed towards where he had left his horse, looking fearfully around as he walked.

From his horse, Leroy examined the creek road. No one was in sight. At a gallop he quickly covered the half-mile back to his farm, and in a high state of animated excitement revealed to his wife who sat listening with bulging eyes, what he had discovered. "The dream!" she cried, "The dream! It weren't no weddin' what I seen. It was a funeral!"

"You can't have no funeral without a dead body," Leroy protested. "Who was the buryin' fer and who did the buryin'? How come nobody knowed nothin' ' bout it? We was in Bolton three days ago, we stopped by two farms on the road and nobody said nothin' 'bout no funeral. This is mighty strange!" Leroy turned his head sideways and looked around suspiciously. "Mighty strange!"

Cora was anxious to share the new information with the McMillans. "Well, what is we waitin' fer. Hitch up the wagon."

"Wait!" Leroy advised, "we don't want to tell nobody 'bout this befo' we ken figure it out some mo'." Leroy had already determined that if there were advantages to be gained from their discovery, it should be shared with no one. "There was Millicent Vanderver," he thought, "there were Rebecca McBride and two children. Now there ain't no one, only a grave." There were still chickens in the yard and he had seen at least one cow resting under the shade of a tree. Could it be that Billy McBride had actually returned, found his wife dead, buried her, and taken his children away, leaving the place deserted? Chickens, cattle and all? For over an hour the couple sat behind closed doors, weighing the facts, and hypothesizing as to what could have transpired. Cora kept insisting that the news should be shared. Finally towards the vesper hour, Leroy gave in to his wife's wishes. He rose, and with Cora following closely, stepped outside to hitch up the wagon that rested near the barn. They stopped dead in their tracks while yet on the porch. A dark steed carrying a stranger dressed in a dark gray suit and wearing a dark felt hat was coming down the path into their yard.

The stranger respectfully tipped his dark felt hat and introduced himself. The nervous and suspicious couple listened as Drude explained to them the reason for his presence in the valley. He was a relative of the McBrides, Billy's half brother. He explained to them, standing in front of the steps upon which the couple was planted, how he had come to visit the family knowing that his brother was away. "I am a man of religion and I knew it was the Almighty who said to me in a dream, Drude, go to Rocky Bottom, your people need you." He had arrived at the Bottom just in time to hear his brother's wife speak her last words on her bed of death, "before she departed to glory." She had asked him to bury her right on the place. "She didn't want nobody cryin' and no funeral visits. Just me and the children. I made her a solemn promise, and I kept it." She had asked him to take the children up North, dispense with the property, and use the proceeds to care for the little ones.

Drude described to Leroy and his wife how it had broken his heart to see his brother's wife die, after not having seen her for several years. But she was a "good woman" and he felt sure that she was "gone to glory."

All of this communication transpired in front of the Bentons' house. Leroy audited, attentive and silent, one eye half closed, his head cocked slightly sideways. He eyed the stranger with profound incredulity. "I don't trust the likes of him," he thought to himself. "He look sho nuf like one o' them what if you yawn he'll steal the chewin' tobacco out ya mouth."

It was Cora who gave voice to the suspicion. She directed an observation at the stranger in the form of a comment to her husband. "Leroy, I didn't know that Billy McBride had no brother."

"Same here!" Leroy was still focusing his gaze on the stranger.

"It sure nuf beats me that Billy had a brother and we didn't know nothin' 'bout it!" Cora continued.

Leroy employed the same process to challenge the stranger through comments to his wife. "I knowed Billy's Mammy fer—I say fifteen years 'fore she died. Never knowed her had any other chile. She came here with Billy after her husband died, and growed that boy up right here in Rocky Bottom. When she died that boy went up North and married hisself that Yankee woman."

Drude had perceived the wariness of the farmers as well as their lack of enthusiasm for the northern woman Billy had married. He moved immediately to exploit his observation. He explained apologetically to the couple that he was actually Billy's half brother-- "the same daddy but a different mammy," and he had carried his mother's name. "I advised my brother strongly 'gainst marryin' a northern woman. 'Marry a southerner like yourself,' I said, but he won't listen." Being his brother, however, he had forgiven him "as the Good Book says we must do."

With this apocryphal presentation, Drude could see that the tension had visibly eased. He hastened to further extirpate any lingering doubts or suspicions. He explained to the couple that he had moved the children to Alabama, taking them to family from his side in Birmingham. As soon as he could dispense with the property, he was going to return to Birmingham for the children and head for Ohio, where he presently lived. He explained to Leroy and Cora that he was aware that there was bad blood between their family and the McBrides, but he hoped that with the tragedy of the McBrides, Leroy and his good wife "will fergive and ferget." Seeing that they were the nearest neighbors, he wanted to give them first choice to buy the place. He already had two offers from folk in Bolton, but he had not made a decision.

The suspicion and tension which the entrance of Drude had elicited was at this point replaced by an air of expectation and controlled excitement on the part of Leroy, who had long nurtured the desire to own the McBride place. It was like the submerged glee of an art dealer over the possibility of obtaining at a bargain price a rich art treasure drawn from the attic of an unknowing layman.

Drude, consummate in the art of deception, crooked financial dealings, and a poker player of no small skill, perceived through Leroy's change of expression and growing friendly posture, his interest in the deal. He hastened to further cultivate it. "Of course, I know that the farmers in this area are not exactly rich in material things. And seeing how it is a matter of urgency, since I have only a short time before I must return to Ohio, I am ready to sell whatever can be sold, including livestock, at a bargain price. The two potential buyers in Bolton, I told them I'll be back tomorrow morning. But frankly I'd prefer to sell it to someone from the Bottom. Someone who could care for the place and love it as my brother and his wife did."

Leroy himself, an old fox of sorts, sensed the air of urgency of the man to dispense with the farm. "Why is we talkin' out here in the yard? This ain't no neighborly way to treat a stranger," he said, looking at Cora as if she was to be blamed for not having invited the man inside. His good wife accepted the blame.

"You sho right," she said, "I bin so taken listenin' to the sad news 'bout the death and buryin' at the McBrides, that I plumb ferget we was standin' outside. Come on in." Leroy led the man inside.

Once inside Cora hurriedly placed a pot on the stove to prepare coffee. She listened intently to the continuing conversation as her husband moved to control the situation. "Me and the missus as you said was not close to Billy and his wife, but we is Christian people, poor but Christian. We don't have no hard feelin's 'gainst the McBrides. If we knowed she was sick, we woulda bin the first ones to help." He looked over at Cora, scratching his head

"We sure woulda helped," Cora mourned. "Yes, we had some misunderstandin', but we is all God's chillen."

"Whar is Billy?" Leroy inquired.

Drude responded with a look of embarrassment as if it were a topic he preferred not to discuss. "It is a very sad and long story, one of dem family things I find difficult to discuss."

"Me and the missus sure nuf don't relish meddlin' in people's family business," Leroy said apologetically, studying closely the face of the stranger. "But most of the folk along the creek been saying how Billy ran off and left the po' woman with them two chillen all alone."

Drude shook his head, looking at the floor then glancing up at the man before him. "I reckon what you just said is 'bout the way it is. I tried to get him to return but he refused. He told her she could have the farm, and he moved in with some woman in New York, claiming he wants to start a new life. As I said, is a shameful thing and I feel embarrassed to talk about it."

As the stranger spoke, Leroy was congratulating himself for not having given in earlier to his wife's desire to pass the news on to the McMillans further up the creek. Now with the question of sale being discussed he would wait until it was all over before he would pass on the news of the tragedy. "Of course," Leroy said, "we ain't rich people, but if there is anything we can do, anything to help, we will try. As I said, we don't have much, but we sure want to help."

Leroy inquired of Drude what were the things he wanted to sell. Drude explained that he had not taken stock of all the things on the property, but he knew "there's chickens and some cattle, and some farm implements." These he wished to sell immediately, but he also desired to sell the property—perhaps at a later date. If he could sell it now, however, it would go at a bargain price. Leroy nervously shifted on the bench as the topic of the land came up.

Here was an example of a psychological struggle between a cunning old farmer and an urban con man. Each studying the other closely, trying to gain advantage, and considering the other man not smart enough to perceive his intention. "You mentioned 'the place'?" Leroy followed up. "Of course, we got all the land we need here, but we're willin' to help you, so if we can, we will take the land off your hands."

Drude thanked him for his kindness as he sipped on the cup of hot coffee. "With the help I'll get from you and what I hope to get from other farmers up the creek, I'm sure I should be able to get rid of everything."

With the mention of "other farmers," Drude could see an excited concern in the man with whom he was negotiating. "Well, I doubt if dem folk up the creek will want anything. Dey is a right hostile lot. They don't take to strangers none." Benton turned to his wife. "What ya think, Cora? Think them farmers up the creek will want to buy anything from the McBrides' place?"

"Oh, no," Cora responded. "Not dem. Dey is all dirt poor, white trash—most of them. There ain't nothin' they hate to see more than a well dressed stranger."

Leroy supported his wife. "Dem is the meanest lot you ever seen, Mister. But we'll work with you--me and the missus, once we see what you's got to sell, stock an' all, and maybe, dependin' on the price, we can even talk about the place."

THREE:
MZ. MABEL'S CHILLEN

People in Mudville County, Mississippi, who knew her called her "Mz. Mabel. Mabel had lived in Mudville County all her life. She was born some two miles from where she now lived, in a town that went by the name of Niggerville. Niggerville, an all black community, was formerly part of a large white plantation owned by the Wright family. Bilbo Wright, the last of the owners of the plantation prior to 1864 had remained unmarried after the death of his childless wife and by the time of his departure from life, had sired at least twenty-three children on the plantation, by a number of black women. Before his death he had given the land where the town now stood to its inhabitants, and the surrounding land he had broken into small allotments and given to his former slaves.

The town itself had been originally called Wrightsville by its all-black population, in memory of old man Bilbo. The name Niggerville, by which it now went, was given to it by whites in the county, and within a matter of years had become the accepted name not only by blacks but in official state and county records, though the town itself had never been officially incorporated. Two-and-one-half miles to the east of Niggerville along a dirt road lay the town of Mudville, a predominantly white community and the seat of the county of Mudville from which the Sheriff and other officials operated. Mabel was born in Niggerville, the granddaughter of old man Bilbo, the daughter of one of the planter's sons.

Mabel was married at the age of eighteen to a childhood acquaintance of Mudville County, Jake Hart, who had acquired the total inheritance of his father, twenty acres of land on the banks of the Yazoo River some two miles south of Niggerville and two-and-one-half miles southwest of the town of Mudville. Mabel bore her husband four children, two boys and two girls. But within a few years tragedy had struck. Two of her children, a boy and a girl, caught swamp fever, brought from the swamps of the Yazoo by mosquitoes. In spite of intensive treatment including daily doses of broth made by boiling the bark of the red oak tree, the two children died ten days apart. Malaria had been of epidemic proportions in the county, cutting down whites and blacks alike.

Mabel was yet in the process of accepting her tragedy when mishap struck once again. Mabel discovered that her husband was having a full-blown relationship with Petunia Willis, an attractive young woman from Niggerville. There had been quiet rumors of this relationship in Niggerville for some time, but though Mabel and the woman attended the same Baptist church, somehow it had never come to her attention--that is, not until one Sunday afternoon after church when a deaconess, Mildred Crane, pulled Mabel aside. "Sister Mabel," she said, "It ain't no business of mine and it ain't my habit to meddle in family affairs. But I done says to myself 'If I was in Mabel's place I'd want someone to tell me.'"

"Tell me what, Mildred?"

"That my man is foolin' around with another woman."

It broke into the open on Saturday at the church fall picnic in Niggerville. Petunia was edging up to Jake, "putting her hands all over him" as the other women observed, when she was accosted by Mabel, usually a person of mild manner. Unmindful of the Church members milling around, Mabel accused Petunia of trying to steal her husband. Were it not for the presence of one of the church deacons, there might have been even an exchange of blows. Months after the incident, it was still being discussed by the women of Niggerville.

The day following the encounter between Petunia and Mabel at the picnic, a group of women was gathered under the mimosa tree on the side of Babs and Ann Jacob's shop on Church Street in Niggerville. The mimosa tree itself had been struck by lightning several years earlier and had been split almost in half. Rather than dying it had continued to grow, and now was the largest mimosa tree in Niggerville, with large spreading branches making a unique gathering place under its shade. The women gathered under the shady tree were discussing the incident of the previous day.

"But a scrawny, wiry, little piece of woman like that bitch Petunia! If I was Mabel, I'd break her ass in half," one woman said with contempt in her voice.

"You's talkin' right, chile," another injected. "She look just like a broomstick and her backside is as flat as a white woman."

"Ain't that the truth," said another, laughing huskily. "I can't imagine what Jake Hart see in dat woman, her chest is as flat as a man!"

"But men can be damn fools, yes!" said yet another. "The man have a nice wife, she beat Petunia for looks any day, and yet he foolin' round with that 'ho'."

All of the women under the tree were sympathetic although none was close friend to Mabel, who was not particularly sociable and stayed much to herself. A prime factor motivating this response was the painful fact that they, all married, considered Petunia a threat. Petunia, a very beautiful and salacious woman, was admired by most of the men in Niggerville. She was considered by some women a harlot, and viewed with envy by others.

"Dat's the way most men is," said an older woman, and went on to tell of similar incidents she had known at other places and times. Earlier that evening Ann Jacobs had warned her husband Babs, "If I ever catches you foolin' with that no good woman you is done fer."

"Who me? Fool with another woman?" Babs had protested.

As the women under the tree were deep in their gossip, one of them looked up and said, "You talks 'bout the devil and she appear." And sure enough, there was Petunia coming down Church Street in the direction of the shop. The women stopped talking to look at her as she passed. Petunia must have realized this, for as she walked she swung her hands tauntingly at her side, slightly slowing her pace and accentuating the undulation of her hips. As soon as she was out of earshot, the conversation continued.

"Jus' look at her. As bold as brass. She ain't got no shame, dat bitch," said Ann Jacobs. "I won't be surprised if she ain't done something to him, maybe she done put some goopher dust on him."

"Nah," responded another, "ain't give him nothin', at least no mo' than you or me can give him." They laughed raucously.

∧ ∧ ∧

In the spring, at the time when most of the black people in Mudville County were in the fields—either their own or those of white planters for whom they worked—preparing the land or planting early spring crops, when warm winds blew constantly from the south, when flocks of migrant birds were northward bound from their Caribbean and South American retreats, and even the clouds seemed to be moving northward, Petunia packed up her few belongings and left Niggerville, declaring that she was going north, "an' I ain't never comin' back." Two weeks later Jake Hart disappeared. He left on his mule for the town of Mudville and was never seen again.

There were two explanations drifting around the black community accounting for Jake's mysterious disappearance. It was an open secret that Jake, against the wishes of his wife, occasionally sold moonshine for a white man who ran a still somewhere in the woods by the Yazoo. One rumor had it that Jake was killed by another moonshiner and his body dumped in the Yazoo as a warning to Jake's boss. The second rumor and the one which most in the black community, including Mabel, were inclined to believe, was that Jake "had run off up North" to meet Petunia, according to plans they had made before Petunia's departure. Whether Jake Hart was in the bottom of the Yazoo or left the arms of his wife for those of Petunia was never known. In any case, Jake was not seen or heard of again, though there were rumors that someone had seen him and Petunia in Dayton, Ohio.

Mabel continued to live on the land with her two children, Joshua and Sharon. She reared some hogs and sold the young each year to a butcher in Niggerville, she grew vegetables for her household, and planted some cotton which she sold. But her main means of livelihood was dressmaking which she did for white women in Mudville and for blacks alike. Mabel refused to carry her husband's name any longer, and reverted to calling herself Mabel Wright; her children too carried the name of Wright, and were generally referred to as "Mz. Mabel's chillen."

The land in some areas of Mudville County was exceedingly low and during rainy periods became quickly water logged. The region was a perfect hideout for water moccasins, and indeed not ideal for farming. The few farms were small. There were four white farmers east of Mabel, the nearest being about half a mile away. Between Mabel's place and Niggerville, where the land rose higher, there were mostly white farmers, with a few black plots interspersed. Many blacks farming in the region were sharecroppers, while nearer to Niggerville, much of the land surrounding the town was owned by blacks.

The month of July was usually a busy period for Mabel and her two children--Joshua seven years old and Sharon eight-and-a-half. When there were a few acres to be plowed, Mabel would hire help for a day, but she cherished her independence, and as much as possible she, aided by her children, did what was to be done on the farm.

During the hottest period of the year, Mabel usually worked in the garden from the break of dawn till the sun was well on its journey, and again close to sunset in the evenings. She would rise in the early hours of the morning while the sun yet lay under a blanket of clouds in the east and begin her work, remaining in the field until the heat forced a retreat. Much of the rest of the day would be spent in sewing and other work within the house.

On one particular morning, Mabel was out earlier than usual. The heat of late July was intense during the day, extending even into the night. With much work to be done Mabel was up at the first peep of dawn. She worked for a while in the garden bordering the serpentine dirt road that separated her land from an unworked stretch of pine and brush across the road to the north. After working outside for almost an hour, Mabel returned to the house, quickly prepared breakfast which she left on the table and potbellied stove for the children still sleeping, and returned to the garden plot to the right front of the house.

As she labored, bent over rows of white potatoes, beads of perspiration had already begun to form on her face and neck, and rolled down into the crevice formed at the convergence of her ample breasts. She worked with haste so as to get out of the garden before the sun got much higher in the sky. As she worked she thought of the wedding dress she needed to complete for a white customer in Mudville. She had yet one day to finish the job. Mabel was so involved in the work she was doing and absorbed in her thoughts that she neither saw nor heard the horse-drawn wagon which had appeared around the bend on the dirt road only a few yards away from where she was bent over the row of potatoes.

Mabel had just straightened up to ease the agony of her back, when she turned around and saw the wagon. The mare which drew it was for all purposes under her own control. She would pause, reap a mouthful of leafage from the side of the path, take a few steps, more leafage. On the wagon were two white children. The boy sat in the driver's seat, his head bent forward, and seated beside him, her head laid across his lap, was a little girl. Both children were fast asleep.

Mabel looked at the strange sight in surprise and wonder. She dropped the hoe and slowly approached the wagon, wiping her hands on the sides of her flowered skirt. The horse ignoring her approach continued to munch on shrubbery nearby. "Well, what do we have here?" she said as she got beside the wagon. The sound of her voice awoke the boy. Startled, he looked at the strange black woman, a look of fear and bewilderment on his face. Mabel responded with a broad motherly smile. "I would say you is on the wrong trail, young man." As she spoke her two hands rested on her hips. "This road you is on ain't goin nowheres. Where ya'll headin fer, anyways?"

"We goin' to New York, Ma'am."

Mabel looked at the boy, unbelieving. "Oh! I see. You little uns goin' to New York all by you'self," she smiled.

"Yes'm. We musta lost our way."

"I'll say you have," Mabel replied. "An' where might y'all be comin' from, young man?"

"From Rocky Bottom, ma'am."

"Rocky Bottom? I can't say I ever hear 'bout dat place befo'. Where it near?"

"Near Bolton, Mississippi, ma'am."

"Bolton! Bolton is fifty miles or mo' from here." She paused, still studying the children. "Oh, I see!" she said confidentially. "You little ones done fed up with your ma and pa and is runnin' away."

"No, ma'am. Our ma's dead, and we is goin' to New York to find our pa," the boy replied.

Mabel shook her head in silence. How miserable the children looked. The little girl still asleep on the boy's lap had tear stains on her face, and from the look of the boy he too had been crying. "You young uns had breakfas' yet?" she inquired.

"No, ma'am, but we's fixin' to have it soon. We's got bread, butter and jam."

"Well ain't that strange now?" Mabel said, smiling broadly with a look of pleasant surprise. "I just a few minutes come from fixin' breakfas' for my two little uns. They is just 'bout your age. I jus' place the food on the table and you wouldn't guess what it is? Fried bacon, eggs, with grits and fried potatoes." She smacked her lips tantalizingly. "I can almost taste it with a warm cup of milk." The description of the food set Billy's salivary glands working. He could almost smell the food from the woman's description.

"I tell you what," Mabel suggested, smiling with an air of motherly authority. "Seein' how you both is lost, and seein' how is breakfas' time, come on an' have some breakfast with my little ones, then you can tell me all 'bout where you is going and we will see how we can get you there."

Billy McBride, already having had one close shave with danger the day before when a man they called Uncle Enoch tried to sell him and his sister, was cautious of the stranger beside the wagon, but pangs of hunger tempted him to accept the offer. Mabel saw his hesitation and responded with a warm smile and reassuring voice. "Don't be afraid, son, an' don't you worry 'bout a thing. Ever'thing gonna be all right."

Billy was about to shake his sister Sandy to awaken her. "No, don't wake the poor thing." Mabel reached onto the wagon, took the sleeping child in her arms, and with Billy beside her, walked towards the wooden frame house. "What might your name be, young man?"

"My name is Billy McBride and my sister's name is Sandy."

⌃ ⌃ ⌃

Mabel placed the child she carried in her arms on the old sofa next to the window, seated her brother at the table and proceeded to charge the plates with food. Mabel's two children were behind the house, washing their faces from a bucket of water when their mother entered the front door with the two strange children. As Mabel worked over the stove, she questioned Billy, who poured out to her the full story of their experiences over the last few days: how their mother had died, how he and his sister alone had buried her by the barn and had set out for New York where their father lived.

"Was there no one around you could turn to for help?"

"No, ma'am. The nearest neighbors live far up the creek, and they ain't no friends of ours. They is a mean lot and ain't talk to any of us."

The sound of voices and possibly the smell of food awoke Sandy. She sat up and looked around. Startled to find herself in a house with a black woman rather than on the wagon where she last remembered being, she jumped up from the sofa.

"Don' be afraid, chile. Everything is all right." Sandy looked at her brother seated at the table. He showed no signs of fear or concern. Momentarily she mistook the woman for the wife of the black man who had helped them on their land months before.

"Come an' sit here by your brother an' eat your breakfas'. Eat as much as you want."

Still confused as to the turn of events that had brought her into the strange house, Sandy climbed on to the chair next to Billy. Mabel's two children entered the kitchen from the back door and stood mouth agape looking at the strange children seated at the breakfast table.

"Don't stand there with your mouth open," Mabel called. "Breakfast is ready. This here is Billy and Sandy, they's havin' breakfas' wid us."

The four children were now seated at the table. "Say your prayer," Mabel directed. Joshua led out, clasping his hands together. "Our Father, thank you for safe keepin' during the night, thank you for the mornin' light. Bless this food, and the hands that prepared it, Amen."

This was a familiar experience for Billy and Sandy, for they too had been taught to say a prayer before eating. The prayer seemed to have broken the ground, creating a basis for communication between the two children and the black family. The children smiled and grinned at each other as they devoured the delicious breakfast. As they spoke among themselves Mabel listened closely.

"How old is you, little ones?" she inquired.

"I am seven goin' on eight, an' my sister is six goin' on seven." Mabel was still puzzled that the two children could have traveled over fifty miles without meeting anyone who could help them. "How long you bin on the road travelin' to New York?" she asked.

"Two days," Billy answered. By now Sandy, her spirit rekindled by the food and warm milk, joined in the conversation.

"An' we might have already bin in New York if it weren't fer that bad man that we met."

"What bad man," Mabel inquired.

"A bad man who tried to sell us."

"You mean someone tried to sell you chillen?" Mabel wondered if the child's imagination was not getting the best of her. Who would sell a white child in Mississippi, she wondered.

"He was a bad man, and his name was Uncle Enoch," Sandy said.

"Let me tell it, Sandy," Billy ordered. "You mixin' it all up." Then he proceeded to tell how after the burial of their mother and their departure for New York, they had met a man who had asked that he be called "Uncle." He had offered to accompany them to New York, but had stopped by a farmer's home and was negotiating to sell them for $250 when they had narrowly escaped and headed on the road which had led them to Mabel's place.

"Are you sure that this man you called Uncle Enoch was fixin' to sell you chillen?"

"Yes'm." Billy assured her. "I was sitting outside by the winder an' I heard ever'thing. That's when I took my sister and ran off in the wagon."

"That's how it happened, as Billy says," Sandy injected. "That bad man Uncle Enoch was fixin' to sell us jus' as they used to sell niggers." There was a moment of chilled silence. Then the children all giggled.

'Well, slavery is long over," Mabel assured the children, "and it's 'gainst the law to sell anybody, it make no difference if you is white or colored. That man ought to be locked up in jail."

Billy went on to tell how he and Sandy had hidden in the bush on the side of the road, as Drude rode by calling for them. Heading out once again on their trip to New York, they had traveled into the night until it was too dark to see; then the moon came up and they traveled some more. They had stopped the wagon by the road and had fallen asleep but as they slept the horse must have continued walking and thus they had arrived at Mabel's place. As Billy mentioned the wagon, Mabel rose from the table. "Good Lawd, I hope that horse ain't walked away. He bin carryin' that wagon for two days." But from the porch she saw that the wagon was still there, only a few yards from where they had left it. As she led the tired horse into the yard and unhitched the wagon she could hear the children laughing in the backyard. Joshua and Sharon were showing Billy and his sister their ducks, their pet goat, chickens, and young pigs in the pen. They played with the goat, watched the piglets feeding, then laughing and talking they walked across the field to look at the mighty Yazoo which flowed less than three hundred yards away. Mabel watched them as they walked along the path towards the river. It was as if they had been together and had known one another all along. "How nice it would be if all people were as open and as easy to get along with as little ones."

Mabel thought of all that the children had told her. It sounded incredible. Two children yet babies, burying their mother and then coming close to being sold by the first adult they met after the tragedy. Now on their way to New York two thousand miles away, traveling in a horse drawn wagon, and ending up in front of her house on the Yazoo. Could all this be a matter of imagination? Could there be another explanation for their presence? Were they really from where they said they had come? Mabel remembered the small suitcase in the wagon outside. Fetching it, she examined its contents. There were a few articles of clothing and a framed picture. It showed a white man and woman seated with a little boy standing beside them and a baby on the man's lap. Below it in the left corner was written—Billy, Rebecca, Billy Junior and Sandy McBride, Bolton, 1880.

Billy and Sandy stood gazing at the Yazoo as it lazily coiled its way southward. Its waters sparkled in the morning sun with millions of wavelets stirred by the south wind blowing against the tide, the surface of the water ruffled like the back of a scaled monster. In wonder they looked at the body of water, the largest they had ever beheld. It seemed like a thousand times or more the size of the creek in Rocky Bottom. As they enjoyed the sight, Joshua told how he with his mother and sister had often fished and caught many a big one from the very spot where they stood. Billy, not to be outdone, told of the large catfish he and his dad used to catch in the creek back home.

They threw stones on the water and watched the circular waves that were made. They threw sticks and watched as they floated southward. Some dark brown-feathered mallards were resting on the surface near the other bank of the river. The children watched them as they occasionally disappeared beneath the surface, only to reappear at another spot. They were still enjoying themselves when Mabel called through the bush: "Come up from the river, chillen, I don't want any of you fallin' in."

As they played beside the house in the shade of the oak trees, Mabel took out the wedding dress she had to complete. From where she sat at work, she could see the children through the window. She thought of the possible ways she could help them find their father. "If them children's father is alive, the best I can do for them is to help them get to him." She could give them some supplies and send them on their way, but what would happen to them? They could not hope to reach their destination by themselves. Some adult would have to take the responsibility of getting them to their father.

Mabel thought of seeking advice from the Reverend Jones, who was her spiritual leader in charge of the Baptist church in Niggerville.

She could hear him saying, "You don't want to get involved with white folk chillen. Give them to the sheriff. Let him worry' bout them."

She could also imagine the response of some blacks in the community: "Fancy Mabel, with all her own problems, Jake leavin' her an' all that, takin' on the worry of a couple o' white chillen. We black folk have trouble enough not to go an' worry over white folk problems."

"I will do it my way," Mabel thought. "There must be people in the vicinity of where they live who will be able to tell me more, or lead me to their relatives." Even if it were only an address of the father to whom she could write informing him of where the children were.

The children returned to the house as the sun climbed higher in the sky. They sat on the sofa and paged some children's books that Mabel had recently bought through the church. Stories of the baby Moses, and of the Jews crossing the Red Sea. Mabel looked across the room at the children. "You young uns had a rough night," she said. "You better lean back on the sofa and rest for a while. If you all is goin' to New York you got a mighty long trip ahead of you." Within minutes Sandy was sleeping. Soon Billy too fell into a deep sleep, his sister's head leaning on his shoulder. "Play quiet outside, that you don't wake them," Mabel directed her two children.

When the children awoke the sun had already passed midpoint of its day's journey, and now with the temperature hovering near ninety-five degrees, it hung like a ball of golden fire over the Yazoo River. Mabel prepared lunch for the children. She had to go to Mudville on an errand and she would leave the four children alone, as she had done on recent occasions with Sharon and Joshua. They could remain in the house, play in the yard, but on no conditions were they to go down to the river. "If you all behave, I will bring back somethin' for you from Mudville." To Billy and Sandy she added, "When I gets back from Mudville, we will talk about getting you to your pa."

While the children ate Mabel hitched the mule to the wagon and headed for Mudville two miles away. By the time she returned, the sun was almost at the horizon. The children stopped their play in the yard in front of the house to crowd around to see what she had brought, and each received a share of candy and store bought cookies.

⌃ ⌃ ⌃

That evening, Mabel got Billy and Sandy to discuss the problem of finding their father. She tried to impress upon their minds how impossible it would be for them to try to locate their father without the help of some adult. "Your Daddy is in New York. Do you chillun have any idea where New York is?"

"It's way up North," Billy informed her.

"Way up North is right," Mabel agreed. "That is almost 2,000 miles from here. If you tried to go to New York with your wagon, you couldn't get there till next spring and that poor horse will drop dead long before you gets there." The children listened intently as she spoke. "When you gets to New York, then your troubles just begin. I ain't never bin there, but they say there is as much people in New York as there is in all of Mississippi. So even if you gets there, which you can't on that wagon, you may never be able to find your pa alone. The best way to get to your daddy, is to have him come here and fetch you both."

The children pondered silently what the woman had said. "I'll tell you what I'll do," Mabel continued, "I will go to Rocky Bottom and Bolton and find out where your pa is. There must be someone who will know. Then I will write him a letter, tell him where you all is and in a matter of days he will be here to fetch you." The children were happy with the suggestion. Somehow, within the home of the black family to whom up to that morning they were total strangers, they had perceived an element of safety and security, which seemed preferable to taking to the road alone and facing other experiences such as they had with the man they called Uncle Enoch.

In the house that Mabel called her home there were two small bedrooms and one room that served as kitchen and dining room. Mabel slept in one bedroom on an old brass bed, with a mattress of cotton which she herself had made. The two children slept in the other bedroom on a mattress also of cotton which was rolled out on the floor each evening. It was usually sunned at least once each week since Joshua was still in the habit of occasional bedwetting. Mabel had tried to cure the habit by boiling ground pumpkin seeds, adding honey to the water, and giving it to the boy to drink, and by giving him garlic to eat. In an effort to make the two strangers as comfortable as possible Mabel decided to place them in her bed and sleep on the floor with Joshua and Sharon. "After all," she thought, "it will be strange 'nough for them to be sleepin' for the first time in a house with colored folk."

Mabel prepared the bed on the floor and showed Billy and his sister the bed in the other room where they were to sleep. When it became clear that Sharon and Joshua would be sleeping on the rollout bed, the two children requested that they too be allowed to sleep on the floor. Billy explained to Mabel that in Rocky Bottom, when Miss Vanderver stayed at their home, he and his sister slept every night on a bed made up on the floor. "If you young uns want to sleep on the floor with Sharon and Joshua, go right ahead," Mabel informed them, smiling broadly.

Saturday, the following day, Mabel was up as usual before the sun, and by the time the four children had awakened some two hours later, she had done a good deal of garden work and had come in to the house to make breakfast. While the children ate Mabel explained to them that she would be gone for about two hours and would be back long before midday. They were not to play by the river or even go down there. She promised that in the evening just before sundown, she would take them down to the Yazoo to try their hand at fishing. They could examine the raspberry patch and collect whatever ripe ones they could find. The children accelerated their pace of eating as they spoke of the fun they would have while Mabel was gone. "Don't talk with food in your mouth, and don't eat so fast," she exhorted. "The food ain't goin' no ways. " Mabel latched the mule to her wagon and drove off towards Niggerville.

There were several black families living along the road leading north into Niggerville. Some of these worked their own land, mostly small acreage; others were sharecroppers. The white farmers along the road depended on black labor. On some of these farms black sharecroppers lived and worked for farmers by whom they and their fathers had been owned during slavery. One such worker was Jim Brown. Brown, his wife, their seven children and his mother lived crowded in a small cottage bordered on three sides by a cotton field. Jim's mother, who had been a slave, was a great storyteller and family historian. She often regaled her grandchildren with narratives from the days of slavery, pointing out places in the country, and describing specific incidents that occurred there. She described to them the rebellion of 1862, detailing the issues involved, those who had led out, how the rebellion was put down, who was hanged, even the tree where the hanging occurred. She showed them exactly where she was working the day emancipation was proclaimed. "We was all working the cotton field down by the ravine, when this boy, his name was Benjamin, comes ridin' on a mule and say slavery was 'bolished. We all picks up our tools—forks and hoes and everything—and start fer the village dancin' and singin' "When the Saints Go Marchin' In" when the white foreman comes up on his hoss. "Niggers," he says, "is you all crazy? Get back to the field, it ain't quittin' time yet; get back and work afore I wup the whole buncha you," and we looked that white man right in his face and say, we say, "Boss man, we is now 'mancipated, we ain't working no mo'." With this and other stories Mother Brown entertained her grandchildren and others who would listen.

It was the Brown's place that was Mabel's destination on this particular Saturday morning. Mabel had often employed Mother Brown as a babysitter when she had to be away from the house for a day or more, a service for which she paid cash. Mother Brown usually enjoyed the experience as much as the children. She loved to sit by the Yazoo and look at its quiet waters under the shadows created by the late evening sun. Mabel greeted Jim who was working on the side of the house, and explained to him the purpose of her visit. She had to be gone from home for one day and a night as she was traveling outside of the county to the town of Bolton on an urgent errand, and wondered if Mother Brown would mind staying with the children until she returned. She would pay her as she had done in times past. Getting clearance from Jim, the usual process before approaching the old lady who was now nearing her sixty-fourth birthday, Mabel proceeded into the house where she greeted Jim's wife Gertrude, and formally made the request to Mother Brown. The old lady was glad to comply. It was at least one year since she had babysat for Mabel, and it had always been a pleasant experience. "Come to think of it," she said, "It's been almost six month since I seen your place, and with all this heat burnin' up, I can sure nuf 'preciate the shade of them trees in your yard." Mabel explained that she would be needed for the coming Monday.

Returning home, Mabel informed the four children that she would be gone on Monday to Bolton. "I am goin' to see if I can find exactly where your pa is. Then I will write him and let him know that you both is safe so he can come and fetch you." Someone would stay with them while she was away. An evening thunderstorm prevented the planned fishing trip to the Yazoo.

The next day Mabel gave the children further information on her planned trip to Bolton and Rocky Bottom and the surrounding area. She was sure she would find at least one person who would know the whereabouts of their father. Mother Brown, a nice old lady, would be staying with them while she was away. "Now," she informed them, "Mother Brown is the nicest person you can find anywheres. She loves chillen. Joshua and Sharon knows her well. But sometimes she can be nosy. She may want to ask you lots of questions 'bout who you is and why you is here. Now, I don't want you to tell no lie, you understand, just tell her you both is visitin' for a few days, till your pa comes for you. Don't tell her nothin' else."

Monday morning Mabel went to fetch Mother Brown. On their way back to the farm she explained to the old lady that there were two other children visiting with her for a while. The children were to stay away from the river, and were under no consideration to be allowed to leave the farm. She would be gone for one night only and should be back the following evening.

With Mother Brown watching over the four children, Mabel set out on her journey to Rocky Bottom. She walked to the town of Mudville and from there boarded the train that would take her on the fifty-mile trip to Bolton. From Mudville the train wended its way westward through the flat country laced with cotton fields green with midsummer foliage. They passed a number of small villages along the way; at some of these the train stopped, picking up or unloading passengers and goods. In one small town there was a crowd of white people at the train station and a small band was playing as the train came to a halt. It was apparent that some important person was on the train. It was in fact a senator from the Mississippi legislature—a home-boy who had made it good and was returning on a visit. As the heavy built, cigar smoking, pot-bellied man got off the train, the band struck up the tune of "Dixie."

The train rolled on, passing white and black homes along the track. Children playing stopped to wave at the train. An old black man sitting under a tree at the side of a small cottage looked unsmiling as the train rolled by. A group of black women working in a field bordering the rail line paused as the train passed; some waved laughing, others just gazed expressionless before bending once more over their work. An occasional blast from the whistle heralded the train's imminent appearance to communities up ahead. Some two and a half hours after the trip began, the train pulled into the station in Bolton, Mississippi.

Mabel had never visited this town before, but as she viewed it from the open window of the train, she was amazed at how similar it was to Mudville. The road from the station led to the center of the small town. In the center of the town was a small square with trees, and on the four sides of the square were various buildings. Now in the center of town Mabel could see its distinctive characteristics. The buildings--the courthouse, the saloon, the bank, the small stores and shops--were similar to those in Mudville. The green tree lined square made the difference. Along the side of the square were wooden benches planted into the ground. On one of these three old white men sat, one whittling on a piece of wood as he conversed with the others.

Mabel passed several black persons on their way to work before she stopped a well-dressed lady and asked her for the colored section of town. Smiling but without uttering a word, the woman pointed towards the edge of the town across the track, where the lines curved in a northeasterly direction. When Mabel crossed the track she observed that the first road in the district was Church Street and she smiled, reflecting that black sections of town seemed always to have a Church Street. At the corner about one block away was an old wooden church building. As she turned left on Church Street she observed the rows of small wooden homes on both sides of the road. Some were painted white while some were dark and moldy on the outside. Some had small porches attached to the front, with benches and chairs and flowers planted. On some of the porches old folks sat and little children played. Beyond the church was an empty lot, and beyond that an old building with the sign "Blacksmith" nailed on the front. Two black men sat on a bench that rested against an old oak tree on the lot between the church and the blacksmith shop. Nearby was a small horse drawn buggy.

Mabel approached the two men seated on the bench, who stopped talking to look at her as she came. "Howdy."

"Howdy," the men replied, looking at her carefully, one of them tipping an imaginary hat.

"Mighty hot, ain't it?"

"Sho is," the two men replied in unison.

"Is you a stranger?" the older of the two men inquired.

"Yes, sir. I am from a place called Niggerville, fifty miles up the line."

"I reckon'd you ain't from here," the old man commented. "I figure I knowed every colored woman in this here town. I bin livin' here fer thirty-five years. 'Sides, a woman as good lookin' as you, if you was from Bolton, I musta knowed you." The men laughed heartily.

"This weather is too hot for flattery," Mabel protested, smiling. "Is just as hot back in Mudville County where I come from."

"Is you married?" the old man inquired, a mischievous grin on his face, revealing tobacco stained teeth.

"No, I ain't, least not no more, and I don't plan to."

"Ah shucks," the old man said, slapping his right knee and looking at his younger companion, who seemed to be enjoying the exchange, "an' I bin here all mornin' followin' the direction of a dream. Last night Melda, my former wife, God bless her soul, appeared to me in a dream and says: 'Don't live by yuself no mo'. Go in the mornin,' she say, 'below the ol' oak tree by the church, and the fus woman to come along, she is to be your new wife.' You is the fus' woman." Again the two men laughed at the older man's wit.

It was Mabel who changed the tenor of the conversation as she sought to pursue the purpose of her visit to the strange town. "How far is Rocky Bottom from here," she inquired.

The old man was the first to reply. "What is you, a colored woman, askin' bout

Rocky Bottom fo'?" His legs had been crossed. He uncrossed them, bending forward, his head cocked slightly sideways as he spoke, examining Mabel's face closely.

"Well, I don't see how bein' a woman or colored have anything to do with it. I have to visit down there so I got to know where it is."

The old man opened his eyes wide as he looked at the two men—another had just joined them—one seated, one standing, and at Mabel. "If you knowed anything 'bout Rocky Bottom, lady, you woulda knowed why I said what I done said. Ain't no colored person in his right mind will go down in that there cursed hole o' rattlesnakes. I reckon past twenty years ain't no colored person I know of bin down there."

The last of the three men to arrive at the scene of conversation added further information to the discussion. "Ain't no nigger bin down in that place an' comes out live. Them white trash down there is worser than Satan hisself. Few years after 'mancipation they kill a whole heap a colored folks down there. Yes, sir. They'd left the plantation where they use' to be slaves an' was headin' North. The plantation owner caught up with them down in the Bottom and with the help o' them infidels down there they hang all of the grown men, and wup some of the women to death. Since then ain't no colored person gone down there." The other two men agreed, nodding their heads.

The youngest of the three men who up to now had said nothing, spoke up. "There is an old sharecropper down the road 'bout half way between here an' Rocky Bottom. Says he done some work fer a farmer down in the Bottom. Says he took his whole family down dey with him, but ain't no one believe him."

"Yes," the old man chuckled, "Dat ly'n rascal always saying he done what he ain't. He swore he bin in the Bottom many times an' offer to take me wid him to prove it."

"Well," Mabel responded, "whether you believe it or not I is fixin' to go down there. I've got some business with some folk down there that can't wait."

The men were looking at each other in utter amazement at the folly of the woman, when Mabel addressed the young man. "You said a sharecropper say he bin down there?"

"Yes, ma"m," he answered, "but as I said, everybody know he lyin'."

"How can I get to where this sharecropper live?" she inquired.

"You go back across the line," the old man directed. "Turn right then left. Stay on that road. 'Bout six miles outa town you'll find the sharecropper. His name is Jim Williams."

"Who owns this buggy?" Mabel asked.

"Iz my buggy," said the old man.

"How much will you charge to take me to Jim Williams' place?"

The old man cocked his head sideways, looked up at the sky, scrutinized the clouds as if they were part of the formula he used in determining the charge for use of his buggy. "Is a mighty hot mornin'," he said. "I'll charge you one dollar."

"It's a deal. Let's go." Mabel turned towards the buggy.

"Just here, wait a minute! So we can get somethin' real straight," the man said.

"I is takin you to Jim Williams' place for one dollar, but I ain't going no further. An' I sure nuf ain't goin anywheres near Rocky Bottom."

"I don't expect you to go where you don't want to go," Mabel assured him. "The agreement is for you to take me to Jim Williams."

By the time they arrived at the sharecropper's home it was four o'clock in the afternoon. During the trip Mabel had learned that her driver's name was Stephen Duke. He was born on a plantation near Jackson. Following emancipation, he had traveled to Bolton to find a younger brother and sister who had been sold to a farmer in the Bolton area a few years before. He found his brother and sister, both of whom had married. His mother died shortly after, and he settled in Bolton to be near the rest of his family. His brother had since "passed on," but his baby sister was still "live an' kickin'". Stephen himself had been married but his wife had died three years earlier.

When they arrived at the sharecropper's place, Jim Williams was just returning from the boss man's house where he had been helping the planter to replace a broken backdoor. Stephen saw Williams walking along the dirt path leading from the farmer's house towards the road. "Dat is old Williams comin' overdar." He pointed towards the path, beyond the field of cotton. Mabel could see only the upper part of the man's body, the rest being hidden by the full growth of cotton bush. Williams had a straw hat on his head and took his time as he walked, looking at the cotton field laden with green pods. Williams saw the buggy pull into his yard, but he continued his slow pace, his hands clasped behind his back. Soon he turned onto the road in the direction of his residence. A black dog trotted ahead of him, his red tongue hanging from his mouth, as he panted in the heat of the afternoon sun. The dog passed the buggy without as much as looking at the strangers, and headed for a shallow tub at the side of the house. He stuck his head in the tub and lapped at the water.

Stephen greeted Williams as he approached. "Howdy, Jim."

"Howdy." Williams was looking at the woman who with the assistance of Stephen had dismounted and now stood beside the buggy. "Looks like old Stephen done gone and got hisself a woman," Williams mused. "She ain't bad looking."

Stephen introduced the stranger. "This here is Miss..."

"Mabel Wright," Mabel volunteered, to the embarrassment of her companion. "And you are Mr. Williams."

"That's me," Jim assured her.

"Nice meetin' you," Mabel said. "Mr. Williams, Mr. Duke here tell me that you bin to Rocky Bottom and that you knows people down there. I want to run a message in Rocky Bottom. I've got to visit Mr. Billy McBride's farm and I was wonderin' if you could take me there. I will pay you for your trouble."

Stephen Duke was thrilled to death to see his friend Williams in such a fix. Trying desperately to keep a straight face, he took a piece of paper from his pocket, fidgeting with it, as he looked at Williams out of the corner of his eyes. "Ah!" thought Duke to himself, "this nigger is sure nuf on the spot." He expected Williams to explain how busy he was and maybe how impossible it would be for him to leave the farm now because of his work.

Instead, when Williams heard the name Billy McBride he beamed with satisfaction. "Lawdy, Lawdy," he declared. "Dem white folks you is talking 'bout is friends of mine. Yes'm. I works for dem for two years now. Right nice folks. Mr. McBride is some ways up North. But the missus is down there with the two chillen."

"Do you know where the man is?"

"I don't reckon I knows. Dey is got the best spring water on their place in Rocky Bottom. It's got healin' qualities in it. Last time I was there I had a terrible chest cold. I took me a drink from that there spring and the cold plumb disappear."

"Will you be able to take me down to Mr. McBride's place now?" Mabel inquired. "It is very important that I get there. As I said, I'll pay you whatever it cost."

"I don't need no pay fer dat. Will be a pleasure to take you. I wants a jug full o' that water anyway." He turned to Stephen who had already climbed back on to his buggy, and taken the reins into his hand. "Well, as soon as I gits paid, I'll be headin' back to Bolton," Stephen was saying.

"Stephen, you knows I don't have no buggy. All I's got is a old mule cart. An' you can't put this woman on no mule cart. Les use your buggy."

"Oh, no! Not this here buggy. I sure nuf will like to go seein' how I ain't never bin there befo'," Duke assured him, "but I ain't got the time. Befo' the sun goes down I's got more work to do than I can handle."

"Negro, you know you ain't got no heapa work to do. Come on wid us. 'Side, how you expect Miz Wright to get back to Bolton? Don't tell me you is scared to go down in Rocky Bottom. Dem is nice people down there," Williams said, a wicked grin on his face.

"Jim, you knows I ain't scared. Hell no. Dem rednecks can't scare me none. But I's got to get back to Bolton soon."

"You wait till I tell them on Church Street how you run like a jack rabbit chase' by a houn', while me alone with this here lady went down in Rocky Bottom," Williams taunted.

Mabel Wright added her piece. "Stephen, you ain't nothin' but scared. Come on with us. I is a woman and I ain't scared. Come on!"

Stephen hesitated. "I can't say I like this seein' how I'm busy, but jus' to show that I ain't no scareder than the resta you, come on, we's goin'."

Some two miles south of the sharecropper's house, the land began to undulate. The road curved west, running for a while along a dry creek. Then it suddenly curved south and disappeared in the thicket with its heavy overgrowth. The three people traveled almost in silence, each absorbed with his own thoughts. The road they traveled soon terminated on the Rocky Bottom road, which ran in an east-west direction. When they got to the creek road in the bottom of the valley, Jim Williams glanced over at Stephen and announced, "We's here. Right down in Rocky Bottom. Ain't no colored person in twenty years travel this here road clear through to the border of Bolton County."

Stephen, holding the reins tightly in his hands, was tense and unsmiling as he scrutinized the road ahead of him. "How fer be it to this McBride Place?"

"Not too fer," Jim responded, "but that ain't make no difference. I likes to be down here in Rocky Bottom in the night. Is the darkest dark you ever seen. So dark you can't even see your own hand if you put it up to you' face."

"Come on, Mr. Williams," Mabel said in a scolding voice. "Don't frighten Stephen like this."

"Who me? I ain't frighten, no sirree." He looked up at the sky. The sun was well on its way towards the western horizon. "Come up," he urged, and the horse increased the pace of its movement.

Soon they came to a small path which led from the main road south, and curving disappeared behind the thicket. On an oak tree at the side of the path was a piece of saw board with the name written in white paint. "Billy McBride."

"Here is the place," Williams announced. Carefully Stephen led the horse down the narrow path, the thicket pressing in on both sides. The path emptied into the farmyard. Before them was a silent house, to the left a partly open barn equally silent save for the sounds of sparrows which had taken possession of the loft and wrangled among the thrushes. The buggy came to a stop in front of the house. Mabel dismounted with the help of Williams, while Stephen nervously dismounted on the other side. Jim walked up to the door.

"Ain't nobody there," Mabel said. Jim turned to look at the woman following behind and Mabel pointed to the stone pressed against the front door. When Jim climbed onto the porch, its boards creaked under his feet. He knocked on the door and waited. Silence. Jim knocked again. Silence.

"It don't look like anybody's home."

"That what I done told you," Mabel commented. She had been standing at the foot of the steps which led onto the porch, and now turned to examine the place. West of the house was an unkempt vegetable plot, a hoe resting against the fence. Mabel walked to the left side of the house.

"They must be gone to Bolton," Jim suggested.

"No, they ain't in Bolton. Ain't nobody livin' here now," Mabel commented dryly.

Jim looked at the woman in surprise, thinking to himself, "How comes she knows all this." Mabel headed towards the barn, Williams walked near behind, while Stephen, still standing close to his horse, nervously observed them. Before she got to the barn Mabel saw the grave to her left. The upturned earth stood out against the surrounding green. Some withered flowers lay on the raw soil. A crude cross guarded the grave site. On it was carved the name, Rebecca McBride. Williams was stunned by the sight of the grave. He opened his mouth to ask, "Who buried here?" but held back and said nothing. Quietly he removed his old hat from his head.

"Mrs. McBride is buried here," Mabel said, as if understanding the unasked question of the man beside her. She turned back towards the house with Jim following closely. "Do you know any of the people in Rocky Bottom?"

"No, I can't say I does. There is another family up the road 'bout half mile and some more further up, but I ain't never bin up there."

"Well, we is goin' up there now," Mabel informed him. By now they were back in the vicinity of the buggy.

"What you both bin watchin' over there by the barn," Stephen inquired.

"A grave," Williams said.

"A grave!"

"Yes, it looks like the woman who lived here done died, an' the others done left."

⌃ ⌃ ⌃

"It gettin' mighty late," Stephen commented, glancing at the clouds gathering overhead. "Les be gone."

"Since there ain't nobody here, we've got to go further up the road to the next house. Mr. Williams says is 'bout half mile up the road."

Stephen looked at the woman who spoke as if she had lost her mind. Mabel was already climbing back on the buggy without help.

"But look here, Miz ... er ... Wright," Stephen protested, "I promised, and I am a man to my word, that I will bring you to the McBride place. And here we is. I ain't promised to go no further."

"But it's only another half mile and is still early."

"A half mile make a lotta difference. Specially when you ain't been there befo'," Stephen still protested.

Williams who until now had remained out of the conversation joined in. "He is right, lady. Ain't no tellin' what we can run into up that road."

"I tell you what," Mabel suggested. "Both of you can stay on the road by the entrance out there. I'll drive up to the next house myself."

"Jus' wait a minute! This here is the only buggy an' hoss I got. Supposin' you takes it up the road and som'n happen to it?"

"I'll pay you for it," Mabel said impatiently. "I come all the way here to get some information and I got to get it."

Unwillingly the men decided to accompany Mabel to the next farm. Climbing back on to the buggy, they headed towards the path leading back to the Rocky Bottom Road. As they came around a curve in the path, a mule-drawn wagon was approaching from the opposite direction. It was driven by Leroy Benton with his wife Cora seated beside him.

The occupants of both vehicles were equally surprised at seeing the others. For a brief moment, they stared at each other unspeaking. Cora, startled by the black faces on the wagon which blocked their path, thought to herself, "Dem niggers look mightly dangerous. We is don fer."

Stephen on the other wagon was thinking, "Lawdy, Lawd, I knowed this was gonna happen. What we gonna do now?" as he looked at the formidable and hostile red face of the man on the other wagon. The horse and the mule eyed each other balefully.

Mabel was the first to speak. "Howdy, Mister."

"What you niggers doin' on my property?" Leroy thundered. "You got one minute to git off 'fore I take my shotgun and blast you all."

"Ah, come on, mister," Mabel said reassuringly. "You wouldn't shoot nobody. I can see by the look on your face that you is a Christian, God-fearin' man. Besides, this here is Mr. McBride's place."

"I ain't Billy McBride," he bellowed, brown spittle gathering on the side of his mouth from his chewing tobacco. "An' this ain't McBride's place no more. What you want with Billy?" Leroy's eyes narrowed and his frown deepened as he made the demand.

"I've got business with him. Very important business. I need to find him or a relative of his."

"You ain't gonna find him here. And he aint got no relatives in these here parts. That no good redneck done went up North, married a Yankee woman, brung her down here to Rocky Bottom, lef' her to die, and ran away up North after some other woman. I bought the whole place from his half-brother who took the chillen to Ohio."

"Do you know anyone what knows Mr. McBride's address?"

"He wouldn't leave no address when he done left his wife fer another woman. He bin gone for two years or more. Better don't show his face no more in the Bottom, fer after what he done won't be no surprise' if he ain't lynched if he come back."

There was nothing more to be said. The path being too narrow for the two vehicles to pass at the same time, Stephen tried to back the buggy into the yard, but the horse, disturbed by the presence of the mule refused to budge. Leroy Benton had therefore to back up his wagon almost to the road, before a spot was found where both vehicles could pass.

"Thanks for the information," Mabel said, as the two came abreast. "Oh, by the way, the man you said you bought the place from, might his name be Enoch Drude?"

Leroy, already affronted by the brazenness of the woman, now brimmed with indignation. "The business I got with Enoch Drude ain't nobody's business but Drude and me."

By now the vehicles had passed each other. Leroy and his wife Cora looked back in cold anger at the black woman and the two men as their buggy headed towards Creek Bottom Road.

"She's a right bold and uppity nigger, ain't she?" Cora commented. Leroy never answered. He sent a wad of tobacco spittle on to the grass beside the wagon.

As they traveled back to the sharecropper's home, Mabel learned what more she could about the man whose whereabouts she had come to Bolton County to discover. Jim Williams explained that he had seen the man but had never spoken to him or known him personally. It was only after Billy McBride had left for up North that he had been employed by Mrs. McBride to do some work. The man who had contacted him was a cattle buyer who lived in Bolton but was now on one of his business rounds through the county. Mabel was distressed. Even if, as the man she had encountered in Rocky Bottom had said, Mr. McBride had run off with some other woman, he certainly would want to come and get his children now that his wife was dead, she thought. Before heading back with Stephen to Bolton, Mabel wrote a note. She placed it in an already used envelope that she had in her purse. Handing it to Jim, she requested that he give it to Mr. McBride if ever he saw him.

The following day, after having slept in Bolton in a room owned by an old lady who rented rooms to blacks passing through, Mabel, her mind crowded with thoughts about the fate of Billy and Sandy, headed for the station where she would take the train for her return trip to Mudville. As she approached the vacant lot where she had rented the buggy for the trip to Rocky Bottom the previous day, she saw a group of about nine men crowded together around the bench which leaned against the spreading oak tree on the lot. The buggy was standing there in the shade, the horse brushing pestering flies with his tail. Approaching the group Mabel could hear a voice which she easily recognized as that of Stephen Duke. Stephen had his audience spellbound with his interpretation of what had transpired the previous day on his trip to Rocky Bottom. Overtaken by the excitement and suspense of his own story, Stephen got up from the bench on which he was seated and the crowd of men gave him enough room to perform as they formed a small circle around him. "An' there I was," he was saying, his eyes open wide in concentration, reliving the experience. "There I was down in Rocky Bottom with this here woman from Mudville by ma side in the wagon. She was as scared as a possum cornered in a tree. And there blockin' the road was a mule cart fulla peckerwoods. The meanest bunch you ever seen, dey face all red like devils. Befo' they could make a move I grabs ma shot gun, points it straight at them, and looking them dead in the eye I says, 'the fus one o' you rednecks moves is dead.' Then I says, 'Touch the sky.' They all puts up their hands, then I says, 'Take your gun with one hand and drop dem on the ground.'" He paused for a moment. "They all done just as I said. Then I says, 'Turn that wagon round and clear out.' They turn that old wagon around and with the mule tail flyin', they hightail it for the other side o' Rocky Bottom."

"Stephen, you knows you lyin'," an old man standing nearby said. "How come ain't no one seen that there colored woman but you?"

"Ask Charlie Poole," Stephen said. "He was here yestiday when the woman hire me. Go cross the road and ask old Percy. He was here too." The men were still laughing unbelieving, when Mabel pushed her way through the group to the inner circle. Stephen saw her as he was about to present another level of defense, and embarrassingly turned to sit down. As he sat looking at the group sheepishly, Mabel addressed him: "Mr. Duke, been lookin' for you. I am goin' back to Mudville this mornin', but I just want to say befo' I go, thank you for savin' me yesterday, when you an' me met that wagonload o' mean white folk in Rocky Bottom."

Stephen, not sure how to interpret the woman's statement, remained silent looking at his feet. "Is you the woman who was with Stephen yestiday?" an old man inquired.

"I is, and this here is one o' the bravest men I ever seen," she said, pointing at Stephen. "Well, I got to go now, since the train is leavin' soon. Good day to you all, and thanks again, Mr. Duke."

As she walked away, the men looked at her in silence. Stephen, having regained his composure, was once more on his feet. Dramatically, he looked around at the men, like some scrawny gamecock having unexpectedly won a battle. "Ain't nutten to it. White folk, black folk, all the same to me," he said. "Got brave uns like me, who ain't fraida nothin'—walk right in to the jaws o' death—then there is others." He paused to fill his pipe with tobacco. "Shucks, that ole shotgun o' mine ain' even have no shells in it." Stephen seated himself on the bench. He puffed on his pipe. "That reminds me o' when I fought in the Civil War under Lincoln in 1864, it was. Yes, sirree, I can still see it now." And he proceeded to tell a tale he had told one hundred times before.

⌢ ⌢ ⌢

When Mabel returned to her farm by the Yazoo it was already afternoon. Mother Brown was seated in the shade of the porch watching the children play. The children saw Mabel coming and ran to meet her, hanging on her arms and all trying to talk to her at the same time. As she looked down at the children, she found herself struggling to fight back the tears. Suddenly images of the past flooded her memory, and for fleeting moments she saw her four children including the two that had died a few years before. She thought how the four used to greet her when she had been away for the day. "Mama, we is so glad you is back," they would say. Then they would ask, "You bring anything for us, Mama?" and Mabel would stop where she was and distribute whatever candies or cookies she had brought back. Knowing what little hope she had brought back to Billy and Sandy, Mabel had stopped off at a store in Mudville and bought two small cloth dolls dressed in beautiful gowns and dancing shoes for Sandy and Sharon, and two toy confederate soldiers outfitted with rifle and shining boots for the two boys. She then opened a package of assorted candies and distributed some to the children.

"Dey bin real good chillen," Mother Brown informed her, smiling with satisfaction. "But them two white ones they ain't too much for talking. I tries to ask them who dey is an' where they come from. All I can get is that they is visitin'."

Mabel laughed. "That is how they is, they don't talk much till they gets to know you real well."

Mabel invited Mother Brown to have supper with them; then she would be taken back home. The two girls helped with peeling potatoes but Mabel took her time preparing the meal. With the cooking done, they all went down to the Yazoo to look at the water just as the sun was going down. The evening was windless; below a gray sky the water was like a gray, greenish sheet of glass. A short distance down the river they could see a flock of water mallards cruising on the surface. On the bank across the river, wild ducks were calling to each other. Mabel and Mother Brown sat below a tree on the bank, and watched the children as they played ducks and drakes and counted the skips made by their pebbles on the surface of the water, or threw sticks in the water and watched them float away. Mabel talked about Bolton, the train ride and the black people she had met, but she revealed nothing concerning the purpose of her trip. Mother Brown again commented on the children, how good they had been during Mabel's absence.

"Sharon is surprising how quick she growed up. Was just yestiday she was jus' a baby," she said, shaking her head and smiling.

Mabel was responding appropriately to the comments of the old lady, but her thoughts were on another subject. Looking at the children play, hearing them chatter, she agonized within herself, "How can I tell them I have not found their father. How do I keep their fires of hope burning that eventually they will find their pa, and what do I do with them in the meantime?"

After supper, Mabel loaded them all into the wagon to drive Mother Brown back to her place. By now the sun had fallen behind the trees on the far side of the Yazoo. Gray shadows crept from the forest over the landscape. This suited Mabel well, for she desired not to have to answer questions about two strange white children from anyone encountered along the road. The horse moved at a quiet pace over the bumpy road. The children enjoyed the ride, filling the air with laughter. Fireflies in the field along the road blinked their lights at irregular intervals as they floated silently nearby. When one flew right over the wagon, Billy reached up to grasp the moving light and the creature fell into the wagon, the luminous portion of his body mildly glowing.

They had covered about half of the distance to Mother Brown's place. Sandy, who sat beside her brother, looked towards the east. "Look at that moon!" They all turned their attention away from the firefly to the greater phenomenon in the sky. There it was, with half its body yet hidden behind the trees, across the cotton field. Like a stately bedecked galleon with silver sail, slowly, majestically it climbed over the trees, on its journey across the sea of heaven.

"You can even see it move," Billy observed.

"No, it ain't movin'," Sharon suggested, "Is when the clouds pass by, it look like it's movin'."

"Do you want to hear a poem 'bout the moon that my Mama learned me?" Billy asked.

"Yes, go on," the children urged. Billy looked up at the moon, but remained silent.

"Go on, Billy, say the poem," Joshua urged.

Then little Billy, with the silver glow of the moon upon his face, repeated the words his mother Rebecca had taught him:

> *"How silently, thou silver moon on high*
> *Sails among the islands of the sky,*
> *Slowly glidest thou across the silver sea,*
> *In all the splendor and tranquility."*

Billy paused. Suddenly he could hear his mother's voice, as clearly as the sound of the wind now blowing against his ear. The vivid scene returned to him, and for a moment he could see his mother, her ruffled golden hair, her face beautiful in the moonlight as they sat on the front step of the porch of their house in Rocky Bottom and she led him to repeat those very words of poetry until he had learned them from memory. His soul reached out for her, and the agony of the yearning caused his tears to flow, as from a cup full and running over.

The other children waited in silence for the rest of the poem. His soft voice had brought everyone in the wagon to silence, including Mabel and Mother Brown.

"Go on, Billy. Finish it," Sandy said. But Billy was silently weeping, tears flowing down his face in the darkness. "Billy's cryin'," Sandy said. "Something's wrong with him."

Mabel handed the reins to Mother Brown. "You can drive better than me, jus' hold it for a while." She turned around into the wagon, took the weeping child into her arms, and held him close to her breast. "Don't cry, son," she said tenderly. "Hush, hush, little darling, and don't you worry 'bout nothing. Everything is gonna be all right." Mabel's eyes were tear-filled. Her teardrops fell on the hair of the child pressed against her bosom. Sandy, seeing her brother weep, broke into crying. Mabel drew her close. "Don't cry, little angel, don't cry," she repeated. Her voice was soft, sweet, and low, filled with the pathos of motherly understanding. "There ain't no reason to cry, your daddy will soon come, and your Ma, you'll meet her in heaven one day." Mother Brown heard little of the reassuring words Mabel spoke to the children. With her aged eyes she tried to keep the wagon on the road, as she strained her ear to hear what was transpiring in the wagon. When they got to Mother Brown's place, Mabel left the children in the wagon. She greeted Mrs. Brown and her husband, thanked them for letting the old lady stay at her place while she was away, and promised to be back soon with the children for a visit. Mother Brown stood by the door, looking over the shoulder of her daughter-in-law as the wagon headed out of the yard and turned south on the dark road. After it disappeared into the night they could still hear the wheels rolling over the stony road.

"We missed you very much," her daughter-in-law said. "You being gone made the house feel like it was empty."

"Thanks, chile," Mother Brown replied, still looking in the direction where the wagon had vanished. "Mabel's got two white chillen stayin' wid her."

"What!" her daughter-in-law asked.

"I says, she got two white chillen stayin' wid her."

That night after the children had prepared for bed, Mabel called Billy and Sandy to her. She told them of her trip to Rocky Bottom. She had been to their home. She had also talked to a man, a colored man, who had worked for their parents. "Do you remember him? His name is Jim Williams."

"Yes," Billy responded. "He had two chillen and a wife. They use to help us on the farm."

"Well, it was he who took me down to the farm." She paused before continuing. "I found out that your daddy is really up in New York. Nobody I spoke to know exactly when he is comin' back. I left a letter for him telling him where you all is so he can come and fetch you. Now all yous got to do is to wait. You see, New York is such a big place and is so far away ain't no way you can find your pa by goin' up there. The easiest thing is fer him to come and get you. Now," she continued, "You both can stay here till your pa comes or if you prefer, I can take you to the town of Mudville and let the Sheriff help you. He can get some nice white family where you can stay, till your pa comes."

"We don't want to go to town," Billy said. "If we is goin to wait fer pa we want to wait here. We like it here with you, Sharon, and Joshua." Mabel looked at Sandy who was biting on the thumb of her right hand.

"Me, too," she said. "We can have plenty of fun playin' with Joshua and Sharon till pa comes."

Mabel again questioned them closely about relatives. They knew of none. Their Mom had told them about relatives in a place called Massachusetts, but they had never seen them. Billy had heard his mom say that her folks in Massachusetts didn't want her because she had married a Southerner. "The people in Rocky Bottom was unfriendly to us—most of them—cause my Ma is from the North."

"Well, that ain't nothin for you lil' uns to worry 'bout," Mabel assured them. "There is plenty of people in the world like that. Some don't like others cause they is from the North, or from the South, some don't like others cause they is white or cause they is black, some people will hate you if you is a Catholic or a Jew or a Baptist, but God likes us all cause he made us all. Jus' remember that for every one person you can find who will say, 'I don't like you,' you can always find ten who will say, 'I like you.'"

The last days of July flew swiftly. Days accumulated into weeks. August came and merged with September. The rapid passing of time in the house by the Yazoo was accompanied with joy and laughter, as Mabel did her best to bring happiness to the lives of the two children waiting for their father. The more she grew to love them, the more she hoped that their father would come, yet from what Leroy Benton had told her, deep within her heart she realized that their father might never come. Mabel spent much time with the details of the daily lives of the children. Regularly they fished in the evening hours and sometimes early morning on the banks of the river. Chores to be done were shared equally by the children.

Mabel sewed clothes for the two children just as she did for Sharon and Joshua, out of cloth that she purchased in Mudville. She purchased storybooks for them to read, and shortly Sandy was able to read almost as well as her brother. Mabel read to them from the Bible, and saw that they said their prayers before going to bed at night and before meals each day. By the end of August close ties had been forged among the children. It was as if they had always been together. One day in early September as Mabel worked in the kitchen, Sandy, who all along had addressed her as Miz Mabel called her "Ma," the name used by her own children. Soon Billy, too, began addressing Mabel as "Ma."

For Mabel, too, changes were occurring in her relationship to the children. One night in late September, before retiring she made her usual round of tucking in each child's blanket to protect against the chill brought in by a brisk night wind blowing from the northwest. She bent over and kissed the four children on their foreheads, and as she took one last look at them before blowing out the candles, it was as if her own children who had died some years before had returned to her. She suddenly realized with a stab of anxiety, how much she had grown to love the two white children. She did not know how long they would be with her, but she would in the meantime give them all the love and affection of a mother.

Since the experience with Petunia at the church picnic, Mabel no longer attended church regularly. Not that she had rejected religion; for Mabel not only read from the Bible to her children, she also taught them to read it, and each Sunday directed her own Sunday School for the four children. But there was an element of resentment within her, that the church had offered no help in her conflict with Petunia. Further, though Petunia's behavior was known and had become a regular topic for gossip and discussion in Niggerville, Petunia was never officially reprimanded up to the day she packed up and left town. Some people had it rumored that Parson Swibbs had had a brief relationship with her during the past, which was why he was reluctant to touch the issue. In any case, Mabel had stopped attending church. A deacon who came to her place earlier to encourage her to return was told, "Until the church gets a new preacher I will be worshipping God right in my own house by the Yazoo."

"Your home ain't the same as the church," the deacon pointed out, at which Mabel quoted to him from the Bible, "Where two or three are gathered in my name, I will be there, said the Lord."

"And what if we ain't never gets a new preacher?"

"Then I ain't never goin' back," Mabel assured him.

Mabel's resolute refusal to attend church was secretly supported by some members of the congregation. She stuck to her decision and returned to the church only after a new preacher arrived on the scene to care for the "flock."

In a way, Mabel's absence from the church had its advantages, for with the two white children in her home, there were even more reasons to stay away from the church. Already, probing questions were being asked in the black community about the children. Rumors were drifting around. The main one which Mabel had made little effort to suppress was that she was being paid by some white folk outside of the county to care for the children while they were away. This particular rumor had been a byproduct of Mother Brown's overnight stay with the children. The day after Mabel's return, Mother Brown and her daughter-in-law tried to piece together what little information the old lady had gathered during her visit. "Dem chillen was sure nuf tightlipped," the old lady observed. "I ask them plenty questions but all they say is that they is visitin'. Dey ain't from round here. I knows all the white folk in these parts. I suspect dey is from Bolton County. Dat's why Mabel bin there visitin'."

"An you notice how strange she acted las' night? Didn't even bring the chillen in to greet nobody, an' was so anxious to hightail it out the yard. Now dat she got white folk chillen stayin' by her place, she probably thinks she is better than we," Mrs. Brown suggested.

"No," the old lady responded, "Mabel ain't like that. I done known her since she was a chile."

"Maybe them is some o' the Wright chillen," the daughter-in-law suggested. "Don't forget that she is a Wright, and her granddaddy was one o' the white ones. There must be still lotsa white Wrights in Mississippi. It could be some o' them Wright chillen stayin' with her."

By the next Sunday after church in Niggerville, people were talking about the white children at Mabel's place. It was mostly curious women involved in the gossiping. "I wonder who they could be?"

"Mother Brown says she stayed overnight with them while Mabel went to Bolton. She says she think some white folk from Bolton is payin' Mabel to keep the chillen. "

"I'll sure nuf like to know who they is and where they is from," said another.

"Well, don't bother to ask Mabel, fer dey say she ain't talkin'," advised another,

"Why she would want to go and get involve' keepin' white chillen in her place, it beats me," Mrs. Jacobs commented. "She got enough problems keepin' them two of her own without a man."

"I don't know what all this fus 'bout keepin white chillen is fer," Sister Ebenezer said. "Black folks bin always keepin' white folks chillen here in Mississippi. You look all across this here State an' you'll find that some o' the richest and most successful white folks bin raised an' even nursed by colored women. So I don't see nothin' so strange with Mabel Wright keepin' a couple of white chillen."

News of the strange children at Mabel's place led to a spate of visits by people "jus droppin' in to say howdy." "I was jus' in the area," they would say, "So I drops in to say hi." "An' how are the little ones?" "Well, I see you got company! Nice chillen they is." To all such probing Mabel had a fairly standard response: "Dey is very well behaved, an' they like it here."

"Will dey be stayin' much longer?"

"I don't know. It all depends when their daddy comes to fetch them," Mabel said to the probing woman, and added, "It don't make no difference. We Wrights always takes care of our own."

The woman went back to Niggerville and spread the new information she had garnered. "Is just what I suspected all along. Dey is chillen from one of the white Wrights--Mabel's granddaddy's folks."

 ⌒ ⌒ ⌒

There was little of what could be called fall in Mudville County. After a few cool nights in September, warm winds continued to blow into October and November. Only in early December did nights chill regularly, with the first touch of frost encrusting the countryside on the night before Christmas. The leaves on the trees browned or yellowed and fell to the ground--save the leaves of the oak, which even in death continued to cling to the trees through the winter months.

During the winter the bonds between the McBride children and Mabel and her two children grew in strength. The children worked, played, sang, and explored every acre of the farm together, taking advantage of the cold period when snakes lay in hibernation. The speech patterns of Billy and his sister were showing audible signs of change. Their accent was becoming closer to that of the black children with whom they lived.

In the winter when the wood in the stove died down and the house grew cold, it was customary for Sharon and her brother Joshua to climb into bed with Mabel and cuddle up close to her. This winter Mabel had to cope with four children climbing into her bed during cold nights. Joshua with his occasional bedwetting was the only one who presented a problem to Mabel by this nightly invasion. According to Joshua he would have a dream which was the cause of his problem. "Whenever I wets the bed I always dream I is peein' outside the back door, and sho nuf when I gets up in the mornin' I find that I peed in my bed." To deal with this problem Madel made a law that anyone coming into her bed at night had to first use the chamber pot under the bed.

The first encounter of Billy and Sandy with a white person since coming to Mudville County occurred in December. The children were gathering black walnuts which still lay on the ground–though the squirrels had started to save their allotment. There was a patch of walnut trees about one thousand yards east of Mabel's place, along the low dirt road which ran east and curved north, finally ending in the town of Mudville some three miles away. The children had collected a large supply of nuts and were returning home when they encountered Mr. Mathis, a white man who worked a small farm about a mile and a half up the road from Mabel's place. Mr. Mathis had been fishing at his favorite spot on the banks of the Yazoo, and had just emerged from the woods on his way home. It suddenly dawned upon Ben Mathis that he had seen the four children together on more than one occasion, in the neighborhood of Mabel's farm, and at least once in a wagon as they returned from Niggerville. Mathis determined to investigate the purpose and origin of this togetherness. "I notice you chillens is always together," he said as he passed them. "Who you be?" he demanded.

"We is Miz Mabel's chillen, sir," Sharon informed him.

"I ain"t speaking about you. I know who you and you is. Is them there I is talkin' to. You, boy! Speak up!" he raised his voice sternly.

"We is from the same family, sir," Billy informed him, looking at the ground and digging his toes into the dust.

"The same what?" Mathis bellowed.

"We is kinfolk," Billy repeated calmly.

Mathis looked at the boy and his sister for a moment, frowning in displeasure, then his frown turned into an uncertain smile. "Oh, yes," he nodded. "I see. Mabel's granddaddy is a Wright." They is either some white Wright chillen from north side of the county, or some of them near-white half-breeds, he thought to himself.

When the children returned home and related to Mabel the details of their encounter with Ben Mathis, she almost had a heart attack. She inquired concerning every detail of the encounter. "What did he say?" "Was he angry?" "What did you say to him?" She was told how Billy informed the man, "We is kinfolk," and how Mr. Mathis had smiled and said, "Ah, yes," nodding, "Mabel's grandpa is a Wright."

"Why did you tell him we is kinfolk?" Mabel inquired from Billy.

"But Ma, you'self said we is all kinfolk in the eyes of the Lord."

Mabel remained silent.

The encounter reinforced in Mabel's mind the conviction that sooner or later there would be a direct challenge from some segment of the white community with regards to the identity of the two children, possibly involving the sheriff. She was glad that the children so far had followed her suggestion, not discussing with anyone their experience in Rocky Bottom or their purpose for being at the farm on the bank of the Yazoo. Mabel determined in her heart that she would do all she could to enable her to continue to care for the children till their father appeared. From what Leroy Benton from Rocky Bottom had told her, she doubted that the man would ever turn up, but she dared not give such cruel information to the children. In any case, she felt herself just as capable as any person, white or black, to take care of the children in the absence of their true parents or relatives, and this she determined to do.

⌃ ⌃ ⌃

Mabel lived a relatively independent life in the black community, and had cultivated few close friendships. Following the affair between Petunia and her husband, she had withdrawn even further to herself. On the other hand, like many of her race in the South, she had developed a careful relationship with a number of whites in the county.

Through the years Mabel had developed a reputation as one of the best seamstresses in the county. Most of her customers were white women. There was not a month of the year when Mabel did not have work to do for a white family in the town of Mudville or in the county. Mabel never advertised her skills, neither did she go about canvassing for sewing jobs. Jobs usually came to her based upon work she had already done. Two years before the McBride children joined her family, Mabel had been given the assignment of making the bridal gown for the sheriff's daughter. She had acquired this particular job as a result of having sewn a formal dress for one Mrs. Plumefeather, whose husband was a veterinarian in Mudville. And this job she had acquired as a result of a dress she had made for the fourteen-year-old daughter of the proprietor of the store where Mabel bought goods occasionally in Mudville. Mrs. Plumefeather had seen the beautiful silk dress, which the girl wore at a party, and inquired of the mother about it. "It was sewn by a colored woman—my personal seamstress," the lady informed her. This, of course, was a gross exaggeration since it was the first time Mabel had done work for that family. "She is," the girl's mother boasted to Mrs. Plumefeather, "the best seamstress in the county."

While the mother had failed to mention the name of the dressmaker, Mrs. Plumefeather found out from the girl herself when she saw her a few days later. "Mary Ann," she said, "I adore that dress you wore at the party the other day. Your mother was telling me the name of the colored woman who made it, but I can never remember the names of colored folk."

"Her name is Mabel. Mabel Wright," the unsuspecting girl informed her.

"Oh, yes, that's right. Where does she live?"

"I am not sure, Mrs. Plumefeather, but I think it must be in Niggerville."

Mrs. Plumefeather on her return home asked her colored maid if she knew a seamstress named Mabel Wright who lived in Niggerville. "I knows her," the maid replied, "but she don't live in Niggerville. She lives in the country south of Niggerville."

"Do you know how I can get in touch with her?"

"I sure do. I knows some folks who live not far from her. I'll send a message through them an' have her get in touch with you."

In dressmaking, Mabel would use pattern books ordered from New York, or she would work by her own patterns. She could simply listen to a description of a dress pattern, and sew a perfect facsimile. When Mrs. Plumefeather wore to church the white dress which Mabel had made, it was the envy of the other women. The dress gave the woman a sort of stately, royal appearance. When Sheriff Tate's daughter decided to have her wedding the following spring, his wife, who was an acquaintance but not a close friend of Mrs. Plumefeather, inquired about the seamstress who had made her sensational dress.

"The colored woman who works for me is my personal seamstress," Mrs. Plumefeather informed her, "but seeing how it is your daughter's marriage, I will give you her name with the understanding that it is not given to anyone else." Thus Mabel's work advertised itself, along with the egotism of some white women in the county.

∧ ∧ ∧

Following the encounter of Billy and his sister Sandy with Ben Mathis, troubling questions began to frequent Mabel's mind. What would she say, how should she respond if she were confronted by this or that white person, concerning the identity and presence of the children at her home? Suppose she was confronted by the sheriff, what would happen? Mabel recalled that she had made the sheriff's daughter's wedding dress and she determined to use this as an avenue of establishing contact with the sheriff's family.

On Monday morning before leaving for the town of Mudville where she had to buy some cloth for a dress she was making, Mabel went into the garden and picked an assortment of fall greens—collards, turnips, kale—which had done well in the mild winter weather. These she placed in a basket and took along with her.

Sheriff Tate lived on the eastern entrance of the town in a small white colonial house, four blocks away from his office. It was just after twelve noon when Mabel walked into the yard, up to the back door of the sheriff's house, and knocked. She greeted Mrs. Tate who immediately recognized her as the colored woman who had sewn her daughter's wedding dress. Mabel expressed the hope that the daughter was doing fine, and informed her, "If you ever have more sewing to do I will always be glad and ready to help." For this offer Mrs. Tate thanked her. At this point, Mabel offered Mrs. Tate the greens, telling her, "My garden is running over with greens and since I was coming to Mudville, I thought I should bring some for the sheriff." Tate, home for his midday meal, heard his name mentioned, and called to his wife to learn who it was. "I thought I heard some lady out there say 'sheriff.'"

"Yes, dear. This colored lady, the one who sewed Marian's wedding dress, brought us some greens." Tate came to the back door.

"Oh, yes, thank you kindly."

"Don't mention it, Sheriff," Mabel laughed. "I always say that there is two men in the county who's got to be fed well, seeing how they have important work to do, the sheriff and the parson."

"You hear that, Mrs. Tate?" the sheriff said, patting with huge heavy hands his belly which slightly hung over his pants. "This lady here knows what she is saying." He laughed. "Ah, let me see— you are from Niggerville."

"Oh, no, sir. I's got a little place about two and a half miles south of Niggerville, right near the Yazoo."

"Oh, yes," the sheriff said, "There are so many people in the county I will never get to know everybody. Well, thanks for the greens; let me pay you for them."

"Oh, no, sheriff, sir, please, no. I didn't bring this for money. However, if the missus will like fresh greens this winter, I'll be happy to sell her all she wants."

"I sure can do with fresh greens," Mrs. Tate commented. "We use a lot of them every week."

"If you ever need to order anything, you can send the message to me by Sally Maud, who works for Miz Plumefeather. She is the cousin of Jim Brown, and he lives just above me."

That winter, Mabel was a regular supplier of greens to Sheriff Tate's household. Aside from providing food for her husband, Mrs. Tate usually prepared meals for every person being held in the county jail.

One day in late February, Mabel was in Mudville on an errand. Passing by the train station, she saw a very fair-skinned black woman coming from the station. The train had just pulled in and Mabel assumed that the woman had arrived on it. She was dressed in black as if in mourning. Two girls around the age of fourteen walked beside her. It was the girls that held Mabel's attention, and had a direct influence on the direction of Mabel's future efforts to protect what she saw as the interest of Sandy and Billy. The two girls, like the woman with whom they traveled, were black but extremely fair of complexion. In fact, it would have taken very close scrutiny on the part of a stranger to ascertain that they were not white. Mabel watched them as they crossed the road and disappeared around the corner. "Indeed," she thought to herself, "If those children tell someone they are white, there's few who could tell them that they ain't. They have blue eyes and is the spittin' image of white folks." The woman, who appeared to be their mother, looked over them as proudly as a hen over newly hatched chickens. As Mabel traveled back to her farm, she thought to herself, "If it comes to it, I sure can pass Billy and Sandy off as fair skinned colored children. We got relatives in Soso, Mississippi, and in South Carolina, who as white as them kids, yet they is colored. Some of them is so white, they don't even think 'bout their selves as colored. A few bin up North and marry white folk who didn't even know they was marrying colored."

When Mabel returned to the farm, the two children were seated on the sofa. Billy was reading from a Bible storybook to his sister. "They don't look no different from them two girls I seen today," she thought. "Besides, when you look at their olive hue and Sandy's unruly hair, there is few people white or colored who would know the difference if I say them children is colored."

∧ ∧ ∧

Winter, which had been relatively mild, gave way to an early spring. By the second week of February, warm winds blowing across the Yazoo up from the Gulf of Mexico caressed the earth; and as rays of sunlight shining through the bedroom window onto the face of a sleeping child in early morn awakens her to the new day, so the warm southern winds gliding across the Yazoo sent shivers of joy through the land. The wind embraced the bodies of naked trees with their myriad bony fingers pointing skyward. It made soothing sounds against their empty branches, whispered in their ears "awake, awake from slumber," and the branches stirred in response. By the end of February the stems on the dogwood swelled and burst into small leaves. Lavender crocus pushed their heads from the damp soil and the forsythia bush at the side of Mabel's house was displaying its deep yellow blooms.

With the early spring, some farmers took to planting earlier than usual, while others described the warm weather as a freak situation, and waited to see if the cold would return. Ground worms revealed their presence, leaving cylindrical patterns on the surface of the soft soil. Frogs began to croak in the marshes along the river, where water lilies emerged from under the surface.

The blue jay and the sparrow began their nest building about three weeks earlier than usual. Jim Brown, with his boss, Mr. Brentwood, was working in front of the barn on a plow that needed repair. When Jim observed the blue jay building a nest in a tree nearby, he shook his head. "We is in fer trouble this spring."

"What trouble are you talking about?" Mr. Brentwood inquired.

"Them jay birds," Jim said, pointing towards the tree. "They is building their nest early, I'd say, three weeks early. Birds have sense us humans ain't got, an' the jay know that bad weather is a'comin so he is hurryin' to get over with the raisin' of chillen befo' the drought."

The farmer laughed. "That's nothing but superstition, Jim. There ain't no substance to it."

"I bin workin' on the farm all my life," Jim retorted. "I worked fer your daddy and I work fer you, and I ain't once bin wrong in predictin' the weather from birds. Dem birds know what is happening in the future. That's how come befo' a bad winter they allays go away, and if they know the winter will be warm, they don't go nowheres. If we humans can study birds, we can learn a lot."

"Well," Brentwood responded, "We'll wait and see if the birds are right."

^ ^ ^

Mabel returned from Niggerville one day in the spring to see a pile of soft brown hair on the table in the kitchen. She looked at the hair in disbelief. Outside in the yard, the children were building a tree house. There was Sandy, but her hair, which normally fell below her shoulders, was short and plaited in the same cornrow pattern as that of Sharon. For the first time since the children had arrived at the farm, Mabel became truly infuriated. "You chillen come inside right away, all of you," she demanded.

"I told you Ma will be mad," Joshua reminded. "I'm gonna tell Ma that me an' Billy had nothin' to do wit' it."

"That's right," added Billy. "We didn't even know what you two was doin' inside the house."

As soon as the four stepped inside, Mabel confronted them. "Whose hair is this on the table?"

"It's mine, Ma," Sandy said meekly.

"An' who told you, you can cut off all you hair like this?"

"I wanted my hair to be just like Sharon, so I could comb and plait it the way she do hers."

"So you cut all your hair off?"

"I done it," Sharon said. "Sandy wanted her hair like mine, so I cut it."

"So Sandy is a woman in this house, is she? She decides if her hair can be cut?"

"No, Ma," Sharon answered.

Mabel ordered Billy and Joshua to go outside and cut a whip from the sassafras tree. "I goin' give you two a good wupin'." Sandy hadn't been spanked for over a year, the last time by her mother Rebecca, but still she remembered how she had begun crying even before the whipping started, with the hope of softening the heart of her mother. I'll try the same thing on Ma also, she thought, but Sharon beat her to it.

"Oh please, Mama, not this time. We ain' never gonna cut no more hair again," Sharon pleaded.

Sandy chimed in, "Please Mama, give us one more chance." They both were crying bitterly. "That the first wrong thing we done in a long time an' if you give us a chance this time, we ain't never goin' do nothin' wrong again."

By now the boys, Billy and Joshua, relishing the idea of seeing the girls whipped, had cut a sizable whip, trimmed off the leaves, and brought it back to Mabel. Having delivered the whip they planted themselves by the back door outside, from where they hoped to witness the spanking.

"What are you both standin' there for?" Mabel demanded. The boys quickly retreated to the side of the house, below the window, from where they could hear what was transpiring inside.

Mabel surveyed the crying children. Her initial annoyance now partially abated, she had already decided against whipping them. "I have a good mind to really put it on you both," she informed them. From the tone of her voice the children sensed that things were moving in their favor, the scales were tipping in the direction of no whipping. "Oh, please, Mama," they pleaded. "Give us another chance."

"Both of you come and sit on this sofa." They quickly complied. "I don't know what craziness entered both of you to make you do this. Do you have any idea how long it will take for this hair to grow back?" They were silent. "Since I never talked to either of you before about cutting hair, I'm gonna let it pass this time. But the next time it happens, ain't no crying will save you both from a good wuppin. Now both of you sit right where you are until I tell you to move."

Billy and Joshua went back to their work on the tree house, somewhat let down over the change of events. "How hard does your Ma wup?" Billy inquired. "My ma before she died, boy! Could she wup. She used to use a small leather strap if it was a small thing you done, but if you done real bad, like playin' with fire or saying a bad word, boy! She will drop your pants and wup you straight on your behind."

"Ma is zackly the same," Joshua observed. "A little wuppin for a little thing and a big wuppin for a big thing. One day, me an Sharon went down to the river and went in the shallow water. Ma sho nuf let us have it. While she was getting the whip, me and Sharon ran inside and put on some more clothes. It didn't make no difference. Mama took off the two pants I had on, an' right on my backside she put it. She done the same to Sharon. We ain't bin back in that water no more since."

That spring Mabel proceeded with the idea that had come to her that winter day in Mudville when she had seen the fair colored woman with the two almost white children. She hitched up the wagon and drove over to Mr. Mathis' farm. Mathis farmed thirty acres, about one mile east along the dirt road. His house, a bit larger than Mabel's, had an actual fireplace built of stone. He kept a few cows and planted a few acres of cotton from which he and his wife, a childless couple, made a meager but satisfactory livelihood.

Mathis was just leaving the barn when Mabel drove into the yard. "Howdy, Mabel," Mathis greeted her. "Since that man o' your'n left we ain't seen much of you or the chillen."

"Don't even talk 'bout that man, Mr. Mathis. He ain't no good. When I was young there was three men come courtin' me, an' I had to go and marry the worse of the three."

"It sure surprised me that he'd do a thing like that," Mathis commented, shaking his head.

"Well, with God's help I'm makin' it. I bin doin' a lot of sewin' and growin' enough food an' vegetables to support myself and the chillen. We need a lot of food in the house, seein' how I got two of my cousin chillen staying with me."

"Cousin?" Mathis said with surprise. "You mean them two white chillen I seen back in December is your family? I kinda figured they was Wrights, but I didn't know they was as close as cousins."

Mabel laughed. "Ain't it strange how if you is colored and real fair skinned people find it hard to tell if you is white or colored."

"You mean dem chillen is colored?"

"They sure is, Mr. Mathis," Mabel responded. "Their mammy is fair skinned and their pappy is white. The mammy died and the father is somewhere up north and I'm takin' care of them."

"Well, they sure nuf fooled me," Mathis said. "I took one look at them and I figured they was white chillen."

"I got lots of fair skinned family like them in South Carolina and in Soso, Mississippi," Mabel informed the man. Then abruptly she changed the conversation. She was looking for a pony to buy for the children, and wondered if Mr. Mathis knew where she could find one. Mathis recommended to her a farmer north of Mudville who raised ponies, and after thanking him for the information Mabel departed.

Before returning home Mabel turned the wagon on which she rode north on the road to Niggerville. Some two miles up the road she pulled into Jim Brown's yard. "Anybody home?" she called.

"Yes, I is here," came the voice of Jim's wife, Edith. "I heard the wagon roll into the yard, but I thought it was Jim. He's gone to Niggerville to fetch a wheel he took up there to repair three weeks ago. The man shoulda finished it since last week, but each time Jim bin there he says it ain't ready. You'd think he was doin' it for nothin'. I told him, if it ain't finished today, to take it to Mudville."

Mabel sighed. "Chile, there is problems all over the place, there is me without a man trying to take care of two chillen, suddenly I finds myself with four." She laughed. "But what can you do. You can't put your own family out."

"I knowed it all along," Edith said triumphantly. "I told Jim that them white chillen was your family."

"Dey is my family, but dey ain't white."

"Dey ain't white?"

Mabel shook her head. "Down in Soso, Mississippi, you'll find dozens o' Wrights what look just like them. Some of them is so fair skinned they demself don't know what dey is."

When Jim returned with the repaired wheel and Mother Brown who had gone along for the ride, Edith related what she had learned from Mabel. Mother Brown scowled her leathery face. "It sure beat me," she murmured. "Sure beat me. I thought I knowed what black folk and white folk look like. It sure beat me. I could swear dem chillen was white."

Before the week was out, it was all over Niggerville that the two strange children at Mabel's house were actually some of her fair skinned colored relatives. The children had been to Niggerville on only one occasion, late in the evening. To most people in the town they were just a rumor since they had not so far been seen. But those who had seen them had taken it for granted that the children were white. Only Babs Jacobs took a different view. When he heard some women in his shop talking about the newly obtained information with regards to the children, he announced triumphantly, "I knowed it all the time. From the fus moment I seen them chillen, I says to myself, I says, 'Babs, you ain't lookin at no white chillen. You is looking at colored folk.' But I kept my mouth shut. I ain't said nothin' cuz I knowed how you women always gossipin'. So I said, let them think what dey want. I knows what I knows."

That week on Wednesday Mabel took the children with her to Niggerville. The town was having a yard sale to collect money for building a school. This effort coincided with the departure of the residing preacher for a new post in Montgomery, and the arrival from Tennessee of a new shepherd for the local Baptist flock. Immediately upon his arrival, Parson Jones had declared the need for a school and had launched the program to add a room on to the side of the church for this purpose. Meanwhile a school was started in the church.

In keeping with her earlier commitment, Mabel returned to church now that a new preacher had arrived. Participation in the sale was the first overt signal that her return to the church was imminent.

Mabel coached the children on how they should behave while in Niggerville. "Don't pay attention to no nosy questions," she directed them. "If people ask you where your parents is or who you is, tell them to ask me."

There were no problems. The children played on the grass beside the church where the wagon was tied, while Mabel attended the sale spread out on tables in front of the church. The money collected at the sale, along with financial gifts by members of the community was enough to add the new room to the church in time for school the following September.

In spring, Mabel planted a larger than usual garden. The children helped as much as they could, especially in the planting of peas and corn. When spring peas came in, Mabel picked several pounds, part of which she took to Sheriff Tate, whom she now regularly supplied with greens. Greens were not expensive nor difficult to grow, but the sheriff's wife, not the gardening type, preferred to buy whatever such commodities she needed.

Mabel arrived at Sheriff Tate's home just after midday. The sheriff had already finished eating and sat now under the shade of a spruce tree in his back yard, on a bench which he had placed there for that purpose. The sheriff's wife who had just been talking to a neighbor across the fence, greeted Mabel as she entered the yard. When Mabel presented her with the peas, Mrs. Tate turned to go to the kitchen to get some money, but the sheriff had some change in his pocket and offered to pay for the peas.

"The peas really came early this year!" the sheriff's wife observed.

"Yes, ma'am," Mabel answered, "and since I got more help than usual this year, I was able to plant a little more. Two of my cousin's children, a boy eight and a girl seven are staying with me. They is young, but the boy especially knows a lot about planting, and with my two little ones they bin a great help."

"I was brung up on a farm and when I was about their age, I used to help my Ma and Pa in the garden," Mrs. Tate commented. The sheriff glanced over in the direction of his wife with a look of curious surprise on his face. He knew full well that his wife, though brought up on a farm had no farming experience herself. Her father had had an entire army of black workers who did all the labor. The wife saw the curious look on her husband's face, but she ignored it.

"Is difficult to take care of four children without a man, but I had to take these two in, seeing how they is my relative and they had nobody else to care for them," Mabel continued. "Trouble is, these two their skin is so fair, seeing how their daddy is white, that wherever I takes them even black folk callin' them white chillen." The black woman chuckled.

"Well, it's lucky they have someone like you to take them in. God will bless you," Mrs. Tate said.

"I sure need it, Miz Tate," Mabel replied.

∩ ∩ ∩

Mother Brown like some other elders of the black community was a source of living history and homespun philosophy. In the early days of spring, she would sit by the window of their small wooden cottage or in the shade of the sycamore tree on the side of the house and look in silence across the field, where she and her parents had worked for well over one hundred years. She would see the land being upturned in early spring in preparation for the cotton crop. Mother Brown would watch as the cottonseeds were planted by a row of black men, women, and children, as with backs bent they worked and sang under the sun.

Mother Brown would sit by the window for days and look at the dark soil as it lay in silence, with the millions of cottonseeds implanted in its womb. Then one morning after an overnight light shower of rain, Mother Brown, after breakfast, would take up her post by the window, and lo, it would be as if a greenish yellow, only barely-visible carpet had been rolled out during the night over the field. By the next day, the green would be more pronounced, as millions of seeds in response to some imperious call of nature, each opened its heart and released a small, fragile pair of leaves. Soon the land would be covered with a thick carpet of green as the young plants sucked the nitrogen from the rich humus laden soil, absorbed the sunlight, and transformed them into life.

Within weeks, Mother Brown could go to the edge of the cotton field, and walk for a few yards among the youthful plants, already so grown that her ankles were hidden and the stretching stems of their pliant branches touched the hem of her long, sweeping dress. Mother Brown would sit by the window and look at the cotton bushes each day as they grew, as the small pods appeared on the stems and slowly swelled to full maturity, like the breasts of young virgins changing from childhood to puberty. Mother Brown from her window would look at the cotton field as, one by one, in the fall of the year, aging cotton pods, no longer able to contain the pressure of their contents, burst at the seams, exposing their white soft substance to the sun. She would look at the aging field, leaves withered and dry, white with matured cotton, and say, "The cotton tree is jus' like us humans. They grows, develops, bear fruits, gets old. Soon the cotton gonna be picked, and the trees with nothing else to do gonna be plucked up."

Late in the fall, Mother Brown commented to her son Jim, "Time is like a creek running over level flat ground. It sure nuf run slow."

- 110 -

Jim thought for a while as he sat by the kitchen window. "Ma, time ain't really slow or fast," he said respectfully, "Is us humans who make it look that way. It don't ever change, ain't have no reason to change. Time is more like a mule pulling a cart in the heat of the sun--it don't go fast or slow, it just keep goin'."

⌢ ⌢ ⌢

But Mabel Wright had reasons to perceive the swiftness of time. The first and second winter since the arrival of Billy and Sandy had come and gone. It seemed to her that their arrival had marked a new beginning, so that much of her thought was tied to occurrences defined as "before the chillen came," or "after the chillen came."

There was little unusual about the second spring. Winter had been mild; then towards the end of February a massive snowstorm swept from the north across the delta. Mother Brown and other elders described it as the worst snowstorm in memory. Some people gave a religious interpretation to the phenomenon. The preacher at the white Baptist church in Mudville declared from the pulpit on the coldest Sunday in the city's memory, that it was the hand of the Lord, "showin' his displeasure with all the moonshining and other deviltry in the county." By the end of the second week in March, spring had enveloped the countryside. Winds blowing across the Yazoo brought with them a freshness and an indescribable smell of new life. There was little rain during the spring, but the land was saturated by the moisture from winter.

In the month of September, the church school in the town of Niggerville opened under the direction of Mrs. Thelma Jones, the wife of the new preacher, Parson Malcolm Jones, a man in his forties. The parson who had formerly shepherded a flock in Madison County, Alabama, and in Birmingham, for reasons known only to himself— accepted the position in Niggerville, a place he had never known before.

School started. Billy and Sharon, both nine years old and Joshua and Sandy, eight, were among the first students. Mrs. Jones had attended school in Atlanta and prior to her marriage had worked as an assistant teacher in a Baptist school in that city. She had met her husband at a convention for Baptist workers held in Montgomery, and had since been his faithful wife and inspiration, eager to advance the cause of education in the black community.

Mabel's children walked to school each day. Usually they met some of Jim Brown's children, and together they would walk the remaining two miles to the school. For Mabel's children school soon became a fascinating experience. All four children had learned to read from the storybooks that Mabel bought, and had memorized a few short poems and Bible verses. Eagerly the children absorbed that which they were taught by Mrs. Jones, and soon settled into the rhythm of school, nine to three o'clock from Monday to Friday.

In late October, some eight weeks after school started, a young boy, the son of Zell Hines who resided in Niggerville, brought a squirrel to school in a shoebox. He had caught the creature when it made the mistake of going into a cul-de-sac in the back of his father's barn, attracted by some grain that had spilled on the floor. Starky blocked the escape of the squirrel, which he called Brownie, and tied a string around its neck. Sandy and Sharon were allowed to take the squirrel out of the box during recess to play with it. In the process of being returned to the box, the squirrel bit Sandy on the thumb of her right hand and scratched the back of Sharon's left hand.

The encounter with the squirrel was almost forgotten until two weeks later when Sandy fell ill. Returning from school the children were caught in a thunderous rainstorm that soaked them thoroughly. Over the weekend, two of the children became ill with sore throats, spells of coughing, and by Monday a high fever. On Tuesday, Sharon's fever had disappeared, her coughing had diminished, and she felt well enough to go outside. But not so with Sandy; her condition grew worse. The fever increased so that by Tuesday she was literally burning up as she lay in bed.

Mabel had interpreted the child's complaint as a severe cold and had been treating her with the simple remedies she had used so many times before on her own children. She made tea of special herbs sweetened with honey. She kept Sandy's forehead covered with a cool, wet cloth and sponged her with soda water to keep the fever down.

Mother Brown, a woman versed in home medicine, having successfully nurtured seven children of her own, when she heard that Sandy was sick, came for a visit to see if she could be of help. Mother Brown's knowledge of home medicine had gained her respect in the community. For simple cuts she administered powdered resin to stop the bleeding, for arthritis dry ginseng roots ground up and mixed with vinegar, for asthma a tea of chestnut leaves or a plaster of lard and black pepper; for a bee sting she would apply moistened snuff or tobacco, for snake bites Indian tobacco leaves, and for boils, catnip leaves cured in boiling water. For treating a cold Mother Brown would boil pine needles, strain and add sugar; for chills and fevers boiled dry peach leaves; for swollen breasts collard greens and milkweed in hot water; and for rheumatism, boiled ginseng, pink root, and slippery elm.

Listening to the conversation of the children as she talked with Mabel, Mother Brown learned that two weeks earlier Sandy had been bitten by a squirrel. Later that evening, Sandy, who had eaten nothing all day save a few spoonfuls of soup, was given a cup of water to soothe her burning lips. The child took one sip of the water and rejected it, crying that her throat was hurting. Billy, who had taken the water to his sister, related the incident to Mabel and Mother Brown: "She won't take it. She took one look at it, and pushed it away like if she was 'fraid of it."

Mother Brown heard the words "water" and "'fraid of it" and responded with alarm. "Let me see that water." She took the water and with it returned to the bedroom where Sandy lay. She offered it to the child. "Here is some water. Drink it, it will help your throat."

"No, no," Sandy cried, turning her head towards the wall. "Take it away, take it away." Mother Brown placed the tin cup on the small table near the window, drew Mabel aside and whispered in her ear, "That chile is got hydrophobie. There ain't no medicine fer that but prayin' an' miracles." She explained to Mabel that the child's frightened response to the water was a sure sign.

Mabel panicked. Rapid scenes passed before her mind of her two children who had died five years earlier from malaria. Mabel sent Billy and Joshua to Niggerville to get Parson Jones. She wanted to scream and pull her hair out, but she kept telling herself, "You've got to be calm, Mabel." While she awaited the arrival of Parson Jones, Mabel sat at the bedside of the sick child. Holding her burning hands in hers, feeling her face, she prayed that the fever would subside. She kissed the child's burning cheeks. "It's all right, baby," she said reassuringly. "Mama is taking good care of you, you will be better soon."

When Parson Jones got the message carried by the two boys, he came immediately. He was motivated by his religious responsibility, but was also aware of the problems Mabel had had with his predecessor and her recent return to the church. He determined to leave no stone unturned in his effort to help.

By the time the parson arrived at Mabel's place, other interested parties were there. Jim Brown, informed by the two children on their way to Niggerville that Sandy was suffering from hydrophobie, hitched his wagon and took his wife to see the child.

Parson Jones greeted members of his flock, and talked soothingly to Mabel, commenting that about one-third of his members presently seemed to be under the weather with a cold or other complaint. Mabel with Edith standing close by her side told Parson Jones the diagnosis which Mother Brown had made.

"She coulda catched hydrophobie from the squirrel that bit her," Mother Brown told Parson Jones. "That child's bin bit by a squirrel, and such critters and skunks carry hydrophobie. The way the child is afraid of water is a sure sign."

Parson Jones, himself far from being a novice in matters of local medicine, was aware of the fact that one symptom of rabies, locally called hydrophobie, was the display of a fear of water. The parson asked for a cup of water, which was presently fetched. He went into the dimly lit bedroom where Sandy lay, her body partly covered by a colorful homemade quilt. She was groaning softly. The preacher got a piece of cloth, and in the sight of the girl he poured some water over the cloth. Taking the wet cloth he passed it over the child's face. "Here, my little one, this water will cool the fever a bit." He placed his fingers in the cup of water, and as a priest baptizing an infant he sprinkled the water over the child's face then dried her face with the cloth. She continued to groan, but there was no other response.

Returning to the room where the other people were talking in a subdued voice, he placed the cup on the table. Then humbly but in a voice of authority, he said, "That child ain't got no hydrophobie. She's got something all right, a bad cold, maybe pneumonia or something else, but there ain't no sign of hydrophobie." He advised Mabel that should the fever continue to the next day she should get the child to a doctor. Before departing for Niggerville, the parson led those gathered in the house in prayer for Sandy. Speaking to God on behalf of the group, the parson pleaded: "Place your healin' hand of mercy on little Sandy's head, and heal the chile even as you healed the sick in days of old." The older ones kneeling with the parson joined in with cries of "Amen," "Do, Jesus," and "Yes, Lawd." The prayer was ended with the parson leading the group in the Lord's Prayer, which he signaled them to repeat with him when he said, ". . . in the name of the One who done taught us to say when we pray. . . . "

Wednesday, Sandy's condition seemed to stabilize, but by Thursday she grew worse. Mabel sent Billy and Joshua, accompanied by Edith Brown's eldest daughter, to Mudville to ask Dr. Beadle if he would come and visit the child. The doctor directed that Sandy be brought to Mudville. "Tell her mother to wrap her up in a blanket and bring her to my office." The doctor was extremely busy with several cases of illness in Mudville. He was also standing by to aid a woman who was having difficulty in childbirth.

Mabel received the doctor's message with alarm. "The child is too sick to take outside in this chilly weather." Getting Edith Brown to care for Sandy, Mabel hurried to Mudville and to the house of the county veterinarian. With tears in her eyes she told Mrs. Plumefeather of the condition of the child, how she had had a high fever since the weekend, and was so weak she could hardly raise her head. Mrs.

Plumefeather's heart was touched. She knew Dr. Nicholas Beadle very well; in fact, she had been one of his early sweethearts. Using her charm and her long acquaintance with the doctor, she related to him the condition of the child and pleaded with him to pay the visit.

The pregnant woman by now had had a stillbirth. The mother was in satisfactory condition, making it easier for Dr. Beadle to make the trip out of town.

Following Mabel in his stately coach, the doctor arrived at the farm on the banks of the Yazoo. He examined the child closely, looked into her mouth, felt around her neck and her throat. He listened carefully to her coughing, which was deep and painful. He listened to the sound of her breathing through his stethoscope. There was a heavy ooziness in her chest. The fever remained high. Completing his examination, he placed the cover over the child. "She needs an extra blanket. She must be kept warm by all means." He gave some medicine in a brown bottle for the child. "Keep her forehead covered with a cold, wet towel the way you have been doing. Give her the medicine in doses as directed on the bottle. Can you read?"

Mabel nodded her head. "Yes, sir."

"I believe that the child has pneumonia. Don't give her anything cold to drink. Feed her with broth or soup, as warm as she can drink it."

Mabel was thanking the doctor profusely for coming to her humble home to visit the child. She knew he had a lot of other work to do, but she was sure that God would bless him. As he walked towards his coach, he turned to face Mabel. "Er, what's the girl's name?"

"Sandy."

"Is Sandy a white child?"

Mabel looked at him in his eyes. He was looking beyond her. "Her father is white as well as her grandfather on the mother's side."

"Oh, I see," the doctor replied thoughtfully. "Let me know how she is progressing. Get in touch with me should she appear to be getting worse."

Again Mabel thanked the doctor. She paid him the visitation fee of two dollars, and directed Sharon and Joshua to place a sack of potatoes as well as two dozen eggs in the back of the doctor's coach.

Thursday and Friday, Sandy's condition remained unchanged. Her fever would decrease in the morning, only to rise again to a high point at night. Mabel remained close to her bedside throughout the day, while at the same time seeking to meet the needs of the rest of the family. All night she remained with Sandy. When Mabel awoke from a troubled sleep the following morning, she looked at Sandy. The child was so still Mabel shook her slightly to see if she was still alive. The child turned and groaned weakly. Early that day, Mabel sent a message to Dr. Beadle, telling him that Sandy had taken a turn for the worse. While her fever was behaving the same, she was growing visibly weaker.

Dr. Beadle rode the two-and one-half miles from Mudville to Mabel's place, even allowing Sharon, who had brought him the message, to ride back with him on his coach. He spent several minutes with Sandy, carefully examined her, listening to her breathing, the rattling sounds coming from her chest. "What a lovely child to die like this," Beadle thought to himself. When he left the room there was an ominous seriousness on his face. "She is very weak," he said to Mabel. "She has declined since last I saw her. We must continue giving her the medicine. There is nothing else we can do now. It's out of our hands, we just have to pray."

As soon as Dr. Beadle left, Billy and Sharon were sent to Niggerville to get Parson Jones. The parson jumped on his wagon and with the two children who had brought the message headed for Mabel's farm, three miles away. When he arrived, Mabel was almost in a state of shock over what the doctor had said. She struggled to keep from falling apart in front of the children, knowing there was nothing else she could do to save the child.

Sandy lay on her side, her body on fire with the fever. Her breathing was harsh and shallow, and Parson Jones could hear the slight rattle deep in her chest as she breathed. Mabel explained to him that the doctor had called her sickness pneumonia. "That's the first thing that came to my mind when I saw the child the last time I was here."

When Jim Brown's wife arrived, Parson Jones was saying that faith and prayer could save the girl's life. "It's never too late with Jesus. Dr. Beadle may say it's out of his hands, but it ain't never out of the hands of de Lawd." Mabel accepted the parson's comment, but with the grim memory that prayer and fasting had not saved her two children five years earlier.

Parson Jones led the group—Mabel, Ethel, and the children—in a session of prayer at the bedside of Sandy, and when the prayers ended, Parson Jones suggested to Mabel that he anoint the child. Mabel was now fully awakened to the tragedy about to befall her: anointing had been the last act performed by the former minister on her two children before they died. She shook herself out of the gloom that was seeking to engulf her. "The doctor says there ain't nothing we can do and we done prayed and asked God to heal Sandy. I ain't gonna sit here and watch the chile die without trying everything I can. Since Dr. Beadle can't do no more, I'm gonna try my own method. It may fail, but is better than sittin' here and doin' nothing. I gonna give Sandy a fomentation.

People who have pneumonia is suppose' to have heaps a cold on their chest. Fomentation is suppose' to loosen up colics. In any case, I can't sit here an' see my chile die without fightin'."

Mabel heated up a pot of water. Removing the clothing from Sandy's chest, she covered her with two pieces of linen up to her chin. Taking a large towel she soaked it in the hot water, wrung the water from the towel, then folding it in two, laid it over the linen on the child's chest. The towel was then in turn covered by a third piece of cloth. With the help of Mrs. Jones, Mabel continued this process for over an hour, at the same time keeping the child's forehead wrapped in a wet cold towel. After about an hour, Mabel removed the hot towels from Sandy's chest, dried her well, then rubbed her chest and neck thoroughly with eucalyptus oil. Mabel repeated the process twice during the day, and once more after sundown.

About eight o'clock that evening Sandy fell into a deep sleep and slept till the following morning. Reverend Jones had left during the night to return to Niggerville, but his wife remained to assist Mabel until it was time to start school for the day. Sandy accepted small amounts of liquids and her situation remained stable. Mabel repeated the fomentation treatment, with the help of Edith Brown who returned to see how the child was doing. That night after Edith left, with the other children asleep in the adjoining room, Mabel fell on her knees beside the bed where Sandy lay. Holding the limp hand of the child in hers she poured out her heart to God on behalf of the child. As she prayed silently, her lips visibly moving, tears flowed down her face and on the hand of the child she held. "Oh, Lawd," she cried silently. "I ain't complaining, but like Job, I is weighted down with grief and anxiousness. I don't know what I done, what sin I committed to deserve this. I have carried silently the burden fer years. My man went and left me, then my two lil' ones the joy of my life I buried within three months in the grave. I thought I would die, that my heart was breakin', but I bit my lips, hid my tears, and struggled on. Then you sent me these two chillen, strangers, white. I took them and I bin lovin' them an' carin' fer them like my own chillen these two years. Now little Sandy is lyin' here burnt up with fever, weak and helpless. I done done all I can do. I done tried all I know, even after Dr. Beadle done gave up on her. Don't take her from me, Lawd. I can't bear the agony and the pain. She is just a lovely, innocent chile. She lost her real mother and father, that was pain and sufferin' enough. I beg and beseech you, save Sandy's life." Mabel prayed and fell asleep on her knees, her head resting on the bed, and there she slept till morning.

Mabel was startled awake by the voice of Sandy calling, "Ma. Ma." She wondered how long she had been asleep. "I'm so thirsty I need some water." Mabel rushed into the kitchen and fetched the water.

"Take a few sips, darlin'," she urged, placing the cup to the parched, blistered lips of the child.

Sandy gulped the water down. "Thanks, Ma."

Mabel let her head rest back on the pillow. "How you feelin', chile?"

There was a weak smile on her face as she looked up at the woman bending over her. "I'm feelin' much better."

Mabel held her hands in hers, she kissed her face. The fever had departed. The crisis was past. Within two days Sandy was out of bed and walking around the house. She had lost some weight and was still weak, and it was one full month before Mabel allowed her to return to school. The experience of Sandy's illness drew the family closer together than ever, forging an even greater feeling of kinship among them.

ᗘ ᗘ ᗘ

One Sunday afternoon, in spring, three years after the arrival of Sandy and Billy in Mudville County, Mabel and the four children on their return from church stopped at Jim Brown's yard for a social call. Edith had taken two of her children to church. Jim, not particularly a church person, had remained home with Mother Brown, whose rheumatism was acting up. Edith returned with her children only minutes before Mabel arrived.

The old folk sat on the porch and talked while the children played in the yard. The conversation centered on the church service of the day. The children's choir, in which both Sandy and Sharon sang, as well as Jim's girls, Milicent and Juliann, had provided the music for the divine service. The music had been beautiful. The youthfulness of the voices, the melody of the music, and the words, taken together, were moving to the congregation. The choir had presented three renditions before the sermon. A solo part in the last song had had been done by Sharon, who had a melodious contralto voice. As her voice rang out with the choir humming in the background—"Keep pressing on, De Lawd is on our side," tears came to the eyes of many, and one old deaconess "caught the spirit" and fell to the ground. By the time Reverend Jones stood up to preach, the congregation was already in a state of spiritual excitement.

The conversation among the women in the verandah shifted to the children playing outside. "Jus' yestiddy that little Juliann was born," Mother Brown commented. "Edith had so much trouble birthin' that chile, some o' the women thought she won't make it." She shook her head. "I'll never ferget that night. Stormy and thunderin' outside—a real

- 118 -

gully washer an' all of us prayin' inside. Look at the chile now. Fifteen years old an' as big as her Mammy."

"Yes," Edith added, "already almost ol' enough to marry and have her own chillen."

Jim, who was seated on the steps, looked back at the women. "She is still my baby. It gonna be a long time befo' I allows any man to come courtin' her. She is got plenty mo' learnin' befo' she can even think of courtin' much less marryin'."

"When I was one year older than she is now, I done had my fus chile," Mother Brown reminded her son.

"Dat was long time ago, Maw. We is livin in a new age now. Black people ain't slaves no more. They can get schoolin' and make somethin' o' their self. When you was young like Juliann, if the master caught you learnin', readin' or writin', he could wup you."

Such was the tenor of conversation among the adults on the verandah when the slow rumbling of thunder like rolling drums began to swell from the distant sky beyond the Yazoo. Streaks of lightning like the aftermath of cannon fire flashed on the horizon and danced across the face of dark gray clouds that formed an unbroken line across the South. The sky overhead was deep blue and empty, save for a few fleecy clouds which had the appearance of a caravan of white camels in the sky.

Slowly the cloud line advanced from the south, engulfing more and more of the sky, obliterating the sun and spreading a dark shadow of gloom across the landscape. As the clouds drew nearer Edith and Mabel almost simultaneously moved to call the children inside. "Chillen! Come in the house. Dem clouds comin' yonder looks like tornado clouds," Edith called. "An' look at that section over there. The clouds is so low they looks like they is touching the trees. Hurry, youn'uns, cut your playing out and come in."

As the clouds drew nearer, they were preceded by winds blowing in violent gusts. The clouds were moving in a northwesterly direction at remarkable speed, as if pressed from behind by some malignant force. As they drew nearer, all the family withdrew into the house. Clashes of thunder reverberated over the cotton fields, shaking the house. The dog, which had been hunting rabbits in the field, yelped as if struck by a whip, and ran below the front steps.

Within minutes the clouds, the thunder, and the lightning were gone, and the sun reappeared. Not a drop of rain had fallen in spite of the low hanging dark clouds. Within twenty minutes the children were back in the yard playing and the adults had returned to the porch. "I is sorry fer the people wherever dem clouds decide to break," Jim commented.

Mother Brown looked at the sky towards the northwest, where the rear line of some of the clouds could still be seen. The whites of her eyes, which in her youth had been spotless, were brown with age. She frowned, her heavy eyelids drawn close as she focused her eyes on the horizon. "I seen in my time, many tornado clouds pass over this section of Mudville County like those what pass today. Sometimes they brung rain, sometimes only fear and darkness," she said thoughtfully. "After they passes we always say the same thing, 'We is sure lucky the tornado ain't touch down here.'" Mother Brown remained silent for a few moments, then added, "One day it gonna come down. The tornado will strike, and there ain't nothing we can do 'bout it."

FOUR:
THE WHITE LEAGUE

Changes were taking place in Mudville County that would inevitably challenge the fragile equilibrium that had existed between whites and blacks. It was an equilibrium based on the principles of inequality, but the relationship had been largely devoid of the ferocious hostility and violence now commonplace in other counties within the sovereign State of Mississippi. One of the possible variables accounting for the relative absence of open hostility between the races in Mudville County may have been tied to facts of the social history of the area. The final decades of slavery in the county had been among the least oppressive of any area of the state. Many blacks had won or were granted freedom prior to 1865, the official year of emancipation. By the beginning of the Civil War, Bilbo Wright, one of the largest plantation owners in the county, had already emancipated his slaves, provided some with land of their own, and proceeded to pay wages to his ex-slaves, some of whom had elected to remain and work on his land. The Crane family, by far the most powerful landowners in the county, had also been known for their relative humaneness to their slaves, and were both a pre- and post-revolutionary political force in the county.

By 1884, in many parts of the Southland, organizations had emerged, some dedicated to the restoration of pre-1865 conditions of black people in the social and economic formula of the South. Other organizations were geared to the goals of white supremacy in a Southern environment where, in many counties and towns, black people comprised the majority of the population.

In Mudville County an organization had emerged with the majority of its supporters from the northwest corner of the county in the region known as Limestone Hills, an area inhabited by a preponderance of poor whites, many whose economic conditions were no more attractive than those of blacks in the county. There were practically no schools in the region. Few of the people could read or write, and most were nurtured in a state of benign ignorance. This organization, which went by the name of "the League" or "the White Christian League," had been founded by a man named Obadiah Manson, who had unsuccessfully run for the state legislature on two occasions and eventually was incarcerated for second degree murder of his wife. The League had since remained largely dormant.

In the summer of 1884, a man named Julius McMosby entered the scene of Mudville County. He was a businessman from Jackson and had purchased months earlier a section of about one thousand acres, a portion of which was situated on the Yazoo River between the property of Ben Mathis and Mabel Wright. The property had on it everlasting springs that emptied into the Yazoo, one of which had been the source of Ben Mathis' secret fishing holes through the years.

It was never absolutely clear what McMosby planned to do with the property he had acquired, but it soon became clear that his interest for land ownership in the area extended beyond the one thousand acres, and included the properties of Ben Mathis and Mabel Wright.

McMosby, a man with a disarming smile and a congenial personality, approached both families with proposals to purchase their farms. McMosby first called on Ben Mathis, to whom he introduced himself as "your new neighbor next door." Mathis, not particularly known for his friendliness to strangers, listened in stoical silence to the man's glowing description of all the economic benefits he planned to bring to the area before responding dryly, "Well, it sure different to have a neighbor so close to us. The nearest people from here is a colored woman up the road 'bout half mile."

The following day McMosby returned and without much ceremony offered to buy Ben Mathis' farm. "I'd like to take this place off your hands," he informed him. "I got plans for developing this area, but in order to carry out this development I need this piece of property." He offered Mathis "a good price" and the opportunity of working for him and earning "regular money."

"This place not fer sale," Mathis informed the man coldly, "so Mister you better plan to do whatever you want to do without this here property." McMosby rode off on his stallion, promising to call again.

⌢ ⌢ ⌢

Mabel saw the man from the window as he entered her yard, and went out to the verandah to greet him. The stranger introduced himself as the "owner of the property next door," and broadly smiling proceeded to pour words of praise and admiration upon Mabel's children who had come outside to observe the man.

"I would say, what a beautiful family you's got here! Oh, how beautiful it is. I always say all people is the same to me. Color or religion ain't make a bit o' difference. The good Lawd made us all. Some of the best friends I got in Jackson is colored folk. The colored people have a heart of pure Christian gold," he informed her, "to forgive us white folk fer all the evil we done done to them—slavery an' all that."

In spite of the air of friendliness generated by McMosby, pinching Sandy's cheek and patting Joshua's head—"I say, what a right strong boy he is!"—Mabel, though smiling pleasantly, eyed the stranger with suspicion. Experience had taught her that whenever a stranger, and a white one at that, came to her place with so many nice words he either had something to sell or some scheme to unfold.

"Mr. Mathis, your neighbor, told me that you lives here alone with your children."

"He told you right. I have lived here with my chillen alone for five years."

"How noble and brave," the stranger said, an expression of surprise on his face. "It must be very difficult living out here in these woods by that river, with all them water moccasins and skeeters. It's a miracle you ain't had death in you' family, or some tragedy."

"Two of my chillen died from malaria five years back. They died within weeks of each other."

"Lawd have mercy!" McMosby exclaimed. "Such bravery, such courage, to remain here in spite of your grief. My visit here is much more timely than I realized. Maybe it's Providence who sent me in such a time like this. I am proposing, Mrs. Wright, to take this place off your hands. In spite of the skeeters, snakes and all. I'll give you a decent price, so you and your loved ones can move to Niggerville or Mudville, or some other place where you can be happy and ferget the tragedy of this place."

Mabel's suspicions of the man had been justified. "So this is what he is after," she thought. "We are all very happy here," Mabel assured the man, "We have problems, but we also have lots to be thankful fer. This place is the only property we's got and I ain't never gonna sell it."

"Well, think about it," McMosby urged her. "Maybe you'll change your mind after a while." With this he departed, saying that he would keep in touch. The man had not been threatening, yet a feeling of apprehension crept into Mabel's mind over his parting words.

One week later on Sunday night Ben Mathis was awakened by the hysterical barking of his dog. He grabbed his shotgun and felt his way through the darkness to the window in time to see a lighted torch moving towards the barn at the side of the house. Mathis let both barrels fly in the direction of the torch. The torch carrier dropped the torch and fled into the darkness. The torch sizzled on the ground, caught the grass on fire, and blown by a brisk northwest wind, began to spread towards the barn. Mathis, dressed only in a pair of long underpants in which he slept, got two shells from the shelf by feeling in the darkness, and stumbled outside loading the gun as he went. Using a piece of damp canvass that hung on the rail on the side of the house, Mathis beat the advancing flames and finally smothered them before any damage could be done to the barn.

The following evening two white horsemen trotted into Mathis' yard. Ben saw the men approaching. They were both strangers. He stood in front of the partly open front door of his house waiting to see what they wanted. Without dismounting, one of the men, the meaner looking of the two, informed Mathis that he represented the League. "Niggers bin acting up in this area," the man said, looking at Mathis from eyes set deep in his face. "They is even talkin' bout burnin' people place down. You and your wife living here alone may be the first to suffer.

"I won't be surprised," he continued, "if one night they wouldn't creep up on you and burn your house down. If I was you," his tone was confidential, "I would get out of here, move closer to where there is more white folk. We is members of the White Christian League. Our job is to advise and protect white folk, and our advice to you is to sell the place."

As the men turned to depart, Mathis responded, "You can tell whoever you is workin' fer—niggers or white—tell them, I'll be waitin' and I ain't goin' to use a shotgun next time. I'm goin' make sure they ain't leavin' if they comes on my place." Without responding the men rode off and headed west on the dirt road.

Mabel saw the two men riding side by side into her yard. "Go inside all of you," she directed the children, " and stay inside until I tell you." The children obeyed.

"Is you the owner of the place or is you a sharecropper?" one of the men inquired.

"This is my place, all twenty acres of it."

"You heard 'bout what happened to Ben Mathis up the road last night?"

"No, what happen?"

"They almost burn him out. You better take our advice and get out of here. Sell the place and go to Niggerville where there is lots of niggers like you. Livin' out here by that river, with all the trouble brewin' in this area, I won't be surprised if something don't happen to your children. Maybe when they playin' by the river or maybe when they walkin' on the road. If you know what is good fer youself, you'll sell this place and git out." Mabel looked at them in silence as they left.

⌃ ⌃ ⌃

As soon as the two men departed, Ben Mathis saddled his horse and rode into Mudville. He stopped at the sheriff's office and informed him of the incidents leading up to the appearance of the two men claiming to be members of the League. He recounted the visit by McMosby and his offer to buy the place, which he refused, the attempted burning of the barn, and the threatening behavior of the two most recent visitors. Tate promised to look into the matter and followed Mathis back to his farm before riding on in the direction of Mabel Wright's place.

Mabel greeted the sheriff. It was the first time he had actually been on her property. "Seen anythin' strange round here recently?" the sheriff inquired.

"That's all I bin seeing these last few days," Mabel replied. "First comes this man, with lots of nice friendly talk. I can't remember his name. Then today come these other two white men. They threaten me that if I don't leave here something gonna happen to the chillen."

"Your neighbor up the road, Mr. Mathis, been having the same trouble," Tate informed her. ""I don't know what it's all about, but I aim to get to the bottom of it."

"Well, I sure hope that you can, Sheriff," Mabel said, "cause I don't want no trouble here. I got all I can already taking care of my family."

"Don't you worry none," Tate urged her. "Everything will be all right."

⌒⌒⌒

Back in Mudville, Tate inquired around about the identity of the man who called himself McMosby, and discovered that a man by that name had indeed acquired some property near the Yazoo. McMosby was temporarily residing in rented quarters on Jackson Street on the eastern edge of town, where some of the more prosperous of the community lived.

McMosby was just leaving the house when Sheriff Tate approached the gate. He greeted the man wearing the star with a pleasant smile. "Good day to you, Sheriff."

"Howdy," Tate responded. "Are you Julius McMosby?"

"Why, yes. That is my name. I am just in the process of moving into your friendly community. I plan to establish business in this county that will bring money into Mudville and raise its status in the State of Mississippi."

"It's mighty nice that you plan to bring business into the area. We can always do with more money and more jobs. But what I came to see you about is your interest in property on the Yazoo a few miles southwest of here."

"Yes, indeed," McMosby added in a most congenial voice. "I bought some property in that area. As a matter of fact, I plan to buy some more in the immediate vicinity."

"Yes. I understand that you approached Ben Mathis and a colored family about buying their property."

"I sure did. I sure did," McMosby replied. "And you have no idea, Sheriff Tate, what this will do for your county. I got plans to--"

"What I'm trying to say, Mr. McMosby," Tate interrupted, "is that those people don't want to sell their properties—neither Mr. Mathis nor the colored woman. Now, there ain't nothing illegal 'bout asking them to sell, but I understand someone tried to burn Mathis out last night, and today two men went around, trying to persuade them to sell. Now I don't know if these men, whoever they be, is taking orders from you, but I don't want no more of this kind of thing in my county."

"I am not a man of violence," McMosby protested. "I am a businessman. I build and create things, not destroy."

"Well, I'm just telling you, Mister, that I have received complaints from these people, and I don't want no more of such behavior."

The following morning Tate got a message that Mayor Simpson of Mudville wished to speak with him at his convenience. Tate took his hat and walked over to the mayor's office at the end of the block. He and the mayor, Charles Simpson, were best of friends, having known each other for years. There was thus no formality between them.

"Come in, John," the mayor greeted him as he knocked, pushed the door, and entered the mayor's office. "Sit down and rest your legs a while. I just been working on a report for the council meeting tomorrow." Simpson pushed the papers before him to the side of his desk. The two men spoke of fishing, problems of tracking down moonshiners in the county, and a few other trite items before Simpson changed the topic. "Say, John. A friend of mine—a new acquaintance I perhaps ought to say, his name is Julius McMosby—you know who I mean, you met him yesterday, is in the process of establishing himself in the county. He plans to start a major beef industry in the area, including possibilities for leather making, which will bring money and jobs to the area. He is trying to acquire some land on the Yazoo along the southern edge of the county. I understand you had some hard words with him yesterday."

"I wouldn't call it hard words," Tate responded. "I simply told him what he ought to be told. I think he has hired some men who are trying to use wild west scare tactics to get people to sell their land. I just don't want McMosby to start no trouble in this county. If he wants to set up here, well and good. But I cannot allow people to be pushed or scared into selling property against their will.

"Someone tried to set fire to Ben Mathis' place, and the very next day, these two men turn up, declaring that niggers are about to start trouble, and advised Mathis to sell his place. That was after McMosby had already proposed to buy the place and Mathis had refused. The same two men went to the colored family next door and tried to get them to sell. McMosby also visited that family. I don't believe these visits are coincidence. They seem part of a strategy to me, and I aim to stop it before it gets out of hand. So far we been lucky not to have the kind of racial trouble that is taking place in just about every county around us. I aim to keep it peaceful here as long as I can."

As Tate spoke, Simpson took the cigar he had lit up from his mouth. "Now, look here, John," he said. "There ain't nothin' wrong with a little sales pressure. It's all part of the free enterprise system. In the case of the fire, it may have been just an accident. Now I should tell you what I'm sure you are already aware of. Julius McMosby has joined the White Christian League. The League is getting active all over Mississippi and the South. I predict that in a few years time, ain't nobody will be able to run for a political office and get elected as sheriff, mayor, state legislator, or what have you, without the support of the League. That is how it is already in many other parts of Mississippi. The way I understand it, the League is supporting McMosby in his desire to set up business in the county. Frankly, I think the county needs a man like him. He represents economic progress, and more money for the region.

"Why should we allow a small matter like a few acres of land to stand in his way? He is ready to pay the people for their land, and there is property for sale in other areas of the county. You ought to encourage them to sell McMosby the property for the good of the county, and our own future."

"Where does he plan to stop in his quest for land along the river? If he succeeds in pressuring these people to sell, what assurance do we have that he will not try the same process with others?"

"I don't know that," Simpson responded, "but I know that he will be a great boost to the county's economy, and therefore to the town of Mudville. You tell me what contribution that dirt farmer and nigger is making." The challenge seemed rhetorical. "Look, John, nobody is going to get hurt, and all of us will gain if the man settles in this region. What will I tell my constituency come election when they learn that we drove an important investor out of the county in order to protect a nigger and a white dirt farmer?"

Tate could see his own position being threatened by this alliance between McMosby and the League, which now seemed to be coming out of its dormancy in the county. "You said that there ain't going to be any violence," he repeated.

"No violence," Simpson assured him. "They may use some pressure tactics to get them two to sell, but I can tell you there won't be no violence."

Tate was disturbed as he left the mayor's office. He did not like the new development. So far, his job as sheriff had been a relatively uncomplicated one. There were occasional problems with moonshiners, drunks, and petty crime, but these were all in the normal line of duty. He disliked the tactics of McMosby, and was distressed over the support the man was receiving from the Mayor of Mudville, but he was also aware of the potential challenge he faced, should he find himself standing alone in confrontation with the League. Tate decided to be watchful and let things develop.

For two weeks the McMosby incident appeared to have quieted down. Then, on Saturday night, Mabel and her four children were returning from Niggerville where she had been shopping that evening and later visiting with friends. A late moon occasionally emerged from behind dark clouds, to envelop the road in a pale sickly glow. The horse drawing the wagon, anxious to end his journey, increased his pace only to be slowed down by Mabel's gentle tug at the reins.

They were about a half mile from their home when a torch emerged from the nearby woods. From the distance it appeared that the torch propelled itself through the night. Mabel slowed the pace of the wagon as the torch approached while the children, startled by the flickering light, huddled together in the wagon. Mabel stopped the wagon as the torch drew near. Only now could they see that the torch was being borne by a rider, accompanied by three other horsemen. The men planted themselves across the narrow road, the foremost rider holding the torch high in his left hand. By its light they could see the frightened faces of the children pressed against the woman, her dark, expressionless face glistening in the glare of the torch. For a moment there was only silent staring, as Mabel's horse rocked its head restlessly, disturbed by the glow of the torch. Finally the torchbearer spoke. He pointed his finger at Mabel as he spoke. "Look here, nigger," he said, his face harsh and contemptuous, "this is the last time we plan to talk to you. We don't want you in this area no more. Sell that place to Mr. McMosby and clear out. If we's got to talk again there's goin' to be a whole heap o' trouble for you, an' 'specially for them young'uns. This is your last warning."

With this the riders turned and galloped away into the darkness. As the men drove away, Mabel tried to reassure the children. "They ain't from round here. They is only tryin' to stir up trouble, but they can't scare me none. Next time I travel late like this I'm gonna bring along my shotgun."

Sunday following church service, Mabel Wright drove her wagon into Mudville and stopped in front of the sheriff's office. A deputy was on duty, but intent on talking to the sheriff himself, Mabel drove to his home. When she knocked at the back door, a colored maid appeared. Mabel asked for the sheriff, who heard her voice and came to the door to determine the purpose of her visit. Mabel gave Tate a detailed description of what had occurred the previous night.

"I can see they is tryin' to chase me from my place," she said, "but I ain't leavin'."

Tate looked at her thoughtfully, then shifted his eyes beyond her. "Mabel, don't you think perhaps it will be better and safer for you and the children to move near to where there is more colored folk? There is property for sale east of Niggerville. Maybe it will be better there."

Mabel spoke respectfully, without ever raising her voice, but she was insistent. "That piece of property and my chillen is all I have in this world. I lived on it for years. We don't trouble nobody, we don't cause no problems. We are law 'biding folk. They ain't got no right to come an' frighten us like that, and drive us from our own place. I like it there by the Yazoo. The chillen likes it. We don't want to move, and I ain't fixin' to sell it." She paused under the gaze of the sheriff.

"Well, if you intend to stay, if you don't want to sell the place, stay. They may try to scare you—whoever they be—but they ain't going to harm you or your children. I'll see to that."

Mabel thanked the sheriff and drove home.

⌃ ⌃ ⌃

Niggerville was rife with rumors. Everyone knew what had transpired at Mabel's place, and about her Saturday night encounter with the horsemen. Talk had it that the League was reorganizing for the purpose of driving black people off their land. Another rumor had it that the League was working on a plan to diminish the size of the black population in the county by "scaring black folk into going up North." Blacks outnumbered whites in Mudville County and the League viewed this as a threat. "They is spoilin' fer trouble," some of the youth of Niggerville declared. "We must be ready, so if they try here what they been doin' in other parts of Mississippi we can fight back."

"What the sheriff doin' 'bout all this?" one inquired.

"That peckerwood! I bet he is one of them."

"I don't believe so," another added. "I hear that he told Mabel he is gonna see that she ain't bothered."

"I don't know 'bout the sheriff in this county, but in Meridian where I lived the sheriff, the mayor, the deputies, all o' them is either members of the League or sympathizers. The League control politics in the county."

An older man sitting nearby commented, "If I was Mabel Wright I would take my young'uns and clear out from that place. It's right dangerous to live down there alone with all this trouble brewin'."

"Clear out and go where?" demanded a young man. "Why is it that we colored folk always has to clear out as soon as we gets pressure from them rednecks. Go north and leave the place that we an' our parents help to --"

"I ain't says go up North. I simply says leave the place by the Yazoo," the older man explained. "I knows them rednecks. I seen them act in other parts of Mississippi and in Alabama. Once they gets organized an' start attacking black folk, all the other white folk suddenly don't see, hear, or know nothin'. Is every man fer hisself. The League ain't strong in this county yet, but if they ever take this county over, it's gonna be hell. Now, it's right brave for Mabel Wright to stay down there by the Yazoo, but it don't make no sense to be brave and dead, or have them chillen livin' there in fear all the time."

The following Sunday, Reverend Jones preached about harmony and love. He expressed concern that some members of the community were talking about fighting and getting weapons to protect themselves. "We in Mudville County," he said, "are fortunate that we have so far escaped some of the aggression being directed against colored folk in other counties across Mississippi. We have to continue to pray to the Lawd to keep out the forces of evil and destruction from our county."

"I see storm clouds gatherin'," he continued, "but these clouds don't have to break upon us. We need prayer and faith. We can achieve a whole lot more with Christian love than anger. For whether we like it or not, we can't protect ourselves forever, regardless of how much arms we have, except we have God on our side. Let us put on the whole armor of Christ's love"—his voice was fervent—"an' we will be able to stand."

⌃ ⌃ ⌃

The question of how to respond to what was being seen as a growing threat from fanatics in the white community remained the main issue of discussion for several days, prompting the convening of a special meeting at the Baptist church to discuss the issue. It was presided over by Parson Jones himself. Mabel Wright attended the meeting with her four children, and for the first time gave a concise but detailed account of the incidents, including the most recent encounter the Saturday night before. Mabel also provided some information on what had transpired at the farm of her neighbor, Mr. Mathis. This item of information provided a new dimension to the entire situation. Parson Jones used this information to support his suggestion that the incident was not entirely racial.

"This ain't no colored/white confrontation. A white farmer has also been molested." He preferred that word to "attacked," which for the psychology of the moment he perceived would be more threatening. "An' it therefore don't make no sense giving racial meaning to it."

A young man stood up to speak. "I understand that Mr. Mathis was told that it was colored folk who tried to burn his place down. Seems to me they's tryin' to set white folks 'gainst coloreds. An' since it's the White League who done this, we can call it what we please, it involve the issue of race. We must consider the intention of these people. If we sit down an' do nothing—not even raise a voice in protest—we may wake up one day and find there is a war on our hands, and our hands are tied."

"Don't talk 'bout war, son," Parson Jones urged, in a fatherly voice. "With God's grace, this whole thing will blow over."

Jim Johnson, a church deacon who had listened with care to the different presentations; joined the discussion. "I agree with Parson Jones that we don't want no trouble between coloreds and white folk. But the question is, how best to keep that trouble from happening. Mr. Brentwood, my boss, say that the League is trying to make trouble in order to gain power in this county. There ain't too much we can do now, but I feel we ought to send a delegation to Sheriff Tate an' express our concern."

"I agree," the young man who spoke earlier said. "We could form a committee and go to the sheriff. Let him know that we are law-abiding people, but we can't stand idle and see our own attacked."

"Careful, brethren, careful!" another deacon counseled. "If we go talkin' to Sheriff Tate this way, he may feel that we is threatening him!"

"I agree," the parson said. "I reckon is best to let things rest an' see what happens." It was decided to accept the wisdom and moderation of the parson's suggestion.

Sheriff Tate had been out of the office most of the day. With two of his deputies he had spent much of the afternoon in Limestone Hill, where conflict had been brewing for some time between two moonshiners. Each one, seeking to put the other out of business, had secretly passed information to the sheriff as to the location of the other's still. But after searching all afternoon, Tate and his two deputies had located neither of the stills. Apparently, counter-intelligence from each side had learned of the planned raid, so that by the time the posse arrived, the stills had been dismantled and hidden. The sheriff found a few jugs of bad tasting whiskey—nothing more. One of the moonshiners, who went by the name of Billy Squeeze, in a high-pitched voice suggesting a voice box partly eroded by the highly potent drink, protested to the sheriff, claiming that he was insulted by the allegation of illegal whiskey making. "Fancy me, a law-'biding citizen, who never done knowingly anything 'gainst the law. I goes to church every Sunday, fancy me bein' accused of moonshinin'. It's real downright shameful an' humiliatin' that anyone—especially the sheriff of the county—will think of Billy Squeeze that way."

By the time Sheriff Tate and his deputies returned to Mudville, night had fallen. The men sat in the office smoking and reviewing the events of the day. "I can't figure it out," one deputy commented. "How come they knew we was comin'? Do you think maybe someone from this office told them?"

"I sure would like to know," Tate said. "That Billy Squeeze really makes me laugh with his talk of innocence. Everybody knows he is the biggest moonshiner in Limestone Hill. Yet if you listen to his protests you'll swear he's innocent. I am going to catch that rascal one day." Tate smiled pensively. "Well, I think I am calling it a day. I'm going to get a long sleep."

The men were rising to leave when they heard a fumbling outside the front door. The door opened, a man stumbled through and fell to the floor. Tate and the two deputies rushed to his assistance. They lifted him from the floor, and helped him onto a wooden bench against the wall of the office. Sheriff Tate at first did not recognize the man, but a closer look at his face revealed him to be Ben Mathis. There were bruises all over his face, one eye was partly closed, his lips were hanging and swollen. The shirt he wore was torn, and close examination revealed swollen welts across his back.

"Who done this to you?" Tate asked.

"The League. They say I bin cooperatin' with niggers against a white man. Say I bin workin' hand 'n glove with niggers to oppose what the League want fer the area. They say next time they will feed me to the fish in the Yazoo."

Tate was livid with anger. He hurried over to the gun rack and took down the rifle he had replaced only minutes earlier. The deputies quickly armed themselves. Ben Mathis was still talking. "Says they is takin' over this county, an' who don't cooperate is got to leave one way or the other. I ain't leavin'. Is my place an' nobody is goin' to make Ben Mathis run away."

"Do you know who they are?" Tate asked.

"I didn't recognize none of them. It was real dark, an' they had masks on their face."

"In which direction did they go?" Tate inquired, as he loaded shells into the rifle.

"I heard them say somethin' 'bout the nigger woman is next."

"Go over to Dr. Beadle's place, tell him I sent you. Can you go there by yourself?"

Mathis stood to his feet. He tottered slightly, then steadied himself. "I'll make it."

The sheriff with his two deputies hurried through the door, and climbed on their horses.

⌢ ⌢ ⌢

Sandy, Sharon, Joshua, and Billy were already asleep. Mabel, tired from a long day of work, hurried to put the finishing touches on a dress she was to deliver the following day. The heat of the summer day lingered into the delta night and she kept the window open to benefit from a mild wind blowing in from the west. From the corner of her eye Mabel caught glimpses of lights approaching, and looking up through the open window she saw four torches approaching the house. Mabel rushed into the bedroom, grabbed her shotgun from the ledge behind the bed, and with a box of shells returned to the front room. She blew out the lamp, leaving the house in total darkness.

By now the bearers of the torches had dismounted and stood close together at the far end of the yard. They had seen a light in the house, but now it was gone. "Hey, you in der, woman! Come outside. We wants to talk to you," the voice of a man called from behind a torch.

Silence.

"We don't want to hurt you and you' chillen. We jus' want to talk to you."

Still no answer.

"Listen here, nigger, if you don't come out, we is comin' in an' we can't be responsible if dem chillen of your'n gets hurt."

Mabel's voice penetrated the darkness. "Git out of my yard. Git off my place. I is got a gun pointed at you right now. You come nearer my house an' I'm gonna shoot. "

The men were hesitant. "See anything?" the leader asked. "I can't see a damn thing. We got to get nearer the house."

"You come one step closer an' I'm gonna pump you full of holes," Mabel warned.

"Do you think she's really got a shootin' iron?" one of the men asked.

"I don't believe she's got no gun," another said, grinning mischievously, his eyes glazed in the light from the moonshine he had been drinking earlier.

"That nigger bitch ain't got no gun. She's just a stallin' to get us to leave," the leader concluded. "Look here, you black bitch," he hollered in the darkness. "We's come here to talk to you, friendly like, but if you want to make trouble, we can give you all you want. Now is you comin' out or is we comin' in to get you."

Mabel remained silent. The loud voices had awakened the children. Mabel could hear them feeling their way in the darkness. "Git back in the bedroom. Git back!"

"All right," the leader called. "If that's what you want, we is comin' to get you." Before they could move forward, a flash of fire lighted the spot where the window stood, and the deafening sound of a shotgun reverberated across the yard.

Boom!

The men beat a hasty retreat to the far end of the yard. They had been beyond the range of the shotgun, but could hear the pellets as they danced on the ground in front of them and see the little red balls of fire.

They were still in the process of deciding the next move when the sheriff arrived with his deputies. The three dismounted a few yards away and walked over to the four men. "Who is in charge here, and what's goin' on?" the sheriff asked calmly.

"Oh, it's you, sheriff. You know me. I is the new head of the League in the county, an' we is just havin' a little talk with some trouble makin' folks around here—ain't that so, fellas?" he turned to the three men beside him.

"It sure is," "Yeh," they repeated almost in unison. The leader, a resident of Limestone Hill named Festus Slime, grinned confidently. He was in the process of turning back to face the sheriff, when Tate's right fist caught the side of his chin and sent Slime plummeting to the ground. The torch he carried rolled over the ground, sending off eerie sparks. One of his followers, obviously drunk, moved towards the sheriff. It was not clear as to his intention, but as he moved towards the sheriff, at the same time reaching with one hand under his coat, Tate raised the butt of his rifle, striking the man across the chin. He stumbled and fell backwards. The butt of a forty-five pistol stuck out from under his belt. The four men were searched and disarmed. Along with the paraphernalia they carried were a whip and a long portion of rope.

"I'm taking you all under arrest for assault of Ben Mathis. Get on your horses. If anyone tries to escape, shoot him," he directed the deputies.

Turning to the house, Tate called to Mabel, "Mabel Wright, this is Sheriff Tate."

Mabel opened the front door of the house and cautiously, with her gun still in hand, stepped on to the verandah.

"Are you all right?" Tate inquired

"A bit scairt, but we is all right. It just ain't right at all," she continued, "fer them to come here at night an' scare me an' the chillen like this."

"Well, don't you worry. This ain't gonna happen no more, as long as I can help it," he assured her.

The men were taken back to Mudville and jailed. "You jus' wait till Mayor Simpson hear about this an' all the brutality you used against us," Slime said to the sheriff.

"Neither the mayor nor McMosby can save you from at least two years in state prison for what you done to Ben Mathis," Tate replied. A deputy was left to watch the jail during the night.

Before retiring for the night, Sheriff Tate rode over to the home of the mayor. It was just past ten and the mayor had retired to bed. Tate apologized for his intrusion. "Charlie, I don't usually call on you this time of the night, but with the kind of trouble that is building I thought I should inform you right away."

"What trouble are you talking about?" Simpson asked.

"I just arrested four men, all apparently members of the League. One of them is Festus Slime. They went over to Ben Mathis' place—the white man I talked to you about the other day—and beat him up badly in an effort to force him to sell his place to McMosby. They say you support them in what they've done. Once this news of what happened spreads to white farmers across the county, there is bound to be a hell of a lot of trouble."

"Just a minute, Tate, let's get this straight," Simpson said. "You know I wouldn't support no such thing as the beating of a white man by the League or any other group. That man Slime, I've seen him a couple of times but I don't even know him."

"Well, he's obviously working for McMosby, and McMosby must have told him that you are in his corner."

"Well, I'm telling you right now, that I ain't in nobody's corner who would do a thing like that."

"You told me there was not going to be any violence," Tate said.

"Yes, and I meant every word I said."

"Well, I just thought I'd let you know what these men are saying. They said what they said in the hearing of two of my deputies. If this gets around town tomorrow, you can imagine what people will be saying. I am just warning you as a friend."

Simpson was emphatic in his response. "If you hear anybody say I support this, you just let them know, it ain't true. I am the mayor of a respectable town, and no bunch of rednecks is goin' to drag me down."

Once again, Tate apologized for calling on the mayor at so late an hour, and went home.

By the next evening, white farmers throughout the area knew of the beating of Ben Mathis. Tate himself made no effort to hide the fact, when questioned, that the four men had been acting on behalf of McMosby. Festus Slime and his companions, somewhat more sober the morning after the attack, were more objective in the evaluation of their situation. As it became clear that they would receive no help from the mayor, their courage began to falter. One of them, Fred Holland, released from prison only a year and a half earlier, was the first to blame McMosby for what had occurred.

"I is ready to swear on a stack of Bibles that it was McMosby's fault. He done filled us up with liquor and sent us to do the job on Ben Mathis and the nigger woman. I ain't goin' back to jail for nobody." Holland was ready to turn state's witness if the sheriff would give him a break.

By that evening all the men were ready to cooperate with the sheriff for some consideration, and were pointing their finger at McMosby. Tate decided that there were grounds for McMosby's arrest. The mayor, perceiving the unfriendly reaction of local farmers to the incident, publicly dissociated himself from McMosby, leaving the man to fend for himself. It was announced that the Farmers Association would call a meeting to discuss the matter. Realizing that his efforts had backfired, McMosby suddenly left for Jackson. Tate, mostly for political reasons, made no move to arrest the man before his departure. Ben Mathis, on his part learning that McMosby had fled the area, and assured that he would be no more molested, decided not to press charges. The four jailed men had among them a total of twenty dollars. This the sheriff took and gave to Ben Mathis for compensation. Tate himself, not wishing to have a confrontation with the League, readily released the men, after getting a signed statement from them, implicating McMosby and promising to abstain from disturbing the peace in the future. Two of the men, unable to write, signed the statement with an "X."

Following the McMosby incident, Mudville County settled down to a period of uneasy quiet. Many white farmers in the region had reacted in anger to the violence directed against Ben Mathis, and at a meeting of the Farmers Association, had called for action to prevent such violence and "stirring up of trouble" in the county. The response of farmers along with the careful response of the sheriff placed the League on a temporary defensive. The men released from jail returned to Limestone Hills to lick their wounds.

In spite of the retreat of the League and the departure of McMosby, an air of disquiet and uncertainty settled over the black community. The relative quiet of the county and the comparative sense of security which black people in Mudville County had known were being eroded by the awareness that the League which in other counties was a source of terror and oppression of black people was now knocking ominously at the doors of Mudville.

In some sections of the white community, concern was also being expressed as to the significance of the League-McMosby episode. Among the white farmers expressing concern over the implications of what appeared to be growing League action in the county, was Urick Brentwood, on whose farm Jim Brown worked, and whose father had sold Jim the ten acres he now owned. As a boy Urick had been cared for by a black maid, Jim Brown's mother, and had even been breastfed by her when his own mother had taken sick during his infancy. Urick, while taking for granted his own superiority, had never had problems dealing with black folk. Not highly educated nor exceedingly religious, he had occasionally through the years attended black religious services in Niggerville, at funerals or other special occasions. As a farmer, Urick Brentwood understood the economy of the South as one involving white social, economic, and cultural leadership, with the black community providing the critical variable of labor. The white race he perceived as superior in intelligence and other God given abilities. These, he was convinced, should be used to govern black people with understanding and kindness rather than through oppression and fear. "Colored folks is just like children," he would say to his wife. "Treat them with discipline but with kindness."

Opinions such as those of Urick Brentwood were simply part of a wide range of beliefs with regards to what was and what should be in the county and other parts of Mississippi. Among the numbers of active and passive supporters of the League were white people who sincerely believed blacks in the county were a threat to the future of white people. "Them niggers is multiplying like rabbits," they would say. "We done talk about the yellow peril from China, but ain't no one payin' much 'tention to the nigger peril."

"You mark my words," Jeb Tyson, the owner of a small store in the town of Mudville, and a League member of some influence, would say to anyone who cared to listen. "One day dem niggers is goin' to rise up like one man, just how the inferior classes in ancient Rome an' Greece rose up and help to destroy them great nations. They is goin' to rise up all over this state an' this county because of their numbers."

Such opinions were given religious sanction by some white preachers such as Reverend Mike Minnows of Mudville's white Baptist church. Minnows was always ready to give chapter and verse from the "Holy Writ" to prove that "niggers is inferior," and that this inferiority was pre-ordained by God through the mouth of His most sacred servants. Minnows would become intense, his voice solemn as he spoke with authority of the "divine direction to the white man" to dominate the tribes and peoples of the world. "It all began," he would tell his followers, "when them three sons of Noah, Shem, Ham, and Japheth, was livin' in de hills with their daddy. One day the old man drank some homemade whiskey, an' he took his clothes off. While he was naked one of dem boys, Ham, done went and peeked at his daddy's nakedness; the other boys hide their face an' covered up the old man. We white peoples"--his voice was triumphant--"is the descendants of them two what cover up the old man, and niggers descend from the no-good brother Ham.

"You see," Minnows would continue, "when the old man found out how Ham looked on his nakedness, and how dem other two respectfully cover him up, he called on God and God cussed Ham through the mouth of his pappy. God made him an' all his descendants— that include all niggers an' other non-white people—forever servants to the two brothers an' their children—who is we white folk. God took their intelligence away, an' to mark them wherever they be, he turned them black."

Matthew Bradley, a white farmer who lived west of Mudville town within the county, was one of those who openly criticized the behavior of the League and its intent of stirring up racial strife. "Ask yourself what will happen to us economically," he urged members of the Farmers Union, "if those people (referring to the League) succeed in stirring up racial trouble to a point where they drive black laborers out of the county." As it emerged, it was this question rather than the Mathis incident that dominated the farmers' thinking.

A few days later Bradley visited his friend Urick Brentwood, and the League was the main topic of conversation. "If they will just leave things alone, there would be no trouble here. White farmers like us and negro workers are contented with things as they is. As you know, I got coloreds working on my place as sharecroppers and laborers, and I declare, you ain't never seen a more contented group o' people. Not a word of dissatisfaction come from their mouth. They always greets you with a smile, and when they's working in the field they's always singin'. You ever hear folk laughin' and singin' and unhappy and dissatisfied at the same time? That just ain't natural. The only dissatisfaction in the county is from the League, an' mark my word. If we let them be, they'll cause our economic ruination."

Brentwood was not as eloquent a speaker as his friend Bradley, but he supported much of what Bradley said. "You take my boy, Jim Brown, for example," Brentwood pointed out. "He is a good boy, he takes care of his family—his wife, children, and mother, he works on his little piece of land my Daddy Winston Brentwood sold him years back, and he works my place. You ain't never seen a more dedicated worker. Jim was born here, he grew up here, and he is my right hand man on the farm."

"Jus' like on my place," Bradley affirmed. "I got me some niggers I've trained over the years, they not only work in the field, they repair my machinery. One of my boys, William his name is, came up with an addition for the plow; he invented it hisself. I even got one of my boys to keep my books. If they should pack up an' leave, I'll be ruined. A few of them left some years back. When they came to me an' say they was goin' up North, I said, "If you wants to go, go, and if you ever want to come back, remember there always be room for you on the farm."

"It's really strange, ain't it, that all these years the League was quiet, and suddenly they start actin' up," Brentwood commented.

"It sure is," Bradley agreed. "They obviously tryin' to do here in Mudville County what they done in other areas of the state. Their aim is to get control of the county. When you look at it, they ain't from round here. I understand most of them is rednecks from Limestone Hill. Ain't none a dem got nuf sense to come in outa the rain. They don't plant cotton or corn, all they do is lumberin', hunting, and drink cheap whiskey. Far as I'm concerned, they can stay up in them hills fer good."

The encounter between Mabel Wright and the League heightened concern and gave an element of credibility and support to those in Niggerville who were calling for a definite response to the situation. Suggestions were being forwarded that a team of men from Niggerville be sent to guard Mabel's place, but Mabel poured cold water on the scheme.

"I 'preciate your interest an' concern," she assured them, "but I think I can take care of the situation myself." Mabel, in fact, had become a sort of heroine to black people around the county over her standing up to the League. The story of her defense of her place by blasting away at the four men with a shotgun had spread like wildfire among blacks throughout the county, and within a few days of the incident was being discussed in every black home.

As the story traveled, it assumed new proportions and greater elements of drama so that within a few days the number of men had grown to twelve, and the shooting to a fifteen minute stand-off—"with empty shells all over the place." Mabel herself, perhaps unwittingly, added to the situation by her calm, almost naive and casual response to the incident, and by her genuine reluctance to discuss the matter.

On her visit to Niggerville following the incident, friends and others gathered around closely auditing each word, hoping to hear from her lips what actually transpired. "Jus' once mo'," they urged, "tell us once mo' zactly how it happen."

"There ain't nothing to tell," Mabel protested, "an' there ain't nothin' to be excited 'bout as far as I'm concerned." She spoke of it as of the weather or some casual topic. "I done what any person coulda done. These idiots come to my place, scarin' the chillen, an' carryin' on. I warned them to leave my place, an' they didn't heed the warnin' so I let them have it."

"They ain't scarin' me from my farm," she continued, as she walked away. "I don't care what color they be, red, white or yellar."

Mabel's apparent reluctance to accept the role of a heroine was not shared by her four children who attended the Baptist Church school. They reaped a windfall of benefits from their peers, especially Billy and Joshua, who accepted every compliment about their "brave Mama." They not only exploited the situation, but in a boyish manner, and with a liberal amount of imagination, they held their peers in school spellbound during recess, by their own interpretation of what had transpired that night at their house by the Yazoo.

Boys who heretofore were selfish with their playthings and favorite artifacts, now became generous and altruistic to Billy and Joshua. "Hey, Joshua, take a spin with my top. You want to borrow it fer a while?" one boy offered. Another gave Billy his favorite marble--a crystal with a brown eye inside. Both boys had a larger supply of candy from gifts than ever before, and Zell Hinds' son, Starky, whose squirrel had bitten Sandy one year earlier, allowed Billy to take home his favorite frog which he usually kept in his pocket. During lunchtime, it was almost like a picnic for the two boys, sampling food and other goodies offered them. Sandy and Sharon, though accepting the accolades from other children in school, showed less readiness to take full advantage of the situation.

In the middle of a game of marbles, one of the players raised the issue. "Tell us once mo', Billy, how it happent. How yuh Mama drive 'way them peckerwoods."

"Is jus' like we said it happen. There ain't nothin' mo' to tell," Billy replied.

Interpreting his reply as a reluctance to discuss the incident, Starky Hinds pressed him further. "My pa says your Mamma is the bravest woman in the world. He say she in a 'sparation to all black folk in America."

This stimulus was enough to get the boys going. "Well, there we was," Billy started, "Me an Joshua lookin' outta the window at them peckerwoods. They face was a' red as blurd, all shinin' in the light from the torches. Yes, sir, when Mama grabbed that gun, me an' Joshua was jus' handin' her shells an' she was shootin' from one window to the other. Every time they rush the house, Mama will let go another blast, an' me an' Joshua will hand her mo' shells. We kept that up till the sheriff came."

"Wow! You all is sure nuf brave," the boys exclaimed. The compliments were graciously accepted by the boys. As time passed, the excitement over the incident subsided, and with it, the special treatment to which the boys had grown accustomed.

Among the adult black population of the county, there was serious concern. It was noted that the League had been rebuffed by the response of the sheriff and the farmers' association, but there remained an abiding and overriding conviction that this was not the last to be heard of the League. The main concern of the white community was seen by many blacks as having more to do with the projected economic impact of the League's activities, than with the welfare of black people. Among the young men of Niggerville, the idea was being circulated that blacks should prepare themselves for the worst, and make preparations for the defense of their community.

"We must defend ourselves like Mabel Wright did on her farm," one of the young men declared. "If we just sit and sing and pray, one day we gonna look up the road and see the League comin' down on us, like they came down on Mabel the other day. They will march through this town and do as they please, and as long as they don't bother white folks in the area, no one will raise a finger on our behalf. If they know that we're not lookin' for trouble, but we're ready to defend ourself, they will think twice before they bother us."

"Mabel Wright set an example fer the rest of the community," another said. "She didn't threaten nobody, or make no big noise, but when the time came to defend herself she made sure her powder was dry."

When these points of view being expressed by the young men of Niggerville came to the knowledge of Parson Jones, he immediately disapproved. At a Sunday service, he described such arguments as "unacceptable, dangerous, and unwise." He advised, "If we serve the Lawd, and do what He says, He'll protect us. Our future is tied like a knot to the white folks of this county. They can't do without us, and we ain't never done without them. They are the mediators of our physical and economic wellbeing. They ain't gonna sit back an' see no harm come to colored folk." Parson Jones, who spoke perfect English when he so desired, would readily recourse to any level of the local dialect necessary to get his point across. "Who chucked the League out when they came down from the hills last week to make trouble?" he asked rhetorically.

"Mabel Wright done it," a young woman at the rear of the church responded.

"You's wrong, sister. Mighty wrong. Mabel Wright sure nuf played her part, but it was Sheriff Tate, and the voice of the white farmers who done it."

That evening in a private conversation with his deacons, Parson Jones expanded upon his argument. "Sure, we can beat off the League's attack if they came 'gainst us in Niggerville, but how long can we stave them off? And who's gonna protect the sharecroppers, the small black farmers and all others across the county? The problem we are talking about don't relate to Niggerville alone, it includes the entire county. If the League move into this county an' take it over, colored folks can no more stop them than the Red Injun was able to stop the white man. Our only hope is God Almighty. He can use the good people he's got among white folk, to check the advancement of the League."

As discussions of the incident heated up in Niggerville, some people began talking about "heading North."

"I'll say, let's all pack up and leave this damn place to them peckerwoods, and see how they make it without us. See who will pick the cotton or do all the work colored folks bin doin'," Babs Jacobs' son suggested. "If every colored person leave the area, they will be beggin' us in no time to come back."

On this issue father and son strongly disagreed. "The North ain't no better than the South," Babs Jacobs pointed out to his son and other young men gathered below the mimosa tree in his backyard. "Goin' North ain't no better than remainin' South. There is some no-good white folks up North, jus' as we's got some here in Mudville County. The same thing they's doin' to black folks in Mississippi, they's doin' right in the nation's capital in Washington, as well as in Chicago and New York. They's killin' an' lynchin' colored folk up there too."

The young men were silent. "As fer as I is concerned," Jacobs continued, shaking a finger at his listeners, "if I leave here, send me back to Africa, the native home of the soul of all colored folk—but I ain't leavin."

"An' who made America the homeland for white folk?" Josie, the seventeen year old son of Azalea Petrus inquired later that evening, searching the faces of the men all older than he, gathered in the circle, for a reply. "This is the red man's country. If the white man can live here and claim it as his own, we can live here too, an' do the same. Further, is us colored folks who done all the hard work to build this Southland. We cut the trees, hacked the roads, an' help build the towns an' cities in Mississippi. Our claim to this land is just as valid as the white man's. This land is littered with the dried bones of our fathers who did all the work without pay. We plowed the land, we planted the tobacco, we planted the cotton, we set the South movin', we made cotton king, we placed him on his throne. I ain't goin' to Africa, I ain't goin' up North, or nowhere else. I am stayin' right here. This is my home and as Mabel Wright said, 'Ain't nobody goin' to drive me out.'"

The Mabel Wright incident had elicited divergent views among the coloreds of Niggerville and the surrounding areas of the county, but it also had a centripetal effect on the community. There was strong and growing conviction among folks that some whites in the region wanted to see colored people back into formal slavery. Some of the younger adults of Niggerville, while sharing this view, also perceived their existing state in itself as a form of slavery.

"We are still slaves!" Josie Petrus insisted. "Look at black people across the South, and right here in Mudville County. Thirty years after the Civil War, which it is claimed freed us from slavery, and yet today, while the federal government and leadership of both the Democrats and Republicans turn their backs, one by one the southern states have denied black folks the right to vote. They say we have been free since 1865, yet today, there are thousands of colored mechanics, carpenters, and other technical craftsmen, who are denied the right to pursue their trade because certain jobs are declared for whites only. We are free and yet we are being forced by the system to be drawers of water and fetchers of wood." There was a look of derision on his face as he applied the Biblical analogy. Many nodded their heads in agreement. And this egged him on, as more men joined the group. "We talk about being threatened by the League," he said, searching the faces of the men. "Well, let me tell you all something. We are a much greater threat to ourselves, by our whole frame of mind, the way we look at ourselves and the world around us. Look at this town"—he swung an arm in a half circle—"Its real name is Wrightsville, after the man who started it. A white man, yes, but one who during the days of slavery had a heart. He set his own slaves free willingly and happily. Now I ask you the question, what do we call it today? Niggerville! Why? Because some white folk in this county decided over twenty years back that that was a more suitable name. Did we challenge it? No. We accepted it and without protest we refer to our town today as Niggerville. I'll tell you again, as long as we remain within our present attitudes, we will continue to be the greatest obstacle to our own progress. We have to realize that we are caught in the vice of a new form of slavery, and emancipation must come by our own efforts."

⌃ ⌃ ⌃

As the youthful Tallahatchie merges with the upland to form the Yazoo which flows lazily into the meandering body of the incessant Mississippi, so the days and weeks in Mudville County in their unending onward motion emptied into the months of summer, and with the passing of time black people settled down to the routine of life. The disquieting episodes of spring remained an uncomfortable reminder of the fragility and uncertainty of the peace under which they existed.

Billy and Sharon were both eleven years old, and Sandy and Joshua ten. The four children had taken to studying and were doing well in school. Mrs. Thelma Jones, the school mistress, had informed Mabel Wright of the good performance of her children. They were all towards the top of their classes. Sharon and Sandy had developed an extraordinary love for reading and consumed the few books in the school's library, as well as their readers, as fast as they became available. Both boys, Joshua and Billy, seemed intensely interested in insects, birds, and natural things around them; in school they read all they could find about science.

Mabel kept constantly before the four children the importance of education. "Schoolin' is the most important thing next to religion," she repeatedly told them. "I never had no opportunity to go to school. What little learnin' I got, I got from my mother. She taught me how to read an' write and do sums. If you get a good edgecation, then you can one day work for yourself an' be independent. That's the best way to remain free. You won't have to go an' pick nobody's cotton to make a livin' or work in nobody's kitchen. You will be able to be your own man an' woman."

Mabel drilled these ideas into their minds until they knew them from memory. As the children grew older, Mabel had become more protective. She spoke to them quietly but sternly about "keeping good company" and "not wasting time, but making the most of every moment." "In a few years, you all will be growed up, so you don't have no time to waste."

During the early fall of the year following the incident with the League, the four children came home from school one Friday, and Sharon as spokesperson for the group went to their mother while the other three stood in the background. Mabel knew that some important request was about to be made, and stopped from her work, wiping her hands on her apron.

"Well, what is it now?"

"Maw," Sharon said hesitatingly, "Can we go with some of our friends from school to pick cotton? They all is talkin' about makin' some extra money by pickin' cotton for Mr. Brentwood."

Mabel pulled a chair and sat beside the table. She invited the children to sit on the old bench near the window. There was an element of tenderness in her voice, but it was also firm and decisive. "Listen to me, my children," she said, "and listen to me carefully. I don't want you pickin' nobody's cotton. There ain't nothing wrong with pickin' cotton. I use' to do it myself until a few years back. There ain't nothing illegal or immoral 'bout it. The colored folk who go out on the plantations an' pick cotton are mostly good God fearin' people, hard workin'. Most of them do it because there is little else 'round left for them to do to stay alive. Others do it cause they are sharecroppers an' if they don't, the white man can throw them off his land. Now, if you all was starvin' or if you needed money an' there was no other way, we all would go out there and pick cotton at Mr. Brentwood's place. But you don't need to go and pick cotton 'cause you don't need the money. We ain't rich, but by God's grace we will always have nuf to eat and clothes to wear.

"From next year we're going to plant a few acres of cotton. We will save the money for your edgecation. I want you children to stay in school and get all the edgecation you need so you can be you' own man an' woman, and be proud of what you is. Pickin' white folks' cotton don't bring us no pride. We done it as slaves, and now many have to do it though they is free. As long as I can help it, by God's grace, we ain't pickin' nobody's cotton. Now, Jim Brown have a few acres up the road. He an' his chillen usually pick it. If you wants to go up there one evening and help him for free, I have nothing 'gainst that, but I don't want you workin' for pay in nobody's cottonfield."

The children were entering the early years of adolescence. Billy and Sandy seemed to have completely forgotten the traumatic episodes of their early life, the workings of fate that had brought them to the small house on the banks of the Yazoo. Of their father, they knew, for Mabel had felt obliged to tell them, two years after their arrival when she felt they were old enough to understand. The information she passed on to them was based upon what she had learned from Leroy Benton in Rocky Bottom—that their father had deserted their mother, and like her own husband, had disappeared in the haze of the distant North. The love, warmth, affection, and care they had experienced at Mabel's place, the struggles of sickness and survival, by now had forged an unbreakable family bond among them.

Mabel was to the four children a father and mother, but also a friend in whom they could confide. "Don't ever hide no problem from your ma," she would tell them. "Matter not how bad the problem, nor how serious whatever you done, don't you ever ferget that your Ma loves you, and there ain't nothin that you can possibly do, that can change that love. If you ever gets in trouble, come to your Mammy. "

Mabel taught Sandy and Sharon how to sew. "You mus' know how to sew every kind o' clothes," she informed them. "Clothes is very near and dear to people, and when you can sew clothes and do it real good, people won't ferget. Sometimes when trouble comes you can turn to them whose clothes you sew and they will help you."

Mabel taught the girls how to cook and perform other functions expected of women in the colored community. The boys, too, learned to work and to perform manly tasks around the house, but Mabel kept ever in their minds that their future lay in education. "Never be satisfied to be jus' part o' th' group," she pressed into their minds. "Don't ever feel that you is better than other people, but always aim so you can be a leader, and a help to your community. Whatever you does, be the very best you can. It don't matter if it is something very important or simply pullin' weeds in the garden. Always do what you do so that you an' those who see it can be proud."

Each morning before breakfast, the family would have prayer followed by a brief lecture from Mabel. "Your mind is what will help you to make it in life. They can take away everything from you, but not what you's got in your mind."

As the children grew, Billy and Joshua took on more of the responsibility of gardening and other outside chores. They turned over the land and prepared it for planting. They plowed with the mule, and by the time they were fourteen, performed much of the labor on the four-acre cotton patch which Mabel now planted each year, saving the proceeds for the future education of the children.

Six years had passed since Billy and Sandy arrived, both asleep in an old horse-drawn wagon, in front of Mabel's house on the Yazoo. Even Sandy's name had experienced a change over the years. During the first year of her attendance at the school run by the wife of Parson Jones, some of the children had taken to the habit of calling her Samandra. The name Samandra had stuck with her through the years, so that now even in her home, rare was the occasion when her true name Sandy was used. Sandy herself seemed to prefer the new name, and with the passing of time, inquiry as to her name invariably brought the response, "Samandra Wright."

One day, the four children returned from a wagon trip to Mudville and complained to Mabel that some white children had molested them. "They call us black nigger, and they call Billy and Samandra red nigger." Joshua was upset. He was sure that he and Billy could take on the three boys who had molested them. "Next time they call us names, me and Billy gonna wup the stuffin' out o' them."

"You'll do no such thing," Mabel warned. "I don't want you all gettin' in no fight or trouble with white folk. If they attack you, naturally you's got to defend yourself, but don't start no fight with them. Words don't mean a thing." She paused as if to be sure the children were listening intently and then continued. "Any fool or crazy person can call others names, but it takes one who is brought up decent, to know that people who call others such names is ignorant and should be ignored."

As the children grew older, Mabel stressed, with increasing emphasis, the importance of avoiding conflict with white folk. She was keenly aware of the potentially disastrous consequences of aggressive response to whites by children growing into adulthood in the colored community. The potential dangers were particularly acute for the colored male. The South allowed a colored woman some latitude in response to perceived hostility from a white person, but the colored male had to be much more circumspect. Even justifiable display of hostility to a white person by a colored adult male carried with it the potential for awakening of tribal instincts among whites, cutting across law, order, and justice with disastrous consequences. These were among the reasons why Mabel encouraged her children to be independent. "Independence would make it less necessary," she thought, "for the children to have to come into daily contact with the white community, and this would diminish the chances of problems."

"Be respectful to older white folk," she warned the children. "Don't put yourself out of the way to talk to them, but when you have to talk to them, say 'Yes, sir' or 'yes'm' and 'Thank you, sir.'"

The children had long begun to show awareness of prevailing racial issues in the community. Of the four, Joshua seemed more ready to stand and fight when confronted, and this severely troubled his mother. In school, when two boys who had recently moved into the community picked on Billy, challenging him to a fight, Joshua readily accepted. The fight would have occurred had not Mrs. Jones intervened in the nick of time. Following this incident, Joshua gave Billy some backyard lessons on "how to fight." Though a year older than Joshua, Billy was a quieter child, reluctant to fight or take up a challenge. Not so with Joshua. He was ready to confront anyone who troubled a member of the family.

Two white boys living along the road between Niggerville and Mabel's farm threatened to beat up Billy, and on two occasions chased him for almost a mile when he was on his way home from Niggerville. Rather than telling Mabel of the episodes, Billy on both occasions told Joshua. The next time Billy met the two boys, Joshua was with him. Joshua confronted the bigger of the two boys—walked right up to him, so that only a few inches separated their faces. "Both o' you bin chasin' my brother?" he inquired, making his face as mean as he could, cocking his head sideways and looking the boy right in his eyes.

"We ain't got nothin' gainst you," the boy informed him. "Is him we's after. My friend here say that he made a face at him a few days back."

"Well, you don't have to chase my brother no more," Joshua informed him. "Next time I gonna pulp your face with this," and he showed the boy his right fist. "Now it won't happen no more, will it?" he asked.

"We don't have nothin' 'gainst him no more," the boy assured him.

⌒ ⌒ ⌒

Mabel sat on the porch of her home, relaxing in the shade of the evening and observing the four children as they played in the yard. "How rapidly they are maturing," she thought to herself. There was an element of joy and satisfaction in her heart, but it was mixed with anxiety. The girls, though one year apart, eleven and twelve had both reached puberty. Sharon seemed suddenly to be pushing up towards the sky, like a pliant spruce tree. Samandra, rather smaller and frail of body, was experiencing similar growth.

As she looked at the four children, concern for their future gave rise to worrisome questions which lay siege to her mind. In Mississippi, the safest and most secure period for the colored person was the period of childhood and innocence. Childhood, before the severity of racism in its many facets made itself felt in all its reality on the individual. The colored child was relatively safe from the overt abuse and physical dangers with which the colored adult had to contend. As the colored person evolved into adulthood, the whole perspective tended to change. It was as if the person had entered a new dimension with its own rules and regulations.

While the colored man whose life did not reflect humility and gentleness in his interaction with the white world was seen as an immediate threat in the white community and was thus constantly exposed to the dangers of losing his life, the colored woman, rather than being perceived as a threat, faced the possibilities of sexual and other forms of abuse.

It was the consciousness of these realities in the world of the South that disturbed Mabel's mind, as she pondered what the future held in store for the children. Should she encourage her children to adjust to the system and remain in Mississippi? Should she make plans to send them up North to live?

It was clear to Mabel that changes were coming to Mudville County. The actions of the League in the past few years followed a typical pattern as in other counties. For Mabel, it was just a matter of time before things would grow worse. Mudville was fortunate to have a sheriff who apparently was not under the control of the League, but how long would this continue?

The feeling of disquiet in Mabel was shared by colored folks all across the county. But with Mabel Wright, there lingered still the hope that in the end somehow things would be all right for her and her children. "I will have to watch over them with greater care than ever," she thought. "I'm gonna teach them, and teach them quickly—for there is not much time—how to live as colored folk in Mississippi—how to survive. I'm gonna have to teach ma boys how to understand white folks, how to relate to them in order to stay alive. Ain't no use encouraging them to go up North," she reasoned. "I hear say they is lynchin' colored folk up there just like everywhere else. As soon as they is old enough, one by one I gonna send them off to school maybe in Atlanta and in Tuskegee, Alabama. I hear say there is some good schools for black people up there."

Mabel's anxiety and uncertainty of the future inevitably drew her closer to the church. Somehow, the religious milieu, the social union, the religious assurances seemed to have a mollifying effect on her anxieties. To hear Parson Jones on Sunday say, "everything gonna be all right," provided comfort and hope to her that nothing else could offer.

Elections in the State of Mississippi were just around the corner. In Mudville County, candidates running for the state legislature and for local offices were warming up for their campaign. Throughout Mississippi, political machines relatively dormant since the last elections were being greased, cleaned, and set in motion. In Mudville County, an election fever with its concomitant air of expectation was beginning to rise. Though the campaign was not yet in full gear, trial runs were being made, forces organized. Those running for office had suddenly become concerned with the affairs of the community, and had commenced to visit the homes of farmers, asking questions about problems and needs, and seeking suggestions about what should be done. The perceptive farmer had only to think back a few years to realize that the interest suddenly being displayed by these men was cyclical and seasonal, with little relationship to actual problem solving. But such is the character of these election campaigns, in which the electorate become fixated upon words, artificial or imaginary issues, and promises, rather than on an evaluation of past performance or the character of the candidates.

Julius Crane, the son of Jacob Crane the local representative to the state legislature who was about to retire, was intent on taking his father's place in the legislature and announced his candidacy for the post. The Cranes, a rich farming family from the county, had a very heavy stake in the local cotton industry. In spite of his affluence, Jacob Crane, known for his arrogance and contempt for the poor whom he conceived with Calvinist outlook as responsible for their own conditions, had barely won during the last elections. Indeed it was the voice of wisdom encouraging his retirement, for he faced almost certain defeat at the hand of growing numbers of electorate who desired nothing better than having the Cranes "removed from the throne." There were two other candidates challenging young Crane for the Senate seat; one was George Walton, a teacher from Limestone Hills, and the other Charles Jason, a county businessman.

George Walton had attended Peabody College for Teachers in Nashville, Tennessee, and had returned to his native region to teach. A member of a family known for its prodigious multiplication, George had relatives throughout the region among the mostly poor hill people. Almost in every town, settlement, or village he visited in the hills, there were people who called him "Cousin George." So much had the name stuck that now, many with no blood connection addressed him affectionately as "cousin."

Ever since his return to the county a few years earlier, George had a vision, and it centered around revolutionizing politics in the region. As one who had read extensively and had closely scrutinized the political process at work in the area, George Walton felt that he understood the maladies of the county and indeed the State of Mississippi, and determined within himself to do something about it through political action. Long before his announced intention to seek the office, George had been talking to relatives and friends about his ideas, as it were testing the atmosphere.

Like most of the Walton clan, George was slight in frame, tall, with deep, intelligent, searching eyes and a look of yearning. He was mild mannered, but persuasive with the passion of a lawyer. Observing him, one had the distinct impression that he had seen hard times during the past, a trait he shared with most of his kinfolk. Born during the closing days of slavery, George had had little personal contact with it, but he learned much about that period from his father who was now aged, bedridden, and rapidly losing his sight. When not in the classroom of his private school, George Walton was traveling across the South, and what he saw, felt, and heard convinced him that his evaluation of the malaise of the Southland was correct. He had already decided to seek a place in the government, but before announcing his intentions he would share his ideas, his observations, and convictions with persons whom he could trust, and on whom he could depend to provide him with objective feedback. The first with whom he spoke were close members of his family and a cousin with whom he had grown up and shared many a boyhood experience, a small farmer named Bigsby Walton. George presented to his cousin the following argument:

The political structure that had run the affairs of the South before the Civil War—the wealthy planter and the rich urbanite—had once more returned to power. "It is most amazing," George told his cousin, "to stop and look at it carefully. The vast majority of the South, the poor white people, the landless, the small farmer, who before the Civil War lived in a state of penury and powerlessness, are still in the same social and economic condition.

"The small wealthy class," George pointed out, "very cunningly has got the powerless and relatively unlettered whites to view the black man as his worst enemy, a threat to his survival. And while across the South poor white folks are focusing more of their attention on blacks, the rich minority has very cleverly returned to power and has consolidated position in every county.

"We the ordinary white people of this county have got to open our eyes and see who our real enemies are, who are the real threat to our survival. If we look coldly and carefully at the total scene, we will discover it is not black folk, it is those who control the politics and the economy of the nation.

"I see a pattern developing over the past twenty years," he said analytically. "The pattern involves identifying the former black slaves as a perpetual threat to the poor white, many who themselves are descendants of former white slaves. They hope through this means to maintain perpetual control of our destiny. Note what happened in Yazoo County before the last elections." George paused before making the point. "When the white trash, as they called them, began to make demands for improvement in their lot, for better pay, better opportunities to share in the affairs of the county, what did they get from the political leaders? I'll tell you what they got. Almost to a man, the politicians brought on the Black Boogie. Rather than addressing real problems or promising improvement, they told the people, 'Keep your eyes on the nigger, if you know what's good for you; he's out to get you.' To prove their point, they got the league to lynch a couple of men, whose only crime was that they happened to be black.

"Simpson was trying to use the same procedure in Mudville County during the last election, but it didn't work. Old man Crane was better at it, and he used his money to reinforce his position.

"Now I ask you," George Walton continued as his cousin listened intently, "what would happen if someone comes along and begins to open the eyes of the poor whites to what is really happening, open his eyes to the game that is being played on him?" George provided the answer to his question: "The entire political process across the South—in Alabama, in Tennessee, in Mississippi, all over—would have a good chance of being revolutionized, with power going into the hands of the people, rather than staying with the small aristocracy where it is now."

Bigsby had listened carefully as his cousin spoke, and his mind had wandered back to recent efforts to revive the League in the county. He recalled the cyclical interest of local politicians in the League. He himself had heard during earlier election campaigns, how politicians warned the people that "the niggers is fixin' to take over." It is interesting, he thought to himself, that he had not taken note of this before his cousin George had pointed it out.

"So is you suggesting, cousin, that us po' whites should form some kinda alliance with niggers and control the politics of the South?"

"No, that is not what I am saying," George replied. "In the first place, as I see it, many blacks don't seem to have much interest in politics; in the second place, in most Southern states including Mississippi, blacks are being barred from the polls by various measures both legal and illegal; and thirdly, most blacks who work on white farms or who are sharecroppers, usually vote the way their boss tells them to vote. But even though negroes can't vote or run for office, the politicians, most of them rich, from old pre-Civil War stock, are still using that technique of setting poor whites against blacks, and while we spend our time guarding against the nigger, the rich man is living off the cream of the land."

"What you is sayin' makes sense," Bigsby confessed, "but I can't see how you plan to change the thinkin' of people in these here parts. People bin 'customed to hear the politicians blame niggers fer ever'thing that's wrong. To change their way o' thinkin' will be like changing the course of the Yazoo."

"I feel it can be done," George answered. "It should at least be tried. A lot of the poor folk in this neighborhood can't read or write, but they have a lot of common sense, and that is what I want to appeal to. These rich politicians are convinced that they can keep us forever under their control. They call us trash. They have no more respect for us than they have for niggers, and they don't desire anything better for us. The main weapon we have in our favor is our numbers and our right to vote. If we use these intelligently, we can succeed in making this place a better world for ourselves and our children."

"George, you have my support," his cousin assured him, "but remember this. Once you present this kind of argument in public, it will be a matter of sink or swim. You will be layin' down a challenge to a lot of people who will see you as a threat to their way of life, and may stop at nothin' to silence you. If you succeed, your name will be written in school books, but if you fail, the only writin' may be on your tombstone."

Following his discussion with Cousin Bigsby George proceeded to discuss the issue with other members of his family. Among them he found reactions ranging from support to skepticism, objections, and reservations. To these he responded with a range of arguments, seeking to remove doubt and opposition. Having made the rounds of several members of his extended family, George decided to test his argument on a more difficult subject. The man he selected was not a complete stranger to him. In fact they were related by marriage, the man's wife being a second cousin to George. The man himself was a member of the League, in charge of recruitment. His name was Phil Instant.

By the time George Walton had arranged a meeting with the husband of his second cousin Gladys, news had already reached the League about the strange line of argument that "Cousin George" was presenting to members of his clan. The two men met at Phil's place--a small house at the side of a creek somewhat off the county dirt road.

As soon as George had greeted his cousin, commenting on how well she looked, jokingly inquiring about her "secret of youthfulness" and exchanging observations about her two rapidly growing girls, Phil initiated the discussion.

"Cousin George," he began, "what is this I bin hearin' 'bout you goin' round an' tellin' folks that whites and niggers is equal?"

"That's what's wrong with rumors," George answered. "The more they go round, the more they change and drift away from the truth. Now, I never said such a thing. I have no way of determining who is from who ain't equal."

"But what I hear is that you preachin' that us po' white folk is just like niggers," Phil insisted.

"What I said, is that poor whites an' niggers are in the same position in the South, in that both groups are being exploited by the same bunch of people."

"An' who might them people be you is talkin' 'bout?"

"I am talking about the people who ran and controlled the politics of the South during slavery, and who today continue to rule and dominate the South. In what way have the poor white people of the South improved their lot since the Civil War?" George inquired of Phil Instant. "Consider what was our position before the Civil War. We were the outcast, the landless, and largely despised. The white wealthy class viewed us as the scum of the earth. We did not even have the financial worth of a slave, for a good slave often cost two thousand or more dollars. Since the war, has anything changed? A few of us by hard work and sheer luck have been able to improve ourselves, but to the white ruling class we are still trash. Though we the poor people of the South are in the majority, we are ruled by a small white upper class. As soon as we begin to think of power, they says to us, 'The niggers are coming,' and they set us to fighting niggers while they continue to cream us and the entire South. So long as we continue to focus on colored people as our main enemy"--George was confident--"so long the small ruling class will continue to rule."

"We in the League," Phil said, studying George's face carefully, "we in the League is convinced that the nigger is our greatest threat an' that is the basis of our teachin'—the protection of the white race."

"In what ways is niggers a threat to us, and what white race are you talking about protecting?" George asked pointedly. "What we represent, the rich class of the South despises. You talk about protecting the white race, but the truth is that the only people you are protecting are the white class who run the state. And we are not protecting them from niggers, because niggers aren't any threat to them. In fact, they see

- 154 -

us as the ultimate threat, because they know we would like some of the economic and other benefits that they enjoy, and that we, the poor, are in the majority, and if we organize we can take over the South politically. So they set us against niggers, and while we are fighting niggers, they, the rulers of the land, continue to reap all the benefits."

"But look here, Cousin George," Phil persisted, "you know just as me that there ain't nothing niggers want mo' than to get their hands on white women an' rape them."

"I'm sure there are some niggers who won't mind raping a white woman, but tell me this, cousin. How many niggers have you known to rape a white woman, as compared with white men who have relationships with black women? Look again," George suggested."Look at all them fair skinned niggers--maybe as much as half of the niggers in Mudville County aren't all black. How come? Do you think it was because black men went after white women? It's just the opposite. You can trace every half breed nigger to a white daddy somewheres back."

"The point we must understand," George pressed home, "is that whatever we may feel about black folks, they aren't our enemy. They don't have nothin' we want, and we don't have nothin' they want--we don't have wealth, property or education in general. When we understand this fact and we ask ourselves what is it that ordinary white folks want, then we will see clearly who are our main enemies."

"I say," George continued, "what is needed is a broad movement among ordinary white people like you an' me, to assert our rights, and demand a better deal. If we get control of the political machinery, then we can make the changes necessary to use the resources of the state and county to help improve our lot."

⌒ ⌒ ⌒

During succeeding weeks, George had other discussions with Phil on the changes he felt were needed in the South. He had answered most of the questions raised by the man, and had apparently convinced him that at least part of the problems of the South lay with the nature of the power structure rather than with black folks.

"If all niggers left and went back to Africa today," George assured him, "it wouldn't help us a bit. We will become the cotton pickers, the sharecroppers. We will be the new niggers, and the law which today they like to say is for niggers and white trash, will then be for white trash only. This system that the upper class operates must have some niggers if it's to run properly. So if Blacks weren't there we would be it."

By the time electioneering began in earnest, George was already in full swing. Like a racehorse warming up, when the starting bell rang he was already in a state of momentum. Night after night he crisscrossed the hills preaching his new doctrine to audiences of his kinfolk and their neighbors. His message was simple: "The struggle in this state ain't white against black. They ain't got nothin', no money, no land, no education, no power. Many of them still live like slaves. The struggle is between us who don't have no political power, and the small white ruling class who are our oppressors."

As he traveled around, George Walton got bigger and bigger audiences. There were scattered hostile responses and catcalls, but there were more and more questions being asked, and he left his audiences thinking.

"It sure nuf stupid," one man commented to his companion one night as they left a rally, "that the politicians always tell us, we is got to protect ourself 'gainst niggers. As fer as I can recall I ain't never heard 'bout no niggers attackin' white folks in this county." The man paused reflectively before continuing, "I don't care for niggers m'self, but I agree with cousin George. We's got to face our real enemies."

When Julius Crane, son of the retiring legislator, kicked off his campaign for the post being vacated by his father, he was greeted in several areas of the county by calls of "the upper class is our real enemy," and "political power to the masses." Within a matter of days, it became clear to young Crane that his electioneering was having little positive effect on the people. There were even elements of hostility among some who came to listen to his speeches. On many occasions he heard such cries as, "We don't want no upper class to represent us."

A close examination of the territory by Julius Crane revealed that primary responsibility for negative response to his campaign was the dangerous doctrines being preached across the county by George Walton. But this was only partly true. Many residents of the county, with the arrogance of the elder Crane still fresh in their minds, were demonstrating to the son their feelings towards the old man.

Julius Crane, like his father, had used the "nigger" theme in his campaign but it seemed to no avail. Realizing that his election campaign yet in an early stage was floundering, Julius in desperation wrote a letter to his dear friend Henry Wippingthorp, a former schoolmate at Vanderbilt University in Nashville, Tennessee, who was now a member of the legislature of that state. In it he described the situation he was facing in his campaign, and sought his friend's advice.

Dear Henry,
      Since the initiation of my political campaign for my father's seat in the legislature, a campaign I had

expected to be relatively easy based upon the political record of my father, a new and startling element has entered into the politics of this (Mudville) county. This element is represented by a man, George Walton, a former graduate of Peabody College, but a member of the lower class, with extensive family connections among the worst white elements of the county. This Walton fellow is preaching a new and dangerous doctrine among his people. He is seeking to generate a sense of solidarity among the white trash, telling them that they are the majority, and they, the poor whites, must unite and take over political control of the county. His message which seems to be making inroads among the ignorant and illiterates of the county, is that the wealthy class who today controls the politics of the area is the enemy of the poor, and must be overthrown. It appears that many are taking this Walton seriously, for wherever I carry my campaign in the county, I seem to encounter hostility or impassivity.

I am hoping that you, already having "passed this way"—I mean as far as experience is concerned-- can advise me as to some positive approach to counter this development. With only a few weeks left in the campaign, I must turn the tide soon or face defeat.

Please reply immediately.

Sincerely,

Julius

The letter traveled by train to Nashville, and within a week of its arrival, Julius Crane received a reply from his friend Charles Wippingthorp.

Dear Julius,
Greetings. Your letter came only last night, and I immediately set about to reply, realizing that the matter was one of urgency. Let me start by saying that the problem you face in Mudville County is not unique to your area. In other parts of the South--right here in

Tennessee--there have been voices among the less reliable elements of the white community, who have tried to rally their kind against the so-called ruling class.

It is widely recognized that if such a movement becomes fully organized, we who through our own labor and intellect, through the process of natural selection have come to inherit the land, will be in grave danger. In the process of struggle and survival of those that are most fit, we have been brought by nature's laws to the forefront of society, and it behooves us through our own intelligence to assure that our position is not usurped by an inferior group.

Here in Tennessee, as in other areas of the South, the ruling class has been successful because it has been able to turn the attention of the lower elements of the white community to the "negro encroachment." It is an established fact that the lower elements of the white community have certain pre-inclinations that make them quite susceptible to tribal calls against the negro. This fact has proven to be a blessing to the white upper class. For even as we despise the white trash, so the poor white can be made to despise the negro, and assume a mentality of siege with the clarion call that the negro is about to surpass him, or is about to take the little that he has.

The fear of the negro is in fact the most clever card being played today in the game of politics here in Tennessee and in the South, to control the restlessness of the lower white element. The most horrifying spectacle you can shake before a poor white is that of a Negro--former slave--surpassing him socially and economically. If you can use this approach, get your constituency convinced that "the niggers are coming," all other considerations will become meaningless to him, and his entire energies will be geared towards confronting the niggers. A new organization recently started in Tennessee in a village not far from Nashville, is serving this very purpose. Its founders and moving supporters are among the least intelligent of the white community. But it feeds like a vampire on the "threat of the negro," and has shown the capacity to generate a religious frenzy against negroes.

I am sure that should you support the organization of such a movement in Mudville, your opposition will be submerged by the resulting flood, and your problems will be solved.

Please keep in touch and let me know the progress of your campaign.

Sincerely yours,

Charles

Julius Crane was delighted by the response he received from his friend. What Charles told him had simply reinforced ideas already in the forefront of his mind as he had contemplated a possible model of counterattack against George Walton. Following his friend's advice, Crane enthusiastically launched into the attack, using the almost pictorial rhetoric he had learned from college days as a leader of student activities. He warned his audience wherever he went that "a black shadow like a mighty tornado is sweeping across the South. It is the shadow of niggers determined to take over this place lock, stock, and barrel, and the ones who will suffer most," he warned his listeners, "are you the ordinary hard working people of this land. It will be too late," he preached across the Limestone Hills and the farming areas of the plain, "if we wait until tomorrow. We must recognize that we all have one thing in common, we are all white folk. It is we against them. Let us all hold hands together like a grand dedicated family, and make sure that this land is secured for us and our children."

At one such meeting at Cross Roads, a farmer standing at the back of the crowd of listeners challenged Crane in the middle of his presentation. "Where is the niggers who is fixin' to take us over? How come we don't know nothin' bout it and most of us have niggers on our place?"

"It is all working underground," Crane informed the man. "They are planning. There are plots in Niggerville, in every black community in this country."

"And yo' pappy have over one hundred niggers workin' on his place," the farmer persisted.

"Oh! Our niggers ain't involved. We see to that, but that don't change the fact that the greatest threat to white people in Mudville County is that of niggers, and I am dedicated to see to it that white folks is protected."

Like a Biblical prophet, with burning eyes and a hoarse voice, Julius Crane crisscrossed the county with his message of fear, calling on white people to seek safety under his banner. Some listened in stony silence, some nodded their heads in agreement, some jeered, others challenged. "Where is the niggers you is talking 'bout?"

"They is all around, like darkness of the night creeping across the land. They is in Niggerville and in every other colored community."

"How come no one else but you is talkin' 'bout them?" another asked.

"The eyes of most of us whites are blinded," Crane explained. "While we are fighting among ourselves the niggers are creeping up to take what we got."

"You mean what you's got?" one said. "We ain't got nothin', an' yo' daddy used to call us white trash. Fer as I is concern' the only niggers what fixin' to do us in is them what have white face and right now is running the government an' everything else that's worth owning in Mississippi."

"You are wrong, my brother, so wrong. There is lots that you have that niggers want." He lowered his voice like a preacher making an altar call. "They want your daughters, your wives, they want freedom to sleep with your womenfolk. The only people in this county who is worse off than niggers, are those who are trying to set white against white."

⌃ ⌃ ⌃

Towards the end of July, the days are hot and dry. It has not rained for several days and the grass along the road is parched and brown. There is a sense of stifling in the air, but each night, the wind like an angel of mercy brings water from afar and deposits it upon the cotton bush as a delicately woven jeweled blanket of dew. In the early hours of the morning before sunrise, the mockingbird and the cardinal fly into the field and drink from the dew. Then the sun rises, and the wind which during the night showed a mood of giving, now gustily, greedily, laps up with invisible tongue the remaining water on the leaves. By the middle of the day, there is an eternal sultry haze in the heavens, and beyond the heartless blazing sun. Here and there piles of clouds like bizarre creatures sculptured in cotton move listlessly across the infinite expanse. By evening, the sun, well on its way, hangs in a bluish haze beyond the Yazoo.

The white farmer, perspiring in the evening heat, rides his steed to the border of the cotton field, along a small dirt path where the aged blackberry bush mingles with the withered honeysuckle and wild rose. The farmer looks across his expansive field of cotton, and a feeling of satisfaction fills his heart. He sees that the crop is strong and sturdy, the leaves are dark green, and the pods are heavy. "It will be a good crop," the farmer says to himself, and with a sense of joy and delight he turns his steed towards home.

But, alas, his joy will be short lived. For within a few days a colored field hand, who has examined the crop of cotton more closely, will come to the back door of the farmer's house and say, "Masa! There is plenty o' bole weevil in de cotton fiel'." Now the farmer realizes that what appeared to be healthy from a distance, bore the seeds for economic ruin and disaster.

So it was with George Walton as he traveled the community with his new political doctrine, as he looked into the faces of the people who came to see and hear him, people mostly silent and thoughtful. "The people are listening," he thought, "the people are thinking. Their eyes are being opened. The new day that I seek will begin here in Mudville County."

But the words of Julius Crane were having the intended effect on the people. Like the boll weevil, the message of hate was silently working its way into their hearts. George Walton was given regular reports on the political meetings of Julius Crane. "Julius is laying it on thick," his cousin Bigsby Walton told him. "Some don't take him seriously. But many questions are being asked, people are thinking, and some people, even though they don't care too much for the Crane family, feel that there may be some truth to what the boy is sayin'."

"Further," Bigsby informed his cousin, "Julius has joined the League. He is goin' to try to use them to rile up the whole county. Luke Atkins is the new head of the League in the county."

"Who is Atkins?" George inquired.

"He moved in here from Yazoo County a while back. He was right in the middle of it when they lynched those two niggers down there three years back. As soon as you say nigger his eyes turn red, like an Indian mongoose seein' a snake. I suspect there is goin' to be plenty o' trouble before this campaign is over."

"I am not going to let the League or no one scare me in this county," George said. "The white people around here are no fools. They wouldn't allow a fringe group to scare them into submission. My response to Julius Crane will be a public challenge to discuss the issues." And so it was. At a meeting where farmers and village folk were gathered to hear him, George accused his opponent of trying to direct the attention of the people away from real problems by using the same trick used by the wealthy politicians in other counties to scare white people into supporting them.

"Who has the guns, the police, the army, the political power under their control in the State of Mississippi?" he asked rhetorically. "These are all controlled by the ruling rich white minority. Then tell me," he continued, "where is this colored attack coming from, from the share croppers and cotton pickers of the plains? From Niggerville? How come Julius Crane is the only one who knows about this impending attack? How come the sheriff of the county don't know nothing about this threat?"

Then came the challenge. "I challenge Julius Crane to an open debate before you the people. Right here among these hills I challenge him. I challenge him to share a platform with me and to argue his case. For he has no case except what he has created in his own mind in order to win the election."

There was a cheer from the audience. Even supporters of Crane were enthusiastic. "Fancy Crane and Walton sharing the same platform," one man said, grinning in anticipation. "That's goin' to be the best thing I ever seen in these here hills."

∧ ∧ ∧

News of the challenge spread through the hills and across the cotton fields of the plain and arrived at the doorstep of the Crane mansion by the following day. The challenge was repeated again and again by Walton, and with the passing days it became obvious to Julius Crane that he could not afford to ignore the challenge and hope to win the election.

A few nights later, Crane responded to the challenge. "I will debate George Walton any time, any place, and I will uncover him before the people as a traitor to the white cause."

The place of encounter was to be a small town in Limestone Hills which went by the name of Summit. The time agreed upon was Saturday evening at six o'clock. By five forty-five, the square, usually a place where children played and old men whittled on benches below the oak trees, was filled with people from the surrounding hills. A few enterprising persons had set up stalls and were selling drinks, confectionery, and watermelons. There was fiddling, guitar and banjo music, and a general air of gaiety and anticipation. The platform to be shared by the two contenders was a four-wheel cart pulled into place by a mule.

At five minutes to six, George Walton pushed his way to the front of the crowd and climbed on to the cart to noise and cheers of the crowd. Next came Julius Crane, dressed in an impeccable evening suit, a large gold ring on a finger of his left hand, and an expensive London-made felt hat. Three chairs had been placed on the cart. The contenders sat at the two ends, and the mayor, a short, stocky man uncharacteristic of the hill people but very much one of them, sat on the middle chair.

Standing with one foot on the side of the cart, the mayor welcomed the crowd, recognizing a few persons of special importance—the banker, the owner of the only hotel and restaurant in town, and a lumber mill owner, an important contributor to the local economy—and making a few comments which brought laughter from the crowd.

"But we ain't here for a picnic or a circus," he reminded them. "We are here to listen to politics, and to hear what these two men have to say. There won't be no vote on who win or who lose this debate. You all will be the judges in your heart and I believe that I express the will of all the people when I say we is highly honored to have this debate here in our little town." The crowd cheered. "I ain't gonna take no more time, 'cause I ain't part of the debate." Cheers. "So I will turn the meeting over to these two gentlemen."

George Walton was the first to speak. He said that Summit was his part of the county, and as a matter of courtesy he would allow Julius Crane, the man from the flatlands, to speak first. Then he sat down.

Crane's presentation was largely an intense summarization of the message he had carried to the people over the past two weeks. "A dark shadow is creeping up upon us. They are fixin' to remove themselves from the position of fetchers of wood and drawers of water which the Almighty assigned them in the Bible." This latter statement was a new element introduced by Crane. "They plan to leave the cotton fields and other places where they now work, and move into positions of power, and to use that power to suppress you the white people of this county. Like the Philistines and the Amorites in the Bible, they look upon us to whom God has given this country with envy, and there are dark plans on foot to improve their position at our expense.

"First they plan to exchange their place with you, the jobs you have, the economic security you have worked so hard to create for yourself. Their goal is to create the conditions so that you will be the sharecroppers and cotton pickers, and they will be above you. This threat from the nigger population is not only an economic and social threat, it is a threat against your womenfolk—your wives, your daughters—and a threat to destroy the purity of the white race. Their method is to set white folk fighting against white folk, poor against rich, and while we are so involved, they are creeping up upon us to take over. Rather than listening to the voice of those who will set white against white, the time has come for us to clasp hands together and like one big family, shoulder to shoulder, resist this evil force. I am asking the people to support me for the seat in the government, because I am dedicated to the task of keeping this land free for us and our children."

Julius Crane turned sideways to look at Walton seated behind him. "It is with pain in my heart that I have to accuse this man, George Walton, a white man like you and me, of unwittingly working to split the white community, and making it easier for niggers to take over the county."

George Walton was on his feet before his opponent was seated. He faced a silent crowd seeded with several of his own relatives. Immediately he launched into a counter attack against Crane.

"Julius Crane, like his father before him who publicly showed contempt for the poor white people of this county by referring to them as 'white trash,' has the gall to accuse me of working against my own people. My campaign and my challenge to him have drawn him out into the open like a copperhead from his crag. What he has just said before you is an example of what a lot of upper class politicians and others who choose to follow their example are doing all over Mississippi. They seek to get votes and the support of ordinary white folk like you and me, not by promising us jobs, not by promising us programs that will improve our economic conditions, not by promising us schools to educate our children, or better roads, but by trying to get us to look away from our own problems and needs, by telling us that niggers are fixin' to take over. He has tried to give you the impression that I am working with niggers to destroy you, many of whom are my own family, and all of whom are my own people. I am not a nigger lover, but I am not a nigger hater either, and if I have to use nigger hating to win an election, then I will never be in the government. What kind of man is this who is ready to set white and niggers fighting just so that he can occupy his pappy's seat in the government? He says that the main issue in this election is the threat of niggers. Ain't it strange that it is only now that elections is around the corner that suddenly Julius Crane picks up so much interest in saving us white folks from niggers? Ain't it strange that in spite of this so-called 'nigger threat' Julius Crane has over one hundred niggers working on his nineteen hundred acres of land? Ain't it strange that this man is so concerned about the purity of the white race, when in fact he's got half brothers with black mammies on his farm."

"Shell the corn!" someone yelled from the crowd.

This was "hitting below the belt," and Julius Crane could scarcely contain himself. He sprang to his feet, to the delight of the audience many of whom thought a fist match was about to occur, and headed for George; but the mayor was between them.

"Jus' now, here, let's keep this calm. Your turn will come to reply, but we don't want no boxin' match here."

Julius Crane was protesting over the attack on his father.

"You will have your time to answer," the mayor, tickled by the incident, assured Crane.

"I am not attacking anybody," Walton continued when the crowd had settled down. "I am just pointing out the facts to you. It is not necessary for Julius Crane to try to ride on our backs to the state legislature by telling us to protect ourselves from niggers. We know how to protect ourselves from any enemy, colored or white. Not once has he promised to help to improve your living conditions.

"My message to you has been and is, that we, the majority of this county, must get together and elect one of our own to represent us in the government. One who will fight for us, look after our welfare, see to it that we get a fair share of the resources of the state.

"They set us on while they live in luxury and grace, with black servants attending them. I don't know much about niggers, cause I ain't never been that close to them, but my guess is that they don't want to fight us any more than we want to fight them. You name one incident in the last twenty years," he challenged Crane, "where niggers have attacked white folk in this county." George paused, and in the pause Crane jumped to his feet.

"My opponent is suggesting to you that black and white people are equal, and that niggers are entitled to the same treatment as you. The truth is that God Almighty direct in the Bible that niggers who are descendants of Ham be servants forever to white folk. It is not by chance that the nigger was a slave, neither is it by chance that they are the cotton pickers of the South, and the sharecroppers. The threat exists because the nigger is rejecting his historical role, and is trying to move up to the position of white people, and George Walton is making it easier for them at your expense."

"I am not trying to do such a thing," George protested. "I am trying to open the eyes of my people to the antics and the methods of control being used by Julius Crane and other politicians like himself to maintain political control by putting fright into us about a nigger threat that doesn't really exist."

"Julius Crane said that niggers were made by God to be slaves and servants of white folk. If that is so, how come right in this county there is poor white folk working as servants to other whites, picking cotton, and living as sharecroppers? And if God intended niggers alone to be slaves, how come my own great gran' pappy was a slave and had to buy his freedom in Virginia? Was he a nigger?" he asked rhetorically.

"Is possible he coulda been, cousin!" called a voice called from the crowd, causing a fit of laughter.

Crane, who had been seated as Walton spoke, rose to respond. "As far as white folk being slaves, it was the doin' of Britain and not of God Almighty, and it wasn't predicted in the Holy Book. But we need to go back to the main issue at hand. George Walton says that you don't have nothing niggers want, and niggers ain't standing in your way, but I ask you, is it not a fact that a lot of niggers are mechanics, masons, carpenters, and do other skilled jobs that unemployed white men should be doin? If you don't wake up before it is too late, you will find one day that there 're no jobs in the towns or on the farms left for white folk. If they are competing with you for jobs, they are taking food from your mouth and the mouths of your wives and children."

George Walton interrupted, "It is a fact that there are a number of black folk with skills and doing jobs that white men could do. They work as mechanics and engineers of the farms. There are black builders and bricklayers. But I ask you the question, where did they get the skills from? Who taught them? They got it from white families like the Cranes, who preferred to teach these skills to a slave and use his free labor rather than pay a white man to do the job. If there is such a problem this man has his father and grandpappy to blame. But an even more important point is that if the politicians would promote the development of this state as they ought to, there will be enough jobs in the black community for the black skilled person and in the white community for the white skilled worker."

The political rally broke up, not because both candidates were through with each other, but due to a drizzle which had descended on the place with sounds of thunder breaking over the hills, and streaks of lightning chasing the clouds over the town. As the drizzle increased, the crowd began to disperse, some seeking shelter, others heading out of town along the trails and narrow roads.

A third candidate running for the seat was a farming machine salesman by the name of Jason Bilbo. His campaign was rather low-keyed, going from farm to farm and from community to community talking to people, informing them of what he would do if elected to advance the interest of the community.

As the days of election approached, the campaign intensified, and attacks by Crane of "nigger lover George Walton" reached a high point. The League, stimulated by funds provided by Julius Crane, was in a county-wide membership drive, with drums, bugles, and marches through Mudville and other towns. Before them they carried a white banner, with the words written in bold black letters, "Beware of the Black Shadow," and "White people of Mudville County, Awake."

Little by little a snowball effect was being achieved. Fringe elements, the unemployed, religious fanatics, and extremists were joining the ranks and marching to the drumbeat of the League. Visitors were being brought in from outside the county to give speeches on what niggers were up to in other counties, and what the League was doing to stop them.

The mayor of Mudville, with his eyes on his own upcoming election for a post he had occupied for two terms, perceiving the attention being given to the League declared that while he was not anti-nigger, yet he had nothing but support for the League in its effort to protect the interest of white folk. The white preacher from the church in Mudville, encouraged by a sizable offering from Julius Crane, had joined the bandwagon, pounding his pulpit as he declared support for the candidate whose family had traditionally provided protection for the county against the threat of colored insurrection.

⌢ ⌢ ⌢

The upsurge of the League was being discussed by white farmers across the county and by blacks in the many villages and rural places where they lived. It seemed to many that the issue was no longer the election but the growing power of the League. Farmers were expressing the fear that excessive action by the League could drive blacks out of the county and create serious economic problems on the farms. "Is just them politicians," Urick Brentwood explained to Ben Mathis who had been earlier attacked by the League for "working with niggers against the interest of white folks" and had reason to be fearful of the developing situation.

"I wouldn't give too much attention to it," Brentwood assured him. "Once this election thing is over they will settle down."

"I don't know," Mathis said thoughtfully. "The League is like a pack o' dogs. You train them to hunt and let them loose and there ain't no telling what they'll hurt. Like dogs, if they can't find real prey, they turn on cattle, sheep, or anything they can find. But mark my word," Mathis was somber, "once they start attacking niggers, you goin' to see a stream o' niggers headin' North, and when it's all over, it's the farmers who will suffer."

"I hope to God it don't get that far," Brentwood mused. "One of my best colored workers, Jim Brown, is sure nuf upset over all this League business. He says there is tension an' fear building up among colored people in Niggerville an' all over. I told him just to lie low and keep quiet, and tell other colored folk to do the same. I told him this whole thing will blow over once election is done and dem League people will go back up in Limestone Hills where they belong."

"I hope you's right, Urick. I sure hope you is right," Mathis replied.

A few days before the election, the League added a new slogan to its repertoire: "Those who ain't fer us is fer the niggers." Some farmers, uncertain as to the allegiance of their neighbors, were refusing even to discuss the developing situation for fear of being found on the wrong side. When a farmer asked his neighbor, "What do you think 'bout the League?" "Well, I reckon I don't fully know," was the reply. "I's still watchin' an' thinkin'."

In the colored community, the political campaign was observed with growing alarm as it developed more and more into an insidious anti-black crusade. In fact, developments in Mudville County were very much a reflection of conditions transpiring throughout the State of Mississippi. During the previous decade, the involvement of black people in the political affairs of the state had been drastically reduced by the evil machination of some white political leaders led by men such as Zachariah George and Lucius Lamas. The policy they pursued was one of white supremacy and the complete elimination of blacks from the political arena of the state.

Where alterations in the State's constitution had failed to deter the black voter, force, intimidation, and violence with the passive or active support of the law were utilized. Thus, in campaigns involving Democrats and Independents in Mudville County, blacks could neither vote nor run for office. Sharecroppers and workers on white farms were being assured by their employers, "Ever'thing is going to be all right," but such assurances in no way compensated for the fear that was being generated by the tenor of the political campaign. As rumors spread in Niggerville and other areas where blacks lived that the county sheriff and the mayor of Mudville had come out in favor of the League, some of the more vocal members of the black community began to speak out.

"I told you so," Babs Jacobs was saying to all who cared to listen. "All this talk 'bout white farmers gonna protect you cause they have an economic interest in you" is just hogwash. I been sayin' it all the time and I's sayin' it now. We coloreds need to arm ourselves, have guns like white folks, and be ready to protect ourselves. Them whites are building up to a frenzy; all they need is a crazy leader overloaded with moonshine, and they'll be marchin' on Niggerville. If they attack my family they may kill me, but I sure gonna take some o' them with me."

Parson Jones was against any action that would give the League an excuse for attacking colored people. "There is a battle taking place," he told his congregation on Sunday. "It is a battle between the powers of good and the powers of evil—for the souls of white folks in Mudville County. We can only pray that the forces of good will prevail, and let us do nothing that would encourage the evil one."

There were a few families who decided not to wait for the outcome. Some of them, already attracted by news of opportunities up North, and having relatives or friends living north of the Mason Dixon, took what little belongings they could and headed northward. During the last week of the campaign, twelve black families left the county on the northbound train. On some farms in the Cross Roads area, the situation had become so tense that blacks were staying in after sundown. On one farm the day before election, the white farmer, observing that long after sunrise no field hands were at work, went to investigate. The two houses on his premises where the black sharecroppers lived were empty. During the early hours of the morning, the two families had left with what belongings they could carry.

As news of the flight reached neighboring farms, some farmers began to voice complaint and issue threats. "Let it be known," one of the more vocal farmers warned, "that any of them leaguers come on my place to molest my niggers is goin' to be dead. I ain't gonna stand around an' face economic ruination 'cause a politician gets with some crazy rednecks and decide to stir up nigger hatred in order to win an election."

Sheriff Tate was caught in the middle. On the one hand observing the growing strength of the League he desired not to offend them, yet he determined not to sit by and see violence explode in his county.

"It's you politicians," he complained to Mayor Simpson, "who will be responsible for whatever happens. I've seen this before in other counties, where politicians get people riled up about the 'threat of niggers.' All you need is one incident or a rumor that some white person been attacked and the lynching and beatings is goin' to start."

"Don't blame me," Simpson protested. "I ain't running fer nothing."

"You tell that to them farmers who are complaining to me every day that their niggers are refusing to go into the fields in some places because of the League."

Simpson hurried to warn Julius Crane of the growing reaction of the farmers. Crane at the next political rally warned his followers, "I say to you, don't take the law in your own hand. If you are attacked naturally you have to defend yourself, but don't give the enemy any excuse for actions they may be planning."

Rumors were flying that there was a plan to shoot George Walton. The League had dubbed him "Nigger Agent," and had further spread it around that he had a nigger woman as a concubine. Friends and relatives warned him that there was a plan to kill him. Even some who supported him secretly hoped that he would not win, for the League was already saying through its spokesmen, "George Walton may win the election, but I guarantee you he will never make it to Jackson."

As tension mounted during the last week leading up to Election Day, Mabel kept her children at home. She stayed away from Mudville, and when she traveled to Niggerville, she took her children along and returned home before sundown. Memories of her experiences with the League a few years earlier were yet clear in her mind. "I'm sure some of them remember what happened and may want to seek revenge," she thought.

Mabel's children were sharing the excitement in the discussions in school and in Niggerville generated by the election campaign. Daily they brought back to their mother news of what the League was "fixin' to do" and the different opinions being voiced in Niggerville. But Mabel was not so confident. She realized that it was only providence and the intervention of the sheriff that had averted a disaster during the earlier encounter. Eagerly she prayed, waited, and hoped that with the passing of election day, things would return to normal.

∧∧∧

Julius Crane won the election, but it was by no means a landslide victory. One hundred and fifty-one votes separated Crane from George Walton. Many of Walton's friends and relatives breathed a sigh of relief, for it had become increasingly clear that had Walton won, his life would have been in danger not only from the League but from the entire apparatus his policies would have had to confront.

Crane went on to the legislative assembly but he left a fully organized League behind him, one that had successfully flexed its muscles and called the county to attention. It had unnerved the mayor, stymied the work of the county sheriff, and injected into the county a psychosis of fear and uncertainty.

"We is calling the shots now," the leader, a man who could neither read nor write, told his close lieutenants, "We is on the move and ain't nothin' can stop us now."

On the surface things seemed to have returned to normal. George Walton returned to his teaching career at his school in Summit. With election past, interest in the League began to wane. A continued public drive by the League to recruit members among the farmlands had little or no success. Sheriff Tate with the support of the farmers' organization warned that no public disturbances would be tolerated from any quarter. With the cotton season coming on, it was necessary to have peace and quiet so that the crops could be harvested.

The League continued to declare its purpose as being "to keep an eye on the niggers," and in response to criticism from farmers who during the campaign had lost some of their workers, the League was now saying, "the ordinary niggers who is respectful and knows their place ain't got nothing to worry 'bout. Continue to work for your boss, continue to pick the cotton and do what you is told. The ones what need to worry is dem uppity niggers, dem what tryin' to be like white folks an' causin' trouble."

Parson Malcolm Jones of Niggerville saw the calm following the elections as the working of the Almighty. "As I done said it befo', everything will be all right. Good will prevail over evil."

In early September, Mabel Wright had a surprise visit from her neighbor Ben Mathis. Though living less than a mile away, Mathis had not visited the place since Mabel's husband had left several years earlier. The last visit was when Mathis needed some work done on his barn, and had employed Mabel's husband. This day, Mathis drove his wagon into the yard. On it were two large watermelons. He had had a good crop and at his wife's suggestion had brought two over for the children.

"Just yestiddy," he told Mabel, "my missus says to me. 'Bin a long time since you visited the Wrights' place. That lady is there alone with dem four chillen'."

Mathis did not climb down from the wagon. He called Billy and Joshua to unload the melons. "How is you makin' it?" he asked Mabel, looking at the four children in the yard.

"As well as can be expected," she replied. "The drought almost killed the vegetable garden, but we pulled water from the Yazoo and keep some greens alive. The heat was so intense that even though we watered the tomato and sweet peppers, still they burn up in the sun."

"I don't reckon the League bothered you none out here?"

"I ain't seen any of them since that time three years back. They been actin' up but they don't come out here."

"I ain't forgot what they done to me," Mathis assured her, looking beyond Mabel towards the house, "and I ain't never goin' to. As I done told Sheriff Tate, if I ever catches them on my place again I'm gonna shoot fus' an' ask questions after." He looked at the children as Joshua cut one of the melons in halves and portioned large slices to the other three children. "Lordy! How them chillen growin' fast! Just yestiday dey was little bitty ones, now look at them." He looked at Sharon, her rapidly growing breasts protruding in her blouse. "I see yo' still got them family ones with you," he observed.

"Yes, dey ain't got nobody to go back to, so I adopted dem. Dey is my chillen now."

"Well, I is sure God Almighty will bless you for carin' for them."

"He already done that," Mabel assured him. "Dey is healthy, well, and all obedient and good chillen. I can't ask fer much more."

"Yes," Mathis pondered. "Me an' the missus ain't got no young uns, but we sure wish we did. As folk gets older, is more important to have young ones around the place." With this, Mathis turned his wagon and departed, assuring Mabel, "If you needs any help me an' the missus can give, make sure you let us know."

Mabel thanked him kindly both for the melons and his expression of readiness to help. As he drove from the yard, Mabel observed him. He seemed to have aged much since last she saw him. "Is strange," she thought, "how similar white folks and colored folks. You have some good, nice ones, and you have some no good ones."

⌃ ⌃ ⌃

During the early fall of the year, the dry spell which had brought unbearable heat to the county through July and August persisted. Hill county folk were saying "Is hot nuf to roast the devil." Towards the end of September a bush fire started among the Limestone Hills; within two days it had traveled several miles and was visible for miles across the plains of Mudville County. It was not clear as to the origin of the fire. Some said an overheated chip of stone had ignited the dry leaves nearby, some said it was a lightning fire, while others had it that the fire was caused by an exploding moonshine still. In any case, by the third day vast areas of the hill country had been destroyed. Smoldering blackened stubs marked the spots where formerly pine and oak trees stood. Several homes along the creeks were destroyed, leaving families homeless.

One front of the fire was heading directly toward Summit. The people of the town and nearby areas organized into teams and, aided by the sheriff and some of his deputies, fought to contain the blaze. They felled trees ahead of the approaching fire and cut a path about thirty feet wide to check the blaze, but the tongues of flames, urged on by heavy winds, sucked into the heat filled zone and lapped across the gap. At night an eerie red glow illuminated the skies over the hills and during the day a bluish gray haze of smoke enveloped the region.

Colored people from Niggerville and other parts of the county saw the glow from across the plains. Some concluded that it was "the judgment of God being brought upon the hill people 'cause there is where the League has its nest.'"

"Look at that eerie glow in the heavens," Parson Jones commented to a deacon as they stood in front of the church building after the Sunday night service. "It sure looks jus' like what Abraham might a seen when he looked towards Sodom and Gomorrah that night."

"Sure nuf," said the deacon. "Is de hand of de Lawd. I reckon is de way de Almighty is showin' his disapproval of what dey been doin' an' sayin' across the county."

The parson shook his head sadly. "The Lawd is callin' on his chillen both white and black to repent."

A group of boys sitting on the steps in front of Babs Jacobs' house was also observing the spectacle in the sky and along the hillside.

"Ain't that look nice," Babs' boy Benjie commented. "Them ol' troublesome Leaguers are bein' paid back by the Lawd."

"That's it, Lawd," he said gleefully, "I is in your corner, burn dem peckerwoods out."

"I wonder what dey is all doin' up there now?" another asked.

"I hear a whole heap o' houses done burnt down."

"You feel the strong wind blowin' towards de hills? Is the fire that drawin' it," Benjie observed.

"How come?" a boy inquired.

"The fire burn up all the air on the hill, an' pulls in more air to keep it goin'."

In the environs of Summit, over two hundred men organized in teams of ten and fifteen, now retreating in the face of intense heat, now standing and resisting, continued to struggle in an effort to check the advancing fire line. Members of the League stood shoulder to shoulder with others who had supported George Walton in the past election. One League member, as he paused momentarily to drink a cup of water commented to his companion, "I is ready to bet that this here fire bin set by niggers. If you ask me, I'd say dey sneaked up here, set the fire, then hightail it back to the flats."

"Oh, come on, Jake," his companion, a distant cousin of Walton, replied. "There is one thing 'bout you Leaguers. You blame everything on niggers. Next thing you'll say is that the niggers cause the drought weather."

"It ain't impossible, it sure ain't impossible!" Jake answered raising his voice to emphasize his convictions. "The Almighty have ways of showin' what he likes and what he don't likes. It won't s'prise me none if he didn't send the drought to show that he don't favor all them cotton pickin' niggers we harbor in this here county."

"Well then, how come he didn't send the fire to burn up no niggers' place, rather than white folks?" the man challenged.

"He sent this fire against us to make us unite," Jake informed him. "See here, me a member of the League, an' you a Walton, we both fightin' the same fire. Lawd want us to unite the same way to fight niggers."

On the following Tuesday, a cloudburst over the hills brought an end to the fire. Two days later, an interesting phenomenon appeared over the plains. A single dark cloud, seeming only a few hundred feet across, hung like a massive beast from an almost cloudless sky, and from it rain was falling—a swath of rain only a few hundred feet across. Men working in the field removed their hats to receive its cool drops, but others only yards away were untouched.

"Ain't dat somethin'," an old man said, looking up, grinning in the rain. By the end of the week the rains came out of the south, and the drought was finally broken.

Winter was extraordinarily mild in Mudville County. Encouraged by winter rain the grass continued to grow in green patches, and the vegetables in the garden in Mabel's front yard continued to flourish in the face of an occasional mild frost. In the month of January, the temperature rose to heights breaking all former records in the county. By the end of the month, what little existed of winter was for all practical purposes gone, as the forces of spring, encouraged by the weak performance of winter, emerged from ambush for a final onslaught. Black field hands, though accustomed to relatively mild winters, were saying, "This is sho nuf the strangest one we ever seen."

Mother Brown recalled a winter back in the eighteen forties that was similar, but concluded, "Seems t'me, this winter been even warmer." Some county folks were saying that it was so warm "the snakes didn't even worry to hibernate." But others were not quite sure as to the meaning of the warm winter and so early a spring. "Don't likes the looks of it," Jim Brown said to his boss, Mr. Brentwood. "See them blue jays buildin' their nest early again." He pointed to a pair of jays flying back and forth from the field to the pine tree not far away. "That mean bad weather is comin'." Brentwood, who had heard this line of reasoning before, did not reply; he simply looked at Jim and laughed.

Buds sprouted on the sassafras trees and reddish tender leaves began to appear on the rose bushes in front of the Baptist Church in Niggerville. Butterflies and insects were fluttering around in early February.

Spring rains came making the land soggy and difficult to plow. The fourth Sunday of March was one of the few mornings in three weeks in which it had not rained. The sun climbed on to a bluish morning sky, where white fleecy clouds floated peacefully across the dome. For farmers in the county the sunny morning was a welcome sight. To many it signaled a change in the weather and a chance for the water soaked land to dry out.

But by three o'clock in the evening the weather began to change. Fringes of dark clouds appeared from the southeast across the Yazoo. Distant peals of thunder could be heard faintly rising and falling as the echoes of cannon fire from some distant battlefield. Flocks of birds flew in haste northward as if pursued by some unseen predator of the sky. An ominous stillness settled over the land.

Jim Brown, feeding the sow and her litter in the sty at the back of the yard, observed the strange behavior of the animals. Rather than eating the slop, they were running around in the sty as if in a state of confusion. Jim glanced at the line of black clouds climbing onto the skies from across the Yazoo, heard the distant thunder peals and saw the yellow flashes escaping to the surface of the clouds. "This don't look good," he mused. "The pigs don't behave so fer nuttin. I reckon we is in fer real trouble."

By four o'clock the entire landscape was overcast. Dismal jet black clouds, now rushing in abnormal haste across the Yazoo, hung low over the trees. Scattered heavy raindrops began to fall, resounding on the earth. "A gully washer is a comin'," Mother Brown announced, looking from her window.

⌒ ⌒ ⌒

"Tornado!"

A white farmer, his wife and two children scrambled from the horse drawn open wagon on which they were riding, and dashed across an open field towards a trench not far away.

"Tornado!"

A colored horseman riding towards Niggerville looked over his shoulder and saw the monster descending from the southeast. He placed his stallion into a gallop, looking ever over his right shoulder. It appeared as if the funneled cloud was heading directly towards him. In panic he swerved the horse off the road across the field towards a patch of young spruce trees.

"Tornado!"

Terror filled the hearts of those who heard the sound. People, black and white, sought shelter and safety wherever there was a hole, an indentation, or a spot that appeared to be relatively safe.

Traveling at a speed of about thirty miles an hour, the tornado came from across the Yazoo River. A huge funnel protruding from the abdomen of dark laden clouds moved horizontally across the land, the tip of the funnel like the trunk of a crazed elephant raking the surface of the ground. From its body issued forth a constant greenish glow, a rapidly flickering light as from some massive bizarre furnace, and as it moved over the land, it emitted an ominous roar as of a freight train in full steam, or of rushing waters of a broken dam through a narrow mountain gorge.

The tornado passed across Ben Mathis' farm. As it touched the little farm house the building exploded, its fragments dispersing as far as three miles away. It passed just east of Jim Brown's place and Urick Brentwood's white painted house. The strong wind at the periphery tore part of the roof from Brentwood's barn, and several cows were killed in the field. Passing along the eastern rim of Niggerville, the tornado leveled everything in its path. It passed over a small pond and greedily sucked out the contents, leaving it empty; next day dead fishes were among the rubble found on Church Street. It approached the small, neatly kept home of Deacon Johnson of the local Baptist Church. As it touched the house there was an explosion. Deacon Johnson, huddled in the bedroom with his wife, found himself sailing through the air. During that brief moment of space travel, his entire life passed before him. The deacon imagined himself floating up towards the gates of heaven. But utter darkness enveloped him! He considered himself dead, and marveled that though dead he was still conscious. "This can't be heaven," he thought to himself. "It is so dark! It must be hell! Oh, Lawd, save me from this here pit of darkness."

Slowly it dawned upon his consciousness that he was wet. Rain was beating down upon his upturned face where he lay some two hundred feet away from where his home once stood. The deacon opened his eyes; he could see slivers of lightning like red hot swords slashing the skies. "I'm sho nuf 'live," he thought to himself. He realized now what had happened. His house had been struck by the tornado. He wondered what had become of his wife Muriel. The deacon struggled to his feet. Aside from being soaked he was all right. He walked and felt no pain. "Praise de Lawd," he exclaimed.

The tornado continued its path across the county. Cutting a hundred foot swath, it climbed up the face of Limestone Hills, clearing the trees and other movable objects in its path, mixing twisted, broken and uprooted trees with the mangled remains of houses. Then, as suddenly as it had descended, it ascended into the heavens and dissipated itself as it traveled northward. Even before the storm passed, people emerged from their homes and places of hiding to inspect the damage done by the tornado. Rescue work was initiated. It grew from spontaneous action by people who, realizing that help was needed by a neighbor or others in the community, were drawn together by the desire to assist. In the county, people, ignoring the factor of race or creed joined together to assist those in need. When news of the damage wrought by the tornado reached the town of Mudville, Sheriff Tate with a group of volunteers headed for the disaster area.

⌒ ⌒ ⌒

Sunrise Monday. The extent of the havoc wrought by the tornado was apparent as information on property destroyed and lives lost spread from farm to farm. Aside from the injured there were nineteen dead, including nine black and ten white persons. In the town of Niggerville there were three deaths, five houses destroyed, and others damaged. The dead included Muriel Johnson, the wife of Deacon Johnson, and an old couple who lived in a shack at the edge of town. Among the white victims of the tornado were Ben Mathis and his wife whose bodies were found the following morning in the field across the road several hundred feet away from the spot where their little farmhouse had stood.

Tuesday was a day of mourning throughout Mudville County. Whites and blacks wept alike and shared in common the sorrow over the untimely departure of so many of their friends and relatives. In the Baptist Church in Niggerville funeral services began in the morning. The first involved three coffins containing a mother, father, and only daughter. They were churched and buried side by side in the churchyard cemetery. By sunset, nineteen bodies had been funeralized across the county.

Mabel and her family were fortunate: the tornado had passed about one-half mile west of her place. The only damage to her farm was a few broken branches. During the storm her pigs escaped from the pen. The following morning Joshua and Billy found them wandering near the Yazoo.

Babs Jacobs and a group of rescue workers from Niggerville, having toiled all night in the county, were returning home just before sunrise when they came across an object partly wrapped in a blanket. It was the body of an infant. At first sight the infant appeared to be dead, but on being lifted from the muddy ground it began to cry. Subsequent search of the county failed to reveal the origin of the child. The baby, a little girl about eight months old, was placed under the care of an old widow, Mrs. Thelma Phillips, in Niggerville. The child's discovery and the mystery surrounding her origin gave rise to rumors and myths about where she actually came from. Some speculated that the tornado had picked up the child in another county and had carried it through the air all the way to Niggerville. Others suggested more supernatural origin. In any case, the child was given the name of Jane by the old lady, and was to be known through the years as "Tornado Jane."

The period of reconstruction following the disaster began almost immediately. Four houses in Niggerville had been destroyed, and indeed there was no home which had not lost at least a few shingles from the roof, a windowpane, a door, or had an outhouse damaged. All except the church, and this was interpreted by Parson Jones as a sign of the "power of the Almighty."

"God is tryin' to show black folk in this here county," he told members at the emergency Saturday evening prayer meeting, that "when all others fail, when everything else seems lost, His church will stand as a shelter in de time of storm."

Following the tornado, community spirit among blacks in Niggerville and the county area affected by the disaster reached a level not experienced in recent memory. A spirit of cooperation among whites and blacks emerged. As many worked together to restore damaged and destroyed homes and to provide aid to the many families made homeless by the storm, the pernicious racial emotions generated in many areas by the elections during the previous fall were replaced by a surge of optimism. Mabel Wright was among those who shared in the expectations that engulfed the community. With Billy, Samandra, Sharon and Joshua she had attended the funeral of Ben Mathis and his wife. She and the children wept as the two coffins were lowered into the graves. The Mathises had not been bosom friends to her family, but in a way they had shared much in common. They had lived as neighbors for years in a relationship devoid of hostility. They had both experienced the wrath of the white League, and the Mathis family had revealed their humanity by their occasional expression of interest in her family.

This new upsurge of interracial cooperation in the community had raised Mabel's level of expectation that time would be on her side. "I don't know how long this feeling of goodwill will last," she told the four children, "but I pray the Lawd it will allow us more time for you chillen to grow up and go off to college." The evening following the Mathis funeral Mabel sat on the front porch of her home with Samandra and Sharon. Fugitively the incident of the League returned to her. "Ain't it strange," she observed to the two girls, "how it is the good people who often die befo' their time, leaving the evil ones to inherit the earth."

The spirit of togetherness set free by the disaster was having a dramatic impact on the town of Niggerville. Suddenly there were feelings of excitement and a growing sense of community pride among the townsfolk. People were working together as never before. "I am really proud of my people," Parson Jones declared. "Look at the spirit of giving. Look at the spirit of cooperation! Niggerville has suddenly become a beehive of activities, as people work together and show an eagerness never before seen in these parts to help each other. These past few weeks I have seen white and colored folk workin' together, helpin' each other in a spirit of cooperation never seen before along the Yazoo. It is the hand of the Lawd," he pointed out to his church on Sunday. "Yes, we have lost loved ones, yes, we have suffered, we have experienced heartaches and anguish over our human an' material losses. But even as God made Israel to suffer in Egypt so that they could turn back an' serve him, so I feel we have been made to face tragedy— both white and black—in order to save us from ourselves."

The momentum of activity generated in Niggerville by the disaster continued through the summer and fall and into the months of winter. The homes destroyed and damaged were rebuilt through group action including contribution of money and material by white folks in the county, Mr. Brentwood being among the most altruistic.

In the town of Niggerville and its environs, there had always been a spirit of cooperation among black people. It was in part a function of the history of their condition, and by the more recent sense of siege growing out of the actions of the League. Though there had been no external outpouring of cooperative action embracing the entire community through the years, there was always in the hearts of blacks a yearning to work together, to draw together in the face of danger and uncertainty, and to stand shoulder to shoulder. But this desire, particularly in the hearts of the old, was counter balanced by the apprehension and fear that open signs of togetherness would be seen by some whites as a challenge and a drawing together for combat, and accelerate the process of confrontation. This perception by some of the elders was accompanied by an element of reverse psychology. Rather than projecting an image of unity and strength to the white community, security lay in being perceived as weak and helpless. Such perception would stimulate the better elements among whites to come to the defense of black folk. Some who supported this position even claimed to have seen it operational during threats by the League in the last elections.

⌒ ⌒ ⌒

Another winter came and passed. A new spring, and with it memories of the disaster now a year gone. Yet as the young new leaves appeared on the trees, as wild flowers blossomed, and warm winds wafted across the Yazoo, a spirit of new life, of optimism and positive expectations filled the air of Niggerville and the hearts of its citizens. People in the town planted more flowers in their yard during the spring, there was a movement led by the women to keep Niggerville clean, many found time to put new paint on the outside of their homes. Parson Jones had been the first to verbalize observations of these changes, as he sat at the supper table with his wife and Deacon Johnson, made a widower by the tornado one year earlier. The Deacon was a close friend of the parson and a regular and welcome member at his supper table.

"There is a stirrin' in this town," he mused over the table. "One can see the physical signs of change since the tornado, a new sense of dignity and worth among people, a new self-awareness. The many flowers we see in front yards, the 'keep Niggerville clean' movement, the newly painted houses, are the overt signs, but I sense a stirring of much more profound proportions in the young people. It is like the stirring of spring after a harsh winter. It brings joy to me, but also a touch of apprehension. How I wish," Parson Jones was shaking his head and gazing past his wife towards a picture of Jesus hanging on the wall, "how I wish it were possible to peer beyond the veil of the future and see where it all will lead."

Saturday evening early in June. The youth choir at the Baptist Church in Niggerville had just completed two hours of practice in preparation for the special service that was to take place on Sunday. Dr. Paul Ogese, a renowned Baptist preacher from Georgia, was to be the main speaker for the day's service, which was to end with a program of music by the youth choir and a visiting black choir from Mudville.

After choir rehearsal Julene Bell and three of her close friends, Josie Petrus, Benjie Jacobs, and Henry Hayden, all members of the choir, talked about Niggerville as they walked home together. Somewhere in the conversation Julene casually commented on how hungry the two hours of practice had made her. "As soon as I get home, I'm gonna dig into some barbecue chicken and cornbread."

"Barbecue chicken!" the three young men exclaimed in a chorus.

"I bet that just slipped out of your mouth by mistake. You didn't really want us to know 'bout that chicken," Azalea's son Josie jokingly taunted.

Julene chuckled. "Before my uncle from Jackson left this morning he insisted on Mama preparing for him some of her special chicken. Mama really laid it on him, and there's some left over in the kitchen."

"That's what I get for opening my big mouth," Julene protested as the boys uproariously demanded their share. "I was planning to enjoy all by myself, now I have to share it with you greedy men. Only one piece for each of you!" Julene tried to sound stern.

They walked across the town to the northeastern corner where Julene and her parents lived on their small farm of twenty acres. They reached the wood frame house, which her father, a self-made carpenter, had built. There was a large green front lawn, and a small patch of impatiens and marigolds blooming on each side. The house itself was painted white, and had a lovely small porch, with a grove of tall pines accompanied by a single sassafras tree on the south side.

The boys waited on the porch as Julene went in to fetch the food. Two of them sat on the step, while the other leaned over the banister of the porch looking out into the growing darkness of the summer evening. The sun had already departed. Only a dim crimson glow remained along the rim of gray clouds piled up against the western horizon. From where they waited, the little town of Niggerville seemed so sequestered, peaceful, and secure, as it lay under the magic spell of the Delta evening. Spiral wands of gray smoke slowly rising skyward marked the homes where evening meals were still being prepared. Benjie Jacobs, who was leaning over the banister briefly absorbed in his thoughts as he pondered the evening scene, spoke in a voice low and pleasant:

"It is a beauteous evening, calm and free
The holy time is silent as a nun
Breathless with adoration; the broad sun
Is sinking down in its tranquility,

"Beautiful!" Josie commented.

"It's the words of an English poet, William Wordsworth," Benjie informed him. And the three sank once more into silence.

"Yes! What a glorious evening," Benjie murmured. "There is a peace and a calm that fills the soul during these moments where the delta evening flows into the delta night in Mississippi. There is a magic spell that reaches into the very heart and soul of black folk, and for that brief moment between night and day dispels all fear, doubt, and uncertainty, and seems to say, 'everything gonna be all right.'" As he gave expression to his thoughts, Julene returned with a tray charged with food, and stood at the threshold of the door, listening to Benjie.

"Very well said," she commented. "I've always said you are going to be a great poet one day." With this she passed a plate to each of the three and they sat down to eat in the falling night.

By the time they had finished eating, the celestial threshold, that door through which the sun had departed, closed. The crimson glow was gone; the pinions of night had enveloped the place, making invisible the smoke still rising from homes across the town. The moon, not wishing to share its glory with the sun, only now came from behind a cloud bank in the east. From where they sat, the young people could not see the moon, only its silver glow spilling over the lawn.

Julene collected the empty plates, took them into the house, and returned to her friends on the porch. They had grown up together in Niggerville, and had been close friends as far back as she could remember.

"There have been times when I have seen this town of Niggerville as a prison without walls. There have been times when I have hated it," Julene said, the details of her face hidden by the darkness. "For me the very name of this town has been a symbol of the humiliation that we, not just here or in Mudville County or even Mississippi, but throughout the South and to an extent all America, have suffered. The town of Niggerville has shown me how close we still are to slavery, how meaningless is the freedom that we often say we have won with the help of Lincoln.

"Then there are evenings like this"—her voice had softened—"when out of the darkness appear stars and the moon, and they seem to be saying that there is hope. But you know, the greatest hope that I have had recently is not due to the moon or the stars, but to the people of this town. The way they have behaved since the tornado. In a very basic way I feel that we have helped to dispel from our own minds some of the evil ideas that we have accepted from the white man about ourselves.

"I don't agree with Parson Jones all of the time," Julene continued, "but he is sure right when he said that the tornado was a blessing in disguise. Before last spring I used to feel that most people in this town were scared Negroes, disorganized, afraid of their own shadow, each only interested in himself. But the spirit of cooperation, the self respect that has come from working together over this past year have given me hope for the future, in spite of everything else."

"I feel exactly the same way!" Benjie commented. "I sense, even among some of the older people, a new kind of confidence and a sense of pride in Niggerville. Niggerville," he repeated slowly, and paused to ponder. "Isn't it strange how through the years our parents and we have accepted this name that was thrust upon us? Niggerville!"

"It's the same thing I've been fixin' to say. Both our minds are in the same groove," Julene responded.

"I am in favor of returning to this town its rightful name, Wrightsville," Benjie continued. "We ought to stop using the name Niggerville, and encourage every member of the community to rediscover the original name. One of the best ways to accomplish this is to begin using the name Wrightsville ourselves."

"I don't see anything wrong about this," Julene added. "The proper name of the town is Wrightsville. That is how it was called by our parents who named it in memory of a white man, a slave master who had greater respect for human freedom than money, and gave freedom to his slaves and land on which to settle. So it is just a matter of returning to the town its true name."

It immediately seemed a most brilliant and exciting idea to the four young people. "Isn't it strange how no one has raised this issue before?" Josie asked. "I wonder how folks in this community will respond to the return of the name?"

"I think it is the best thing that can happen. It will be a visible sign of change. It will help to further strengthen the community and increase self-confidence," Josie said.

"I think most people will be glad to use the real name."

"The best way to start things rolling," Benjie added with some excitement in his voice, "is for us to start using the name, and to encourage everyone else to do the same. Spread it quietly among the young people that from now onward the name is 'Wrightsville.' If all the young people use it, after a while the others will follow."

⌢ ⌢ ⌢

Within two days every teenager and young adult in the town knew that the name "Niggerville" was dead. It was a wonderful and exciting feeling to be able to use the old name. To some it was like a declaration of freedom, and to all it was the rejection of a name that had symbolized humiliation.

The first time Babs Jacobs heard the name "Wrightsville," in a passing comment that Benjie made about "the Wrightsville Church youth choir," it did not dawn upon him that he knew what his son was talking about.

"The what choir?" Babs inquired, a questioning expression on his face.

"The Wrightsville choir."

"Where is...?" he paused for a moment. "I'll say is a long time I ain't heard that name, not since I was a boy. That name ain't been used round here in your time. How come you all of a sudden usin' it?" Babs now recollected that he had heard another youth of the town use the same name the day before.

"What you all up to?" he demanded.

"I don't know what you talkin' about, Paw," Benjie responded.

"None of the innocence to me, boy! I wasn't born yestiddy," he informed his boy. "You young uns is up to somethin'."

The following Sunday the issue emerged in church. Josie Petrus, giving the report of youth activities, referred to the town as "Wrightsville." When the call was made for a motion to accept the report, an old deacon rose to his feet, pointing out that the young man had referred to Wrightsville, rather than Niggerville. At this, Josie, the articulate son of Azalea Petrus, informed the church that he had not made an error since "Wrightsville is the real name of what we used to call Niggerville."

Mabel Wright, who with her four children sat in the second pew from the front of the church, smiled with satisfaction as the boy spoke. After all, the town had been named after her granddaddy. That evening as they rode home Mabel recounted to her children the history of the town and the part played by her grandfather in bringing freedom to colored folk in the region. The children were all excited over the new development.

"I never liked that name 'Niggerville' anyhow," Joshua said.

"Same with me," Billy added, "especially how seeing that name was made by white folk. Josie Petrus says that us young people must work for change an' progress and this is all part of change." Mabel listened without comment, though in her heart she wondered where it would all lead.

By the month of August, there was scarcely a person in the town who was not using the new name "Wrightsville." Even with the older folks there was an inner feeling of pride in dispensing with the "nigger" part of the town's name. Some were openly expressing wonder that they through the years had accepted the "Niggerville" with no resistance or protests.

Colored folks all over the county soon knew that Niggerville had changed its name. "Dey don't want nobody callin' deh town Niggerville no mo'," a toothless old colored man laughingly explained to others working in the field around him. "Dey is reclaimin' the original name what was changed by white folk."

"Fer as I is concern' dis Wrightsville name ain't no different from Niggerville," a cantankerous old man working nearby opined. "Both names was given by white folk."

"Dey is a sho nuf difference," the first man protested. "The name Wrightville come from a white man who was godfearin' an' who gave his slaves de freedom and land, even befo' 'mancipation by Lincoln. Further, is the colored folk deyself what called the place Wrightsville to honor the old man. De name Niggerville came from dem rednecks who want to remember colored folks that they is jus' niggers."

One white farmer not far away from the town observed to a neighbor living across the dirt road from his place, "Well, what do you know! Dem niggers in Niggerville ain't callin' Niggerville Niggerville no mo'. It sure nuf beats me why dey will want to change the name of the town! After all, dey is niggers! Beats me why dey would prefer their town to be called by the name of a white man." He picked his teeth with a small twig, a smile of wonderment on his face.

But members of the League saw it differently. "Dem niggers is acting up," the local leader Jeb Tyson, the shop owner from the town of Mudville, declared to some of his followers. "Dey want to be like us white folk. That's how come dey don't want to use the name nigger no more."

Having regained the original name of the town, the young people whose actions had resulted in the change, stimulated by the euphoria of their success, sought now to make the accomplishment formal. Towards this end they decided to erect a signboard at the entrance of Wrightsville. The words on it would read, "Welcome to Wrightsville, the Friendly Town."

The decision to erect the signboard like the one to change the town's name was the work of young people, without consultation of the elders, the church deacons, and Parson Jones, who for all practical purposes through the years had been the center of decision making in the un-incorporated town.

The sign was made from pieces of pine nailed together across the back, forming a surface six feet by four. The sign board itself was painted green, and Benjie Jacobs, who had artistic talents and whose paintings of natural local scenes of spring and autumn hung in many homes in Wrightsville, painted the sign in bold white letters:

WELCOME TO WRIGHTSVILLE
THE FRIENDLY TOWN

The signboard was nailed to two posts cut from an oak tree and planted into the earth at the southern entrance of the town. The new addition to the landscape was greeted with expressions of pride by the young people of the town. Old folks looked at it in the evening as they came in from work in the fields, some smiling in approval. Parson Jones looked at the sign on his way back from visiting a faithful member of his flock. He thought how the youth were pushing the town towards change. Pride mingled with anxiety surged within him as he pondered upon where all this could lead them.

Mabel Wright traveling with her children to church on Sunday from her small farm saw the sign as they approached the town. Shading her eyes with her right hand, she focused on the sign but could not read it from a distance. "What's written on that board up yonderl?" she asked Joshua.

Joshua, whose attention had been elsewhere, focused on the sign. "It say, "Welcome to Wrightsville, the friendly town."

Mabel smiled, "So the old man got his town back," she exclaimed. "Seems it was before I was born they started callin' this place Niggerville. My Mammy said po' white folks started callin' it Niggerville, then other whites picked it up, then the colored folks just fell in line." She paused thoughtfully. "It sure is a good sign. Never thought I'd see it in my lifetime. Colored folks are waking up," she explained to the children. "They are looking for self pride and self respect--two things this county been tryin' to take from them."

"Parson Jones said long ago that it is the tornado that caused Niggerville, I mean Wrightsville, to come awake and to begin to develop a sense of pride. I don't believe the tornado done any such thing," Mabel added. "It was here all the time, but it was covered up by oppression and fear. Many times when people see their lives is threatened, pride and self respect take the back seat," she explained to the four children. "The problem is that when you sacrifice dignity and self respect to save your life, you often end up losing it any way."

"What do you think 'bout the new sign?" Babs Jacobs asked Mabel as she bought some goods in his store on Monday.

Mabel smiled, shaking her head. "Dat old rascal grandpappy of mine musta turned around in his grave and smile when they put up that sign. Is a shame that we allowed them white folk to change the name in the first place. We shoulda resisted, from way back. I always say, Mr. Jacobs, and I ain't gonna change, that if you stand for your rights, you may suffer, but eventually you'll come through." As she spoke, Mabel recalled how years earlier she had blasted away with her shotgun at members of the League who invaded her premises, and were threatening to harm her and her children.

Babs agreed with her. "Come to think of it," he said, "nobody forced nobody to change the name of this town and call it Niggerville. There was some white folk who call it Niggerville, so we just figured that's how it was to be."

"Sometimes, us colored folks is sure nuf like fire bugs," he mused. "We see things only after we done pass them, then we say we wish we'd a done so and so. But I think the young folks today is gonna be different." His voice was confident. "You can tell by how they acting today, that they ain't takin' what we been takin' no mo'."

Exactly one week and a day after the new sign was placed at the southern entrance of the town of Wrightsville, in the morning in early fall, before the sun rose, while a thin layer of mist lazily embraced the land, workers on their way to the field looked up, and lo and behold, the spot where the new sign had proudly stood the previous evening was empty. Upon closer examination the sign was found lying on the ground in the thicket not far away. From marks on the ground and the prints of horse hoofs, it was clear that a rope had been tied to one of the posts of the sign, and with the help of a horse it was pulled from the ground where it stood and dragged into the thicket. Reddish sod on the posts marked the depth to which they had been planted.

By sun-up everyone in the town knew that the signboard had been pulled down during the night. Deacon Johnson of the Baptist church, who had miraculously escaped death during the tornado and who now expanded the drama of the incident each time he told it, heard about the sign from a neighbor, Judith Maud.

"I wonder who done it," he heard her asking someone on the street, as he sat near his open window reading the Bible for his morning devotion.

"I don't know," the other woman replied, "but it sure nuf looks like the work of the League. The way I see it," she continued, "a couple o' them rednecks crept up during the night, pull the sign down, and hightail it back up to Limestone Hills."

Deacon Johnson hurried over to Parson Jones' house and told him over the breakfast table what had occurred. The parson's response was somber. "The devil is not happy 'bout the pride and the community spirit that's been developed in this town since the tornado—the spirit of cooperation between white and colored folks that we saw as we all worked to rebuild the county. He is determined to rekindle the fires of hate that is still smoldering, and to destroy the rays of hope that we have seen shining through the clouds."

Deacon Johnson agreed. As he put down the cup of coffee which Parson Jones' wife had poured him from the iron kettle, his large callused hand showed puffed veins, forming a mosaic from fingers to elbow, covered with graying hair.

"This may be jus' the early thunder of a comin' storm, Parson."

"Not necessarily. It coulda been the work of a couple of drunks returning from Mudville last night."

"You could be right," the deacon conceded. "On the other hand, if it's the League, it could be the beginning o' trouble."

Benjie Jacobs was still in bed. As the early rays of the sun piercing through the window struck his face he rolled to the other side of the cotton mattress, and lay between wake and sleep. From where he lay he could hear his father talking to someone outside.

"You mean dey pulled it down?"

"Yes, dey sure did, and drugged it in the thicket. Everybody sayin' is the League who done it."

"I know they wouldn't a felt comfortable with that sign up there," Babs mused. "They see it as a challenge to them. They say we is niggers, and us by changing the sign says we ain't. You sure it ain't the wind what blown it down?"

"No, sir, that post was mo' than two feet in the ground. 'Sides, you can see the marks where they drug it to the thicket."

The conversation Benjie had heard from the window had driven from his eyes the last vestige of sleep. He rose, pulled on a pair of pants over the underpants in which he had slept, and while his father still conversed at the side of the house, he left through the kitchen door. Benjie cut through the backyard of two neighboring houses before he got to the side road. He crossed the road, walked under a patch of trees and shortly arrived at Henry Hayden's home. As he approached the house he could see Henry in the backyard huddled in conversation with Josie and Jerry Moore. He walked by the garden patch where ripe tomatoes waited to be picked, and joined his two friends under the dogwood tree.

"Is nobody else but the League who did it," he said, gesturing with his hands. His words of greeting had assumed that the boys were discussing the incident.

"The same thing I said," Henry agreed. "I figured that sooner or later they were going to let us know that they did not like what we are doin'. Some people are sayin' that we should leave it down, but I don't agree with them. After all, this is our town, and if we can't stand up to something as simple and clear cut as this, what will happen when real trouble come?"

"You are right," Josie agreed, his hands in his pockets. He had been studying Henry's face intently as he spoke. "I say we put it back up and we do it now. If we wait till later on when Parson Jones, the deacons, and others get involved, you can be sure that the Parson is going to advise that we 'shun the appearance of evil' by letting things be."

"Let's do it now," Benjie said.

They passed behind the row of outhouses that marked the borders of the backyards of houses on Church Street. They walked along the side of an open field beyond which ran the road leading to Mudville. They found the sign board, undamaged but lying on its back in the thicket. Picking it up they carried it back to the spot where it had stood, slid the posts into the two holes which yet lay open and damp with the morning dew. They jammed stones around each post and pounded them in till the posts stood firmly once more in the ground.

$$\frown\frown\frown$$

The meeting at Parson Jones' place was expanded by other elders from the community: Jeremiah Baker, the oldest of the deacons, who lived across the road from Parson Jones; Hosea Moore, Isaac Abraham, and Charles Drake. Each had received news about the removing of the sign, each had walked to the spot to see for himself, and each had made what appeared to be the logical response—heading for a meeting around Parson Jones' table.

Parson Jones, the man of peace and wisdom, who seemed to know the right thing to say at the right time; Parson Jones who, especially to the older and the saintly of Wrightsville, had direct contact with the Almighty. When in church he would say, "I prayed to the Lawd and He told me," it was taken literally by the true believers of his constituency. Particularly to the elders, but also to some of the younger more devout congregants, Jones was a kind of Moses, who at the right time would make the Red Sea open, or bring water from the rock. During the attack by members of the League on Ben Mathis and Mabel Wright a few years earlier, when all in Wrightsville felt that a racial tornado was about to touch down in the county, it was Parson Jones who assured the people that God was in their corner, and during the election campaign when racial tension was high, it was the parson who called on his flock to "look to Jesus, He will see you through." Now the elders and deacons, perceiving what appeared to be the making of a crisis, gravitated towards the parson's place.

There was one conviction among the gathered men, though there existed then no supportive evidence: "Is the League that done it. They was lookin' fer some reason to start trouble, an' it look like we done gave them one," Drake the local elder murmured, scratching his bald head and shaking it back and forth.

"These few weeks of excitement an' joy we done had over the changin' of the name an' all that, maybe the devil made it so that we didn't really see the danger," Hosea Moore commented.

"As I see it," Deacon Baker commented, tapping his felt hat mildly on his arthritic leg, "the hateful attitude some of them white folk have 'gainst us Negroes, they can always find somethin' to use as excuse fo' makin' trouble. As you all know, it gave me a feelin' o' racial pride I ain't never experienced befor'. Frankly, I don't see this as provokin' nobody. The mere fact that we is colored folk provoke some white people. You remember in the Bible"—Baker now spoke in a lowered voice, not wanting to be seen as projecting himself beyond Parson Jones or the other elders on Biblical matters—"in the Bible when the King of Assiri came up 'gainst Hezekiah, Hezekiah tried to buy him off by givin' him silver and gold, but the King only demanded mo' and was fixin' to take everybody an' send them off into slavery. If we get all scairt"—he paused for the lesson to sink in—"an' sacrifice our rights now, ain't no tellin' what they will try to do to us next."

Parson Jones listened in silence, solemnly nodding his head in apparent agreement, studying the faces of the deacons as each expressed his opinion on the matter. Charles Drake pointed out to the men gathered around the table that the "family folk" in the community "didn't have no say in the changing of the name or in the making of the sign board. We jus' went along." He assured his colleagues, "I ain't sayin' I ain't proud over the change, but we's gonna have to take control of this thing sooner or later, befo' dese chillen go too far. We's got to nip this thing in de bud."

Many heads nodded in approval. "The whole thing is the work of Satan," the deacon continued. "I mean what happen last night. Our responses have to be with prayer and special guidance. If we ignore this incident and urge the young people not to respond to it in any way"—he shook a forefinger to make his point clear—"we can deny the evil one the opportunity to make trouble fo' us."

"Amen!" Deacon Moore cried in approval. "I believe we must make a decision here to deny the League any opportunity to make trouble, by leavin' that sign on the ground where it is." Moore added, "The League expect that the sign will be replaced, and such a replacement will be the excuse they's lookin' fo' to cause trouble. So I say let us leave it as it is."

"I so move," said Deacon Drake, looking at Parson Jones in anticipation of a response.

The parson cleared his throat, and looked at each of the men seated around the table. "Well, brethren, you have heard the motion." A knock on the front door interrupted his response. The parson rose from his seat, moved to the door and opened it. It was Brother Pope Festus, a deacon from across town, He had been among the last to learn of the incident and like the other men seated around the parson's table, had visited the site for a personal verification of the facts.

"Good mornin'."

"Good mornin'. Brother Festus, please come in. We just been discussing the matter of the removal of the sign at the entrance of Wrightsville. I am sure you have heard 'bout it." Festus nodded his head. "We been trying to decide what to do about it, and there is a motion on the floor," the parson continued. "Come and join us in our deliberations."

Pope courteously accepted a chair brought from the adjoining room by Mrs. Jones, and seated himself slowly as a man in arthritic pain. "Whoever spread de story 'bout de sign bein' took down sure nuf caused a stir," he said, breathing ponderously. "As soon as I heard it—Stella, my wife, got it from de neighbor—I went where de sign was to see fo' myself and it seem ter me that de sign is still standin' like it was from de start."

"That ain't possible," Deacon Moore cried. "Me an' Deacon Abraham went out dere jus' a while ago an' seen it lying on the ground."

"I don't doubt it was on de ground then," said Brother Festus, "but it sure nuf is standing now."

"That can only mean one thing," Parson Jones concluded. "The young people who placed the sign there in the fus place have restored it."

"We was just 'bout to vote on whether the sign was to stay down or be restored," Deacon Drake reminded the parson.

"Seems to me it don't make no difference now, seeing how it is standing where it was," Deacon Baker observed.

"I don't agree," Moore remonstrated. "We is the elders of this here town, and as we said a little while back, in matters that affect the security of the community we must, with divine guidance, make the decisions."

"I agree," Charles Drake exclaimed, "but are we ready to tell de young people to take down de sign? Such an order will put us in bad light not only wid de youth, but wid many o' de older people in Wrightsville. The way things now stand I would simply let things be, and direct them young people not to make any mo' changes or do anything else without fust consultin' with us."

Parson Jones, adjusting quickly to the new situation, agreed with this suggestion and recommended it for adoption. It was accepted and the meeting broke up as informally as it had started, the men leaving one by one to go to their various duties.

⌒ ⌒ ⌒

Following the replacing of the sign, the pace of life appeared normal in Wrightsville; the act which had caused some excitement seemed forgotten, but beneath the surface a sense of disquiet and an element of tension remained.

One evening several days after the replacement of the sign, Stephen and Henry were walking along the side of the cotton field that separated Wrightsville and the road leading to Mudville when they noticed two white riders on horseback. The men had just turned on to the road leading from the south towards the church and the entrance to Wrightsville. They rode about one hundred yards, then stopped and gazed for several moments across the field towards the sign. Then turning their horses around they galloped off towards the town of Mudville.

Henry and Stephen hurried over to Benjie's place to inform him of what they had seen. Together they discussed the situation and decided that the surprise visit by the white men could only mean that another attempt would be made to remove the sign. The information was passed on to the other young men. All agreed that another attempt to destroy the sign was imminent.

"I think we ought to meet them head on," Josie opined. "If they are going to try it, chances are they will come back after dark or just before daybreak."

"We ought to set up a watch tonight," Benjie suggested. "We can all stay out and hide in the bush. If they turn up, challenge them. Since they won't know if we have guns, chances are they won't use none themselves."

"But we can't stay out there all night, every night, without our parents kicking up hell. I know for one my old lady will have a fit if she know we were out layin' in wait for them rednecks," Josie informed them.

"I have an idea," Henry announced. "Let us get a lantern, light it an' leave it a little off from the sign in the woods. While we are out there we will keep the light out, but when we have to go in, we will light it and leave it there. When they see the light they will figure we're out there an' will stay away. This will allow us to go in before the old folks start askin' questions."

"Great idea!" they all agreed.

They planned to set up watch from that very night, but a severe downpour lasting most of the night hindered them. Next morning the sign was still there.

It was agreed upon that the watch would be conducted by two persons at a time, so as not to cause undue suspicion by the elders. It would last until ten at night, after which the lantern would be put in place. The following night Josie and Benjie and Henry decided to do the first watch. About thirty feet away from the sign among some young spruce they settled in to wait.

By nine o'clock the almost cloudless sky was alight with stars, a partly full moon was climbing on to the stage of heaven, a cool wind blowing from the northwest rustled among the spruce, and above its murmur the sound of insects punctuated the night. About fifteen minutes to ten, they halted the conversation which they had carried on in subdued voices, to listen. The distinct sound of horses' hooves could be heard not far away along the dirt road leading into Wrightsville.

"Perhaps it is someone returning home late," Josie suggested.

"It's two horses," Benjie informed him.

Shortly in the dim light of the moon they could recognize the outlines of two riders on horseback. Having ridden to a point not far from the sign, the two riders stopped, then quietly urged their horses off the road onto the tall grass that grew between the road and the sign. The riders dismounted and carefully approached the sign. In the dim light one of them appeared to be tying a rope to one of the posts that supported the sign. Their plans were to pull the sign from the ground, drag it some distance away, and dismantle and destroy it so that even if its remains were located they could not be reassembled. Suddenly the three boys sprang from the bush. Taken by surprise, the two men swung at the figures approaching. In the scuffle, one of the men was knocked down. He struggled to his feet. Unnerved by the encounter, the two men retreated towards the road with their horses. Then mounting, they galloped off into the night.

News of the struggle with the two mysterious nightriders was carefully guarded by Josie and his friends, already mindful of the alarm and growing concern over recent developments among some of the elders. There was no sign of reaction from the League or any word from the white community with regards to the attack. The night watch by the sign was called off. The young men reasoned that the recent incident had made it clear to the attackers whoever they were that the sign was being guarded and thus they would be unlikely to return.

As days passed and nothing happened, it was further reasoned that were the mysterious visitors bent upon further confrontation they would have responded immediately while the incident was yet fresh in their minds.

⌢ ⌢ ⌢

Josie lived with his mother and younger sister on the eastern edge of Wrightsville. Their small wood frame cottage, built by their father Roland Petrus before he passed, was bordered on four sides by their small acreage on which was planted mostly corn and cotton.

Josie was on his way home from a card game with his friend Benjie and a few others at Babs Jacobs' place. The game would have continued later into the night were it not for Mrs. Philomena Jacobs who at the stroke of nine by the old clock hanging on the wall announced, "Dis is the last game. All of you have work to do or school to go to tomorrow. Is time to go home, an' you Benjie, is time you be in bed." The boys closed the game and reluctantly headed each for his home.

Josie left his companions and headed east on Church Street towards his home which was just one block away, along the dirt road whose borders were barely visible in the darkness. Above his head the sky was ablaze with stars. The Milky Way spread across the dome like a fluorescent cloud. A falling star to the north left an effervescent trail behind.

As he entered the narrow path leading from Church Street to his home, the smell of ripening corn greeted his nostrils. "It shouldn't be too long before we'll be out here pickin' corn," he thought to himself. Ahead Josie could see the light from the lantern shining from the window at the front of the house. On both sides of the path the cornstalks stood in silent rows like soldiers awaiting inspection. To the south the cornfield ran halfway towards the Mudville road before it merged with land where cotton was planted.

From the corner of his eyes, Josie perceived a moving shadow. It had appeared as if by magic from the cornfield beside him. He turned to face the shadow and felt the cold steel of a double barrel shotgun against his forehead. From behind the gun the shadow spoke. "Nigger, you make the slightest sound and I'll blow that nappy head o' yours plumb off your body."

As the shadow talked another appeared beside it. The two men led Josie through the cornfield in the direction of Mudville Road. "You jus' keep walkin'," the man with the gun said, "an' hope I don't get nervous an' pull this trigger."

Josie was paralyzed by the suddenness of the encounter and the precipitate change of events around him. His mind seemed to stand still in response to what was transpiring. Thus trancelike he obeyed every command of the intruders.

The two men led Josie through the cornfield in the direction of Mudville Road. "You jus' keep walkin'," the man said again, "an' hope I don't get nervous an' pull this here trigger."

Josie could smell the stench of the breath of the voice behind his head. It was a mixture of chewin' tobacco and moonshine whiskey. Shortly they entered the cotton field. The cotton bush scratched against his arms and legs as they pressed towards the road. Once on the road, they were met by two other men.

"We caught one o' them," the man with the gun at his back declared triumphantly. With a piece of rope they tied Josie's hands behind his back, then wrapped the rope several times around him, pinning his arms to his body. On the side of the dirt road a horse drawn cart stood in silence. On this they placed Josie, shoving and pushing him on from the rear.

"Don't you think we should tie the nigger's mouth?" the voice of one of the shadows asked

"No, he ain't stupid enough to make no noise," the man who had captured him responded. "I done told him, he is done fer if he make any noise."

Having deposited Josie on the cart, the men barred the rear side with a piece of board which was dropped into two slots towards the end of the side boards running from the front of the cart. The four men mounted horses, two moving to the front of the cart and two guarding the rear. Thus they set out along the road leading towards the town of Mudville, one of the front riders holding the bridle of the horse which pulled the cart while the other lit a lantern and moved somewhat ahead.

Josie lay on his back as the cart rolled over the stony ground. His head bumped agonizingly against the heavy boards which formed the floor of the cart. To relieve the pain of the almost rhythmic bumping of the cart Josie tried to raise himself into a sitting position.

"Lie down!" the rider behind him bellowed. Josie obeyed. His head ached from the incessant pounding against the cart. He turned on his side to relieve the discomfort. There was a dark object not far from his face. He moved his head towards it. It was a piece of canvas. Josie placed his head on it. The canvas had a strong scent of pigs, which for Josie made breathing uncomfortable.

Shortly, the cart turned south off the Mudville road on to a stonier path across the field. It was clearly a very narrow path; the branches of the trees reaching across the path hid much of the sky above. Josie could see the rider at the rear of the cart, his body moving rhythmically up and down in the darkness, like the mast of a ghost ship on a wave filled ocean.

As he lay there in the darkness the entire incident seemed to Josie as a bizarre dream. One moment he was walking along a familiar road on his way home, now only minutes later he was bound, lying on a foul smelling cart, in the power of four strange men, going on a journey of unknown destination. Slowly the reality and the severity of the condition he faced dawned upon Josie. The men were white. He could tell from the sound of their voices.

"Is this really happening to me?" he thought to himself. "I wonder where they are taking me, and what do they plan to do with me? Why was I selected? Could I have done something to escape? Am I the only one they have captured? Could it be that at this very moment others are being picked up—Henry, Benjie, and others?" These and a myriad of other questions infested his mind as the cart bumped over the stony path.

The thought that the men were going to kill him entered Josie's mind, but it was dispelled in fear. He reasoned to himself that were they going to kill him, they would have done so in the cornfield. He thought of his sister and mother back at home. How would they get along without him if he were killed? He saw visions of his mother and sister attending his funeral service. He wondered how his friends would take it. What will happen to Wrightsville? Was this the beginning of the terror from the League which many had predicted? Perhaps Parson Jones was right after all.

After what appeared to be hours of travel the party stopped. The riders at the rear of the cart dismounted and proceeded to open the back of the cart. They were joined by the other riders. Removing Josie from the cart, they deposited him on the ground.

From where he now lay Josie surveyed the unfamiliar environment. There was a small clearing bordered on three sides by trees, their silent dark boughs silhouetted against the ink colored sky. On the other side of the clearing was an emptiness. As Josie looked in that direction, his eyes caught a faint glitter. The late moon climbed on to the sky over the trees, its pale sickly glow reflected on the ruffled surface of the empty space. It was water! Josie had been brought by his mysterious captors to the banks of a river, which the Choctaw Indians had named from earlier times the Yazoo—the River of Death.

"So this is where I am to meet my end," Josie thought, "in the Yazoo, this river in whose bosom the white man, through the years, has thrown the bodies of thousands of blacks they lynched or murdered." He thought of the disappearance of Mabel's husband years earlier, and the rumors that he had been murdered and dumped in the Yazoo.

One of the men placed the lantern on the rear side of the cart. From its dim light Josie could get a better view of the men who had captured him. Each wore a white sack pulled over his face, with holes cut for the mouth and eyes. The tallest, the one who had actually captured Josie, had huge hairy arms, and eyes which gazed frightfully from behind the white mask. One of the other men was short and stocky, and the third and fourth were meager in frame like spruce trees nurtured in the shade, away from the sunlight. They wore overalls with ill-fitting shirts.

The tallest of the four appeared to be the leader of the group. He gave commands—brief, tribal mutterings, which Josie did not understand. Following one such command the men went to their horses and returned with whips, one of which was handed to the leader. "You hold the rope," the leader gestured to the short, stocky fellow. He obeyed. The men formed a circle around Josie. The leader who had fetched the lantern, held it to one side and towards the prisoner. From where Josie sat on the ground, the leader towered over him like an oak tree.

"Get on your knees, nigger," the leader commanded. The stocky man jerked the rope which tied Josie to urge immediate obedience. The leader was bending over, lantern in hand, examining his catch. Looking at his gleaming eyes behind the mask, Josie observed that one eye was slightly larger than the other.

Josie hesitated but a second to the demand that he kneel; a whip exploded on his back. The shock of the blow threw him forward to the ground. He rolled in agony. Though dazed he could see the man who had wielded the whip standing like a mountain over him.

"When I talks to you, you obeys immediately, nigger! I's gonna ask you some questions an' we don't want no double talk, no lies. If you cooperate with us you may jus' come out of this alive, jus' may. But if you don't, you is a dead nigger!" He paused, "Do you hear me, boy?"

"Yes, I hear you."

"Yes, sir! Yes, sir! Say sir when I talks to you." The whip exploded again across his back.

The other three men, whip in hand, who had stood there as restless as hounds on a leash, in a fit of frenzy started to lash away at the hapless body lying on the ground. Josie rolled in the dirt, biting his lips in agony. Perspiration covered his body and face and dissolved the dirt into a muddy mixture on his cheek. All his constitution urged him to scream in response to the pain, yet he struggled against the impulse.

"Hold off a minute," the leader urged. "He can't give us no information if he's dead."

The men visibly strained to contain themselves.

"Get on yer knees, nigger."

To Josie, the voice came to his ear like a sound from afar, an echo rolling across a canyon. Struggling to his knees, Josie obeyed.

"Now," the huge man was standing over him, his whip held ready, "was you one of them niggers what attack them two white men I sent to remove the signpost in Niggerville?"

"No. "

"No, sir," the man bellowed. He lashed again with the whip, but it struck the rope that was wrapped around the prisoner's arms and body.

"You ain't lyn' to me, boy, is you?"

"No, sir."

"Was you one of them what put that sign up?"

"I didn't put it up myself, but I helped make it."

"You have the cotton pickin' gall to tell me that, nigger? What make you and them other trouble makers in Niggerville figure they can change the name of that there place if us white folk don't want it change'?

"We didn't change the name, sir. The original name was Wrightsville. We just gave it back its right name."

"You lyin', boy, you lyin'," the leader bellowed.

A cold wind was blowing out of the trees from the northwest, yet perspiration poured from Josie's body. On his back it was mixed with blood oozing from the lacerations made by the whips.

"If you look in the county records you will find that the original name was Wrightsville," Josie said respectfully.

"Well, ain't that interestin'," the leader said sardonically, looking at his companions, and then back to Josie. The men grinned bizarrely as they nervously twitched the whips in their hands. "Dis nigger know the history of the county even more 'n us white folk."

The sneer on his face froze into a menacing serious stare. "What was the name of them niggers what beat up my men the other night?"

"I don't know," Josie lied.

"Don't know! And you jus' said you help make that sign an' support it?" He screamed.

"I didn't say I support any fight with white men. I only supported putting up the sign."

"I want to know who they be, them niggers what beat up my men, and you is goin' to tell us, boy, even if it mean whippin' you to death. Now is you goin' to talk or is we goin' to start wupping again?"

"I already said I don't know." Before the last word left his lips the lashings began. He was being struck from four directions as the man holding the rope joined in. Josie rolled in pain on the ground.

After what appeared to be an eternity, the leader muttered a tribal sound and the whipping stopped. "Is clear to me that you is one of them proud, haughty niggers," the leader said conclusively. "The everyday cotton pickin' nigger woulda been beggin' fer mercy by now, but you be too proud to beg, ain't you, boy? Well, I is goin' to tell you like it is. Either you beg for mercy an' then tell us the names of them niggers I ask fer, or we is goin' to wup you to death and throw your body for the catfish and crabs in the Yazoo. I wants to hear you say, 'Have mercy on this nigger,' then after that I wants the names of them boys. Now is you goin' to make it easy on yourself?"

The man had placed Josie's life in his own hands, or at least so it appeared. He could have his life by cooperating or he could sign his death sentence by refusing to cooperate. Perhaps he should beg for mercy and give them some false names. At least this might allow him to live to see the light of another day. These and other ideas rushed through his mind. "Perhaps it is true they do not want to kill me. Why else would they wear masks to hide their identity?" he thought.

The profound human impulse of survival urged him to play along with his captors; but another force, one which had come to dominate his life during his last few years, and had found expression in the self pride and black consciousness that had emerged in Wrightsville, suppressed the desire. Josie looked at the men around him, the eyes and the shape of their mouths barely visible in the flickering light of the lantern. His face was expressionless.

"I've done said to you all that I am goin' to say."

The men were startled by the effrontery of their captive. Taken aback by the defiance of one who was helpless, at their mercy, for several seconds they only gazed at him as if hypnotized by what they had just heard. The leader broke the spell. "In a few minutes I is goin' to have you crawlin' on your black belly like a pig an' beggin' fer your life." His voice trembled with rage as he spoke and spittle appeared on the side of his mouth.

The leader raised his whip for a careful aim, but his restless companions beat him to it. Relentlessly they lashed away at Josie. During the earlier whipping, Josie had become aware that the rope around his arm had somewhat loosened. Now as he lay on the ground, he found that the rope was loose to the point that with little effort he could extricate his arms. The men were so involved in the inquisition that the loosened rope had escaped their notice.

Suddenly, without warning, with the help of his partly freed hands, Josie sprang to his feet, and before the men realized what was happening, he dashed to the edge of the river bank not far away, and dived headlong into its dark waters, almost dragging behind him the man who had held the rope.

The four men rushed to their horses, grabbed their rifles, and raced to the riverbank. Holding the lantern high to the side of his head, the leader and his followers searched the water for sign of their captive. The light of the lantern reflected on the slowly moving water; a myriad of ripples ruffled by the winds like scales covered the surface of the water. For moments the men gazed in dumbfounded silence, straining their eyes to search the darkness for signs of life. Frogs and other creatures of the night punctuated the darkness around them with an incessant chorus. They could hear the sound of the water as it swirled and eddied around the water shrubs that bordered the banks not far from where they stood. The midnight moon emerged from behind an invisible cloud bank and briefly illuminated the place with a baleful glow.

"Well, I'll be damned," the leader finally said, still searching the water as if expecting to see their captive rise to the surface at any moment.

"Well, I'll be damned," he repeated. "I declare I ain't never seen no nigger behave that way befo'."

"Same here," one of his companions agreed. "Most niggers I knowed woulda been so scairt, they would be beggin' an' crawlin' like a mudworm. They woulda done or said anything we tell them. Ain't nothin' niggers fear more than guns, darkness, an' death. Dat nigger acted like he was a white man!"

"Don't s'prise me none," the leader said, still searching the water of the Yazoo in disbelief. "I been sayin' this fer some time now but nobody is listenin'. That there town of Niggerville is producin' a special breed o' niggers. They is more dangerous than all the other niggers in the county. They ain't got no humbleness, no respect fer white folk." He paused, and lowering the lantern, turned to his companions. "When a young nigger like that there boy prefer to drown hisself rather than be 'umble an' beg a white man fer his life, we is in fer trouble. That boy coulda saved his life, all he woulda got was a good wuppin', but you seen how he looked at us." He searched the faces around him for confirmation. "He curled up his fat lip like he scorn us, like we was trash." The leader paused again before continuing. "I'll be damned if that no-good scoundrel nigger didn't drown hisself just as a final insult to us."

The men turned and slowly walked away from the banks of the Yazoo. They mounted their horses and headed on to the trail leading away from the river. As they disappeared among the trees, the leader turned for one last fleeting look into the darkness in the direction of the Yazoo. "Well, I be damned!" he muttered.

⌒ ⌒ ⌒

Josie lay in the mud among the water shrubs downward from where he had entered the river. Long he lay with his body partly submerged under the yellow muddy water. Then slowly and noiselessly he crawled from the Yazoo and lay in the darkness in the muddy thicket. He could hear the beating of his own heart and his heavy breathing, which merged with the sounds of the many creatures of nature serenading the night. As he moved the frogs nearby ceased their croaking, as if conscious that some intruder had entered their habitat.

Once in the water, Josie had used his feet and one free hand to swim under the surface of the river, allowing him to move downward with the undercurrent. He had felt his way in the darkness to the side of the river, and had remained motionless for long moments before venturing to crawl closer to the bank of the river. He lay in the muddy darkness, reviewing the episodes he had just experienced. To his benumbed mind, it seemed like a bad dream. It had all transpired with such swiftness. His capture, just seconds away from the front door of his home, the bumpy trip to the banks of the Yazoo, the merciless beating, and his frantic dash for freedom. So sudden had been the events of the night, so traumatic, unbelievable to his benumbed mind, each separate episode harrowing enough to disorient the bravest soul.

Josie's eyes combed the darkness of the trees. He wondered where his captors might be. Had they left, giving him up for dead? Or were they at this very moment hiding, waiting there in the darkness? As his eyes became accustomed to the darkness, he could see with the help of the pale moon, now hiding, now emerging, the outlines of the trees and thicket further up the bank of the river, but there was no sign of human life. Yet an element of fear and anxiety had taken hold of Josie, keeping him fixed to where he lay in the mud.

Hiding among the shrubbery on the river's edge, Josie actually felt a sense of security and relative safety which pressed upon him to stay where he was for the moment, rather than explore the darkness beyond the river bank. There, where the water moccasin and cottonmouth lay perhaps only feet away, there in the muddy underbrush where even during the day Josie would not have ventured for fear of poisonous snakes, there in the mud and slime of the Yazoo, he felt a sense of safety!

The Yazoo, the river of death, the daughter of the Yalobusha and the Tallahatchie; a river which from his childhood Josie had hated and secretly feared. The Yazoo, the ignoble grave of many an innocent black. The murky Yazoo, a river which had symbolized the hate and irrational hostility generated by a brutal political system against black people. How often had Josie heard rumors of black men being murdered and their bodies disposed of in this river; how many times in his own short lifetime had black bodies, often unidentified and decomposed, been taken from the Yazoo and buried in unmarked graves. Moments earlier, when the coarse, cruel voice of one of his tormentors had threatened to kill him and give his body to the Yazoo, it was to Josie as if the Yazoo were alive and part of the conspiracy to destroy him. Yet here he was, lying among the water grass, the muddy Yazoo's waters enfolding his body; and here Josie felt a sense of safety and security.

∧ ∧ ∧

In the darkness Josie could still hear the coarse voice and see the huge form of the rugged man who had led out in his humiliation. As

Josie knelt on the ground, he could still see behind the mask the hateful mouth of the man towering over him as it uttered threats, the voice which had ordered him to kneel, to beg for mercy.

"There is something about that voice," Josie thought, "something that is familiar to me. Somewhere I have heard it before." Maybe it was his imagination playing tricks with him, yet it seemed to Josie that the voice of that particular man and even his eyes had something familiar. The answer seemed to hang just beyond the reach of the fingertips of his consciousness. He tried to get the image of the man out of his mind and to focus upon the immediate problem of staying alive, but each time, it imposed itself upon him—the voice, the distorted eyes, the mouth.

What seemed hours later, Josie cautiously crawled onto the bank of the river and emerged among the trees. His legs were cramped and cold. He steadied himself by holding on to the trunk of a tree. Slowly, Josie felt his way, limping in the darkness. A sleeping bird disturbed by his movements exploded in flight and the sound momentarily petrified him with fear. "It's only a bird, as scared as I am," he assured himself.

The first faint gray of early dawn was beginning to touch the dark dyed rim of the eastern horizon when Josie stumbled onto an open field. There on the edge of the field he sat for a while, hoping with the coming of dawn to get a sense of direction. The wind had changed its course. Now it blew through the trees from across the Yazoo, yet it was chilly like the winds of early morn. Josie rose from the tree stump where he sat and started across the field. It was still too dark to see more than a few feet away. Before him, out of the mist that seemingly clung to the land, rose a mound. As he neared it, he could see it was the remains of a building. To his right the vague outlines of an old barn appeared, starkly lonely and silent. This was the remains of Ben Mathis' place, which had been destroyed by the tornado a few years earlier. Josie now had his bearings. Cautiously he headed down the dirt road, traveling west then east, past the Browns' place towards Wrightsville.

~ ~ ~

Josie was seventeen going on eighteen. His mother Azalea Petrus, herself only seventeen years older than the boy, had been unusually successful in keeping him under control. When his father, Josie Petrus senior, had died ten years earlier from typhus fever, Azalea resolved that she would dedicate her life to caring for her two children, and since that day Josie and Irene, his sixteen year old sister, had been the center of Azalea's interest. Together they had worked the few acres of land left by her husband. It provided them with the food they needed along with the few dollars required for other necessities.

Irene had grown into a beautiful young woman, and Josie at seventeen was healthy and strong of body as of will. When the surge of Negro awareness began rolling through the town following the tornado episode, both of Azalea's children became involved, with Josie playing the more active part. While admiring the improved self-image of her children, Azalea had advised them, "Don't get so taken up in this thing that you go and get yourself in trouble," and when the signpost incident occurred, Azalea had warned Josie, "you been involved enough. Don't go out there and do no more. I don't want you or Irene getting in any kind of trouble with white folks around here. Furthermore, Parson Jones and many others are sayin' that you young'uns have done enough. It is time to break off."

Josie would give his mother, at each such interaction, assurances that he was not over-involved and her worries were unnecessary.

When Josie did not return home by midnight, Azalea was angry. She had forbidden him to stay out late at night without her permission, and only one year earlier had "slapped him up good" for coming in at eleven-thirty.

"I done told you don't stay out of this house later than nine o'clock without my permission. You's still a little boy an' can get in plenty of trouble by stayin' out late. I don't care if you become as tall as a pine tree," she had warned him, "as long as you is in this house, you obey yer mother."

Josie had a strong love for his mother. He never questioned, at least in her hearing, her authority, and accepted with only an occasional grumble her regulations with regards to staying out late at night.

On this particular night, Azalea looked at the old clock ticking away on the mantelpiece. It was ten past midnight. "Now, tell me what that boy is doing out this late on a Sunday night?" she asked herself, for Irene was already in bed asleep. "He knows we have a lot of work to do tomorrow. 'Sides, I done told him a hundred times, he is not to stay out late without my permission."

Azalea opened the front door and looked towards Wrightsville. The pale light of the late moon washed over her face, revealing the look of concern in her dark eyes. Outside nearby, the dew upon the cornstalk glistened in the moonbeams. A light flickered from an open window across the town. A moth, attracted by the light flowing through the doorway where Azalea stood in the night, flew past her into the living room, towards the glass shaded lantern on the table.

"I wish that boy's father was 'live," she mused, passing her hand across her forehead. "He's got to the age where he needs the strong hand of a man to control him." In the silence that followed, she could hear the deep breathing of Irene asleep in the front bedroom which the girl shared with her mother.

Azalea pulled the front door shut, but left it unlatched. She dimmed the light and lay down beside her daughter. She expected Josie any time now. After all, it was past midnight.

Azalea thought of what she would say to her son when he entered the house. Perhaps she should say nothing until the morning, or even better just remain silent and see what Josie would say. See what excuses he would give. After all, he must be expecting her to make a lot of fuss. To remain strangely quiet would be a good way to deal with him. These and other ideas passed through her mind before she fell into a troubled sleep.

Josie walked into the yard from across the cotton patch and through the same rows of ripening corn through which his captors had led him earlier during the night. In spite of the long walk his clothes were still wet. His body ached but he ignored it, focusing on the task of getting into the house. The early morning sun was just beginning to peep over the rim of the east.

Josie intended to try the front door, but even as he raised his hand towards the knob, he stopped and went around the house to the back door. The rooster was still crowing from the hen house in the backyard, and was being answered by others across town. At the back door, Josie took from his wet pocket a small penknife. He placed the blade in the curve between the door and the wall, and pressing it upward he flipped the inside latch. He opened the door. It creaked as its hinges responded to the weight of his hands. In spite of the noise it made, Josie hoped to effect an entrance without waking his mother.

Quietly he entered the house, removing his mud soaked shoes and leaving them outside the door. Cautiously he entered the rear bedroom. He removed his clothes, dropping them in a damp heap on the chair against the wall. He put on a dry pair of underpants and undershirt. Taking the wet clothing, he tiptoed outside the back door and spread the articles of clothing over the side of the shed where the early sun was shining. Suddenly, a feeling of joy at being alive swept over Josie. He smiled, filling his lungs with the cool, fresh morning air. "It's good to be alive and home again," he thought.

The village roosters were still issuing their vocal challenges to each other outside when Josie crawled into bed, covering himself with a flowered sheet that belonged to his sister but had been spread over his bed, since his bed linen was in the wash. He lay down on his back but the pain was unbearable. Wincing, he turned on his side with his face towards the wall, and shortly, like a heavy burden, sleep descended upon him.

Less than half an hour later, Azalea was up and about in the kitchen. She had been awake when Josie came in, had heard the creaking of the door, and the cracking of the boards as he walked into his room. Now she rose to the duties of the morning. The movement of his mother in the room next door, along with the agony from his lacerated back, snatched sleep from Josie, though his weary body longed for more.

Josie could hear his mother chopping wood on the block outside the back door to light the fire and prepare the morning meal. Usually she would sing as she worked in the morning, especially when it was not raining and the morning sun was shining. But today, Azalea's voice was silent. Only the chop! chop! sound of the cutlass cleaving the wood.

Azalea began murmuring to herself. Josie could not discern what was being said, though he could tell from experience that her voice reflected displeasure. As she bent over the woodpile, Azalea's eyes caught the clothing Josie had spread on the side of the shed. She straightened up, walked over to the shed and carefully examined the clothing. They were wet, and the pants were caked with yellow mud.

"Where the devil did he get this from?" she asked herself aloud, looking in the direction of the house and the room where her boy lay. "It didn't rain last night, and asides from the pond, there ain't no body of water within two miles of here. And what would he be doing in the pond at night?" she questioned herself, frowning. Her feelings were more of puzzlement than anger. "I'll see how he'll explain this." She filled her arms with firewood and returned to the kitchen.

Azalea was busy over the potbellied stove when Irene walked into the kitchen. "Mornin', Ma."

"Mornin'. We got a lot o' work to do today," Azalea replied without looking up from her work.

Irene stuck her head through the door of her brother's room. "Hmm," she taunted. "Boy, we so big now we can afford to stay out all night."

Josie heard her sardonic remarks but remained silent, his eyes closed. Irene went outside, a towel over her shoulders. She drew a pail of water from the well and poured it into a basin on the stand near the back door. Bending over the basin, she washed her face. Her partly opened blouse revealed a pair of full developed breasts, their brown jeweled nipples slightly upturned. After drying her face with a white towel, and pouring the used water on the ground, Irene placed the pail on the stand against the house and went into the kitchen to help her mother with breakfast.

Josie climbed out of bed and dressed. He could hear the plates being placed on the table, but his mother had not called him. He understood this as an indication of displeasure. His shirt touched against his mauled back causing him to wince in pain.

Sheepishly Josie entered the kitchen. Food was already on the table—grits, fried eggs, and bacon. "Mornin'!"

No one answered. Josie headed for the door, a towel he had brought from the bedroom over his shoulder. Azalea observed him from the corner of her eyes. "Don't know where you goin'," she commented without looking up from the stove, "why you will want to wash your face when you didn't sleep here last night—or maybe you slept in some other house?" Her voice was a little higher pitched. Josie continued out the door past Irene who grinned at him. He remained unsmiling, paying extra attention to his feet as he descended the two steps behind the house.

Before he returned to the kitchen he could hear his mother's voice and he knew he was the subject of conversation. The sizzle of frying eggs rose from the saucepan on the fire. Azalea dumped the fried egg onto Irene's plate, beside the bacon. Taking another egg, she struck it skillfully against the edge of the saucepan, allowing its contents to pour from the shell into the pan. It sizzled loudly as it touched the hot oil.

"I was married to your father for fourteen years before he died, and he never, not once, stayed out all night." She was speaking to Irene, but her voice was loud enough to assure that Josie, for whom her comments were actually intended, would hear. "But Josie is more man than his father. Stayin' out till morning without as much as a word to anybody. . . . So this is what it come to, eh? You slaves an' you works your arse off, day and night. And you think you get any thanks or respect in return? Well, I ain't gonna stand for this damn nonsense. Anybody who want to stay out all night should find their own house to live in."

Josie sat listening silently, his elbows on the table holding up his head. He listened, and the words of his mother, the agony and frustration in her voice tore at the seams of his heart.

"Ma, you just don't understand," he said, partly covering his face in his hands, his elbows still resting on the table.

"What the hell is there to understand?" she raised her voice to a new pitch, looking at Irene while responding to her son. "You left befo' sundown, say you gonna play a game of cards with your friends over at

Babs' house. You stay out all night, comes back the next day, an' I is suppose to understand?"

Azalea took Josie's plate. She unceremoniously deposited the fried egg beside a serving of grits and bacon and pushed the plate towards him. As she did, her eyes caught sight of a swollen welt on the side of Josie's neck. The welt was caked in blood and the welt line disappeared under his shirt. She gazed at it momentarily. Azalea held the boy's shirt at the end of the collar, gently pulling it back. "What in the name of . . . !"

Josie pulled the edge of the collar from his mother's hand, covering the shoulder she had exposed. "Stand up, boy!" she demanded.

"But Ma—"

"I say stand up, son."

Obediently the boy stood up. Azalea held up both sides of his shirt and spread them apart. Almost in a state of shock she looked at her son's chest. Swollen lines marked by blood stains crisscrossed his body. Without Josie saying a word, somehow she knew what had occurred. The last time Azalea had seen welts of this sort on the body of a black man, he was dead, and it was the result of an encounter with some white men. Azalea grew dizzy. She held on to her son and sobbed loudly. "Oh Lawd, what dey done to my boy, what dey done to ma boy." Irene was also crying as Azalea removed the shirt revealing the full extent of the mauling he had received. Horizontal welt lines ran the entire length of his back.

"Who done this to you, boy?" Azalea asked.

"Some white men. I don't know who they be." Josie tried to quiet his mother and sister. "No use crying. It already happened. Actually I'm lucky to be alive." As they listened unbelievingly, he related to them his experience of the night.

"I knew it was gonna happen. I seen it befo', an' it always mean trouble. But at my own doorstep, Lawd! And to my own child? . . . It's all over. There will be nothing but trouble from here."

"Ain't nothing over, Ma, this has happened millions of times before to black folk. Ain't nothing over."

"But why did they pick you?"

"I don't know."

"Parson Jones must be told about this," Azalea said, wiping her tears. "He will tell us what to do."

"No!" Josie said sternly, looking at his mother's face. "No, Ma. Not a word to anybody. An' that goes for you, too, Irene. The best way you can cause real trouble is by spreadin' this around."

"But at least the Sheriff should know 'bout this. Even if he don't do nothin', we should report it. Don't forget how he helped Mabel Wright a few years back when the League was makin' trouble."

"I don't want Sheriff Tate, Parson Jones, or no one else to know about this, " Josie said. "Maybe later on after things cool down, but not right now. If this gets out, I know people right here in Wrightsville who will want to start shooting. The best thing both of you can do is to not say a word to anybody about this incident. I suspect, as it now stands they are not going to bother us for a while."

Azalea walked away from her son. She gazed through the window at the ripening cornfield. "This kinda white mens who go round pickin' for a fight with a black man, is like a pack. If you gets in a fight with one, the whole pack gonna turn on you. As hard as this may sound," she continued, "the only way to deal with this kind of white man, and to stay live in Mississippi is not to fight back. Not to react to him in any way that suggest you want to resist. Is like when a pack of dogs turn on a small dog. If he lie down an' stay real quiet, they may leave him alone. But if he tries to fight, he is dead." She turned around and faced her children as she continued speaking. "Since you chillen was young uns I been teaching you how to stay 'live in Mississippi. If you is a black woman is bad enough, but if you is a black man then yous got to learn how to accept humiliation, not because it's right, but because if you gets in a fight with the white man, you can only end up dead."

"But Mabel Wright fought back 'gainst the League a few years back," Josie reminded his mother.

"Yes, she sho did, but Mabel is a woman, and had an added stroke of luck, since the sheriff came to her support. But if you thinks you can fight white folks here in Mississippi and expect any sheriff to support you, you is crazy. He ain't gonna raise a finger to help you." There were still the stains of tears on her face as she spoke. "Come spring, I'm sending you up North. You's got an aunt and uncle in a place called Harlem in New York . . . I been thinkin' 'bout this for some time. If things go good for you up there, maybe I'll sell the place later, me an' Irene will come an' join you. But I tell you this one thing. You ain't stayin' down here no longer than spring. Once the white man put his finger on you, ain't no tellin' where it will end."

Josie pondered what his mother had said, and elected not to respond. "In any case," he said finally, still sitting before the unfinished breakfast, "I don't want any of you talking 'bout this to nobody. The only people know 'bout it in Wrightsville is three of us, and it must remain so."

⌃ ⌃ ⌃

Three weeks had passed since the incident with Josie. July had flowed into August. By the middle of the month the summer heat appeared to be broken, for cool winds from the north blew for two consecutive days, bringing rain and heavy clouds and causing some farmers to predict "Gonna be an early winter this year."

In the town of Mudville, four white men sat around an old table under a large oak tree in the backyard of the all-purpose store operated by Jeb Tyson. They were drinking whiskey and playing a friendly game of poker. There was Jeb himself, Festus Grubb, James Moab, and Henry Ames. They shared in common an abysmal ignorance of the world, none of them having had any formal education. But Jeb, having taught himself to read and write, was treated by those who followed him as a man of one eye would be in the land of the blind. Even greater than their shared ignorance was their shared conviction of the "danger of niggers" and the "threat of niggers who is fixin' to take over the God given rights of the white man in the southland." Whenever they sat together below the spreading oak—and this was almost daily—regardless of the theme of their initial conversation, the issue of "niggers" would inevitably emerge.

On this particular evening the conversation focused on a black man, and the interest was intense, to the disadvantage of the poker game on which none of them was concentrating.

"Is real strange," Jeb remarked, chewing on a sliver of wood as he waited on Festus to play. "Is real strange how that nigger boy disappeared and nobody done ask a single question 'bout it. Dem niggers is something else. Now if that boy was white, everybody woulda done knowed that he ain't around no more. His family woulda started looking around, an' askin', an' reportin' to the sheriff an' all that."

"There you is," James Moab agreed. "Niggers is jus' like rabbits in a hole. You kill one an' the rest go on eatin' grass an' livin.' They don't even miss him. Is like if he never been there."

"Maybe we ought to leak something out 'bout what happen' to him," Festus suggested.

"Yes," Henry Ames agrees. "Let the news spread that the nigger been causing trouble an' he ended up in the Yazoo. It will sure nuf put the fear of God almighty in dem niggers."

"You crazy?" Tyson looked up from his cards. "It may put fear in the niggers, but it will also get to the sheriff, an' if he trace it back to us, we will be in a whole pecka trouble. I don't think Sheriff Tate love niggers any more than you or me, but he see this county as his, and don't want no trouble started. So I figure if he find out that we got rid of that boy, we will all end up in jail. Not that any jury will find us guilty, I jus' ain't ready to tangle with Tate." Tyson paused for a while to allow the men to ponder what he had said. Then he continued: "There is some misguided white folk 'round here who don't want nobody messin' with niggers. Dey say, 'Leave the niggers alone, let them be, they ain't causin' no trouble.' He spat on the ground near the trunk of the oak, with the sliver of wood on which he chewed still in the side of his mouth. "They ain't botherin' nobody? Ha! You wait an' see. Dat Niggerville is a dangerous place. It is breedin' the worse kind o' nigger you can ever have. Now in Mudville we got some niggers but they is 'umble an' respec'ful to white folk an' know dey place. Look at ol' Charlie who work for me sometimes, you can't find a better nigger than him nowheres. He is obedient, an' he don't have no interest in bein' like us white folk."

"So what you think we should do 'bout that boy?" Festus interrupted.

"We ain't doin' nothin' fer now. Jus' wait an' see what happen."

^ ^ ^

Charlie Brown was the older brother of Jim Brown who owned the small farm situated along the road between Mabel Wright's place and Wrightsville. Charlie had grown up on the farm but moved to Mudville after he got married. Now he earned a living by doing odds and ends for white folks in Mudville town, and working his garden plot located behind his small house, north of town. The day following the conversation between Jeb Tyson and his friends, Charlie Brown came to Tyson's shop to get his supply of chewing tobacco and to see if Tyson had any work to be done. Tyson was busy putting on the shelf a new batch of goods that had come in that morning by train from Jackson. Charlie walked in, and without invitation joined in the task of stocking the goods on the shelves.

"Oh, say here, Charlie!"

"Yes, Mas' Tyson?"

"You ain't heard 'bout any a dem boys goin' up North lately? I hear say dey sometime jus' disappear, jus' up an' shell out and head up North without tellin' anybody they is goin'."

Old Charlie scratched his head as he searched for a reply. "No, sir. I reckon I knowed just 'bout everybody in Niggerville, an' ain't none gone up North lately."

"Well, that mighty strange," Tyson commented. "Jus' the other day some nigger came in the shop an' I heard him say that dat boy what live in the house in the field on the east side of Niggerville—Josie, I think his name is—left an' went up North without tellin' a word to his folks."

Old Charlie scratched his head again. "I sho don't know who told you so, Mas' Tyson, but dey done told you wrong. Why, jus' yestiday I be in Niggerville an' I seen that boy you is talkin' 'bout. Josie Petrus is his

- 210 -

name. He ain't gone nowheres. I seen him an' his sister Irene goin' home from church with their mother Azalea."

Tyson paused from his work and looked at Charlie. "You sho you seen that boy?"

"Sho am shure, Boss, I seen him jus' as I is seein' you now."

"Mighty strange, ain't it," the shopkeeper commented. "Mighty strange!"

∩ ∩ ∩

Josie's dramatic encounter with the four white men had effected a significant change in his life. His very personality, it appeared, had been altered, something his friends could not help but observe. Normally convivial, forthright, and outgoing, always eager to participate in a debate or discussion, and somewhat of a philosopher on where Wrightsville was and where it was headed, Josie had now lapsed into a state of strange and foreboding silence. He spoke only when it was necessary. Other times he would sit pensive, listening to the others as they spoke. Some of his close friends had tried to explore the reason for his change in behavior but to no avail. "Ain't nothing wrong. I haven't changed a bit; is only your imagination," he would say.

"You think Azalea been putting pressure on him lately?" Julene asked when the topic came up among Benjie, Henry, Dickie, and herself.

"Maybe Azalea is pressuring him to stay away from us because of the incident with the sign. After all, some of the older folks are saying that we are causing trouble."

"I don't know," Henry responded as they waited beside the church for the Sunday evening service that would begin in half an hour, "but he is sure acting strange—come to think of it, all of the family been acting strange lately. The other day I asked Irene what was wrong with Josie, how come he was so quiet all of a sudden. As you know, Irene has always been nice to me, but when I asked her this question she got real mean and ask' me to mind my own business. I don't know what it is, but something has gone wrong and I aim to find out."

∩ ∩ ∩

Evening. The delta sun hung pallid in the west. The sky was a patchwork of cloudlets. In the yard, under the large mimosa tree at the side of Babs Jacobs' place, where various groups met on different occasions to discuss whatever was worthy of discussing, some of the young men of Wrightsville sat. There were Benjamin, Josie, Henry, and three other fellows from the county. A game of cards was in progress. Four of the boys were playing while the other two stood looking at the game from over the shoulders of the players, laughing and joking as they observed the progress.

- 211 -

In the midst of the game, Charlie Brown from the town of Mudville, "Ole Mudville Charlie," as the boys called him, who had been in Wrightsville visiting a sick friend of his, Sister Ebenezer, walked into the yard. He had known Babs Jacobs for many years, and was just dropping in to say "Howdy." Pausing to look at the boys at play under the tree, Charlie spotted Josie and stopped. "Well, well! Some niggers sho know how to get poplar wid white folks," he muttered. All of the players turned to look at the old man.

"What do you mean, popular?" Benjamin inquired.

"I ain't talkin' to you, boy," Charlie informed him. "Is him, ah, watchymacallhim," he said, pointing.

"Josie?"

"Yes! Him, Josie. Mrs. Petrus' boy. I'd say he's sure rite popular with white folks. Why, jus' the other day I was talkin to that owl-eye peckerwood, watchymacallhim, and he says, 'I understand that that boy Josie Petrus done cleared out and gone up North. I understand he plumb disappeared without tellin' anybody he was goin' way. So I says, 'No, no, Mas' Tyson! Dat boy Josie ain't gone nowheres. I seen him only a few days back. So whoever gave you that information sho nuf told you wrong."

Josie listened expressionless as Charlie spoke. "Which white man you talkin' about?" he inquired. "And how come you call him owl-eye?"

"If you knowed who I is talkin' about you call him Owl-eye too. One of that peckerwood's eyes is all right, but the other one is kinda half closed and crippled like."

"But you still ain't said who you talkin' about."

"I's talkin' about Mr. Tyson, what got dat store on Main Street back there in Mudville. I'll say Mas Tyson was real interested in you. I ain't heard him show that kinda interest in niggers befo'." Old Charlie laughed, bending over and exposing his polished bald head as he removed his straw hat..

Josie's hands began to tremble. He let the cards drop to the table, exposing his hand. An icy coldness swept over him; he bit upon his lower lip.

"Oh, come on, Josie, what you gone an' expose' your cards for?"

"I'm done playin'. I'm goin' home," Josie answered.

"But I got a good hand. Let's finish the game," Benjie insisted.

"Let me take his hand an' finish the game," one of the boys who had been looking suggested.

"Nigger, you won't finish nothin'," Henry informed him. "You been standin' here lookin' in everybody hand, now you want to finish the game." He spoke, but his eyes were focused on Josie, as were his companions', all amazed by his strange behavior.

"There I goes causin' trouble with ma big mouth again," old Charlie was grumbling as he headed away from the table towards the front door of the house where he hoped to find comfort from his old friend.

∧ ∧ ∧

Charlie had unwittingly helped Josie solve the problem that had hounded his mind since the night four weeks earlier when he was attacked by the four white men. Long had Josie agonized and stretched his mind in an effort to gain the identity of the man who had humiliated him that night. During those four weeks there were times when the entire incident would return to Josie in a disturbing dream, with the clarity and reality that would jolt him from his sleep. But although that hidden face, those eyes and that voice seemed strangely familiar to Josie, the identity of its owner lay tantalizingly just beyond the reach of his memory. Until this uninvited intrusion of Old Charlie Brown. Now Josie knew who that man was. Now all the pieces like a puzzle had suddenly fallen together,

"I should have figured it out myself," he thought as he walked home. "I have known that man with his crooked eyes for years. I should have realized it was him. He has always been rabid in his denunciation of black people, though he trades with them—those who are stupid enough to go in his shop." There was no doubt in Josie's mind that his attack and the removal of the sign in Wrightsville had been the work of the League. After all, Tyson was and had been a known member of the League for several years.

∧ ∧ ∧

In spite of the rancorous nature of Jeb Tyson, his arrogant hatred for "bad niggers" and his theory about the threat of niggers from Niggerville, there was little doubt among those who knew him that he was one of the more enterprising personalities of Mudville. Committed to keeping "us white folk of the Newnited States in control of the land God Almighty gave us," and dedicated to the task of "keeping niggers in their place," Tyson was also committed to what he called "the free system of enterprise," and in his own manner saw the two as closely linked. "Niggers takin' white folks jobs or "gettin' in business dey ain't have no right in," were part and parcel of the threat to the free enterprise system.

Living alone above his shop on Main Street, Tyson was esteemed by his followers as a luminary and authority on issues relating to black folks. Tyson, who claimed he had never been married, at least since moving to Mudville thirteen years earlier, had shunned all advances of women wishing to share in the profits of his enterprise. "I is a calebate," he would say to the men who hung around him.

"What does that mean?" Festus Grubb, one of his followers who could neither read nor write, asked him one day.

"Calebate is men what ain't married 'cause they know the womens is a whole heap of trouble."

When Festus decided that he, like Tyson, whom he admired greatly, should also be a celibate, he was quickly discouraged by Tyson. "To be a calebate, a man is got to have certain moral and spiritual strength what only few men in the Newnited States is got."

Strangely enough, Tyson's economic enterprise was closely tied to blacks in the county. He pointed out with care to his followers that there "is good niggers what know their place an' is respectful to white folk," but the very mention of Niggerville would throw him into a conniption, wiping any smile or laughter from his face, and leading him to prophesy as to where "Niggersville's niggers" were leading the country.

How many of his creditors were blacks was never known, but from the traffic at his all purpose store, it was clear that there were significant numbers, mostly from the town of Mudville, but also a few from the county. In an old notebook brown with age, some of its leaf pages barely holding together, Tyson kept the names of his creditors, and the money they owed for flour, sugar, kerosene, tobacco or whatever they bought. Among his black customers were those who were allowed to pay on a monthly basis, and some at even longer intervals.

Tyson also ran an unofficial money-lending agency, usually to black folk who had some property, and would put down the property or a mule or whatever they had of worth as collateral. Through this process, he had gained several pieces of property including a total of one hundred and twenty acres in the region.

Like the few other shopkeepers in Mudville, Tyson usually closed shop at sundown. That is, except on Saturday night when folks from the county would be in town. Then he would light his lantern and keep business going well into the night. But there was never a night when one could not call at the back door, particularly his regular customers, and get whatever goods were wanted.

Tyson had already closed up for the day. The latch was placed across the front door. He had only a few chores left to be done. He placed his money in a bag which he usually took upstairs with him, and as a matter of habit, reviewed the account book of "people that owe me." As he performed this final chore he spoke with Festus, who closely observed the man as he worked. Festus lived in an old shack south of the train station with his woman who had borne him no children. Almost daily he visited Tyson's place to drink and listen to his leader talk about "niggers." How they were, and how they should be. In fact, Festus was one of the two men who at Tyson's direction had removed the sign from the entrance at Wrightsville, and had participated in the whipping of Josie Petrus.

That evening Tyson related to Festus the information he had received from Charlie. "Remember the other day we been wonderin' how come dem niggers in Niggerville ain't made no ruckus 'bout the disappearance o' dat boy? Well, I been talkin' with old nigger Charlie an' he says that he seen wid his own eyes that boy Josie in Niggerville."

"Ain't no way possible," Festus responded with emphasis. "Ain't no way dat nigger coulda escaped; his hands was tied when he jumped in the Yazoo. Once water hit dat rope ain't no way dat boy coulda untie his self."

"Well, dat's what old Charlie says, an' he ain't never lied to me befo'."

"Dat old nigger brain is all dried up wid corn whiskey," Festus suggested. "I is ready to bet my last penny dat he ain't seen dat boy. He musta seen somebody else. His eyes not none too good."

"Well, I is got a mission fer you," Tyson said, changing the tone of his voice as he usually did when he desired to assert his leadership.

"A mission for me?"

"Yeah, a job. I want you to go over to Niggerville an' see what you can. See if dat boy Josie Petrus is really live an' come back an' let me know."

"You is sayin' I should jus' walk in to Niggerville and search around. I can't even remember what the nigger looks like."

"You is got to jus' use ya brains," Tyson pointed out. "Don't just walk in there barehanded. Take some pots and pans from the store here, an' go round, say you selling pots and pans. Go to the house east of Niggerville in the field next to where we caught the boy. Tell them you represent an integrated company in Jackson. If the boy ain't there act like say you is interested in the family. Say 'what a right nice family you is got!' Ask the woman if she is got more chillen an' where they is."

Festus listened closely, overwhelmed by the assignment and element of intrigue involved. He reviewed the approach that Tyson suggested he take. In the back of his mind there was some apprehension about going into Niggerville, partly from all that Tyson had said about the character of its inhabitants.   Tyson perceiving the trace of apprehension in his eyes and voice had assured him that claiming he was from Jackson, and describing his firm as integrated, would break down any initial suspicion among the simple minded black folk. It was decided that the visit was to be made on the evening of the next day, Tuesday. Nine-thirty struck the wall clock when Festus rose to leave. "Be seein' you tomorrow," he said as he departed through the back door out into the night.

Moments after Festus departed, Tyson placed the scribbled book in which he kept accounts aside and took down the lantern from where it hung on the nearby wall. He took the strong box in which was kept the earnings of the day under his arm, and was about to climb the creaky stairs leading to the room above where he slept, when someone knocked at the back door. Almost out of habit Tyson placed the strong box below the counter as he spoke. "Who there? The door is open, come in." Another knock. "It must be Festus," Tyson thought, "but why the hell don't he come in?"

"I says the door ain't locked," he said, as he walked to the door. Simultaneously it dawned upon him that he had been about to go upstairs without locking the door. "Is a good thing somebody knocked." If it were not Festus it had to be one of his customers trying to make a late back door purchase.

Tyson pulled the door. It creaked as it opened, and instantly a shadow leaped from the darkness outside. It struck Tyson with a force that knocked him over backwards.

The sudden attack stunned the shopkeeper for brief moments. But shortly he regained his presence of mind enough to realize that he was struggling on the floor with a human being. The shock of the blow had knocked the lantern from his hands, snuffing out its light, so that the room lay in utter darkness. As Tyson struggled with the intruder his hands touched his hair. "Dis here is a nigger who attack me," he thought in darkness. "His hair feel like a nigger, an' he smell like a nigger."

The intruder struck Tyson a vicious blow on the abdomen and Tyson grunted as the wind was knocked out of him. The intruder, now on top of Tyson, struck away at his face. Tyson made a swinging blow with his massive right hand, knocking the mysterious attacker off him, sprawling him out on the floor. Tyson now had the upper hand. A fiendish grimace came over his face in the darkness. His eyes glowed as he thought of what he was going to do with this nigger who had been brazen enough to attack him in his own house. Even in the heat of the struggle, Tyson's thoughts flowed swiftly. "This is sho that Josie fella. Ole Charlie was right. He ain't drowned."

Holding the intruder down with one hand, Tyson used his other hand to search the corner of the room in darkness. His hand touched what it sought—a piece of wood about three inches thick and two feet long which lay in the comer—part of the table which Tyson himself was building during his spare time.

"I is gonna smash this nigger's face to bits," he thought to himself as the intruder continued to grab and swing at him in the darkness. He struggled to free his head from the clutch of the intruder. His head free, Tyson raised the piece of wood now clutched in one hand. Just at that moment the intruder swung a mighty blow with his fist against the side of Tyson's forehead. It knocked him sideways, striking his head against the oak siding of the room, momentarily dazing him. The intruder placed Tyson's neck in a lock with one arm while with the free hand he struck away at his face. Tyson grunted in pain. As he struggled to free his head, he could smell the odor of the man's armpits, and feel the sticky perspiration of the body against his face. Tyson shifted his body in an effort to get loose of the man, but the intruder held the grip on his neck. As he turned, his mouth came in contact with the fleshy side of the intruder's body. Opening his mouth, Tyson sank his teeth into the flesh. The man yelped in agony, releasing his hold. Tyson held on. The intruder, in desperation, grabbed at Tyson's neck and proceeded to choke him. Gasping for breath Tyson released the bite, blood and slime dripping from his mouth.

The stranger sent a series of rapid blows to Tyson's face and head. Tyson pushed the man off. Getting up, Tyson struggled towards the door, intent on calling for help. But before he could reach the door he was struck over the head by a chair. He felt his feet giving way under him. His body became as light as feather. He saw himself floating away, drifting into deeper and deeper darkness.

As his helpless body crumbled on the floor, the stranger continued to pummel him with the chair, but seeing that the man now appeared to be dead, the stranger fled from the place.

When Josie staggered into the house that night, Irene, his sister, took one look at him and screamed with terror. He looked like one who had grappled with a grizzly bear. His shirt was almost torn from his body, his left side some inches down from his armpit was soaked in blood. His face was swollen on the right side, and scratched all over. Without waiting to learn what had occurred, Irene conjectured that her brother had had another run-in with the men who only two weeks earlier had brutalized him. Without raising questions or waiting to hear answers, she bolted out the door and headed in the direction of the Baptist Church where her mother Azalea and other women of the town were meeting to plan the upcoming church picnic. The meeting was just breaking up when Irene poked her head into the room. Azalea looked at her daughter and knew something was wrong. Taking up her hat she hastily excused herself and departed into the darkness with her daughter.

By the time they arrived home, Josie had washed the bleeding bite wound on his side and cleaned up his face as well as he could. His blood soaked shirt lay over the chair. Without waiting to be asked what had occurred, he calmly related to them the entire incident: How through old Charlie's statement he had found out who the white man was who had led the assault on him weeks earlier. How he had gone after the man in Mudville, and in the pursuing fight may have killed him. This information almost threw his mother into a swoon. "Ain't nothin' to cry about now," Josie said, "it happened already. I was thinking of heading North in the spring. It looks like I must leave tonight."

The shock of the occasion was worse on Azalea than had been the night of the beating by the Yazoo. Then it had been the work of white men. Now it was her son, and if his assessment that he had killed a white man was correct, not only Josie but all of Wrightsville, and perhaps black folk in the entire county, were in for trouble. There was no time to waste, no time to quarrel, to scold, or moralize. "Dear Jesus, help us," was all that Azalea said.

Immediately she turned to get some of his clothes together. She took some fruit from the kitchen shelf, and wrapped a few pieces of smoked chicken in paper, placing them all in a sack. "They won't be coming after me till morning," Josie assured his mother as he followed her around. "It will take them some time to figure out who done it."

"You sure no one seen you?" his mother asked.

"No. It happened in his house, it was dark, an' he was all alone."

"They are going to have every road blocked off before you can get out of here," Irene said despondently.

"Before they know how to look they will have to know who done it," Josie responded. "As far as the men that beat me up are concerned, I am dead, drowned in the Yazoo. They won't know who to look for at first. By the time they find out, I want to be far away from here."

He sent his sister to Jacob's house. "Tell Benjie to bring Henry and Jerry. Tell him it is real urgent."

Irene ran as fast as her feet could carry her. Rather than calling at the front door and having to answer questions from Babs and his wife, she knocked at Benjie's bedroom window, which was standard after dark. Benjie looked out and she gave him the message. Within a few minutes Benjie Jacobs, Jerry Moore, Henry Hayden, and Stephen Baker, Josie's closest friends, were at the front door of his house. Josie walked out in the darkness, and briefly and hurriedly explained what had occurred, beginning with his whipping weeks earlier and the battle with the shopkeeper.

"I know I have not been myself for weeks. I been acting as if I was crazy, but the truth is, I didn't want to let you all know about what had happened 'cause I felt it would only cause more trouble. I'm leavin' tonight "—each of his friends mutely tried to come to terms with the information they were receiving—and I ain't tellin' none of you where I is goin' 'cause when the Sheriff ask questions you can say you don't know. . . . I don't know what will happen. Perhaps they will never know it was me, perhaps they will be here in the mornin'. But whatever happen, take my advice. Don't pick no fight with them. If you have to fight to defend yourself, fight, but don't go lookin' for them as I just done. I had to do it. I had to get revenge for what they done to me. I didn't mean to kill him, but that is what happen'."

Josie seemed to forget the danger in which he was. His voice reflected a deep resignation. The sky was dark ashen gray. A wan moon cast a dim pale light on the place, setting the scene for sadness. "Somehow, deep within my heart I knew that the time was approaching when I would have to leave this place, which in spite of all its problems, I love, and call my home. Now I must run away from it, leave my people. What will happen to mom and Irene?" he asked, not expecting an answer.

"Don't worry about that, Josie," Henry assured him. "We'll all help. Ain't nothin' will happen to them."

"I wish I could stay," Josie continued, "but remaining here will mean sure death, and a lot of trouble for Wrightsville. Yet I know that as far as Wrightsville is concerned my running is not going to help. If they ever find out I am responsible, the chances are they may descend on this town to destroy it."

"There is a good chance they may never knew who done it," Benjamin tried to assure him. "In any case, the main thing now is to be sure that you are safe."

While Josie spoke with the boys, Irene had raced through the darkness to Julene's house and told her what had happened. So that while he yet spoke Julene appeared out of the darkness. She had been uncomfortable since her mother returned from church and told her that Azalea had rushed off following the appearance of her daughter.

"What is going on?" she asked.

"It's a long story, a long, long story," Josie replied. He looked at her face as he spoke but he could not see her eyes in the darkness. "I have to leave Wrightsville, Mississippi and the South, and I have to leave tonight, if I plan to stay alive." Briefly he gave Julene a summary of what had happened.

"Where will you go, Josie?" Julene asked, unable to hide the concern and emotion in her voice. The two had known each other as children, had grown up together, and from their early years had been in love with each other. On more than one occasion they had talked about marriage and raising a family, but these were plans for the future. Now without warning an important part of her life was about to become separate from her. Josie pulled her aside from the others. "I must not tell you where I am going," he explained. "If you are faced by the Sheriff, you must be able to truly say, you don't know where I am. I don't believe I shall ever be able to come back. But I will never leave you, Julene. I have loved you since I was a boy and I always will." He pressed her hands in his as he spoke. "I will make something of myself, and I will send for you. All the things that we have talked about, our plans, they will come to pass, but not here."

Julene spoke, her voice breaking. "Josie, I am not going to press you to tell me where you are going, but I hope it will be somewhere way up North. If you can go North of Mudville and get to Bonsville—it's only about twenty miles away, you can catch the eight o'clock for Jackson, and from there head straight north."

"That's exactly what I plan to do. My biggest challenge will be to get to Bonsville before morning."

Stephen suggested that he could borrow two of his father's horses and ride through the night with Josie to Bonsville. He would have the option of bringing back the horse used by Josie, or leaving it on his uncle's farm a few miles outside Bonsville and retrieving it at a later date.

This was the plan decided upon. Stephen would respond to any question the next day by telling his father the truth of what had transpired. His father, a pious, saturnine soul, one who had morally supported efforts by Henry and his friends to change the name of the town, was a brother of Deacon Baker and the town's blacksmith.

By the time Stephen returned with the horses, Josie was ready to depart. His belongings were packed in a small leather suitcase. In a small sack were placed articles of food for the trip. Azalea took from beneath her mattress a few dollars she had carefully saved for emergencies. This was added to what Josie had saved from little jobs he had done during the summer months.

Indeed the parting would have elicited greater emotions had it occurred in a situation of less urgency and danger. But the grim reality of what had occurred and its possible consequences for Josie focused the energy of all those gathered at the house on his escape.

It was past midnight when Josie and his friend Stephen departed for Bonsville. Already in a few homes within the town there was an air of alarm and apprehension. Babs Jacobs, having missed his son when about eleven o'clock he rose to ease his bladder and looked into the boy's room, dressed and went out on to the road in search of him. Seeing the light in the window of Azalea's place he headed there and walked in on the group at the front of the house. Immediately his anger departed for he sensed that something of moment had occurred or was about to occur. Azalea, in lowered whispers, told him of the situation. Silently Babs looked on, standing a few feet away by himself. It was time to depart. As Josie hugged and kissed his mother he could feel on his face and lips the taste of salty tears.

"Don't worry, Ma, I'll be safe," he whispered. "I will get a job, and once I am settled I will send for you and Irene. We will be together again soon."

"God bless you, son," Azalea said, holding him closely. "Please don't get caught. We all will pray for you." She would have held him much longer, but he had to release himself. He hugged and kissed Irene.

"Bye, baby sister. Take care of yourself and Mom. Don't worry. Everything will turn out good in the end. I will send for you and mom when I get a job."

Then he turned to Julene. Embracing and kissing her, he whispered in her ear, "I'll always love and adore you. Wait for me." She was too choked up with emotion to reply. But these were to be the words that would linger in her ears for years to come. Having said good-bye to all those gathered there, including Babs, the two young men rode off into the night. Within moments they were swallowed by darkness, save the fading sound of pounding horses' hoofs on the parched dirt path leading north from the town.

^ ^ ^

In the town of Mudville there was a sequence, a temporal pattern in which the town awoke to the vicissitudes of each day. This pattern had emerged over time, and had persisted through rain and sunshine, cold and heat through the years.

First at the graying of the dawn, with the crowing of roosters and the barking of dogs, life would begin to stir. The wind blowing from across the train tracks would bring with it the aroma of bacon, fatback, and other items of breakfast from the black community.

Before the sun graced the eastern skies, while gray shreds of mist yet hung over the land, black folk, men, women, and often children, would begin their trek from across the train tracks, trudging along individually or in groups, heading for the fields, land where their fathers, and indeed some of their older members, had worked as slaves. Some of them on the road would be heading for their own plots. Next to be seen would be black women in bright flowered dresses and colorful head ties. These would disperse through the well-kept area of the town of Mudville, where they would work through the day, beginning with the preparation of breakfast for white families yet asleep.

Next to be seen on the dusty roads as the first rays of sun touched the trees would be white folk, the poor heading for their various duties in the fields or the town where they performed much of the unskilled or semi-skilled tasks. Later on as the sun climbed further in the sky, the more fortunate of the town would begin the day's activities. The bank would open for business and the small town hall across the road would become occupied.

In spite of his age of sixty-five, Charlie Brown was an early riser. On this day he had risen before sunrise, and attended to some chores in the backyard, including the preparation of a small area of land for the planting of winter greens. He removed the dead and withered plants, which, partly due to the dry spell and lack of care, had ceased to bear and had withered. With a fork, Charlie turned over the earth, removing the weeds. Following this, he had a breakfast of eggs, grits, and fatback with bread. Then with his pouch of chewing tobacco he headed across the tracks towards Main Street. Today he had several tasks to fulfill. There were two yards where the grass was to be cut and the fence trimmed, but first he had committed himself to help Tyson unpack some boxes of merchandise which had arrived by train the previous day. His next job would be in Sheriff Tate's yard, and the last, hopefully during the evening, would be the yard of the white Baptist Church which he helped to maintain. Finally he would drop in to Tyson's for a drink of whiskey before turning in for the night.

Most of the businesses along Main Street were already open when Charlie came around the corner beside the prison and the sheriff's office. His rheumatism was acting up a bit, but not enough to impede the plans he had for the day. Across the road, he approached the front door of Tyson's and was surprised to observe that it was still closed and locked.

"Musta oversleep this morning," he thought to himself. "I bet he done drank too much corn squeezin' last night." He smiled knowingly. Charlie peered through the front window between the dirty torn curtain. He was near sighted and with the darkness inside could see nothing except the vague outlines of the silent shelves behind the counter. Charlie walked around to the back door. "It sure nuf ain't like him to be sleepin' this time of the mornin'." Charlie raised a hand to knock on the door, but he let it drop to his side. "He may be thankful to me fer wakin' him up, but on the other hand he may be plumb mad if he ain't feelin' well and don't want to be bothered," he thought to himself. He decided to sit by the table below the oak tree for a few minutes, and if by then Tyson was not up, he would go over to the job on Sheriff Tate's yard.

Charlie was about to turn to go to the table when he noticed that the back door was in fact only partially closed. A small space still separated the door and the doorpost. He pushed the door and it gave, creaking as it opened. Carefully he climbed the two steps from where he had been standing on the ground at the side of the steps.

"Mornin', Mr. Tyson!" Opening the door a bit wider and bending forward, his right arm supporting the doorpost, Charlie stuck his head cautiously into the building. The scent of ham, stale butter, and coffee greeted his nostrils.

The light entering the room from the open door dispelled some of the darkness inside. A chair was lying on its side, its broken back on the floor beside it near the table. Not far away a lantern, its shade broken, lay on the floor. A huge bluish housefly buzzed by his face and disappeared in the shadows at the other end of the room. Charlie's eyes carefully searched the room.

"Mars Tyson?" he said softly. His eyes caught a pair of boots on the floor. Their tips were close together and pointed upward. Moving his body slowly through the door and stretching his neck forward, his eyes caught the tip of a pair of pants above the boots. Charlie looked cautiously over the table, his two hands partly suspended in the air, as if fearful of touching the top of the table. It was Mr. Tyson lying there on the floor.

"Lawd God in heaven have mercy," he cried softly. "Mars Tyson!" he called, an element of alarm in his voice. He moved cautiously around the table, keeping his eyes on the body. He bent over the body intending to shake it, but then he observed the death-like stillness of the man and he drew back in horror. From all appearances he had been murdered. A cold sweat of fear broke over Charlie. He walked backwards towards the door keeping his eyes on the body, or the point behind the table where it lay. Then he bolted from the door as fast as his old legs could carry him, his rheumatic pain forgotten. He dashed around the side of the building and headed across the street for the sheriff's office. But even as he ran in his terror, the thought disturbed him that he had been the one to discover the body.

"Suppose dey say I is the one what done it," he mused. "Lawd is I in trouble." Maybe he should just go on his business and pretend that he hadn't seen a thing, he thought, but even this was now too late. Several persons on the street had seen him running towards the sheriff's office. Two white women had turned to watch him as he passed. He could not turn back now.

Panting for breath, Charlie climbed the step. He pushed the front door and it opened. Sheriff Tate, a cup of coffee in his hand, had been conversing with one of his deputies. He turned around as Charlie entered.

"Good Lawd, Sheriff Tate, somebody done gone an' kill po' Mars Tyson," he panted. "Right now he is lyin' in his room cold and dead. Ah'd some work to do for him dis mornin'," he explained. "The back door was open an' I seen him lyin' cold an' dead."

Tate without saying a word dropped the cup of coffee on the table, spilling part of its contents. He grabbed his hat as he moved towards the door followed by two of his deputies with Andy Hennessee, known by some as the town's drunk, trailing behind. Old Hennessee lived alone in a shack at the edge of town and for the past ten years had spent much of his time in and around the sheriff's office.

The procession of men hurried across the street, led by Charlie looking back and mumbling agitatedly, "He was a good man, always gib me free tobacci, always gib me a job. Can't amagine why nobody would want to do a thing like dat."

Charlie stood by the back door allowing Tate and the deputies to enter. Henessee followed. "Behin' the table," Charlie directed. Tate walked around the table and bent over the body lying there. "Don't move anything before I inspect the premises," he ordered. "Is this exactly how you found him, Charlie, or did you try to move him?"

"Lawd in heaven, no, Sheriff Tate, I ain't touched him. Dat's zackly how I find him when I walks in de door. Fus I seen the boots, then I seen the pants, then I looks over the table an' seen po' Mars Tyson."

Tate moved the table aside. Bending over the body he examined it carefully. There were bloodstains and swollen welts on the face. His eyes were swollen, closed, one eye slightly larger than the other. "It never dawned upon me to ask him why one of his eyes was larger than the other," the sheriff thought to himself.

His thought returned to the tragedy. "Must have been a robbery," Tate mused audibly, calmly, with authority. "Guess it happened some time last night, maybe just as he was closing up." He walked over to the counter, looked in the cash drawer. It was empty. Then he saw the strong box on a shelf below the counter. He picked it up and opened it. Inside was twenty-five dollars and some change in notes and coins. While Tate examined the strong box and the store area, the two deputies and Hennessee stood around the body. Hennessee had stood looking on. Now he bent closely over Tyson, looking into his face. Then getting down upon his knees he bent his head low over the man's face.

"Don't touch him!" Pete, one of the deputies commanded. "You ain't tryin' to bring him back to life, is you?" he asked with sarcasm in his voice.

Charlie, still standing outside, his head poking through the door, was mumbling to himself. "Can't amagine who coulda done a thing like that. If I knowed who done it, I be the fus one to tell the sheriff, 'cause it jus' ain't right to do what whoever done it done."

Hennessee who had been kneeling beside the body, ignored the sarcasm directed at him by the deputy. Taking up his hat from the floor where it had fallen, he stood up dusting the hat against his knee. "Ain't necessary fer me to bring him back to life," he said, looking at the man on the floor. "In the fus place, I ain't God Almighty. In the second place, he ain't dead, jus knocked out. I'll say he's jus' as live as me an' you."

He looked the deputy straight in the eye. "Since I ain't no deputy, jus' an old drunk, one o' you deputies better run an' call Doc Prichard."

Tate had heard the entire conversation and now returned to the body. Hennessee, having made his diagnosis, had turned away from the body, pretending to concentrate on the picture of General Lee on the wall. "What do you mean alive?" Tate demanded. "Can't you see the man is cold and dead?"

"He ain't cold, and he ain't dead," Hennessee responded, looking at Tate from the corner of his eye.

Tate bent over the man and touched his forehead with the tip of his fingers. Then he placed the palm of his right hand on the forehead. His hands touched the brownish graying hair on the side of the man's head, causing specks of dandruff to fall from it. Kneeling down, Tate placed his ear on the man's chest and listened intently. A slow rhythmic sound, as the beating of a distant drum, greeted his ears.

"He sure is alive!" Tate announced, an element of surprise in his voice. "Go call Doc Prichard quickly," he directed Pete.

"Praise the Lawd," Charlie now inside the door cried. "Praise his name. He works in marvelous ways."

Hennessee was still standing before the picture of General Lee. He mumbled, looking at the picture as if expecting more sympathy and understanding from Lee. "Trouble is, nobody ever listen to what I says. 'You ain't nothin' but a' ol' drunk,' dey always says. Hah!" he sneered. "There is lots a things I can teach folks."

"Okay, Andy," Tate finally said, nodding his head in recognition. "You made your point. Don't rub it in."

Dr. Prichard was just in the process of opening his office when the deputy came at a trot. He stopped with the key in the lock and turned to the approaching man. "Doc, you better come quick. Tyson is hurt bad."

Dr. Prichard examined the man and announced what by now was common knowledge among the men gathered around. "He's in a state of unconsciousness. The main cause is one or more blows to the head." He could not predict the chances of survival. The man was to be taken to his office in the mean time, and placed on the bed in a small side room which had often served as a sort of one bed hospital. Four men lifted him up, a fifth holding up his head. They forged their way through the crowd of people who by now had gathered outside the back door.

People were already speculating about what had probably occurred. "He musta fell down the stair an' hit his head!" "Nah, Tate says somebody attacked him last night." "Yes, it was an attack all right," another added. "Didn't you see dem dried blood marks all over his face?" "Wonder who done it?" another asked. "Maybe some stranger passin' through town," one suggested, "attacked him fer his money."

"No, dey ain't took no money," Hennessee said, as he passed heading for Doc Prichard's office. "It was all in the box. I seen it."

"Maybe it was some nigger what done it," a thin, wiry man suggested. "If it's a nigger he's sure gonna get a rope when we catches him." The crowd drifted along and stopped outside the doctor's office.

Tyson was placed in the small bed. A white sheet covered all but his face as he lay on his back. "There ain't nothin' we can do but wait an' hope," Prichard told the sheriff as he left the room.

"How long do you suppose he can be that way?"

"I rightly don't know," Prichard scratched the bald spot on his head. "He could come out of it in a few minutes, a few days, months." He threw up his hands. "It depends on the extent of the internal injury."

Festus, Tyson's friend and disciple who had heard the news and hurried to the scene, volunteered to watch the patient during the evening. Others offered to watch at different periods, operating in shifts.

Inquiries around town by Tate produced no insight or clue into the attack or the motive involved. "It surely could not have been robbery," Tate reasoned. "The money was not taken."

No one knew of anyone who disliked Tyson. "It musta been a stranger," was the consensus being developed. Tate heard all this but kept an open mind.

Doc Prichard had returned with some medical paraphernalia to clean the bruises on the man's face. There was nothing else to do at the time. He applied some spirits to the bruises to kill any germs that might be on them. When he applied the spirits Tyson groaned and shifted his body. "He's movin'! He's moving!" Festus cried, rushing to the door and spreading the news to those still gathered outside.

Quickly they fetched the sheriff, who came followed by the two deputies. "He seems to be comin' to," Prichard announced professionally. Tate took off his hat, placing it on the small table at the head of the bed. Tyson was still groaning, low but audibly.

Tate bent over him carefully until his face was only inches from the man's ears. "Tyson! Tyson! This is Sheriff Tate. Who done this to you?" Only groaning.

"Hey, Tyson. Can you hear me?"

Tyson's lips moved slowly, and with consummate effort he mumbled a word, "Tate."

The sheriff smiled with satisfaction and anticipation. "Tyson! Yes, it's me. Tell me who done this to you!" he said eagerly.

Tate could see that the man was struggling to respond. He placed his ear close to Tyson's lips. The man uttered two words, barely audible only to the sheriff. "That nigger." Then he slipped back into the silence of unconsciousness.

Tate straightened up from his bending position, looking at the men around with a frown on his face. "That nigger? He isn't taking about old Charlie, is he?"

"Nah," drawled Hennessee, "How could an old man like Charlie do this to an ox like Tyson? 'Sides, you heard yourself how Charlie say Tyson was a good man to him."

"Then what would he mean by 'that nigger'?" Tate wondered aloud. The sheriff looked at Festus as he raised the ponderous question. Festus' eyes caught those of the sheriff and he quickly looked away, and started moving towards the door as he said, "Don't ask me. How you 'spect me to know? I warn't there."

Festus was nervous and uncomfortable under the gaze of the sheriff. As he left the room Tate followed him. "You," he called to Festus outside on Main Street. "Come over to my office."

"What fer, Sheriff?" he asked.

"Don't you mind that," Tate answered, "just come to my office." Tate headed for his office with Festus walking behind, glancing back to see if the men on the street were looking at him.

Tate sat behind his desk. Festus stood on the other side, his hands behind his back. "I want to know what Tyson meant when he said 'that nigger,'" Tate demanded. "Now you are a good friend of his—almost like his shadow. If anybody knows what Tyson means it would be you."

"I done told you I don't knowed nothin', Sheriff," he protested, trying to make himself look as stupid as possible, a mechanism he had used in dealing with Tate during the past.

"I heard a rumor a few weeks back," Tate spoke, his cold hazel eyes piercing those of Festus to study his reaction. Festus quickly looked down towards his feet. "I heard Tyson an' some of his friends had a run-in with a colored man."

"Don't know what you talkin' 'bout," Festus protested innocently.

"I hear say a nigger been beaten up," Tate pressed him, "though I ain't found out yet who that nigger is. Are you tryin' to tell me that Tyson would leave you out of such action?"

"You ain' got no proof," Festus again protested.

"Let me tell you," Tate bellowed, pounding his massive hands on the table. "Sooner or later it is goin' to come out, you hear me. It's all goin' to come out," he repeated, measuring the man with his eyes. "And I swear to you, Festus, if it turn out that you are lyin' to me, you will be in more trouble than you ever been." Tate paused for his words to soak into Festus' mind. "Of course, you don't have to worry 'bout nothin' if you come straight with me. I don't aim on causin' you no trouble," he said confidentially. "I am only interested in knowin' who done that to poor Tyson, and if you really is his friend, you'll come clean."

Festus remained silent.

"Now sit down," Tate directed. The man, still silent, sat on the chair next to the table.

"I think I need a drink," Tate said, pulling a bottle from the drawer. He produced two glasses. "I bet you need one, too," he said, filling the two glasses. Festus swallowed the contents in a single motion. "Come on, Festus. While you are stallin', who done that to Tyson is probably gettin' away. I want to know who was that nigger Tyson had the run in with."

"I don't see how that particular nigger coulda done it," Festus said.

"Why?" Tate questioned.

"Cause he drownded. That's why. Drownded in the Yazoo."

"You mean you all drowned a nigger!"

"That nigger drownded hisself," Festus cut in.

Then with a refill of his whiskey glass, Festus went over the entire series of episodes with Tate, from the removal of the sign to the whipping by the river.

"This boy, does he have any brothers?"

"I sure don't know," Festus said, "but old Charlie told Tyson the other day that the boy ain't really drownded. I don't see how that could be so. His hands was tied with rope when he jumped in the Yazoo. There ain't no way he coulda escaped.

"Where did the boy live?" Tate asked.

"His name is Josie something. He live in that house east of Niggerville in the field."

Tate found Charlie sitting on a bench across the road, listening to all the conversations around him. From Charlie, Tate learned that the boy Tyson had inquired about was Josie Petrus.

"He's sure nuf live " Charlie assured the sheriff.

"Jus yestidday I seen him. Come to think 'bout it, when I mention to dat boy dat Tyson was askin' 'bout him he gets real mad. I knowed that boy fer years an' I never seen him act like that befo'."

⌒⌒⌒

The incident of Josie and the four white men—his encounter with Tyson and his subsequent mysterious departure from Mudville—were all intended to be kept closely guarded secrets by the small group that was now knowledgeable of the incidents. But secrets known by many, in the environment of anxiety now existing among the small group, are unlikely to be kept. Babs confided in his wife, she in her best friend, and by the time the sun stood at its midday position in Mudville County, there was scarcely a home in Wrightsville that had not been privy to elements of the information. With this new information came a series of rumors roving like waves across the town. One rumor had it that Josie Petrus was beaten up by the League the night before and was missing. Another had it that the League had tied Josie's hands and feet and thrown him into the Yazoo, just as they had thrown Shadrach, Meshach and Abednego in the furnace in the Bible, and mysteriously he had come loose, escaped, and was now in hiding. Yet another had it that he had been beaten up and had killed a white man in his effort to escape, and was now in hiding, and another had it that the League had wupped him and given him twenty-four hours to leave the county.

Naturally, when these rumors in their inevitable progress from house to house arrived at the residence of Parson Jones, he, with the urging of his good wife Thelma—who wanted an authentic version of the story, hurried over to Josie's home to hear the truth of what had occurred. Azalea Petrus, not accustomed to lying to the Parson or holding back the truth from him when it was requested, with much sobbing related to him the gruesome details of what had transpired, imploring him not to repeat to anyone the fact that right now Josie was heading north.

By the time Parson Jones returned home, some of the deacons were already gathered awaiting his arrival. Upon their inquiry, the parson related as closely as he could the series of events that had occurred in and around Wrightsville.

"Where is the boy now?" one of the deacons inquired.

"Well," responded the parson, "He is not under arrest as far as I know, and frankly I don't know exactly where he is at this moment. Not even his mother knows. I would say, only the boy and the good Lawd knows."

⌒ ⌒ ⌒

A corpulent, matronly woman stood at the back door of her house on Church Street. She raised her left hand to her brow and under its shade she squinted as she looked towards the dirt road leading from the south towards Wrightsville. On the road she saw three white men on three horses, and immediately sounded the alarm. "They is comin'. The sheriff an' some men."

Without seeking to ascertain the owner of the voice that had made the announcement, people rushed to back windows and peered from doors across the cotton field. The news, assuming a momentum of its own, spread from street to street: "The sheriff is comin'!"

With the news that Sheriff Tate was about to enter Wrightsville, mothers called their children inside and older folks sitting on the front porch withdrew into their dwellings to view from behind curtained windows the arrival of the sheriff and his men. An ominous silence settled over the place as all waited to see what Tate and his men would do.

The road leading into Wrightsville ends abruptly at Church Street, at the side of the Baptist Church. Along this road the three men on horseback were moving at a casual pace as if in little hurry. They turned down Church Street leading into the heart of Wrightsville. Save a few dogs barking at the horses, and the white strangers, the place appeared deserted.

Tate rode between and somewhat ahead of his two deputies, the hoofs of the horses moving in unison over the stony ground. Tate had visited the town on numerous occasions, but never had he been greeted by such silence and absence of human life. "They know why I am here," he thought to himself. He had never been particularly hard on black folk; on the other hand, he had not been known among blacks for his friendliness.

As they rode down the street, it was about one hour past midday. Five days earlier, September twenty-first, the autumn equinox had officially marked the first day of fall and the equality of day and nighttime. To the west the sky was loaded with cumulus clouds, as white as the cotton fields around the town. An abnormally early chilly wind was blowing from the northwest. Tate was a short stocky man with broad, heavy-set shoulders and a round head covered with slightly graying hair. Through the years he had grown corpulent so that now as he rode, dressed in his sheriff garb, the star of authority shining on his chest, he carried a sizable belly which stood out before him. One of his two deputies was Peter Drake, a deputy of several years of service, nicknamed by some, though never called so in his presence, "snake-eyed Pete." Drake had a history of hostility to blacks, and was rumored to be a member of the League.

To the left of Tate rode another deputy, who went by the name of Bill Brude. Brude had first arrived in Mudville County from the town of Huntsville, Alabama, the morning of the tornado two years earlier. The man had not intended to stay more than a day or two in the town of Mudville, but the tornado, which had snuffed out the lives of so many in the county, white and black, and reduced others to penury by destroying what little property they had, had thwarted Brude's plans for an early departure and had set him off on a new path which was to alter the course of his life.

Following the tornado, Brude volunteered his service with the sheriff, and for several days after, had continued to assist in rescue and other volunteer work. So impressive was his performance in disaster relief work that Sheriff Tate, being in need of a new deputy, prevailed upon Brude to accept the job. "You are just the kind of man I need," Tate told him. Brude, having only a few dollars left in his pocket, had accepted the position, declaring that he could stay only a matter of months, since he was really on his way out West. But now, two years later, he still held the position.

A man in his late thirties, Brude appeared to be somewhat older, with touches of gray running through his hair. Though friendly, he was a man of few words. His face bore lines of hardship. He had a deep look of longing and melancholy in his brown eyes and an expression of cold solitude on his face. He seldom smiled, and reflected a saturnine inscrutability, yet the warmth and dedication he had displayed during the disaster had won him the respect and admiration of many in the county, including the sheriff.

Indeed there was good reason for his disposition, the paradox displayed by the personality of this man who went by the name of Bill Brude. He was a man, as it were, hiding from himself. His real name was Billy McBride. Years earlier he had escaped from prison in New York City where he had been incarcerated on a trumped up charge. He had traveled back to his home in Rocky Bottom, Mississippi, only to discover the mysterious death of his wife and the disappearance of his two children, Sandy and Billy. They were taken away, so he was grudgingly told by Leroy Benton, a neighbor in Rocky Bottom, by a man named Enoch Drude, who claimed to be the children's uncle.

For years Billy had searched in vain for his children, and yet, though having all but lost hope of ever finding them, he drifted from place to place. It was this wandering that had brought him to the town of Mudville. Now as Tate's right hand man, he was riding beside the Sheriff through the town which white folks in the county still called "Niggerville."

⌒ ⌒ ⌒

The three men rode through the town and stopped at the front door of Azalea Petrus' home. Tate approached the door and knocked. Azalea, who had observed the movements of the men from the window, unlatched the door from inside and opened it. "Oh, it's the sheriff," she said audibly, as her eyes met those of the man standing directly in front of the door.

"Are you Azalea Petrus?" Tate asked coldly.

"Yes, sir, I is. Please come in."

The sheriff entered the door followed by Brude, while Pete stood leaning his back against the post of the open door, frowning in displeasure at the odor of bacon that filled the room.

For brief moments Tate surveyed the room. A picture of Jesus hung from the wall. On a small table near the window was a lamp with a glass shade, and near it an old clock ticked away loudly. From the window a shaft of sunlight revealed dust particles like a swarm of minute insects, floating from the shadows into the soft beam of light and back out into the shadows.

"Where are your children?" Tate finally asked, breaking the silence.

"I got one boy," Azalea said, looking innocently on the floor near to where the sheriff stood. "He is going on eighteen; my daughter is fifteen."

"You got a boy named Josie?"

"Yes, sir."

"That's the one we want to talk to," Tate said, looking straight at her.

"I don't know where he is at, Sheriff," Azalea said, almost in a pleading voice.

"Your own son and you don't know where he is?" Tate pressed her. "Your boy is in a whole heap a trouble. You know that?"

"I don't know nothin', Sheriff. All I know is that my boy been beat up something bad by some white men, who left him for dead in the Yazoo. He came home that mornin' with blood and bruises all over his body, an' he ain't been the same since."

"Where is Josie now?" Tate pressed her again.

"I don't know, Sheriff. I is tellin' you de God's truth. I don't know if he is 'live or dead."

"When last did you see him?"

"I seen him las' night. He came in here after ten o'clock then left. He been gone all night." By now Azalea was crying. "He ain't never done dat befo' save that night when he was beat up some weeks back."

"Did he tell you that he beat up a white man last night—almost killed him?"

"Almost?" she grabbed at the word.

"Yes, almost," Tate replied, studying her responses.

"He told me he had a run-in with the white man what beat him up. I been tellin' that boy since he was young," she continued, "that he is got to accept humiliation an' wrong from white folk." The expression of her face and her voice reflected a confession, yet there was in it an element of protest. "It ain't right, but that's how it is here in Mississippi."

If Tate noted her statements, he did not respond to them. "So you tellin' me that you don't know where that boy is?"

"I is sayin' dat my boy Josie ain't here, I don't know where he is, an' I don't know if he is dead or 'live," she answered.

"Where is the other child you say you have?"

"She is over by Parson Jones."

"And where does Parson Jones live?"

"Is the house next to the church."

Tate paused for a few moments then turned to Brude who stood beside him. "Can you think of anything else to ask her?"

Brude shifted on his feet and cleared his throat. "Ma'am, you said your boy was beaten up some weeks back by some white men. Why didn't you report it to the sheriff? "

"I didn't want to cause no trouble. An' round here if colored people go complainin' 'bout white folks dey gets in lotsa trouble. I ain't blamin' Sheriff Tate for nothin', and I ain't sayin' he ain't fair, most colored folks say the sheriff is fair, but I know jus' like everybody else, dat if you is black, an' especially a man, an' gets in a fight with white folk, there ain't no way you can win. Dat's how I been knowin' it an' dat's how it is."

"My job as sheriff is to see to it that everybody keep the law," Tate responded. "I don't make no law or change them. If you or your boy

- 233 -

come and make a complaint, I will check it out like any other complaint. You better understand"—Tate's tone was ominous—"that your boy is in real trouble. There is some people in this county if they find him before me, he don't have a chance. On the other hand, if he come and surrender to me, I'll see that he gets a fair trial. So if you know where he is, you better see to it that he give himself up."

At this point the Sheriff abruptly turned and left the house, followed by the two deputies.

Tate questioned Irene Petrus at Parson Jones' home closely with the Parson nodding his head solemnly as the girl responded, but he got no new insight as to the whereabouts of Josie.

They were in the process of leaving Parson Jones' residence, when Hennessee, who had been left temporarily in charge at the office, came galloping on his horse. He had a message for the sheriff. A white farmer looking for a cow that had escaped through a broken fence early that morning, had seen a black man on a mule hightailing it in the direction of River Trail, near the Yazoo.

Sending Hennessee back to Mudville, Tate and his two deputies headed in the direction of River Trail. The road led south towards the Yazoo. It passed several small farms including that of Jim Brown. Further south they came to the place of the white farmer who had witnessed the rider on the protesting mule that morning.

"I couldn't tell who he was," the man informed Tate. "My eyes ain't as good as they use to be. I knowed he was sure nuf a nigger on a mule, an' he was hightailin' it like if the devil an' all hell was achasin' him."

A few hundred yards down where the road teed off, Tate and his deputies turned west on River Trail and soon arrived at the entrance of Mabel Wright's farm, some one quarter of a mile from the junction. Mabel was in the yard working when they arrived. She paused from her work to observe the men, as led by the sheriff they guided their horses through the hedge into her yard. Mabel smiled and greeted the sheriff, waving her right hand. As they dismounted, she thought how the sheriff had grown heavier since his last visit to her place. His neck seemed stouter and shorter, and the area around his cheeks was bloodshot.

"Howdy, Mabel."

"Howdy, Sheriff Tate. I ain't had the honor of your visit to my lil' place since two years back."

"Yes," Tate replied, as if exerting supreme effort, in the face of some deep weariness, to respond. "It's been two years, ain't it?" he questioned in disbelief. "Time sure flies."

Tate took a white soiled handkerchief from the back pocket of his pants. He wiped his face and neck before looking around the yard.

"Well, what brings him to these parts," Mabel was thinking, and was just about to verbalize her thoughts when Tate spoke.

"Look here, Mabel," he said. His voice was lower than usual. "We lookin' for a black boy from Niggerville who beat up a white man last night in Mudville. He 'bout beat him to death." He raised his voice slightly at the word "death" and paused to allow its meaning to penetrate.

"From Wrightsville?" There was an element of surprise in her voice.

"Yes, from Wrightsville," Tate's eyes briefly, very briefly, slipped from the woman's face to her heavy breasts, which pressed close together slightly protruded from the center of her bodice. It was the first time Tate had used the name "Wrightsville."

"Whose boy is it?" Mabel inquired.

"Azalea Petrus' boy Josie. He's suppose' to be hiding somewhere in this area."

Mabel shook her head back and forth silently.

"You seen him anywhere around here?" Tate asked her.

"No, not here, Sheriff. Dat boy ain't been here since the last church picnic and that was back in June."

"If the league gets hold of him before me, he is just as much as lynched," Tate commented. "There is no way he can hide in this county without being caught sooner or later. His best chance is to turn himself in."

Tate looked away from Mabel in the direction of the mule which, tied to an oak tree at the edge of the yard, gave baleful glances at the three saddled horses in front of the house as with its tail it brushed flies from its body.

"Mabel, I been knowin' you for years, an' as far as I know you ain't never lied to me," the sheriff said.

"I ain't lyin' to you, sheriff. I ain't seen dat boy you lookin' fer."

Tate looked back towards the mule. "Some farmers along the road say they seen a black boy racing a mule in this direction early this morning."

"That rider what was on that mule is my boy, Joshua. Sent him with a message up to Jim Brown. I done told that boy a thousand times not to race that mule. The mule is gettin' old an' can't take dat kinda treatment. He an' his brother is somewhere along the river fishin'."

"Mind if we have a look around, Mabel?" The sheriff glanced at his two deputies with a slight nod.

"Not at all, sheriff," Mabel replied, stepping aside. "You can look anywheres on my place that you want to."

Tate and the two deputies walked to the back of the house and followed the little trail leading to the bank of the Yazoo. Shortly they returned to the yard where the horses stood still critically eyeing the mule, which was returning a defiant stare. As Tate exchanged a few more words with Mabel, Brude and Pete, his two deputies, standing close to the mule looked towards the house and saw Mabel's two girls Samandra and Sharon. They were standing on the porch, leaning on the old wooden banister. Both were now in their early teens, their womanly forms well developed, yet pliant with looks of innocence. Brude looked at the young women and his eyes focused on Samandra, her light sunburnt face, unsmiling. For a moment, he found he could not dislodge his eyes from the girl. It was as if he had been caught in some mysterious snare.

Samandra saw that the deputy was gazing at her. She grew tense. A strange feeling crept over her—fear, anxiety, uncertainty—emotions that were so fused and complex, she knew not what they meant. A cold chill crept through her youthful form. Her hair stood on end. It was as if some primeval force was reaching towards her. Samandra fidgeted nervously. Then cold and unsmiling she turned and, followed by her sister, entered the house, closing the door behind them. Brude continued to gaze at the door for moments after the girls had departed. Pulling his gaze away from the house, he turned his attention to his horse. Pete who had been observing him, smiled knowingly.

"Who is she?" Brude finally asked.

"Oh! She is just one o' dem fair-skinned niggers," was the reply.

"I can tell you ain't from nowhere around here," Pete continued. "Mississippi is full o' dem half breeds. There is a place called Soso, Mississippi—the whole town is full o' them. They is too white to be niggers, and too nigger to be white."

"She sure coulda fooled me," Brude said.

"Not me," Pete assured him. "I can spot a nigger a mile off. My guess is her mammy is a fair-skinned nigger and her daddy is some white buck. Dem kinda mixed blooded niggers is the prurtiest you can find." Pete spoke authoritatively. "They usually get their intelligence and prettiness from the white side."

Brude did not respond to Pete's lecture. As he climbed on to his horse Pete continued to advise him. "In case you's got any ideas about that there gal," he said sneeringly, his beady eyes sparkling, "there ain't no way you can get near to her. If you as much as look at her too long, her mammy is goin' to start screamin' all hell." He chuckled. "Maybe if you can get her in some quiet place one day, you can take it by force," he said tauntingly. "You is a white man an' a deputy at that. Ain't no jury will take her word against yours."

⌒ ⌒ ⌒

On the evening of the second day following the attack, Jeb Tyson regained consciousness suddenly, as if awakened from a long sleep. Immediately he returned to his shop, a bandage wrapped around his forehead, covering some of the bruises of the struggle two days earlier. Festus, who had remained close to Tyson during much of his two days of unconsciousness, and Charlie Brown were in the shop with him. Charlie was assuring Tyson how much he had prayed for him during his unconsciousness. "Yes, sir, ever since I found you on the flo' here, all beat up. Fust I runs and calls Sheriff Tate, then I started prayin'. And the good Lawd done answer my prayers."

Tyson continued taking inventory of his stock "to make sho all is in order and nothin' ain't stolen," but paused when Sheriff Tate pushed open the door. Festus and Charlie made a respectful exit as Tate placed his hat on the counter. Wearily he filled his lungs with the air in the room, scented with a complex of stale merchandise, and slowly released it.

"Well, how you feelin' now," he inquired.

"I'd say fine, Sheriff. Fine," he repeated. "At least for a man who been through what I been through."

"You had us worried for a while," the Sheriff informed him. "We thought this was it."

"Not me," Tyson responded. "It will take much more than a blow on my head an' a few scratches to take me out. Furthermore, I don't plan to die from nothin' but old age."

"Can you tell me exactly what happened?" Tate requested, frowning as he studied the man's face.

"Heard a knock on the door," he pointed towards the back door. "Opened it and bam! This nigger jumped on me like a crazy bobcat."

"Did you recognize him?"

"He moved so fast I didn't get a good look at his face," Tyson replied, looking at the sheriff through eyes yet bloodshot, puffed and swollen. "In any case, if I was you, I won't worry none, Sheriff. I can always take care of my own problems."

"We already know who the nigger is," Tate informed him coolly. "As a matter of fact, we been searchin' for him high and low since yesterday. So far we ain't found hide nor hair of him but we still searchin'. Seems he's gone into hiding." He paused, still studying the face of the man to whom he spoke. "We are going to find him and when we do, he is going to be tried for attempted murder. What I can't figure out," Tate added, "is why that nigger attacked you. He ain't took a penny from your place. He didn't touch the strong box, and it don't look as if he took no goods from your store." He rubbed his chin puzzledly. "Sure beats me."

As the sheriff spoke Tyson had turned away from his stare and appeared to be absorbed in straightening the lines of bottles and cans on the shelf behind the counter. With his back turned to the sheriff he responded, "Don't surprise me none, Sheriff, that you can't find no reason why that nigger attacked me. Who can fathom the mind of a nigger? You can't no more tell why they done something than you can tell why a billy goat or a sheep behave like they do. You know just as much as me that niggers don't think like white folk."

"Well, to be honest with you, Tyson, I ain't interested in that kinda argument," Tate cut in. "There is lotsa white folk I got trouble figgerin' out. But I tell you this. There must be some reason why that boy select you for an attack rather than another person in Mudville. That boy came all the way from Niggerville to attack you and then went back home. Can you think of any reason?"

"It sure nuf beats me," Tyson said ponderously. "Them niggers in Niggerville, you don't have to give them no reason fer attacking white folk. I done said this befo' an' I will say it again. That village of Niggerville is abreedin' some o' the most dangerous niggers in the State of Mississippi. An' the more we sit here an' do nothin' the mo' they is goin' to get bold an' attack white folk."

"I understand," Tate interrupted, "that some white men went into Niggerville some time back and had a scuffle with some boys. Do you know anything about it?"

"Why ask me?" Tyson asked rhetorically.

"I'm jus' seekin' information. It's rumored around that a few nights after this scuffle, some white men captured that same boy what attacked you, took him down by the Yazoo, beat the hell out of him, and left him in the river for dead. Next thing you know, that same boy jumps you and tries to kill you. Maybe he mistook you fer one of them what beat him up? Well?"

Tate scratched the right side of his chin slowly, cutting off the head of a pimple. It lodged under the nail of a finger. He observed his fingers closely, momentarily glancing up at Tyson. "Once I capture that nigger, it all goin' to come out. We will know all the details of why he selected you for an attack." Tate waited for the man to respond, but Tyson remained silent. "Now, I talked to a white man who swear that you was one of them men what beat that nigger by the Yazoo. But I ain't takin' his word alone. It's possible he's jus' tryin' to bad mouth you. Once we capture that nigger boy we'll see what he's got to say."

"Ain't no way he can 'sociate me with a thing like that, ain't no way," Tyson assured Tate.

"Well," Tate responded, "it ain't that I am that concerned about a nigger that been beat up. It's just that I got enough trouble on my hands as it is and I don't want no more trouble from niggers, whites, or nobody. I been in this here job for more than fifteen years, an' I figure I'll be quittin' soon. I jus' don't need no more trouble. There is some people around here—of course, you ain't one of them—would like to stir up a race war an' have people killin' each other. Now, I ain't fixin' to allow that to happen. If niggers in this county get out of hand, I will deal with them, but I don't want nobody tryin' to do my job for me. So I am askin' you, " Tate paused, and Tyson half-turned, looking at the sheriff over his right shoulder, "I am asking you not to take matters in your hands. It's my job. I done talked to his mother, and she don't support what the boy done. I talked to other folk in the black community, they don't support it, neither. Now, if any one go stirrin' up trouble, it will look as if I ain't doing my duty, an' there is no man in this county who can stand befo' me an' tell me I ain't doin' my job."

Without waiting for the man to respond, Tate changed the topic, once more expressing satisfaction at seeing Tyson on his feet again. "If any information turn up an' you hear about that boy, jus' let me know," Tate urged him as he departed through the front door.

∧ ∧ ∧

Eight days passed without a trace of Josie Petrus, the boy who had so viciously attacked Jeb Tyson. Members of the League began to show new activity, seeking to expand its membership on the tension created by the attack. Tyson, now the leader of the Mudville branch of the League, kept relatively quiet, though his followers urged him to do something about the attack. "We need to march in there an' burn the damn place down," Festus suggested.

"Jus' give Tate some time. See what he plan to do befo' we makes our move," Tyson advised.

One Saturday, the middle of October, the League had a meeting at Cross Roads. About three hundred persons attended. Some of the attendees came from as far as Sand Mountain some ten miles away, with most of the curious onlookers being dirt farmers from the nearby area.

The League had had little success in getting the more successful farmers around Mudville town to enlist. Most of the dirt farmers attending were merely curious onlookers rather than members. The head of the county League, a Sand Mountain man named Atticus, was the main speaker. He urged his listeners to enlist so they could "receive the protection of the League." The fiery presentation from Atticus was followed by a speech by Tyson. As soon as Tyson had ended his presentation, a farmer, a man who planted six hundred and forty acres of cotton each year, climbed upon his wagon and proceeded to speak. The crowd turned to hear him

"It ain't my intention to get no argument with you people here. If you want to go an' start trouble that is your business. But I don't see how you all can be talkin' 'bout action against niggers, when there was only one nigger involved. Now let me tell you this, an' I feel I is talkin' for the majority of the big farmers whose work provide the money to run this county, since I am a member of the Farmers Organization. Now this is the cotton reapin' season. We've had a good crop, in spite of boll weevil an' all that. The crop is ready to be took in. I can tell you that the farmers out there ain't goin' stand round no how and have people cause trouble that will leave the cotton in the field. That cotton is got to be picked 'fore the weather change, an' as you know is the colored people in this county who bring the cotton in. Now I don't have nothin' 'gainst the League, but I tellin' you this. If I catch any o' you on my place makin' trouble, all hell is gonna break loose. As a matter of fact, the best way the League in this county can destroy itself is by causing a situation that will drive colored folk away. Last year's crop was the worst since the seventies. Many farmers is in trouble with the bank and I can tell you that they is ready to take up arms an' fight to protect their crop, an' that include protectin' niggers who got to bring in that crop."

Having made his speech he climbed on to his buggy and cracking a whip over his shaggy horse, drove away from the scene towards Mudville. In spite of this damper, the League was able to recruit a few members before the meeting ended.

⌃ ⌃ ⌃

Excitement generated by an equally dramatic incident in the town of Mudville temporarily drew attention away from Wrightsville and blacks in the county. Two weeks following the attack on Tyson, four white men rode into Mudville and robbed the Mudville bank. The men were just leaving the bank when gunfire exploded. Two of the robbers were shot dead by Tate; the other two retreated into the bank, grabbed the banker, a prominent citizen and member of the Council, and threatened to "blow his head off" unless they got safe passage out of town. Walking on both sides of the banker, one carrying the stolen loot, the other his forty-five stuck in the hairy ear of the banker, the robbers climbed into the banker's coach and drove out of town, swearing that if anyone followed within half an hour, Mudville would never see the banker "alive again." Some five miles out of Mudville they deposited the banker on the side of the dirt road, stopping long enough to give him a lighted cigar, and disappeared with the $6,000 they had stolen.

For eight days the search for the robbers continued, with a two thousand dollar reward being offered. Teams of men with bloodhounds combed the banks of the Yazoo, after the horseless coach was found not far from the river. Neither men nor money was found, and as October merged into November, the county settled into reaping its precious crop of cotton.

∧ ∧ ∧

The Josie incident had thrown the town of Wrightsville into a state of alarm. Once the rumors were dispensed with and the authentic details of what had transpired became known to the people, a cold air of pessimism settled over the place. Little by little the story in its entirety had unfolded. The removal of the sign at the entrance of the town, the encounter with the two mysterious white men who had returned by night to the sign after it had been replaced, the capture and whipping of Josie on the banks of the Yazoo by a group of white men, and Josie's counter attack against Jeb Tyson.

Older members of Wrightsville, including Parson Jones, were shocked to realize all that had transpired without their knowledge. The sign at the approach of Wrightsville which most had viewed with a sense of pride was now being described by some older folk as a source of trouble which should be "broke down and hauled away." So intense was the debate and exchange that followed the revelation of the details of the series of incidents, so strong had sentiments developed over the nature of the response that should be made, that Deacon Johnson at a meeting of deacons chaired by Parson Jones, lost control of himself. Springing to his feet in animated excitement he declared, "Ah say let us tear down the damn sign an' get rid of the source of this evil." Then somewhat sobered by the realization of the word he had used, he apologized for his use of profanity: "The devil sure nuf knows how to stir up trouble, and to put evil words in yer mouth."

The movement to remove the sign began among the deacons. Speaking on their behalf, Deacon Johnson in a less agitated state declared, "We are persuaded that de sign at the entrance of this here town which was put up by de young people without our permission, was de fruit of good and evil that Satan tempted us wid. We partook of it, and it has become our undoin'."

Their recommendation was that the sign should be removed, "if this will return us to the peace and quiet which existed befo'. To show that we don't want no trouble, and we don't support no attack 'ginst nobody white nor black, the sign must be took down."

It was on the question of who should remove the sign that the plan floundered. The sign itself was planted on a piece of land owned by Babs Jacobs, and Babs, though not a deacon, had been invited to the meeting since the object of contention was on his property. Early in the discussion, Babs had made his position known. "I ain't takin' down no sign. I is sayin' this respectfully but I is sayin' it. I didn't put up no sign an' I ain't takin' none down. Further, I don't believe that there is anything wrong with de sign."

It was finally decided that a sub-committee of three deacons should take down the sign, but no one would volunteer, whereupon Parson Jones, who up to this point had not made his position known but had simply provided occasional summaries of what was being said, decided to take the matter to a general meeting of the church.

⌢ ⌢ ⌢

The meeting was held on Wednesday night at prayer meeting time. It was started by a session of prayer followed by a brief presentation by Parson Jones, who invited the members to respond and express their true feelings. It was the first opportunity for the young people, temporarily smothered by the Josie incident, to express themselves to the community, and they took ample advantage of it.

Benjie Jacobs was the first among the young people to take the floor. "I don't believe that there is a single person here, young or old," he asserted, "who will support pickin' a fight with white folk, but those who claim that the sign is a problem is mistaken. Why is it wrong or evil for us the people of Wrightsville to put up a sign identifyin' the town by its name? Mudville has a sign. It is not the sign that is the problem; it is the existence of some people in the white community that is bent on humiliating an' keepin' down black folk.

"It is clear that the League is behind all the trouble we been havin'. If we allow them to scare us into submission, then we are done for as a community, and we are heading for slavery once more. I am in favor of doing all we can to assure the white community that we are not trying to threaten them; on the other hand, there is no reason why we should have to crawl before them.

"Naturally, if the sheriff demand that we remove the sign, I guess we'll have to do it, but if we took down that sign on our own, we will be doing more damage to ourselves than the League can ever do."

Benjie's presentation was punctuated by "Amens," particularly from the young people in the audience. Parson Jones continued to play the role of moderator, summarizing what each person had to say. The only comment which he gave reflecting an opinion was, "Sign or no sign, the name of this town has been restored an' will remain—whether that

- 242 -

old sign is took down or it is left standin'. But we want to do what is right."

When Parson Jones had finished his brief comment, Sister Ebenezer, a seventy-one year old deaconess, a sprightly and active woman for her age, rose to speak. Her hair was as white as freshly picked cotton, her face an artistic mosaic of wrinkles. She had lost all her teeth save a few molars, and now when she spoke she would occasionally pucker her mouth as if chewing on something. Aside from being the oldest deaconess in Wrightsville Baptist Church, Sister Ebenezer had become known for, as Parson Jones expressed it, "her courage and bravery even in old age." This latter image she acquired after her husband, Alphonso Ebenezer, had died some two years earlier.

Sister Ebenezer and her husband, a carpenter, lived on a half-acre plot not far from the church. Along with the house in which they lived, Mr. Ebenezer had built an outhouse, a tool shed, a small barn, and a smokehouse on the property. After the death of her husband, the smokehouse was left in disuse, and, attacked by woodlice and other insects, was falling apart.

One day, a man helping Sister Ebenezer with her small vegetable garden noticed a huge snake, a rattler, coiled up next to the smokehouse. He grabbed a hoe, bent on killing the snake, but the wily old rattler withdrew to safety under the smokehouse. Almost every day after that incident, the rattler would be seen in the vicinity of the smokehouse but try as they might, no one was able to corner it. Finally the men in the neighborhood, with Sister Ebenezer's consent, decided to tear down the smokehouse, which was falling apart anyhow, and destroy the snake once and for all. Halfway through the job of tearing down the building, the men had paused for a rest from exertion in the hot summer sun, when one of them hollered, "There she goes!" and sure enough, there was the massive old rattler, winding its way toward Sister Ebenezer's house. Before they could get to the snake it crawled under the small back porch of the house. The men proceeded to dismantle the old porch to get at the snake, but the creature crawled under the house itself. Thus began the coexistence between Sister Ebenezer and the rattlesnake. Neighbors concerned for the welfare of the old lady urged her to move until the snake was caught. Her adopted daughter who lived across town invited her to come and stay with them. She resolutely refused.

The old wooden floor of her house had several holes bored by rats, yet the old lady refused to move. "I ain't movin' no way. My man built this place for me when we fus' married, an' I ain't fixin' to let no rattlesnake drive me out of my own house. If he wants to live below the house by hisself, it don't bother me none, so long as he stay under the house."

During the months that followed, Sister Ebenezer and the rattlesnake got accustomed to each other, though at first the sound of rattles would come through the holes in the bedroom floor, sometimes when Sister Ebenezer would walk in the bedroom. Rumors had it that the old lady occasionally placed food outside for the rattler, and this had encouraged a live and let live relationship between them. Though the rumor that she had grown to love the snake and now had it like a pet was never verified, general opinion was that like Mabel Wright who years back "wasn't afraid to deal with dem rattlesnakes in the League, old Sister Ebenezer done tamed the rattlesnake under her house."

Thus, when Sister Ebenezer arose to speak, all turned around to listen. Sister Ebenezer stood with her gnarled hands holding fast to the pew in front of her and her head upright.

She puckered her mouth once and commenced to address the audience: "I is only an old lady," she began. "As you all know I don't have no edg'cation 'sides what I taught myself, and what Chet my deceased husband taught me. But I is old nuf, an' I seen nuf, an' experience nuf here in Mississippi to understand what dis here meeting' is all 'bout. I was born a slave, jus' like some of the older folk here, an' I spent my early days workin' with my mammy—since I ain't never seen my daddy—in the white man's cotton field.

'"I live right here in Mudville County all ma life. I seen in my time the pain, the heartache, and the humiliation that we black folk got to accept in order to stay 'live in Mississippi. I seen the brutality an' the devilry in white folk, an' I also seen the kindness an' the Christian way of our Lord in others. I seen with these eyes white folk killed 'cause dey tried to help black folk, an' I seen black folk treated the same. So the problem we is dealin' with ain't jus' black an' white, there is different shades in between. We got to teach our young people that all white folk ain't bad , an' all black folk ain't good. Dey is bad an' good all 'round. We got to teach them, don't hate nobody no matter what dey do to you. We got to teach them how to stay 'live in Mississippi. Sometime we got to accept things we don't want to accept to stay alive. Sometime we got to keep silent an' pray when our hearts is tellin' us to cry out in anger. But Almighty God don't want us to teach our young'uns that they ain't as good as anybody else, that they is inferior, or simply 'cause they ain't white that they mus' spend their life tryin' to prove to white folk that they is 'umble and obedient. You can't stop some white folk from wantin' to push you round by bein' 'umble!

"I seen in my time 'umble colored men hangin' from trees. I seen obedient colored folk killed an' thrown in the Yazoo, not 'cause they was not 'umble an' obedient, but 'cause dey was black, an' Satan took possession of some white people an' dey done what dey done to dem.

"The changes I seen in young people here in Wrightsville since the tornado—I ain't said nothin' 'bout it befo'—but it sure nuf brought pride an' joy to my heart. The sparkle in their eyes is brighter, an' they keep their head up higher today, as if dey is proud of what Almighty God made them. When I seen this I says, I says to myself, 'There is hope for my people.'"

Sister Ebenezer paused for a moment. She puckered her mouth, chewing in her customary fashion, and continued to speak. "When the young uns in this town put that sign up, dey was not doin' nothin' wrong or nothin' sinful. They was jus' sayin',' We ain't no niggers. We is God's chillen, we is black folk, we ain't niggers.' Now if white folk come an' break down that sign, I is against fightin' over it. This town will still always be Wrightsville. But if we take that sign down we will be tellin' the League an' its followers what want to destroy us, that dey is right, that we ain't nothin' but niggers—an' we will be tellin' the same thing to our own folk. Furthermo', moving the sign will only encourage them what want to start trouble, to push us some more."

Sister Ebenezer paused once more, and opening her eyes wide in the dim light of the lantern, she said: "I had a dream the other night. I looked up an' lo and behold I seen thousands an' thousands o' black folk, my peoples, like endless rows of cotton on a mighty field, an' dey all was holdin' hands an' marchin' down a mighty road an' dey was singin'. An' I look again, in my dream, an' sure nuf, I see white folk among them an' dey was all holding' hands with the black folk an' singin', an' I seen a huge town, with houses reachin' way up in the heaven, an' I hear a voice from heaven sayin', 'Be not weary, my people, keep your head up high an' keep movin' on!'" She paused. "Let us don't do nothin' that will bring shame an' disgrace on us in the eyes of our own people. But let us stand together an' wait on the Lawd."

Sister Ebenezer had reached into the heart of the entire church, who supported her with a thunderous "Amen."

Following the presentation by Sister Ebenezer, Parson Jones summarized the meeting. "Everyone has expressed his opinion, either through the presentation of their own ideas as to how we should deal with this situation, or by the "Amens" received by other speakers such as Sister Ebenezer. I feel that all the ideas expressed are good, they all have the community in mind, and they all reflect moderation and Christian spirit. Now that I know the feelings of all elements of the church, now that we have expressed ourselves let us unite as one man in the face of danger. I am asking the church to leave the situation as it now stands in my hands. I will agonize with God on the matter, and I feel that the directions I receive from Him will be for the good of the church and the community."

⌃ ⌃ ⌃

On the banks of the Yazoo, Mabel Wright, brooding over her four children, waited nervously upon the development of events over which she had no control. Daily she listened for sounds of the storm which she hoped would never come. As she looked over the children she was struck by how little they seemed to comprehend the full potential of danger inherent in the developments around them. Yet she sought not to engulf them in a psychosis of fear. Scenes of earlier encounters with the League passed before her mind, stirring sentiments of anxiety. Still, she reached out to touch that fragile hope that somehow this too would pass away and peace would prevail.

⌃ ⌃ ⌃

Towards the end of December cold, biting winds rolled over Mudville County. As the winds blew from the North, the earth slowly, reluctantly, relinquished her warmth. Cold soil clamped around the roots of trees, cold air enveloped their bark and branches lulling them into slumber. Only the pine and other evergreens gave the appearance of resistance to the imperious call to rest.

At the beginning of the week of Christmas, Sheriff Tate suffered a heart attack which after three days left him with the left side of his body paralyzed. Along with medicine prescribed by Dr. Prichard, Mrs. Tate, following the advice of knowledgeable friends, gave her husband doses of water strained from boiled hops, a common treatment for paralysis. This illness, according to speculation of some, was due to Tate's overweight condition. Acting on the advice of the sheriff, the Mayor appointed Bill Brude as acting sheriff, a situation which only exacerbated the growing hostility between Brude and Snake-eyed Pete. The mayor, like other leaders in Mudville, had been impressed by the sanity, sobriety, and the business-like manner in which Brude had carried himself; thus, Tate's recommendation was accepted without opposition.

Early the following spring, when warm winds began to blow northward from across the Yazoo and wild azaleas in pink and red profusion bloomed along its banks; when reddish green leaves enveloped the sassafras tree and honey bees buzzed around the redbud; when the mocking bird sang from among the white and pink flowers of the dogwood trees, Sheriff Tate died in his sleep. The next day he was buried in the little cemetery beside the white Baptist Church in the town of Mudville.

Tate's passing was viewed as another reason for concern among blacks in the community. Though he had never been known for his amicability, it was common knowledge that Tate had, on more than one occasion, forestalled acts of violence against blacks in the county. After all, was it not he who protected Mabel Wright a few years back from violence by the League? And was it not his efforts that kept Tyson from stirring up racial violence after the Josie affair? Now with his demise and with memory of the previous fall still fresh in mind, there was an element of anxiety as blacks waited to see what the new situation would bring.

^ ^ ^

Parson Jones was among those who attended Tate's funeral. Dressed in a stiff white collar, black suit, and top hat, he stood in the shade of an oak tree and quietly observed all that took place. Occasionally he turned to greet a member of his congregation or a black person from the county who was attending the funeral. "This is sure nuf a bad day for Mudville County," a sharecropper commented to the parson.

"Yes, I'll say it is," Parson Jones responded, wondering whether the man fully understood the meaning of his own statement.

Standing in the shade of the tree not thirty feet from where Tate was laid to rest, Parson Jones looked at the faces of mourners now moving away from the gravesite. He wondered if any of them was troubled by the same thoughts that now rested upon his mind. He saw Tyson, the man Josie had left for dead, with a group of his associates drawn closely together talking among themselves. He could see the deputy sheriff, Snake-eyed Pete, who was a pallbearer. Now he stood looking at the grave, an ambiguous expression on his face. Not far away stood the new sheriff, Bill Brude. He too was a pallbearer. Now he stood by himself, like Parson Jones, observing the people who had attended the funeral. After all had departed save a few immediate members of the family of the deceased, Brude walked over to Mrs. Tate with his hat in hand. He expressed words of sympathy and departed by himself.

Parson Jones climbed into his buggy and headed for Wrightsville. He casually glanced back at the cemetery, unconsciously touching the tip of his hat as a final courtesy to the departed sheriff. "This is the end of an era," he thought to himself as he rode slowly over the dusty road. "Only God Almighty knows with a new sheriff what lies in store for us. Will the new sheriff be able to control the League as much as Tate did? Oh, if only I could push aside the veil of the future and get a glimpse of what lies in store for my people. How strange it is," he mused, "that it seems always it's only tragedy that brings the people of this county together. The last time it was the devastation and death wrought by the tornado, now it is the death of a lawman. I saw sadness and tears on the faces of both white and black people today. In normal times we remain miles apart, with hostility and conflict always not far off, but humbly are we so ready to sit around the same table and partake of the common meal of grief and sorrow which destiny prepares. Yes, we seem so ready to partake of mutual sorrow, but not of joys; of the bitter but not the sweet. When the days of mourning are over, we return to our racial cubicles with all bigotry, hostility, and fear."

For moments the parson rode in silence, listening to the wheels of his buggy rolling over the stony ground. Casually he observed the quiet clouds drifting northward in their wanderings, then his thoughts returned to him. "There is a sickness in this land," he murmured audibly, "a contagious disease more dangerous than swamp fever, chicken pox, or hydrophobi, for it not only attacks the body, it infests the souls of people, destroys the eyes of justice, and creates an image of God so bizarre that scarce can He be recognized as the Creator. Today we black people use religion as a succor, but I fear I see a time when my people will reject the Christian church, not for its ideals, but because of what it is."

The day following the funeral, Reverend Jones received a letter. On opening the envelope, he found it contained an envelope addressed to Azalea Petrus. He took the letter himself to Mrs. Petrus. It was from her son Josie. He had arrived in Washington, D.C. safely, had found residence with a family from Mississippi, and had found a job. After the parson left, Azalea danced with glee over the letter which dispelled the anxiety that had haunted her since her son's hurried departure from Wrightsville.

⌒ ⌒ ⌒

Since the arrival of Samandra and Billy to the home on the bank of the Yazoo, the life of the family of which they had become a part had been tempered by excitement, expectation, tensions, pain, uncertainty, and hope. All of these had their impact on the minds and developing perspectives of the children.

The early illness of Samandra, the warmth, the love, affection and care with which the children were showered by Mabel, had forged them into a single unit, and had submerged under layers of caring and living the painful experiences of their earlier life in Rocky Bottom where their mother had died and their father had from all appearances deserted them. After ten years on the banks of the river, memories of their earlier existence had receded to remote areas of their

- 248 -

subconscious. The unpleasant experiences were now long repressed as their lives had found new meaning and direction under the loving guidance of Mabel and the companionship of her other two children, Joshua and Sharon.

But developments in Mudville County had impacted their pliant minds. They still clearly recalled the attack on Mabel's house by members of the League years earlier, either from the incident itself, or its repeated description by members of the community. The tornado, its massive destruction, the death of Ben Mathis and his wife, and the multiple burials at the Baptist Church in Wrightsville following the tornado, all remained fresh in their memory. Through the years they had shared the feelings and listened and participated in discussions among their peers about political and racial issues in the county. Their attendance at the Baptist Church School in Wrightsville and their interaction with the youth of the town had exposed them to the influences of the pride and self-awareness existing among the young people of Wrightsville. These ideas and sentiments had profoundly influenced their thinking. Gone was the awareness of their racial origin, gone were the vivid memories of their previous existence. As the children grew into adolescence, the more they understood the vital issues being discussed among the young and old, the more closely they identified with the youth movement that had restored the name of Wrightsville and promoted a sense of pride in the community.

As the four children grew older, Mabel Wright increased her efforts to keep them from becoming embroiled in the conflicts around them. No longer could the use of a switch control the children in these and other matters. Now reasoning, pleading, love, and prayer had to play the major part in influencing their behavior, and these she showered upon them lavishly.

The attack and whipping of Josie Petrus, his retaliation against Jeb Tyson and his escape had shocked Mabel into greater determination and efforts to protect her brood from what now appeared to be an impending storm. When Parson Jones had called the Wednesday night meeting to discuss the Josie attack and its aftermath, Mabel and her four children attended. They rode together with the Brown family into Wrightsville, and were there when Sister Ebenezer made her inspiring speech. They, too, had cried "Amen" to her presentation, their young minds excitedly going over the issues. That night after they returned home, Mabel overheard Billy, who by now had become the most outspoken of her four children, as he spoke with the others seated on the steps of the verandah in the moonlight.

"Josie Petrus is what I call a brave person," he commented. "Even though the League beat him up and threatened his life, he didn't allow none of that to scare him, no sir! He stood up to them, an' the fus' chance he got he took his revenge. I reckon I woulda done the same thing if I was in his place."

"Same here," Joshua added. "I done said, that as long as we sit down an' let the League walk on us an' push us 'round, they will do it. We have to show them that we are ready to fight for our rights. Even old Sister Ebenezer said this evening that you got to show your self pride an' show that you not 'fraid to stand up."

"Look at Ma, for example," Samandra added. "Remember when we was little an' the League came to burn our house, what she done? She didn't stand there an' cry, she grabbed that gun an' 'bam' she let 'em have it. That drove them off. What we need to do is every black family should get a gun. If the League know we is armed an' ready they won't fool with us."

"Actually we is still fightin' for freedom here in America," Joshua said, thinking of the contents of a book he had recently read. "Abraham Lincoln said we free but the white man is determined to keep us in slavery. So though we have our own land an' can pick our own cotton an' sell it, the white man is still determined to keep us under his foot. They say that if the League ever find Josie they will lynch him. If I was Josie, I'd always keep a gun nearby, so I can take some of them with me when they catches me."

Mabel interrupted the conversation by walking out on to the verandah. She stood over her children, leaning against the post at the top of the steps. Silence greeted her presence.

"I know exactly how you children feel 'bout what has been happening here in Mudville county," Mabel said, as she sat down on the side of the bench on the verandah, behind the children. "Ever since you been babies, you been seeing, hearin', an' feelin' what is happening in this county. It is natural to sympathize, to be angry, an' sometimes to even want to take up arms and fight back. It's natural for you to get angry when you see what happened to Josie Petrus, or when you see how the League always lookin' for ways to trample on black folks. Sometimes the blood jus' rise in your veins an' you feel like you can go out there and shoot it out if you have to. But then if you is black here in Mississippi, you got to sit back an' let sense an' thinkin' take over control of you. You got to realize that if you is goin' to stay 'live you have to learn how to be angry an' smile, you have to learn how to suppress your anger, to pray, an' sing it away. An' if dat is not nuf, you got to tell yourself,"Yes, I is mad, yes, I been hurt, I been trampled upon, but by the Lawd's grace I is stayin' alive."

"The fus' lesson of survival," she continued, an element of deliberate patience in her voice, "is to stay alive. You go out there, shooting off your mouth, an' get shot or lynched, and you ain't provin' no point, save to whet the appetite of crazy people. I see the situation changing in this part of Mississippi, an' mostly it's changing for the worse. Mudville is one of the few counties left in Mississippi where you don't have regular lynchin's of black folk by the League, an' it's only a matter of time. I been tryin' for years to prepare you chillen for this time, to teach you how to survive in Mississippi. Is always difficult for a black mother to tell her chillen that they must accept injustice an' oppression with calmness, but every mother wants to see her chillen stay 'live. An' the fact is that if you is black in Mississippi you got to accept injustice sometimes. I am beggin' you chillen as I have done befo', don't become involved in what's goin' on around here. See an' hear, but don't get involved.

"Don't get in no conflict with white folk. Stay away from them as much as you can. If you have to deal with them, be respectful, regardless of how you feel. Actually, I ain't against Josie for retaliating, but if I had to advise him I woulda told him, 'No, Josie, don't do it.' Now you see what happen to him? He is a fugitive from the law. If the League get him first he is finished, and if the sheriff gets him, he won't have a much better chance.

"The only reason why I is 'live today," Mabel continued, "is because my Mammy, God bless her, she taught me what I been tryin' to teach you chillen. Keep your pride and dignity as a human being. God gave you that. Don't let anybody take that from you, but learn to accept with dignity, any indignity thrown at you. If I didn't learn that I won't a been here today."

"But Maw," Joshua interrupted, "remember what you done when the League came to molest us, how you got your shotgun an' drove them away?"

"I sure did, Joshua, I sure did," Mabel replied, "but remember it was in my yard, they was threatening' to kill us and I had to try to save my family. Further, I was jus' lucky, 'cause Sheriff Tate came along. If the Sheriff didn't appear ain't no tellin' what could have happened."

"An' don't forget," she added, "that I am a woman. If you is a black woman in Mississippi you have jus' a little better chance in dealin' with white folk. Black women works in white folk's houses, raise their chillen, an' sometimes even breast feed them. Some of them white men always remember in the back o' their mind how a black woman care for them, an' sometime it cause them to be more kind to black women folk. With the black men it is different. The white man see him as a threat, an' is ready to fight the moment he start talkin' brave an' bold.

"Take my word for it, chillen, especially you, Joshua an' Billy, you have always to watch yourself real close. Stay away from any kind of conflict with white folk, don't pay no attention to white women, an' don't ever start no quarrel with a white man. If he start a quarrel, don't follow it up."

The children were silent for a while, pondering what their mother had told them. Mabel continued, "Part of the problem is that many black folk is dependent on whites for a livin'. Dat is exactly why I'm sendin' you boys away to school next year. There is a school in Alabama, they call it Tuskeegee. Dey say it's run by black folk an' it is for teachin' black people different kinds o' trades an' learnin'. I want both of you to go up an' study so you can stand on your own feet an' don't have to depend on no white man for the food you eat. I been savin' money from plantin' an' sewin' all these years, for you chillen's education. Samandra an' Sharon goin' way to school too as soon as they ready. With good learnin' they will be able to be better women, mothers and wife.

"By God's grace I aim to have you all with enough edgecation so you can support yourself if you have to. When you finish school you can come back here to Mississippi, maybe to Wrightsville or here on the farm. Ain't no use in runnin' up North. This is our home jus' as it is home for white folk. Our parents cut the trees, cleared the forests, planted the cotton and built the roads as slaves. It is our home an' it will be foolish for us to run away from it. Further, the same trouble we is havin' here, dey havin' up North. The white man is the same up there."

That night Mabel stayed longer on her knees praying for her children. If she could only get them through the difficult period of growing up. If she could nurse them to full manhood and womanhood, help them to acquire independence so they could stand on their own feet, and give them the values and attitudes to assure their survival.

෴ ෴ ෴

Between early spring and the month of July, several black families from Mudville County took to the northbound road. Four of these were sharecroppers. Others who owned small farms sold their lands to obtain funds for the trip up North. There were both push and pull forces at work in this population movement. Information entering the county from up north had been mixed. Some described Chicago, Philadelphia, Detroit, and New York in terms of opportunities for work and personal advancement. The push factors were mainly the uncertainties with which many blacks viewed their future in Mudville

County. For one family, a sharecropper named James Jones—no relation to Parson Jones of Wrightsville—the departure for up North was more in the form of an escape from what seemed a new form of slavery. Jimmy's father, Ellis Jones, had been a sharecropper on the same plantation owned by Mr. Williamson. During his life, Jimmy's father, like other sharecroppers and blacks working on Mr. Williamson's place had, by purchasing goods in the all purpose store run by Mr. Williamson on the plantation, amassed large debts. Each year a part of the debit would be paid with a good portion of the sharecropper's earnings, but the size of the debit had continued to grow. When Ellis Jones died, his debit was automatically taken over by his son Jimmy who continued as a sharecropper on Mr. Williamson's place. After ten years of paying on the debt left by his father, Jimmy found that his level of indebtedness to Mr. Williamson had in no way decreased. As long as he sharecropped on the man's place, he had to do his buying of groceries and other necessities at Williamson's store. Jimmy found that his debt was larger than ever before. Mr. Williamson, by his own accounting saw to it that the people he called "my niggers" were always in debt to him. After ten years Jimmy concluded that his dream of owning his own land—a few acres, a few pigs and a mule—was just as far away as it had been for his father, and decided to head north. One weekend, under the pretext of going to visit a sick sister who lived fifteen miles away, Jimmy Jones, with a few dollars he had made by secretly selling a few things, headed up north. Monday morning when Mr. Williamson rode his horse into Jimmy's yard to see why he had not turned out to work, he found the place empty.

Other blacks leaving the county were motivated by the push of uncertainty. With Sheriff Tate dead, they were also unsure as to what they could expect from the new lawman, who was a quiet and stern protector of the law. None knew where he stood on the question of the League and other issues affecting their lives. Some had it that he, Sheriff Brude, was himself a League man. In other surrounding counties branches of the League had been terrorizing the black community with lynchings, whippings, and cross burnings. Mudville was ripe with rumors that the League was about to take control, that blacks, who formed the largest segment of the county population would be driven out, and only whites who were members of the League would be allowed to seek political offices.

Tyson, who had remained relatively quiet since his encounter with Josie Petrus, with the passing of Tate had gone on the war path, preaching to his listeners that "Niggerville is got to go."

"I is sayin' what I done said over an' over," he told all who would listen, "so long as we allow that place to survive, so long as we allow so many niggers to live in one place an' control theirself, so long we will have conspiracies on white folk—especially our women an' chillen never will be safe. I done said it a hundred times that Niggerville is breedin' a whole generation o' dangerous niggers. White folk is got to act afore it is too late."

This kind of rhetoric continued through the summer and into the fall. With another election soon to be held in the county and in Mississippi at large, there was true cause for consternation and concern among blacks.

⌢ ⌢ ⌢

In the autumn of the year that saw the passing of Sheriff Tate, Mother Brown also died. She had lived all of her seventy-nine years either on or near the Brentwood farm, from whom her husband had purchased fifteen acres of land on which her son Jim Brown, the brother of Charles Brown of Mudville, now lived with his wife and four children. Death came as peacefully and unhurriedly as her life had been spent.

In the fall of the year, Mother Brown sat on the west side of the front porch of the small wooden house in her rocking chair—her companion of many years—and looked at the crooked line of black folk as they slowly moved across the level field, plucking white balls of soft cotton from dry and gaping pods and loading them on a mule drawn cart. She watched silently each day as the field was cleared of ripe cotton, save a pod here and there left ungarnered.

Mother Brown watched as the dry plants were cut and burned in circular heaps, the dark grayish smoke forming grotesque shapes, slowly rising into the evening sky over the Mississippi landscape. Mother Brown watched as the field, the weary dark delta soil, was turned over by mule drawn plows in preparation for winter repose. She watched, her aged face laced with the furrows of time, furrows as articulate as those carved by the plow through the dark delta soil, furrows as sublime as the intricate work of some skillful artist, and she saw the leaves of the sassafras tree along the back fence begin to yellow, and nudged by the teasing autumn wind, fall to the ground.

Mother Brown walked below the pine trees at the entrance to her yard, and she heard the anxious cry of the lone cicada calling to the female of its kind among the branches, vibrating its timbales, calling. But alas there were none to answer, for their short lives had ended, their dead remains lay scattered among the pine needles about her feet. Mother Brown stood below the autumn sun and saw that it had lost its fervor. She heard the noisy mockingbird crying its heart out from among the naked branches of the dogwood tree, whose limbs were decked with pink umbrella blossoms in the early spring, but now stood bare and wan. And, when she had heard, seen and felt all of these things, Mother Brown decided that it was time to die.

Mother Brown had shown no signs of illness. Each morning after breakfast she would assist her daughter-in-law with the dishes and the cleaning; then she would go and sit on her favorite chair. In spite of her ripe age of seventy-nine, her mind and eyes were clear and her hands steady enough so that she could thread a large-eyed needle.

One morning in late October, Mother Brown decided to remain in bed. Her daughter-in-law was the first to observe her changed behavior. "Ma, what's wrong? You ain't feelin' good today?"

"I is jus' tarrd of gettin' up. I'm gonna stay in bed, an' when my boy Jim come in for lunch, tell him to come an' talk to me."

When Jim came in, his wife met him at the back door of the house where he was cleaning mud off his boots.

"Maw stayed in bed this mornin'," she informed him. "Is the fus' time as long as I can remember she stayed in bed like this. She says ain't nothin' wrong, she jus' want to talk to you."

Jim went into the dimly lit bedroom where his mother lay on an old cotton mattress, covered over with a flowered sheet. The quilt which Mother Brown herself had made years earlier lay folded across the bottom of the bed.

"Maw, it ain't like you to be in bed this time of the day. With such a prutty day outside I can't believe you ain't been outside to breathe some of that nice air an' rock in your chair," he said smiling, with an obvious expression of concern.

"Ain't nothin' wrong wid me, son," Mother Brown said wearily, "I ain't been sick in years except arthritis in ma elbows an' knees, an' that ain't stopped me all these years."

"I reckon you is jus' a lil tarred, then," her son suggested.

"Yes, son, I is tarred, I is sure nuf tarred," she said with a sigh of weariness. "In fact, I don't got long to stay here. Very soon, I's gonna cross over Jordan an' go on to see ma Jesus."

"Come on, Maw! Don't talk like that," Jim scolded. "What you mean you is goin' to see Jesus? You ain't gonna die!"

Mother Brown looked at her son carefully, a faint smile on her face. With a weak but tender-motherly voice she replied, "You mean you don't want me to go 'n' see Jesus, boy? What you think I been preparin' fo' all these years—livin' a Christian life? I been preparin' fo' to go home, an' now I is ready." She paused briefly, breathed heavily once, and continued. "I want you to call Charles, write an' call you' sisters. Ask dem to come an' bring their chillen so I can see them all afo' I dies an' goes home."

That afternoon as Jim and his boss Mr. Brentwood were working together on a broken wagon axle, Jim mentioned to his boss what his mother had said to him.

"I declare I don't know what come over Ma," he said, as he knelt holding the axle that was being welded. "She says she's goinna die. Gonna go home to Jesus, she says."

"Is she sick?" Mr. Brentwood inquired of the woman who had reared him, breast fed him as an infant, and cared for him throughout his childhood.

"Not as far as I can see," Jim replied. "She says she ain't sick, jus' tarred a livin'. Yestiday she was outside walkin' 'round like always, now she say she is gonna die." Jim shook his head in puzzlement.

"You've got to remember, Jimmy, that your ma is old," Brentwood said. "I would estimate that she is in her seventies."

"Seventy-nine," Jimmy informed him.

"When people get that old, Jimmy, sometimes they say all kinds of things. Their mind get weak and they say what they don't mean to say."

"Her mind didn't sound weak to me," Jim responded. "Why, jus' yestiday she was in the backyard an' was sayin' how the sassafras leaves was yellow an' was fallin', and how empty the dogwood look with no leaves, and how all the cicada dem was dead on the ground."

"It sounds to me," Brentwood said, "as if it is a fall feeling. Some people get gloomy when they see nature dying or getting ready to sleep for winter. If she is still in bed tomorrow, let me know, I will come over and cheer her up."

For the next few days, Mother Brown continued to press upon her son to summon her children, which he finally did. Mary came with her children from Jackson, others came from Birmingham in Alabama and from other areas of Mississippi where they lived. Only Jessica who resided in Chicago did not come at her mother's request.

Mother Brown continued to stay in bed, getting up only when it was necessary. Mabel Wright and her children, on their way from church on Sunday, dropped in to see the old lady. Holding the hands of each, Mother Brown blessed them with kind words. How well they had grown, and what good children they had been. The four children had taken to singing in a quartet, and Mother Brown had them to sing for her her favorite song, "Amazing Grace."

One by one her children came to see her. To each she gave a charge, encouraging them to live well and "stay close to Jesus."

"Things is gonna get worse, as the Good Book say will happen in the las' days," she told them. "But if you chillen keeps close to God, everything will be all right. If I ain't teach you chillen nothin' else, I teach you how to be strong and courageous. If you is gonna make it you is gonna have to love an' have hope in your hearts." She spoke with special tenderness to Amos, her youngest son, who had come in to see her from Huntsville, Alabama. "You, Amos, my baby chile," she said tenderly. "Since you was a little boy, you been talkin' 'bout freedom. But the only freedom that you as a black man is gonna find in this country today is the freedom what is in yourself. In the meantime, you have to show courage an' patience if you gonna live to be as old as I is."

The children listened respectfully to their mother, concluding among themselves that she might be losing her mind. "Maw ain't ready to die," Amos assured the rest, "she may even outlive some of us. An' bein' crazy or losin' her mind? Listen to the counsel she been givin' us. Ain't nothin' confusin' about what is said. Is just a summary of what she's been tellin' us since we was kids. Something may be wrong, but she ain't crazy."

"Is possible," he said thoughtfully, "she jus' said she is dyin' to get us all to come an' visit her."

The day after the last of her visiting children left, Mr. Brentwood dropped in to see Mother Brown. He walked over with Jim that evening. "Let me go an' see if I can get Emma out of bed." "Emma" was what he had called her through the years.

Mother Brown greeted him, her eyes brightening up for a moment. She held his hands as he sat on a chair at her bedside. Her face seemed more wrinkled to him than he remembered, and her hair was as white as cotton.

"Hello, Emma," Brentwood greeted her. "Jimmy tells me you not feelin' too well, so I come to see you."

"Oh, Master Brentwood, is mighty nice of you to come to visit the old lady. The room ain't even made up proper."

"Ah!" Brentwood said smiling. "You want to see how unkept my bedroom is."

"I reckon is been five years since you last visited our lil' house," Mother Brown observed.

"Oh, no," Brentwood responded. "I was here Christmas Eve—you had gone to Niggerville with your daughter-in-law—and I was here the time Jimmy sprained his leg behind the plow." Brentwood paused and looked at the old lady. The light from the window showed a calmness on her face.

"I remember when I was a boy I almost used to live in this house. I remember hearing my mother say, 'Boy, sometimes you act like you living at Emma's place.' I'd be around during the summer. I used to fish with Jim and bring the fish here. You would cook it for us."

"Yes, those was good times," Mother Brown sighed. "You was a right good boy, never been rude or troublesome. I remember when you was six months old." Mother Brown reminisced. "Miz Brentwood took real sick. She had lot of headache an vomitin'. Callin the doctor didn't do no good. So we tried boil' catnip for the headache and peach tree leaf tea for the vomitin', but that didn't help. Nothin' but prayin' kept her from dyin'. An' you, I had to nurse you. I was nursin' Jim at the same time so I had lotsa milk. It got so I almost felt as if you was my chile." She patted his hands. "Dat was a long time ago, yet it seems it was jus' yestidday, an' here you is now a grown man, with even some gray hairs in your head."

"I'm gettin' on too," Brentwood commented. "At the pace I am going I don't think I'll ever live to be as old as you."

"You'll make it, Mars Brentwood, you is a good man," she answered. "You is kind, and I ain't shame to say it, that your daddy was kind to colored folks, though he had slaves—but you is kinder. You gave us the title to this piece of land for next to nothing, an' I can't say I ever seen you actin' inconsiderate to coloreds who work for you."

"I try to live up to what I believe," Brentwood said. "That at times is not easy. It is going to be even more difficult down the road. I've seen it closing in on us here in Mudville County for years. Now it seems just around the corner."

"I jus' hopes you don't ever let anybody change you from what you is," Mother Brown murmured.

One week later Mother Brown passed away quietly, unnoticed, while she slept, and was buried behind the Baptist Church in Wrightsville.

⌒⌒⌒

Election fever descended on Mudville County like an epidemic. Signs of the approaching state elections were once more in the air. New political aspirants were declaring their intention to run, old ones were declaring their intention to return or to try again where earlier they had run and lost, and office holders were expressing their desire to continue "to serve the people."

In Mudville County as in the rest of Mississippi and in many areas across the South, election time was a time of increased racial tension. It was a time when increased hostilities were generated and hate of the most primitive form enervated or crawled from subterranean lairs to stalk the land. It was a time when the eyes of the people were bedazzled by political spectacles. Like the fundamentalist preacher who exhorts his believers to let their "emotion go" as a sign of being possessed by the spirit, so the political practitioners exhorted their audiences to let hate and hostility flow, and let fly; for he who is able to play more successfully the game of racial fear and hostility, stands a good chance of being elected to office.

And, as the preacher sought to instill fear in the hearts of his listeners by proclaiming the imminence of "hell fire," so many a political aspirant generated fear and hate in the hearts of white listeners with the doctrine of "the danger of niggers."

The 1894 elections were developing as a re-run of earlier ones. The issue of race was the "red cloth" which political aspirants held before the eyes of the electorate. It was a time when normally sane and sober men, political aspirants, competed among themselves as to who could be the most vitreous, poetic, and descriptive in depicting the "threat of niggers" to the existence of whites. Those political aspirants who selected to disregard "the nigger issue" were the most likely to end up the losers in the election campaign.

Already a foretaste of things to come during the weeks ahead leading up to the elections was taking shape. The League, realizing that the most propitious season for its activities was at hand was stirring into greater activity. The issue of the voting rights of blacks in Mississippi had already been settled with the entire black population being disenfranchised through the activities of the state government and its law enforcement agencies, some in collusion with the League. Thus in 1894 blacks could no longer participate with whites at the ballot box. The League, which during off-election periods had relied almost exclusively upon the poor and the wretched of the white community for its support, during this period of electioneering, as in earlier periods, acquired greater strength and stature. Politicians, perceiving the League as a convenient ally and a dangerous foe, gave either lip service or open support to its announced programs and goals.

In other counties of the "great and sovereign State of Mississippi," the League or its sister organizations had tremendously grown in power and in capacity to break the law with impunity and even with the support of the political authority. Black people in these areas were brutalized into positions of submission; those resisting were summarily flogged, lynched or killed, often under the eyes and with the tacit approval of the law authorities.

In Mudville County, the League, which was non-existent two decades earlier, was slowly spreading its roots like a cancer through the corpus of the community, so that by 1894, though its active membership was relatively small, it had become both for blacks as well as for aspiring politicians, a power to be reckoned with. Anyone opposing its policies was a "Nigger lover," a nomenclature which symbolized the kiss of political death to the politician and a life of uncertain existence to others of the white community.

Two men were running for the local seat in the state legislature: Julius Crane who had taken his father's place two elections earlier, was now running for a third term; and a local county man, a dealer in farm implements named Jason Bilbo, who had sought the office during the previous elections and had lost by a matter of only fifty votes. Both men now gave public allegiance to the League.

Crane, over the last few years, had supported the League primarily by financial contributions that were usually made with the approach of an election. The League itself, usually a rag-tag group of men of the lowest class of society, had little organization aside from individuals bound together by common ignorance and common propensity for vitriolic actions against black people. Yet as elections approached, the League's power increased as it was courted by politicians of every walk of life. The disinherited, the poor, the unemployed, were being told by both political aspirants that the only road to success for themselves and their children lay in the "control of niggers in the county."

"I have dedicated my life," Crane assured his listeners, "to serving the white people of this county and this state, by seeing to it that both in terms of laws enacted and in terms of local action, niggers are kept in their rightful place. I will see to it," he promised them in a voice with the ring of more preacher than politician, "that not one white job will go to a nigger in this county. I will see to it that the nigger as long as he stays in this county, stays in the cotton field, so that the poor but honest and God-fearing white family could have jobs, many of which, since the revolution, he has had to compete for with niggers. I am talking about jobs such as mechanics, carpentry, masonry, and other professions passed down from father to son among niggers."

Jason Bilbo, the other local contender for the state legislature, though having failed in his last bid, now felt that he had a better chance than ever before to capture the seat. Since the last election, while Crane had largely ignored the League, Bilbo had embarked on a program of careful cultivation of a close relationship between himself and the local leadership of the League. Inwardly, Bilbo detested many of the ideas they espoused as a matter of doctrine, but he realized that any chance to win against as formidable an opponent as Crane lay in support by the League, whose growing influence among the poor and largely landless whites and the dirt farmers, was becoming more apparent.

Tyson, though not the head of the League in the county, was recognized as the local leader in the Mudville area. The violent attack against him by Josie Petrus had made him more visible and more popular among the rank and file. Secretly Tyson, an ambitious man, dreamed of running for the senate, and the popularity he had acquired among certain elements of the population since the attack made it appear to him that the dream could become a reality. If he could only get control of the county league, he would be one step away from the senate. It was Bilbo's proposal, however, which for the moment he found to be most attractive.

"You support me, Jeb," Bilbo urged, "an' we can expose Crane for the fraud that he is. He has used us these past eight years. Once he gets the vote, that is it for the next four years. Has he invited you or other League members over to his place, the way that I have done these past three or more years? What has he really done for the poor white folks in this county? He ain't no better than his daddy, who lived off this county for years, and now he has set up a political dynasty. I tell you, if we keep following the Cranes we will be worse off than we ever been. When he gets drunk, he refers to the League as "white trash." I am running against him again, and with your help, Jeb, I can win. If I win, I'll get you the best job I can in the county or in Jackson, and you won't have to run in elections to get it. It will be a job that will enable you to rub shoulders with the politicians and the governor himself."

This promise resulted in a secret pact between both men. Yet Bilbo realized that to win against incumbent Crane would be no easy task. Together they planned a campaign strategy. "We can say," Bilbo suggested, biting hard on a cigar in the right corner of his mouth, "we can say that Crane's daddy and his granddaddy are mostly responsible for many of the problems we have with niggers today."

"How do you reason that?" Jeb inquired.

"It was them who provided their niggers during slavery with training in building, carpentry, masonry, blacksmithing, and mechanics. Niggers been passing the learning down to their children, and that is the kind of training that niggers carry on now from generation to generation, that they use to take food from the mouth of poor white folk. We can say his daddy got rich by using cheap nigger labor—he is still doin' it today, while many white families get poorer."

They smiled and shook hands on it. "It's a sure winner," Bilbo declared, as they parted.

Tyson was enthralled by the possibilities which he perceived as growing from his arrangement with Bilbo. Working together, he could already see in the eyes of his mind the new situation. He would pay someone to run his store while he operated in the stale capital; with the new opportunities he would be able to make himself rich in no time. Of course, Tyson had only an elementary school background, but Bilbo had pointed out to him: "Is not how much education you got that matters, is what you do with what you got." Following his agreement with Bilbo, Tyson began to let the word drop that he was for Bilbo, and began urging his followers to follow his lead.

"Of course he ain't got as much money as dem Cranes, so we can't expect as large contributions as dem what Crane an' his daddy use' to give. But Bilbo is one of us," Tyson told his men, striking his right hand over his heart; "he come from poor ordinary background, he ain't livin' in no mansion, an' he bin supporting us for the past four years, while them Cranes only show interest in us when come elections."

On Saturday evening Jeb Tyson was returning from a political rally in the county, where he had exhorted his listeners about the "growin' threat of niggers among us," and "what Brother Bilbo will do when he get in office, to secure an' to protect our rights." Now he was returning to the town of Mudville, with his friend and disciple Festus riding at his side.

Up ahead, in a slight misty haze they could see Sand Mountains. About a mile away above the town of Mudville, a flock of buzzards was circling in the sky. Tyson was very pleased with the meeting. He could read from the expressions on the faces of his listeners and from their responses that they supported what he had said. Smiling to himself he urged his steed onward. It was at this moment that Festus raised the issue that had bothered his mind for some time.

"Ah say, Jeb. Between them niggers an' us white folk in Mudville County, who is the mostest?"

"The most what?"

"Which have the most people, them or us?"

"I hear say that niggers is the most," Jeb responded, "but I don't believe it. Us white folks is still the most. Trouble is dem niggers is multiplyin' like rabbits, an' if we don't do somethin' soon, dey is goin' to run this county plumb over."

Festus thought for a while as he listened to the rhythmic beat of the horse hoofs on the sodden country road.

"There is one thing I can't figure out, though, Jeb," he continued, frowning as he spoke. "If dem niggers is so dangerous to us white folk who God gave this here country to as you say He done, an' as you say dey is, how come you sell to so many uv dem niggers in your store? You give them credit, an' you let ole Nigger Charlie stay round your place most of the time!

"If I was you I won't trust no niggers. I won't give dem no credit, I won't sell them nutten'—no sugar, flour, oil, beans or nutten—since when you feed an' help dem niggers you is only helpin' dem to spread like rabbits, how you say dey is spreadin'."

Tyson was completely taken aback by the line of reasoning which Festus had presented. Festus who could neither read nor write, but was now trying to advise him! It had never dawned upon Tyson that such thoughts were capable of being processed in the mind of Festus. Further, he thought, if Festus made such observations in the presence of other League members, it could start them thinking in a dangerous direction, and be his ruination. He must put an end to it right now. "What you is got to understand, Festus," Tyson carefully explained, "is that there is niggers and then there is niggers."

"What do you mean by niggers an' niggers?" Festus asked, puzzled.

"There is good niggers an' there is no-good, dangerous niggers, dat's what I mean!" There was a bit of irritation in his voice. "Take ole Charlie, an' take dem niggers what do business in my store. Dey know we white folks is superior, an' dey accept it. When you talks to them, dey say, 'Yes, sir,' or 'Yes, Mass Tyson.' Dey is 'umble an' respectful. Now dem niggers in Niggerville, dem is bad arse niggers, the kind what we is got to rid the county of."

"Well, I been sure nuf confused," Festus confessed, with a sigh of relief. "The way I hear you talk I figure all niggers was dangerous to white folk."

"Look here, Festus," Tyson replied, lowering his voice soberly, "me an' you been knowin' each other fer years. We been in the League ever since it started in Mudville. I been makin' plans for you when I goes to Jackson after this election." He stopped his horse to make his point. Festus pulled the rein on his old mare and she stopped abruptly.

"I been thinkin' of puttin' you in charge of the store while I is out of town, but you is got to be able to separate politics from economics. Now if you go 'round talkin' what I hear you sayin' here, you is goin' to make folk believe that you ain't as intelligent as dey figure you is. Now I is goin' places after this election, an' there is goin' to be something in it for you. Just don't go shootin' off you mouth 'bout what you don't understand. Let me do the talkin' an' the thinkin'."

Festus assured his friend that he had no intention of "talkin' this kinda talk" to anyone. "I only raise this questin', seein' how we been friends for a long time. I sure ain't gonna make no fool o' myself by discussin' this with other folk."

"Very smart you is, Festus, very smart," Tyson commended as he urged his horse into a trot. "I think you will be a good man to work with in my business once I gets to Jackson."

By now it had become clear that the race for the senate would be a two-cornered fight in Mudville County. It was equally clear that the county League had become dichotomized, one section centered in Mudvile under Tyson's leadership supporting Bilbo, with another section under the county leader Tyrannus Brickman supporting Crane. By the time the arrangement between Tyson and Bilbo had been formulized, Crane had already made a significant financial contribution to Brickman.

Late in September as the tempo of campaign increased, Tyson with some of his closest companions came up with the brilliant idea of holding a political rally at the edge of Niggerville, and to end the rally with a defiant march through the town. This he gleefully announced at a rally in the county, declaring that "the march through Niggerville will be means of demonstrating to the niggers down there an' to the whites of this county that Tom Bilbo means business."

News of the intention of the League soon reached Wrightsville, raising to higher levels the tension and anxiety which already existed under the cloud of uncertainty generated by the election campaign. Reverend Jones sought to assuage the worries of his flock, to calm their anxieties and most of all to maintain some control over any reaction to the planned meeting of the League. As was customary, the stage for discussions of crisis situations was the church, and for this purpose a special Tuesday evening meeting was called.

Such meetings were usually attended not only by members "in good and regular standing" but by some who seldom darkened the door of the church with their presence, and others who were totally alienated from the religious activities of the church, yet the Parson considered all of them to be part of his constituency. "Other sheep I have who ain't of this flock," he used to say. Mabel attended the meeting with her four children, Jimmy Brown and his wife, as well as others from the surrounding area who considered the problems of Wrightsville to be part of their problems. Mabel's children, now all teenagers, sat with the young people in the back pews. Even before the meeting commenced Samandra and the others were involved in heated and excited discussions with their friends, sharing bits of news and expressing opinions on the issues at hand.

Parson Jones opened the meeting with prayer. He then reminded his listeners that it was almost customary during times of election for the League to "cut up some trouble."

"The best way to respond to them," he advised "is to ignore them. If they want to hold a meeting outside our town—is a free country, it suppose' to be—let them do it. Ignore them. If they want to march down Church Street, let us show them that we is a community of Christians. I say ignore them. Groups like the League can't exist if they are ignored. As you all know, it is customary here in Mississippi to use us black folk as political bait during election. Once election is past I expect that things will return to normal."

Babs Jacobs was the first to stand in the audience to express his opinion on the issue at hand. "I agrees with Parson Jones," he began, "that if the League want to keep a meetin' outside of Wrightsville, there ain't nothin' we can do 'bout it."

"Dat's right," Mildred, his wife said, encouraging him on.

"As long as they don't try to keep it on property belonging to anybody in this town," he continued. "I also agree that election season is usually a bad time for black folk in this county, but I believe that we is got to look at what is happenin' here in the light of what is happenin' throughout Mississippi an' in many parts of America. Both in the North an' the South groups like the League is formin' an' is attackin' black people. Right here in Mississippi in counties all around us, seldom a month passes, when some poor, innocent black man isn't whipped, hanged, or killed, or some black woman raped

Babs had taken a small shot of whiskey before leaving home. It was the way he quieted his nerves when he spoke before an audience. Without it he would stumble and stammer, but now his words flowed in a fusillade, and as was his custom whenever he made a point which he felt worthy of special recognition he would top it off with "eh?" and wait as it were for a response. "Yes, I know these is hard words to use in church, but this is reality. Fact is, that there ain't no place in these Newnited States, where black folks today is safe. Way up North an' out in the West, black men are bein' killed an' black families persecuted all the time, eh? Now so long as the League stay out of Wrightsville, they don't bother me none. But I say, I ain't too sure that we ought to allow them to march through our town. Black people in Atlanta and Washington, DC, make the same mistake we is fixin' to make—to allow people like the League to march through their area—an' didn't realize what was happening until houses was burned and people killed. Is only when dey decided to fight back that their attackers backed off. What assurance do we have that once they get in our town they won't start burnin' an' shootin', eh? Are we goin' to have the Sheriff here to protect us or to see to it that the League don't start trouble? Eh?

"I tell you this," he continued, "I is a peaceful man, and I minds my own business, but I ain't gonna sit down an' see my kin folk endangered by the League. If a man don't try to protect his own family he is worse than an infidel, as the good book says. If the League with its crazy followers get in this town, you can bet they gonna try to destroy it. I say that we let them know that we's gonna protect our town with our lives. This town is our town, this land is our land, if we don't protect it, you tell me who will, eh?"

"Dem that is fer us is more than them what is 'gainst us," Parson Jones interjected.

"I agree with that, Parson," Jacobs continued, "but so did our brothers an' sisters in Atlanta and Washington, DC, them that is now dead, an' dem what had their property destroyed by criminals.

"If we's gonna get kilt, let it not be with a lynch mob, but let us die fightin', with whatever weapons we have in our hands, an' let it be in defense of ourselves. We should let the League know that we's gonna be at the entrance of Wrightsville waitin', an' we will defend our town." Parson Jones cleared his throat to speak, but Babs Jacobs continued.

"Now, we can pick up an' go up North, leavin' our land an' property behind, the way many black folk done, an' then face groups like the League up there or we can stay here an' fight for our rights, eh? Wherever we go, we's gonna have to fight, an' I say we fight here."

After several presentations by the youth and the elders, Parson Jones called for an all-night prayer meeting, to seek "the guidance of de Lawd," and urged his members to remain calm and "trust in the Lawd." "I declare to you this evening, as the servant of the Lawd, that even as He helped Israel of old, out of Egypt an' through the Red Sea, even as He saved them from the Philistines, so He can, if we trust in Him, save us from them who want to trouble us."

The following evening Parson Jones climbed on to his buggy and drove to the town of Mudville. He arrived just before sundown. A vespers peace had already settled over the town, save for the gentle rustling of a flock of dry leaves which, urged along by their shepherd the evening wind, hurried in willy nilly fashion along the dirt road that was Main Street. Mudville at this time of the evening seemed devoid of people, yet it was the home of some 1,150 mortal souls. Parson Jones tied his horse to the wooden post across the road from the town hall, a block from the Sheriff's office. Old Charlie was seated on a bench in front of Tyson's store, whittling on a piece of wood. He had observed the parson as he rode into town, dismounted, and tied his horse. As he saw the parson approaching he stopped his whittling and turned to greet him, his curiosity already aroused as to the purpose of the parson's visit to Mudville. Charlie had heard the rumor that the League was planning to hold a meeting near Wrightsville and had overheard Tyson talking about walking through the town.

Parson Jones seldom visited Mudville. "Wonder what bring him here this evening," Charlie thought. "Ain't seen him in these parts more than a year now."

"Well, good day, Brother Brown," Parson Jones greeted him, reaching out his hand and shaking Charlie's heartily.

"Howdy, Parson," Charlie smiled respectfully. "I'll say, I ain't seen you in these parts fer some time."

"Yes, yes," the Parson replied. "Wherever the Lawd's chillen live, I his servant must go." Charlie nodded agreeably.

"Do you know if the sheriff is in his office?" the Parson asked after a few moments of silence.

"Yes, he sure is. Just walked in a few minutes ago," Charles responded.

"And Deputy-ah-Pete Watchamacall him. "

"Oh, Snake-eye Pete!" commented Charlie, looking at his whittling knife. "That no-good peckerwood just left a while back, soon after Sheriff Brude came in."

"I'm suprise' at you, Brother Brown!" Parson Jones said, frowning disapprovingly, "using such terms to describe one of the Lawd's chillen."

"Lawd's chillen!" Charlie protested. "Dat rascal ain't got nutten from Gawd in him. Shucks, you can look at his eyes an' see he's got the devil in him."

"Let the Lawd do the judging, brother," the Parson advised. "It is possible that below that exterior he's got a real good heart."

"There's ain't no exterior an' interior with him, Parson. What you can see is what he is, an' it ain't good."

Not wishing to pursue the discussion, the parson thanked Charlie, wishing him "good day" and "the Lawd's blessing," and headed towards the sheriff's office.

Brude was just about to leave when Parson Jones knocked on the old oak door of the office. Brude recognized the parson immediately. He had seen him on several occasions though never had conversed with him before. It was thus with interest that the sheriff, now seated behind his table, awaited an explanation as to the reason for the visit; though having heard about the League's plans to hold a meeting in the vicinity of Wrightsville, he suspected that the parson's visit was related to the intended meeting.

Breaking the silence, Brude inquired, "Well, Reverend, what can I do for you today?"

Parson Jones nervously fidgeted with his hat as he set himself to respond. But the fidgeting was not really the result of fear or nervousness, for Jones neither feared the man nor felt uncomfortable in his presence. It was in fact a contrived nervous response, something Jones perceived as a necessary gesture of respect in interacting with the lawman.

"I know you are a very busy man, Sheriff," the parson looked at and fingered the rim of his hat, "an' I appreciate the kindness of you givin' me a few minutes of your time." He looked up at the sheriff momentarily. "The Lawd will bless you for your kindness."

"Thanks, Reverend," Brude said somewhat brusquely. The expression on his face, particularly around his lips and across the lower areas of his cheeks, appeared as a smile in the making, but if Jones' eyes caught the expression, he was unsure as to its meaning, more so, by the tone of the sheriff's voice as he spoke. It was slow, deliberate, with a touch of monotony. "Now what can I do for you?" The sheriff placed his two hands on the desk. He drummed the tips of the fingers of his right hand on the desk, as if playing some unseen instrument. Jones interpreted the movement of his fingers as a sign of impatience. "Let's get it over with," clearly he was saying.

"Sheriff Brude," Jones began, "the people of Wrightsville is right troubled and afraid." Jones used the word "is" though he knew that "are" was correct; in fact, he spoke perfect English when he so desired. In his thinking, this was appropriate subservience in dealing with authority such as the law. "They is Christian people, humble and good citizens. Yes, we've got a few hotheaded young people, like young ones ever'where, but we are working with them. What have our people worried is the rumored plans of the League to conduct a march through our little town. Some people are so worried that the town will be attacked they are talking about going up North. Just at the time," he emphasized, shaking his head in grief, "when cotton reapin' season is comin', and focus should be on reapin' the crop. I done told them that there is law and order in this here county, an' the League can't bother nobody. The people fear that something will go wrong during the march, an' shooting will start. Some even fear that," he measured the sheriff carefully as he spoke, "there may be a lynchin'."

Jones was ready to continue with his presentation which he had constructed before coming to see the sheriff, but Brude interrupted, "There ain't goin' to be no shootin', there ain't goin' to be no lynchin', there ain't goin' to be no trouble. The League, like anybody else, can walk on any public road, they can hold meetings wherever they want so long as they don't trespass, so if I were you, Reverend, I wouldn't worry about nothing."

Brude rose from his chair as he spoke, and Parson Jones, taking the cue, also stood. When the sheriff completed his cold comment, Jones heartily thanked him, bowed graciously, and departed. As he rode back to Wrightsville, he thought about the meeting. Though he had not completed his presentation, he felt that his point had been effectively made and the sheriff's response had been favorable.

∽ ∽ ∽

Tyson had originally planned the League meeting to be held near Wrightsville as an after sundown affair. But for reasons known only to himself and his closest lieutenants, the time was changed to before sundown. It was Saturday about one hour before sunset that the men began to arrive for the meeting. The first group of twelve men on horseback was led by Tyson. The place of the meeting was some five hundred yards from Wrightsville on a piece of land that had been owned by a white man but taken over by the county for taxes. Within fifteen minutes of the arrival of Tyson and his group, sixty-three, including a few teenage boys had gathered on the site. The meeting was supposed to be part of the campaign for the election of Jason Bilbo, though Bilbo himself was not present.

Following the directions of Parson Jones, the townspeople gave the impression of ignoring the League's activity, but in fact the town was tense, held in boding silence. Babs Jacobs and several others who owned guns loaded them, and remained on their premises ready to defend their property in case of an attack.

Some of the men at the meeting called by Tyson were bona fide members of the League; others were simply fellow travelers and excitement seekers. Many of them were armed with rifles.

Tyson addressed the meeting from a wagon used as a podium. He spoke in a high-pitched voice, and it was clear from the tenor of his presentation that it was directed at Wrightsville, rather than at his white listeners. Once more he ranted and raved about the "threat of Niggers" who were taking jobs away from white folk and food from the mouths of white children, and the threat against white women. He denounced the "plot by niggers to change the name of Niggerville to Wrightsville," and to the applause of his listeners around him declared, "As far as we is concerned, that there junk heap is still Niggerville, an' will always be Niggerville." The coming election was to make sure "once an' for all that niggers is kept in their place an' the Lawd-given rights of the white people is protected."

Tyson had already announced that there was to be a march down the main road through Wrightsville following the meeting. While some of his followers, their heads clouded by moonshine, eagerly anticipated the action, others rather more sober awaited with apprehension, partly victims of the propaganda which Tyson had spread about "dem bad Niggers of Niggerville."

Towards the end of Tyson's address, a shotgun blast reverberated through the air. It came from the direction of Wrightsville. It was actually the accidental discharge by a nervous resident who sat on the back step of his house fingering a gun he had not used in several years. But the discharge had a sobering effect on members of the crowd around the wagon on which Tyson stood.

"Dey is armed to the teeth an' ready," one man whispered to those beside him.

"Is just like Tyson said," another declared. "Dey is just itching for a shoot out."

Tyson himself had become apprehensive following the blast, but dared not retreat in the presence of his followers. When he looked up and saw Sheriff Brude and a young deputy riding towards them, he breathed a sigh of relief.

"Mark my word," he prophesied to the men around him, "that there sheriff who is comin' right now, is goin' to try to stop us from enterin' Niggerville. Jus' when we is ready to start the march. I say we go ahead. What do you say, boys?"

"Yeh!" was the rowdy reply.

By now Brude and his deputy had both dismounted and edged their way through the men toward the wagon on which the speaker stood. Tyson had concluded his address which had lasted some forty minutes. The sheriff looked up at Tyson as he spoke. "Your meeting is over." It sounded both as a question and a statement of fact.

Tyson hesitated momentarily as the men pressed around, not wishing to lose any of the exchange with the sheriff. "I'd say the talkin' is over but we is jus' about to start marchin', yes sirree," he added.

Brude surveyed the motley group. Most of them he recognized by name. They were mainly the poor and wretched from the town of Mudville, and a few from the county.

"Seems to me," Brude said, looking at the men, "most of you here are from Mudville or the Crossroads area. I can't imagine why you will want to come here and keep a political meeting. Most of the people round these parts is niggers an' niggers ain't got no vote."

"We figure there is a few white folk in the area an' we is aimin' to get them registered to vote come elections," Tyson responded, measuring the sheriff with his piercing eyes.

"I heard of shotgun marriages, but I ain't never heard of shotgun registration," Brude commented. Some of the men grinned gleefully.

"What d'ya mean?" Tyson challenged.

"Look at all these guns," he said, pointing to several around him. "I don't see no need for such weapons at a political rally. A hunting trip, yes, but not a political rally."

The men hollered with laughter. It was an uneasy capricious laugh, however, for it was clear to the men that there was a hidden agenda in the sheriff's remarks. Tyson was becoming fidgety from the presence of Brude and the ambivalent response of his men. But he determined to hold his place in the presence of this challenge.

"There ain't no law 'gainst guns in this county. Is a democratic right for every white man to have a gun to protect hisself an' his famiy from niggers what fixin' to take over this county. The niggers is fully armed there in Niggerville. "

He pointed towards the town now partly enshrouded in the shadows of falling night. As he pointed, the men, almost in unison, looked in the direction of the town as if expecting to see a line of guns fixed upon them.

"We been havin' a peaceful political meetin' here," Tyson protested, "and next thing we knowed they start shoot'n at us." Again he pointed to Wrightsville, bending forward to emphasize his point.

"Yeh, that's right," the men grumbled in agreement.

"Well," Brude said, looking at the dim lean faces around him, "as sheriff of this county, I came here to see that nobody shoot nobody, or threaten nobody, or cause no trouble. With election coming up an' you bunch campaigning 'gainst Mr. Crane, there can be lots of problems."

Having said this, the sheriff turned to leave, but he continued speaking. "Now that your meeting is over, I reckon you all will be heading home to Mudville, Crossroads, or wherever you live. In the meantime, me an' my deputy will ride into Niggerville to make sure that nobody start nothing." The men mounted their horses and headed back in the direction of Mudville. Some were talking and some were laughing, while some aimed verbal abuse at the sheriff. "Dat there is a nigger lovin' sheriff if I ever seen one," Festus declared.

"You sho' right," another concurred. "The way that sheriff is treating dem niggers wid kid gloves is nuf to make a preacher cuss."

"We mus' see to it," Tyson advised, "come next local elections, that Pete be made sheriff. He is one of ours."

FIVE:
THE RAPE

Peter Drake, fondly called Pete by his admirers and nicknamed by some who disdained him "Snake-eyed Pete," had sat for the past forty-five minutes on the crudely built bench that stood against the wall on the porch in front of the sheriff's office. A smoldering cigarette hung languidly from the left side of his mouth. Bole Miles, hired by Sheriff Brude only five months earlier as a new deputy, sat beside Pete. Since Bole's employment, a close partnership had developed between himself and Pete. In fact, the two men had taken to each other as a hungry pig to slop. There was something about Pete's lifestyle, his attitude, his demeanor, his political orientation that enthralled Bole, and almost instantly made Pete his ideal. Brude, who had employed Bole on a trial basis, had on more than one occasion advised him to steer clear of Pete, but to no avail. Sheriff Brude realized that he had made a bad choice in Bole and was only awaiting the appropriate time to replace him.

The September evening was warm and humid. A sultry bluish haze hung listless over the Delta town. The first part of the week had been marked by rain, thunder, and lightning, weather conditions caused by a hurricane that had moved across the Atlantic into the Caribbean, causing damage and death. By the time it reached the Gulf Shores and rolled over the Mississippi Delta, it had disintegrated into thunderstorms that bred several tornadoes across the south land. Now the inclement weather having passed, a late heat wave took possession of the Delta. With Brude visiting in the county, and nothing in particular to do, the two deputies sat before the sheriff's office in the shade of the awning of the building, talking about the recent storm, and exchanging bits of information from the county and across the state about the upcoming election.

Pete leaned forward on the bench where he sat, looked down the graveled road towards the north end of town and announced, "Look what's comin'!" Bole turned and looked.

"Who they be?" he inquired.

"You is lookin' at two of the purtiest nigger womens in Mudville County," Pete informed him, easing the front rim of his hat over his forehead. "Their mammy is a woman named Mabel. She lives next to the Yazoo, 'bout two miles from here."

"A sharecropper?" Bole inquired.

"Naw, she's got her own place, maybe five, maybe ten acres. But she makes her livin' sewin' for high class white folk."

By now the girls, Samandra and Sharon Wright, were nearer to the deputies as they walked up Main Street.

"Yes, you is right," Bole said, eyeing lustfully the two girls, "they sho is purty. Ain't it funny how some nigger womens is purty!" There was an element of surprise and discovery in his voice. "I'll be damned if that one to the right don't look like a white woman."

Pete grinned, revealing a jagged row of tobacco stained teeth. He removed the cigarette from the side of his mouth and flicked it with two fingers. It landed still smoldering some ten feet away on the road. "The same thing Brude said when he fust seen that one two years back," Pete said slowly. "You should a seen how his mouth fell wide open lookin' at that gal. We was down by her mammy's place on the Yazoo, searchin' fer that nigger boy what beat up Tyson, when them two gals come out on the verandah. That fool Brude stood there as if he been hit by lightnin'. Man! He wanted that half breed so bad, he could almost taste it." Both men laughed lasciviously. Pete slapped the side of his thighs with his hands, and placed his boot covered feet expertly on a sawed-off pine stump that was used as a seat on the edge of the verandah, so that only the heels of his boots rested on the stump.

By now the two girls were almost across from the point where Bole and his friend sat. Both girls were decked in flowered cotton dresses, and wore closely woven straw hats to shade the afternoon sun. Completely ignoring the presence of the deputies, Samandra and Sharon, talking intently between themselves, continued on their way, their beautiful, shapely bodies innocently undulating as they walked.

"I'll say that there half-white one coulda sure fooled me," Bole repeated, still showing amazement.

"Not me," Pete replied confidently. "I can spot a nigger a half a mile aways, even if they is only got one drop a nigger blood. There is plenty a niggers like that one around Mississippi. Dey daddy is some white buck, dey mammy is nigger maybe with a little white blood. Some o' the children usually come out real nigger an' some almost white."

Bole scrutinized the two women as they passed. "You can have that half-white one," he said. "I'll take me the real nigger one; dem is the sweetest kind you can ever lay." He chuckled.

"Ever had a nigger woman?" Pete inquired, eyeing Bole curiously.

"Yep. I sure have," he said, nodding his head and smiling mischievously.

"You is lyin', Bole! I can tell by the look in your eyes that you is lyin'. You ain't never had no nigger woman!"

Bole chuckled again. "You is right. I ain't never had none!" he confessed. "But I hear say dey is much sweeter than white womens. I have a cousin in Columbus who wouldn't have no other womens. He used to say, 'layin' a black woman is like drinkin' good whiskey, the more you drink, the more you want.'"

Pete laughed, his eyes slightly glazed as he pondered on the venereal philosophy of Bole's cousin. By now the girls were out of sight, having turned the corner to the right a block away.

"I always wonder if Brude ever got a piece of that," Pete pondered aloud. "I know he wanted it real bad. But knowin' how protective the mammy is, the only way I figure he coulda get it is if she snucked out an' gave it to him. 'cause if the mammy ever know, she'll be hollerin' murder. Notice how dey pass us prim and prissy like, an' didn't even look our way?" Pete pointed out. "I don't believe she'll ever give it up to a white man willingly. Seein' how Brude don't have the guts to take it by force, I'll say the only way he ever got that is in his dreams." They both laughed raucously.

Pete took another cigarette from his shirt pocket, placing it between his lips. He brushed a match against his boots and the sulfur burst into flames. He held the flame against the end of the cigarette, the white paper quickly reddened at the tip and turned ashen gray as Pete sucked air through the tobacco. He made a long haul on the cigarette, then dropping his head slightly backward he blew the smoke towards the awning of the verandah and watched thoughtfully as it drifted under the eaves and over the road. "I is ready to bet you any money that if we plan it careful like, we can get it from both of them," he said seriously.

"Do you really think so?" Bole inquired.

"I don't think so, I know so," Pete assured him.

Bole gazed at the corner around which the girls had just vanished. "I'll give one week of my pay jus' to get five minutes of the real black one." He lowered his voice so as not to reveal the tenor of the discussion to the postmistress, Mrs. Prunedish, passing by.

"Ah!" Pete said, looking at Bole in feigned surprise. "We both can get it all fer nothing. All you need is some brains an' a plan." He tapped a finger lightly against the side of his head.

〜 〜 〜

Since the age of sixteen, Samandra had been assisting in the operation of the church school in Wrightsville, the only source of education available to black children in the area. The school, a one-room affair, was conducted in the back room of the Baptist Church at the corner of Church Street. Now Samandra had turned eighteen, and this was to be her last year at the school. The few dollars she had made as an assistant teacher had all been saved at the direction of her mother. This, with the savings of many years by Mabel, was to be used to send the two girls, Sharon and Samandra, off to school in Atlanta. According to information obtained by Mabel, the school was operated in such a way that its students could assist themselves by working to defray part of the expenses of their education. Samandra had long desired to be a teacher and her sister Sharon wanted to be a nurse-midwife, both skills badly needed in the black community.

There was great anticipation as the girls awaited the passing of weeks and months. Mabel was determined to assist her four children in the quest for higher education. Billy had early declared his intention to be a preacher. He was enthralled by the preaching of Parson Jones, and often during their play on the banks of the Yazoo, Billy would take the role of the preacher. At the age of fifteen during Young People's Day at the church Billy and two other boys had been given the opportunity of preaching a short sermon. Billy had done his on "the Second Coming of Christ," and had tried to preach in the manner of Parson Jones, drawing a lot of "Amen's!" and "Preach!" from the mixed congregation of youth and adults.

Billy's vocational interest never altered as he grew older, and Mabel promised to send him to a Baptist school of black preachers in Birmingham, Alabama. Joshua had always desired to be a farmer. He planned to study farming and help his mother purchase more land so that they could farm "in a big way."

On this particular Friday, Samandra and Sharon were to travel together to Wrightsville; from there Sharon was to go to Mudville to deliver a dress which she and her mother had just completed for the daughter of the postmistress. After fulfilling the errand and purchasing some items needed by her mother, Sharon was to return to Wrightsville, and, at the end of the school day travel home with Samandra.

Earlier that morning, Sharon had taken ill with cramps, a condition which troubled her at least once each month, ever since she had reached puberty. The responsibility of getting the dress to Mudville therefore fell on Samandra.

School in Wrightsville ended at midday. Mrs. Jones herself having a mission to run in Mudville, invited Samandra to ride with her in her carriage, a gift presented to her and her husband by the church a year earlier for their devotion and tireless dedication to education and the preaching of the gospel. Parson Jones had all but given the carriage to his wife. He preferred to ride his chestnut stallion on his rounds in the community.

Samandra rode with Mrs. Jones to Mudville, and the dress was delivered to the postmistress, a very peevish lady who spent fifteen minutes scrutinizing it, criticizing the color of the material which she herself had selected and bought, before delivering to Samandra the money for the work. By mid afternoon Samandra and Mrs. Jones had returned to Wrightsville. Normally Samandra would walk the one and a half miles to her home, but this evening she was able to ride as far as the home of Jim Brown, with Jim who had delivered some produce from his farm to Wrightsville, leaving her with less than a mile to walk to her place on the banks of the Yazoo.

A quarter of a mile from Brown's place, the road which ran south from Wrightsville emptied on to the River Trail, a serpentine dirt path which ran for several miles parallel to the Yazoo River. Less than a quarter mile west along River Trail was Mabel's farm. East, the trail ran for almost a mile before it divided in two, one moving south with the river, the other eastward—a muddy and rocky underpath that ended on the southeastern approach to the town of Mudville.

It was along this same River Trail that Samandra as a lass of six and her brother Billy, at age seven had traveled years earlier on a summer morning, drawn by the hands of fate. It is difficult to comprehend the mysterious working of destiny. Its recondite laws, and the purpose for the processes it promotes, lead mortals on to inescapable destinations. How can we contrive the hands that guided that old mare twelve years earlier to continue on the course that ended on River Trail while the children slept, rather than remaining on the larger dirt road that would have taken them to another future?

It was along the side of this trail that Mabel Wright worked her garden that summer morning, when looking up from the row of cabbages she was tending she saw to her utter surprise the old horse-drawn wagon, the mare quietly munching on dew coated leaves and shrubs along the trail, while on the wagon two white children slept.

It was on this same trail that Samandra, now a young woman of eighteen, turned homeward that Friday afternoon, a path so intricately tied to her past, her sorrows, her happiness and security. It was also to be entwined with the fate that awaited her.

The once vivid recollections of her early childhood were now all but gone. The soothing tide of time had flowed unceasingly over the pebbles of her memory, washing them almost clean, removing the painful edges, so that now, only vague, as an ill remembered dream, were the images of her early life; the mother she and her brother Billy had buried, and the father who had deserted them.

But none of this was on her mind this evening, as she ambled lightly, bathed in the pleasant sunlight, her thoughts resting on her plans for college nine months hence. Above her in an almost cloudless sky, a hawk, unnoticed, floated on outstretched wings.

Absorbed in her thoughts Samandra had just come around the bend in the trail when not more than two hundred feet away she saw a man whom she immediately recognized. He had emerged from the pine that bordered the road. It was Snake-eyed Pete, the deputy she had last seen one week earlier on her trip to Mudville. The deputy was talking to someone in the pine whom Samandra could not see from where she was.

"Can't amagine how that there mule got his leg in that hole," Pete was saying to his yet unseen companion. "That front leg seem sure nuf broke to me. Seems that the best thing to do is to shoot him."

When Samandra reached the spot where the deputy was standing, he spoke to her. "Have you any idea who that there gray mule belong to? He went an' stuck his leg in a hole. It seem broke to me."

"We have a gray mule," Samandra informed him. "Where is it?"

"Over there in the pines," Pete said calmly.

Without any urging from the deputy, Samandra followed him into the pine grove. There were several generations of pines growing together, so that the undergrowth was thick in some areas. Shortly after they entered the woods they were joined by Bole Miles, the deputy recently hired by Sheriff Brude. They walked further away from the road, led by Pete.

What a shock the loss of the mule would be to her mother, she thought as she followed the two men. Indeed if the leg is broken it will have to be shot. How she hoped that by some miracle it would not be their mule. But whose else could it be? There were no other farmers in the immediate vicinity. These were the thoughts running through her mind as she followed the men. "How far in the woods is it?" Samandra asked, the concern for the mule reflected in her voice.

At this moment Snake-eyed Pete, who had been walking ahead of Samandra swung around and faced her. A fiendish smile crept over his brazen face as his eyes surveyed her youthful form. "The truth is there ain't no mule," he said, grinning mischievously. "We, me an' Bole here, just wanted to be with you alone fer a while to talk an' enjoy your company. Seein' how we don't get to talk to you when you comes to Mudville." He paused for a while as he scrutinized her body. "Such a beautiful woman like you, as me an' Bole been sayin' when we seen you last week. We will give anything, anything to have some fun with you, specially seein' how you is mo' white than nigger, an' we both is white men." He looked at Bole, who nodded his head in agreement.

A strange expression crept over Samandra's features. It reflected a mixture of fear, alarm, and disbelief. Innocently she had accepted the story the deputy had told her about the mule, and had allowed herself to be lured into the woods.

Without responding to Pete's comment, Samandra turned to leave, but Bole interposed himself between her and the path, spreading out his swarthy arms. "Like Pete said, we just want to have some fun wit' you," Bole assured her.

"I demand that you leave me alone and let me go," she said impatiently, mustering what courage she could.

Pete, who now stood behind, grabbed Samandra by the wrist, and swung her around. "Listen here, you black bitch," he blurted, "don't you try to tell us what we must do. We is the law in Mudville County an' no nigger can tell us what to do. Now we don't want no noise an' nobody will get hurt includin' your two brothers. All we want is a little fun."

With that introduction, Pete, using a single arm, pulled Samandra towards him. So sudden was the movement that she partly stumbled, partly fell onto him with her body pressed against his. She could smell the stench of his body which had not been washed for several days. Raising her arms, Samandra pushed against the deputy's body, partly separating herself from him. But during the brief moment Pete had felt the firmness of her breasts against his chest, he had smelled the feminine odor of her body. It was slightly different from that of any woman he could remember and instantly it drove him wild.

Pulling her back towards him, he kissed her forcefully, but her lips were locked together like a clamp. Pete began to breathe heavily. Wild, agitated excitement glowed fiercely in his eyes. In the silent struggle being observed by Bole, the top of Samandra's blouse became parted, exposing a portion of her breasts. Pete saw them and immediately his mouth dropped towards them. Mustering all the might she could, Samandra tried to push his head away. In the struggle, they both fell to the ground like a pair of wasps locked in a death grip. The ground was blanketed by more than two inches of pine needles.

Pete pinned Samandra's hands to the ground and tried to climb on to her body, but Samandra, shifting her body, kept him off balance.

Bole, who up to this point had not touched the girl, stood over her head observing the struggle. "Come on, Bole, help me with her," Pete demanded. "What the hell you standin' there fer?"

"Don't ferget," Bole said, bending over the struggling woman, "I won the toss, so I am to get it first."

"Well, you won't get it by standin' an' lookin'. Come an' climb on her," Pete said, breathing heavily.

Bole, who by now had himself become equally sexually excited, bolted into action. Still holding her hands at the wrists, Pete shifted his body, allowing Bole to climb on to the struggling girl.

"Get in between her legs, you fool," Pete said impatiently. Forcing her legs apart, Bole slid between them. He unbuttoned his trousers, but when he reached under her dress, she forcefully kicked her legs and sent him flying. Bole crept back on to her. Once more he fought his way between her legs. He tore open her blouse, exposing her breasts. Slipping his right hand under her dress, he held onto the side of her cotton drawers, and gave a massive pull that ripped them apart, revealing her secret parts. Her perspiring body glistened in the light filtering through the trees. The sight of the partly naked woman writhing and twisting in her effort to escape drove Bole to bestial frenzy.

Pete meanwhile, having lost all sanity, was trying desperately to hold her hands and reach her breast with his mouth. Samandra uttered a loud scream that echoed through the woods.

Pete was livid. His body trembled all over. "You bitch," he said, breathing heavily. "You make one more noise, an' it will be your last, you hear me." He placed his hand on her mouth to smother any possible cry. The wild glare in his eyes struck greater terror in Samandra's heart.

"Come on, hurry up," Pete urged Bole. "I want mine, too." Samandra, her mouth muffled by Pete's hand, fought and struggled, creating technical problems for Bole, struggling to complete his vicious deed yet unable to stabilize his position due to the wriggling of the girl. In the process and intensity of the struggle Bole reached the high point of his sexual excitement. Issuing a bestial grunt, part in disappointment from his unsuccessful venture and part in response to his excited condition, his body stiffened, his eyes glazed and glaring.

So absorbed were the two men in their bestial act, that they neither heard nor saw the person approaching. Bole heard a crashing sound against his head, a strange noise escaped his lips, a million stars exploded in his brain. Total darkness enfolded him and he felt himself falling, falling into an abysmal bottomless chasm of darkness.

Pete, who in the process of fondling the girl's breast with his mouth was distracted by the noise, looked up in time to see a black man standing over him. In his hands was a piece of pine branch that hovered in the air menacingly, ready to descend upon him. Pete reached for his gun but it was too late. The vicious blow caught the side of his head. He made a complete somersault and landed sprawled on his back on the pine needles.

Turning again to the first man he had struck, Joshua raised the stick in the air, aiming it at the head of the silent body. Samandra perceived what her brother was about to do and screamed from where she lay. "No, Joshua, no! You'll kill him."

Joshua halted the blow in mid-air. The man at whom it was aimed was lying on his side. Blood was oozing from his mouth and nostrils.

Joshua helped his sister to her feet. Her legs wobbled beneath her, and she held on to his shoulder so as to keep from falling. Shamefully amid her tears she buttoned up her blouse. She took the torn underclothing from her left foot on which it still hung. In her confused state, uncertain as to what should be done with it, she folded it in her hands, as she and her brother set out for home.

Sharon, looking from the bedroom window saw Samandra holding onto the shoulder of Joshua and crying as they entered the yard. "Ma!" she called in alarm. "Something is wrong with Samandra. She is coming across the yard with Joshua an' she's cryin."

Mabel, who was busy at work on the sewing machine, leaped from the chair and rushed to the door. The first thought that came to her mind was that perhaps something had befallen the dress which Samandra was to deliver to the postmistress in Mudville. But the moment she saw the child—her torn clothing, disheveled hair, the terror in her eyes—she knew with the instinct of a black southern mother, that her worst fears had been realized.

How many times through their uncertain years of existence, had Mabel looked at the children and troubled herself of the many dangers that lurked around them? How many times had she prayed to God and agonized for the safety of her boys and the protection of Sharon and Samandra from the physical and emotional abuse that were such common occurrences to black people of her time. The gray hair which now lined the edges of her forehead bore testimony to her worry.

Like a mother pheasant caring for her chicks, chicks that cannot yet fly, in the cotton field near the Yazoo, while the brown delta hawk hovers above, and the gray coyote and the fox forage nearby. Anxiously she broods over them, yet she knows that should danger strike, there is so little she can do to save them. So it was with Mabel. It was these fears that had motivated so many of her actions over the years. It was these fears that in part had motivated her to save every penny she could so as to be able to send her children away to school. It was in part these fears that years earlier had brought her back to the church she once neglected.

Mabel pulled the weeping child into her arms. The girl still held in her hand the torn underclothing. "What happen, chile, what happen?" she inquired.

"She been raped," Joshua said, stamping his feet on the ground in a fit of anger. "I shoulda kilt them. Both of them was on her like a couple a mad dogs."

Mabel led the girl into the house. Taking her into the bedroom with her sister, she questioned her carefully about what had happened.

Billy, who had been down by the river when Samandra returned, came in through the back door. He heard his sister sobbing and inquired as to what was wrong. Joshua informed him of what had occurred. Without waiting to see his sister, Billy grabbed the shotgun, and a box of shells.

"I will kill both of them if it is the last thing I do." He proceeded to load the gun. By the time Mabel came into the living room they both had left the house.

She ran out on to the porch and screamed at the boys. "Are you two gone mad? Are you crazy? Come back here!" she demanded.

"But Ma!"

"Don't you 'but Ma' me. You both is goin' out there to get yourself killed. Come back in this house this minute." She walked to meet them in the yard, and took the gun and box of cartridges away from them. "For God's sake, Billy an' Josh, use your head, not your emotions. I knows how you feel," she said. Standing before them searching their faces she said, "You think I don't feel the same way? Come inside an' sit down. We's in lots of trouble. Think this thing through."

Mabel, carrying the gun and cartridges, walked into the house followed by the two boys. "I was planning to send you all away to school next year, but you are going this year before winter comes," she said. "If the school can't take you now, you gonna stay with your aunt in Chicago until the spring."

So absorbed had Mabel become over what had befallen her child, that it had not registered upon her consciousness what had befallen the two men who had attacked her daughter. It was only as she further questioned the child about the details of what had occurred that she discovered how Joshua had knocked the two deputies out cold, and one of them had blood coming from his mouth and nose.

A cold chill of rising fear submerging even the terror which she felt over the attack on her child surged within her as she realized the mortal danger that Joshua now faced. He had done what any normal self respecting brother would have done. But the assailants were white men, and law officers at that. Putting these facts together spelled disaster for the boy. Strange was the starkness of the turn of reality, the shock of the attack against her child, and the greater terror over the realization of danger which Joshua now faced.

Mabel realized that whatever was to be done had to be done quickly. Several alternatives raced across her mind. Perhaps Joshua should try to escape the way Josie had done two years earlier. Perhaps he should go into hiding until it was clear what would happen. And what about the two deputies? Were they dead? Were they badly injured, still lying out there in the woods, or were they right now on their way to her home to seek revenge? Had they returned to Mudville to collect a posse to come after her son? In any case she saw her boy in mortal danger. Her daughter had been transgressed, violated, but she was alive. For Joshua what happened in the next few hours could determine his fate.

Rapidly processing these troubled thoughts, Mabel decided they should stay where they were at least for a while and await events. If she saw the two deputies coming into her yard, she would let Joshua run through the back door and hide by the Yazoo, until the sheriff arrived. She hoped that the new sheriff would be at least as fair as Tate had been in dealing with her. She knew that he had stopped the League from marching through Wrightsville. This to her was a straw of hope.

"Keep an eye on the road and let me know as soon as you seen anyone coming," she directed Billy.

Mabel went back into the bedroom to comfort Samandra who lay across the bed crying. Sharon stood at the side of the bed weeping in commiseration. "I shoulda gone with you. I shoulda been there to help you fight them off," she was saying.

Sitting beside the child, the mother took her head into her arms. Tenderly she moved the rumpled hair from her face. "Hush, my little baby, hush. Ever'thing gonna be all right," she whispered. "You is alive. You is strong. You is a black woman in America, and that mean you is got to be able to take persecution an' humiliation. You is got to be stronger than any woman in creation. You is got to be able to sing when you is angry, to smile when you actually feel like hatin'. You is got to use every bad experience like this as a lesson; turn it into an instrument to gain victory over them what will destroy you and your people."

Mabel paused for a moment, still rocking Samandra's head in her arms. "Sheriff Brude must be told our side of what happen'. We will wait for a few minutes, and if he doesn't come to us, we gonna go to him. We will travel the road to Wrightsville, and from there to Mudville. That road is longer, but it will give us less chance of running into the deputies."

⌒ ⌒ ⌒

Slowly consciousness returned, as one approaching the entrance of a cave from deep within its labyrinthine womb. First there was consciousness yet darkness. Pete opened his eyes. A gray confused mist flooded his vision. The broken crisp pine needles pricked against his gaunt face, hastening a return to full consciousness. From the perspective where he lay below the pine trees, the world seemed to be at an awkward angle. Everything stood on its head. Pete tried to move his body. His head was painful and resisting. He blinked his eyes slowly. Presently Pete perceived a rapid turbulence near his face. Startled, using all the energy at his command, he forced his head away from the turbulence. It was a wasp which had just captured a large fly, and was about to transport it to a place of safety where it would lay eggs in its body.

Slowly and painfully, Pete raised his head. There was a throbbing, agonizing ache within. Sitting on the turf of pine needles, he examined his head with his hands. There was a heavy lump on the right side. It was painful, stained with blood. Now the scene of what had transpired slowly returned to his memory.

Indelible were the images of that last fleeting moment before he lost consciousness: a black man standing over him, a club hovering in the space above his head. The face, the look of anger it reflected, left an imprint seared upon the engram of his memory that would haunt him for years to come.

Pete looked over at Bole, who lay on his left side, motionless. Crawling on his knees, Pete moved towards his comrade. The area on the ground near Bole's face and under his head was soaked in blood which still oozed from his mouth.

"Hey, Bole! Bole buddy! Is you all right? It look like you got a good one on your head." He rolled Bole over on to his side. An empty guttural sound escaped his partly opened mouth. Bole remained motionless, his eyes half ajar. An ant struggled to escape from the curdling prison of blood on the side of his face. Bole was obviously dead.

The realization struck dread into Pete's heart. Full clarity returned to his mind. "I have to come up with a good story," he said to himself. "It will be my word against theirs. Perhaps they have already gone to Mudville to complain to Brude." Pete struggled to his feet. He staggered as a drunk man as he walked over to his steed which stood not far away. As he climbed on the animal, Pete wondered how long he had been unconscious on the ground. The rays of the sun pierced at an angle through the pine trees. "Musta been on the ground at least an hour," he thought.

Pete took one last look at Bole lying in the stillness of death on the pine needles, then bursting out of the bush he urged his steed on towards Mudville.

When Pete pushed the door and staggered into the office, Brude looked up from his desk and immediately saw the lump on the side of the deputy's head. Before he could open his mouth to inquire as to its cause, Pete blurted out, "Bole's dead. Got killed in an ambush set up by some niggers. I just barely escaped with ma life." He rubbed the back of his hand across his mouth as he spoke.

"Bole is what?" Brude asked.

"You heard me—dead, I said! He's dead. Them niggers set a trap for us, an' we walked right into it. I jus' barely escaped with ma life. I was lucky." He paused as if searching for words. "Musta been unconscious for an hour or so. When I came to, poor Bole was lyin' next to me dead."

Brude hoped that it was all a joke. But realizing the pattern of relationship between himself and Pete he knew it was not likely that Pete would make such jokes with him. Further, the lump on his head lent credence to his story.

Brude rose from where he sat and walked around the desk. Pete leaned against the wall next to the gun rack.

"Where did it happen, an' who were the niggers involved?" Brude inquired, turning his head sideways as he studied the deputy.

"They got us back there on River Trail. I don't; know who all the niggers was, but I recognized two of them. They was that boy of Mabel Wright who live next to the Yazoo, an' his sister. They use' his sister as bait to draw us in the woods. She said that her mule's foot was stuck in a hole. When we went into the woods to help, they jumped us."

Without further communication, Brude moved to the gun rack. He handed one rifle to Pete, took one for himself. Hennessee, more sober than usual, who from his seat by the window had listened to the communication between Brude and the deputy, rose and walked over to Brude.

"You don't need a gun," Brude said, "but you can come along with us." Brude mounted his chestnut and Hennessee his mule at the back of the office. By the time they rode around the building, Pete was already back on his steed. The three headed west out of town, around the rough dirt trail which emptied on to River Trail about three quarters of a mile away.

Brude could hardly believe that Mabel's children would be involved in this attack on his deputies. The few times he had come across them they seemed so respectful and well behaved. Tate, his predecessor, had always spoken of Mabel as "one of the most hard workin' black women in the county, with the most well brought up brood of children you ever seen." How could these children change so radically over a short period of time, to launch an attack against his deputies and kill one at that?

As they rode in silence, briefly his mind flashed back to that afternoon two years earlier, when he first saw Mabel's two girls standing on the verandah at Mabel's place. He remembered how the fair one had jolted him. Something about her had struck a chord deep within him. He recalled how strangely the girl had looked at him before sauntering back into the house. He had seen her a few times since, but from a distance, and had never sought to communicate with her.

Brude broke the silence. "Which one of the girls was involved?"

"The half white one. She is a real hell cat."

"Are you sure Bole's dead?"

"I'm sure," Pete responded. "When I came to he was already dead, blood running from his nose and mouth. I is jus' lucky they didn't finish me off."

"I didn't even realize you an' Bole were out of town," Brude commented dryly. "I thought you were over at Mr. Jason's place, which is where you said you were going."

"It was Bole's idea," Pete said. "He insisted he wanted to take a quick run down to the Yazoo. Said he jus' wanted to look at the ole river a while."

Brude did not reply, but he thought that the deputies had gone against regulation. When on duty, they were not to leave town without consulting with the sheriff.

"I wonder how they knew you were going to be down there," Brude asked.

"Don't ask me. But they was waitin' fer us in the pine woods."

＾ ＾ ＾

"There is something about all this that sounds fishy," Brude murmured to himself, looking at the back of Pete who now was leading the group towards the spot where Bole was last seen lying on the ground.

"You said you only saw two of them?" Brude inquired.

"That all I seen, but there coulda been more. I heard this noise like a thud, an' when I looked around Bole was fallin', an' this nigger had a club raised over my head. Before I could get my gun, he let me have it."

Brude remembered the experience of Tyson. Everyone thought he was dead, but he wasn't. Eagerly he hoped that the same would be the situation with Bole.

"This county is in for a lot of trouble," Brude mused, "whether that boy is dead or not. Once the League gets this and the politicians pick it up, it's going to be real hell in Mudville County." Urging his horse on, Brude caught up with Pete.

They had just come around a bend on River Trail, when they saw a horse drawn light wagon ahead of them. Brude immediately recognized that its driver was Mabel Wright and that her children were with her. The wagon had stopped beside a grassy field. All attention was focused on the field where a black boy was running. Brude was instantly aware that the boy was in pursuit of something. It was a light straw hat, which blown by the south wind, bumbled along just a few feet ahead of the boy. The boy bent down to grab it but it sprinted ahead, and he dashed after it.

"There he goes," Pete shouted, and before Brude realized what was happening, Pete's rifle bellowed, the sound reverberating through the woods. The boy who had been chasing the hat, uttered a sharp cry, straightened, staggered. He turned around facing the direction of the dirt road two hundred feet away where the wagon stood, his two hands clutching his throat. He pitched forward and lay motionless on the ground.

Pete cranked his rifle again, but before he could get off a second shot, Brude struck the rifle upward. The bullet went aimlessly through the air.

"What the hell you shot him for?" Brude demanded angrily, taken aback by the suddenness of Pete's action.

"What the hell I shot him fer?" Pete asked incredulously. "That's the nigger what kilt Bole an' left me fer dead."

"That still don't say why you shot him. I am sheriff and I saw him just like you."

"Dat nigger was escapin'," Pete said, gesticulating wildly. "Or don't that mean nothin' to you. He was escapin' jus' like that other nigger what few years back near kilt Tyson in his own shop."

Brude was so infuriated he had to contain himself from attacking his deputy. "That nigger wasn't escaping nowhere. He was just chasin' a hat. All of us saw it." Brude looked at Hennessee who nodded in agreement.

"I didn't seen no nigger chasin' no hat," Pete retorted. "All I seen was that nigger what kilt one of your deputies—he's dead in yonder bush—headin' fer the high timber when he seen us comin'."

As Brude spoke he hurried his chestnut across the field, followed by Andy Hennessee. Mabel, her two daughters and Billy were running screaming towards the boy lying on the ground. They reached the spot before the sheriff and his men. Mabel was frantically shaking Joshua, calling him by name. "Joshua! Joshua! Oh, my son." Sitting on the ground she pulled his head and the upper part of his body onto her lap. Brude dismounted and for moments stood over Mabel as if unsure as to what to do or say.

Pete, who had remained on the trail, was screaming after the sheriff. "Seems to me you is got more interest in that there murderin' nigger than in your own deputy who right now is lyin' dead in yonder woods."

Blood from the boy's body smeared Mabel's flowered dress. The two girls and their brother were crying hysterically. "Oh my God, my darling boy, don't die, please don't die. Come let's get him on the wagon," Mabel was saying. "We got to take him to a doctor."

Brude bent over the boy, his head still cradled in his mother's arms. Hennessee stood beside him. "He's dead, Ma'am," Brude said softly. "The doctor can't help him now. I'm sure sorry about this. I didn't give my deputy any order to shoot. He done it on his own. Said he thought the boy was tryin' to escape."

"He wasn't escapin' nowhere, Sheriff Brude," Mabel cried. "He was only chasin' after my straw hat what the wind blowed away. We was comin' to see you. Dat is where we was headin'. We was comin' to let you know how two of your deputies attack my daughter Samandra, tore up her clothes and raped her. My boy Joshua heard her scream, went to help her. Now you knows that ain't right. It ain't right for them to attack my daughter, an' do what they done to her. She is a nice, decent, well brung up girl. It's right inhuman and cruel what they done. An' now they kilt my boy too. All he done is try to defend his sister!"

This piece of information from Mabel justified the suspicion which Brude had felt over Pete's story of what had occurred. "I knew something was not right," Brude thought. He looked towards the trail where Pete, his horse cantering restlessly, had remained.

"Is you goin' to stand there fussing over a dead nigger, while one of your deputies is dead in the woods? Seems to me he is the one we should be interested in," Pete was saying.

"I's got to take my boy home," Mabel cried. "Help me get him on the wagon."

Brude, ignoring the rantings of Pete, turned to Hennessee. "Go get the wagon, Andy." Hennessee went to the trail. Holding the rein of the horse he led it across the field, the wagon bumping over the ground. Together they lifted the body and placed it onto the wagon. Sobs unabated, her children climbed into the wagon and knelt over their brother, while Mabel, almost blinded by her tears, and overwhelmed by what terrible fate had befallen her family within the space of a day, took the reins and led the animal with its cargo back onto the trail. Their wailing voices rose above the sounds of the wagon wheels and the crows in the massive oak nearby on the trail as they headed back towards their home on the Yazoo.

Brude and Hennessee stood and watched the wailing family, as the mule drawn wagon rolled northward on the trail with its cargo of death and sorrow. The straw hat which the boy had been seeking to retrieve still lay in the field. As Brude looked at it, a gust of wind pushed against it, and urged it in an aimless tumble towards the grass merged with the thicket at the edge of the field.

Brude climbed on his horse and followed by Hennessee moved from the field onto the trail where Pete still waited. "Ain't you goin' to arrest that nigger woman that baited me an' Bole into the woods to have us kilt?" Pete demanded angrily, his horse cantering and reeling as restless as its rider.

"I am the sheriff," Brude reminded him. "I will decide who and when any arrest is to be made. Now that boy you killed. It was outright murder, any how you look at it."

"Murder!" Pete twisted his face and squinted his eyes, slanting his head as if about to go into an epileptic spasm. "You call shooting that nigger who kilt Deputy Bole and near kilt me, an' was fixin' to escape, murder?" He looked from Brude to Hennessee and back to Brude, an expression of incredulity and utter surprise on his visage. "You tell that to a jury, tell that to Judge Killjoy, tell that to the League," he challenged tauntingly.

Brude maintained a quiescent calm, but inside he boiled like a cauldron. "It is clear that that yellow skunk has it all figured out," he mused. "I'll be damned if that girl isn't telling the truth when she says she was attacked by Bole and him."

"Where is Bole's body?" Brude demanded, ignoring Pete's ranting. Without answering, Pete turned his steed around and galloped down the road followed by Brude and Hennessee. They passed the wagon with the wailing woman and children and the body of the boy. His head in death was resting on the lap of his sister whose integrity he had defended at the price of his life.

Pete never looked at the body. He kept his gaze straight ahead, urging his steed.

By the time Brude and Hennessee caught up with Pete, they had arrived at the point on the trail not far from where Bole's body was last seen. Pete led the way. About three hundred feet off the trail, they came upon the body. Simultaneously they dismounted. The scent of blood had drawn droves of flies which in the still warm autumn weather were abundant.

"There he be," Pete pointed. "See fer yerself, he's dead." Pete struck his hat against his knees in anger. "Boy, I say, what a fool we was. We shoulda knowed them no-good niggers couldn't be trusted. An' there was me an' Bole tryin' to do them a favor. This is what we gets for it." He pointed to Bole's body, a look of disgust on his face.

Quietly Brude surveyed the body and the area around where it lay. There was a pair of woman's shoes. One lay near a pine tree not far away, the other only inches from the body. The body itself had a ghastly look. Its glossy eyes were partly open, coldly staring at the sky through the spreading pine branches. The partly open mouth was covered with flies; a few were trapped in the blood on the side of his face. Brude brushed his hat over the face to drive away the flies. They swarmed and returned. Brude noticed that Bole's trousers were unbuttoned, his belt unbuckled, and red pubic hairs were partly exposed. Brude looked at the open pants, then at Pete who stood nearby observing the examination of the body.

"You said you seen when he got that blow that sent him down?" Brude asked.

"I didn't see no blow. I heard it, and when I looked around, I seen him fallin'."

"That must a been a mighty blow to cause his pants to open the way it is," Brude commented dryly.

"Well, it sure nuf wasn't dat way when I left him a while back," Pete retorted. "Them two female shoes weren't there neither," he pointed to the shoes. "If you ask me, I'd say that them niggers returned to get rid of us an' when they seen only one body, they done this to give the wrong impression."

Brude remained silent. They placed the body on Bole's horse, which had faithfully stood by the dead rider. They tied the body to the saddle. Brude gave the rein of the horse to Hennessee, and still silent he climbed on to his horse, turned its head to River Trail and started on their way back to Mudville.

On the trail it was Pete who broke the silence. "When is we goin' to arrest that nigger woman what helped to kill Bole and near had me killed?"

Brude stopped his horse and glanced sideways towards Pete. "When you shot and killed her brother back there, they were on their way to my office to report that you an' Bole had raped the girl. Their mother says she was rescued from you two by her brother who you shot."

"That's the damnedest lie I ever heard," Pete said, piercing the sheriff with his beady eyes. "What in tarnation you think we is. Bole an' me will never do a thing like that. We will never mess with a nigger woman, much less tryin' to rape her. I say, you arrest that woman now! Me an' Hennessee can take the body back to Mudville."

"You don't ever tell me who to arrest or when!" Brude reminded him. "Maybe you are the one who really needs arresting."

"Oh, yeh!" Pete blurted, his eyes flashing. "Go ahead and arrest me! Go ahead!" The challenge was heavy with sarcasm. "Take me befo' a jury! Befo' Judge Killjoy. An' tell him I kilt a nigger who murdered a white man—an' a deputy at that. Let him hear that cock an' bull story about rape. Take it befo' a white jury an' see who they'll laugh out of town."

Brude did not respond to the jeering remarks. He and Hennessee continued the slow pace to Mudville with the body of Bole. Pete, his steed cantering in circles on the road, gesticulated with his right hand as he spoke. "You don't arrest that nigger," he warned, "leave her free after what she done an' see what will happen to her. Let this news spread across Mudville County, an' I can guarantee you she is goin' to be hanging from a tree with a rope around her neck befo' you can get a jury together." He flashed his hand under his chin in imitation of the lynch rope.

⌢ ⌢ ⌢

Slivers of lightning issuing from the formless mouth of dark and dismal summer storm clouds strike the delta pines, catching them on fire. Warm winds rushing up from the south over the Yazoo fan the spreading flames, urging them on, on an ever expanding front. Billows of smoke rush upward over the trees and across the countryside. By the middle of the day, the flames are advancing along a half-mile front.

Dirt farmers living ahead of the advancing flames smell the sultry smoke-filled air as they work in the fields, and looking up perceive black billows of smoke clouds rising in the distance. Immediately they know that the forest is on fire. Some talk of fighting the fire. "Let us fell some trees in its path," they say. "This may check the blaze." Others feel the roaring wind sucked by the inferno and see the bending trees around them. "Nothing will stop that there fire save the Almighty God," they declare, and taking their family and what household goods they can carry, they head for safety.

The hunter leaves his cabin on the bank of the winding creek whose crystal waters flow into the Yazoo. He looks up and sees the smoke rising in the distance. "The forest is sho nuf on fire," he says thoughtfully. "I reckon all kinds o' critters—possums, deer, coons,

bobcats and whatnots—goin' be headin' in dis direction shortly."
Entering his cabin, a look of satisfaction and expectation on his face, he takes his gun and a box of shells, and with his faithful mongrel trotting by his side, he heads out along the creek humming -the tune of "Dixie."

The prosperous cotton farmer, a safe distance away, looks from his spacious verandah to which he had retreated from the heat of the summer day. He sees the smoke, driven by the wind, drifting over his wide expanse of cotton. Taking his pipe from his mouth and shading his eyes with the palm of his right hand, he studies the horizon carefully. "The pine forest is ablaze!" he diagnoses. "It looks like the fire is headin' straight for them peckerwoods south of me. There is no way it can harm me, cause my land bordering the south is done plowed up. I bin' tryin' to buy out them dirt farmers for years. If the wind keep ablowin' as it is now, an' that fire front amovin', by evening I reckon it will burn them dirt farmers plumb out. Come tomorrow or the day after, an' I should be able to take up their notes at the bank, or buy them out for nothing,"

Such was the varied reaction, when news of the death of Deputy Miles and the shooting of Joshua Wright, like a bush fire blown by delta winds, spread across Mudville County.

By next morning it was being discussed among the women drawing early water from the town's well in Wrightsville, by sharecroppers and field hands working on the land across the county, by old white men sitting on the bench across from the courthouse in the town of Mudville. It was the topic of excited discussions all day long by the black men who came and went from their meeting place under the big mimosa tree in Babs Jacob's backyard. It was the topic of heated discussion among the group of men, all members of the League, gathered around the table behind Tyson's shop in Mudville. In the front room of Parson Jones' home, the issue was being prayerfully studied in low and troubled voices by a meeting of deacons, elders, and the preacher.

As the news spread it assumed various forms and shapes, eliciting a variety of responses ranging from fear and alarm to ecstasy. When the news of the death of Boles reached Tyson at his shop one block from the sheriff's office, he was momentarily spellbound. The right side of his face near his bad eye twitched and jumped uncontrollably. Then a fit of ecstasy seemed to sweep over him as he looked from one to another of the men around him.

"So ma prophecy is comin' true!" he declared, shaking his head in amazement, his eyes glaring. "I been sayin' this all along and ain't no one been listenin' to me. I been preachin' it up an' down this here county, that that Niggerville is breeding' the most dangerous kind a niggers the South ever seen. They don't only feel they is equal to white

- 292 -

folk, but they is ready to spill white blurd. See what is happenin'?" he lectured to the men gathered around him. "Dem Niggerville niggers is now spreadin' their ideas among niggers all over the county. White folks ain't safe in this here county no mo'." He continued shaking his head. "I say the time's come fer us, law or no law, to take matters in our own hands."

The men nodded in agreement. Not once during these first moments did Tyson utter a word of sorrow or grief over the demise of the deputy. What overwhelmed him was what he saw as the accuracy of his predictions.

Two main contenders for the local seat in the state legislature, Bilbo and Crane, had already selected the theme "threat of niggers" as their political platform. Bilbo was the first to get the news of the tragedy, which Tyson rushed to him. When the news reached him on his farm, like a ball player he grabbed it and made a dash for a political touchdown. He first paid a visit to the room where the dead deputy lay. To the restless group of men gathered outside, Jason announced as he left the room, the opening of a fund to help the widow of the "murdered hero."

He assured the men that he dedicated his life to the goal of seeing to it that "such acts of savagery 'gainst white folk will never happen again in Mudville County." Then Jason proceeded to criticize the incumbent Crane, who "through deception and money claim to represent the people of the county, but ain't done a single thing during his eight years in office to assure the protection of white folk in Mudville County." He then announced a political meeting for the evening after the funeral. The meeting was to be in the town square, across from the courthouse.

"Tomorrow night, following the funeral for our departed hero, a funeral I myself will pay for, we will have a rally in memory of Deputy Bole. We will see to it," he assured the restless men, "that those responsible will end up hanging from ropes."

Tyson had informed Bilbo that some of the men were ready to act. "Dey is as mad as hornets." Not wishing to bring to an abrupt and untimely end the tension, Bilbo cautioned against any acts of violence by the men.

"You keep control of the situation," he directed Tyson. "At the right time we will act." Secretly Bilbo desired the tension to persist for as long as possible, so he could ride on its crest to political success.

Snake-eyed Pete had become an instant hero to the League and its followers in the town of Mudville and the surrounding countryside. Eagerly he repeated and rehashed the incident to all those who would listen, adding a piece of drama here and a piece there. He was the lawman who had been through the attack and had lived to tell the story. Secretly a member of the League for more than two years, now he openly flaunted it. "Tyson was right all along," he confessed. He now saw a bond between himself and Tyson, a bond forged by common experience, of being attacked by a nigger, left for dead, and living to talk about it.

To Pete the incident had opened up for him a golden opportunity to become sheriff. Bitterly he recalled how Tate had slighted him in favor of Brude. Now was his moment of opportunity. He would sit back for the moment and let Brude project himself as a "nigger lover." He would drop it around how Brude refused to arrest the black woman and only did it on his insistence, and how Brude had threatened him for shooting the murderer of Bole, who was trying to escape up north. He was sure that when it all was over and the dust settled, the job of sheriff would be his for the taking.

A white farmer with four hundred acres of ripening cotton in the field walked across the county road to his neighbor, a fellow farmer whose holdings were even larger. He met him by the tool house where he had been overseeing a black helper repairing a plow. The two men sat down on a bench in the shade of a large chestnut tree.

"Heard 'bout that deputy an' that nigger boy?" he inquired.

"Yeh, I sure did. Ma son Jamie jus' returned from Mudville with the news. He says the place is like the night befo' election. He says you can almost light your pipe in the heat. I was jus' fixin' to pass the news on to you."

"I can see nothin' but trouble for all of us," the visiting farmer said. "I understand the League has already taken it up. You mark my word," he took his pipe from his pocket and knocked the bowl against his knee. "The way Bilbo and Crane competing for support right now, the way both of them's using this so called 'threat of niggers' to scare people into voting for them, you mark my word. Once they an' the League get their act together, you is goin' to see the greatest crusade ever launched in this county against black folks. A lot of innocent peoples, decent peoples, is goin' to suffer."

"You are right," his neighbor said, "That is jus' what I been thinking. A lot of decent black folk may be killed or driven by fear to leave the county an' head north. An' further, farmers like you an' me are goin' to face economic ruination. Who the hell is goin' to reap the crop? Look at that field," he pointed beyond where his old hound lay sleeping in the shade of a persimmon tree. "Jus' look at that field. I ain't seen a more promising crop of cotton in years. Now you tell me how we goin' to get that cotton out of the field"—he warmed rhetorically to his grievance—"when the League and stupid politicians done drive the niggers away. We've got to go an' let Sheriff Brude know that we expect him to maintain law 'n' order, an' keep the League from taking things in their own hands."

"Is not the League that is most dangerous," the other farmer added. "If you look at their members, they ain't nothing but trash, and their leader this here Jeb Tyson. You put his brains in a jaybird it'll fly backwards. Is them politicians. I seen them work in Alabama, in Tennessee, an' in other parts of Mississippi. They get the mob all riled up, an' as long as they get the votes, they jus' don't give a damn what happen to ordinary people like you an' me, much less niggers."

"We need to get a meeting of the farmers organization," his neighbor suggested. "If we can get a statement from the organization that we won't tolerate no lawlessness in the area, this just might help to ward off some of the trouble."

News of the shooting of Joshua Wright threw the black community into a state of great alarm. As the news came to them where they lived in the villages, towns, farms and rural places across the county, it was invariably of a different focus to that being dispersed at the same time among whites in the county. As told by Snake-eyed Pete and spread by the League, two deputies from the sheriff's office in the town of Muduille had been ambushed "by a band of renegade niggers" who used a woman as bait. One deputy was murdered and the other left for dead, "barely escaped with his life." The shooting of Joshua Wright was presented from the point of view that one of the attackers was shot and killed.

∧ ∧ ∧

In the black community the news centered on the attack on Samandra Wright. The story went that two deputies had lured Samandra into the woods—"a lovely, innocent, virgin chile"—and was in the process of raping her when her brother heard her scream and came to her. In the struggle to rescue his sister one of the deputies was killed by a blow. The other deputy returned a few minutes later with the sheriff and a posse and killed Joshua "in cold blood." In the body of information there were three items, each the cause for alarm. A black girl had been attacked and raped by two white lawmen, her brother trying to defend her was killed, and one of the lawmen was killed by the black man.

All of this descended upon a black community already under attack by the League in consort with two contenders in the state election, both using the "threat of niggers" as a political platform.

Ominous and pessimistic predictions were being made among blacks as to what lay in store for their community before the election fever was over. Talk of fleeing the South and "headin' north," already in the minds of some, now became a point of discussion as a popular alternative, especially among small black farmers and sharecroppers living scattered across the county.

To Parson Jones, the tragedy was an occasion that called for "prayer, fasting, and faith." He called upon his followers to be calm and to have faith in God, assuring them that "them what be for us is mo' than them who be against us."

Saturday, the day following the attack, was sunny and clear. Only scattered cotton white clouds drifted listlessly overhead here and there, their shadows moving slowly across the cotton fields. About three o'clock in the afternoon, two funerals were in session, one in the town of Wrightsville where Joshua Wright was being funeralized, and one in the town of Mudville where a white deputy was being interred.

∩ ∩ ∩

In Mudville, Deputy Bole Miles' funeral service was in process in the white Baptist church. The Pastor, Reverend Charles Bindle, dressed in a black suit and heavily starched white shirt with a priestly collar, white gloves on his hands, stood by the front door, a face as solemn and gray as the occasion, welcoming the visitors a handshake, a bow, and "Lawd bless you" was the most he whispered. Some thirty feet away from the east side entrance of the white steepled church, a newly dug grave, like a recently constructed edifice, awaited its silent occupant. Less than thirty feet away, but under the shade of the same oak tree, former sheriff Tate lay sleeping, a marble stone and a small red rose bush standing like sentinels above his head.

The funeral was such as had not been seen in Mudville in living memory. Even some of the old sages of the town declared that since the founding days "ain't such a funeral been seen." Yet there were others who disagreed. The seventy-two year old sister of the postmistress certified that the death of old Granddaddy Crane, a man of military background, had been a greater affair, bringing guests from as far as Jackson. In any case, most agreed that the funeral of Bole was indeed extraordinary.

Unlike Tate's funeral, it was an all white affair, even curious blacks having stayed away, motivated by considerations of safety. Members of the League from across the county, sympathizers, family friends, and others silently trooped in and filled the pews of the little church, with hundreds being forced, due to lack of space, to stand outside. The roads in front of the church and on the side land were lined with buggies, carriages, wagons, and buckboards.

News of the incident had reached Crane in Jackson by wire. Alarmed by the news that Bilbo was on the scene orchestrating the response, Crane headed for Mudville by the first train, arriving in town early Saturday morning. He was met at the station by his black coachman, who drove him immediately to the residence of the widow, Mrs. Lizzie Miles. He left some money with her—"to help wherever needed"—and offered to pay the funeral expenses, only to learn that Bilbo had already assumed that responsibility.

Outmaneuvered by Bilbo, Crane hastened over to the home of Reverend Bindle, his old friend and supporter, gave him "a little something" to defray any expenses caused to the church by the funeral, and was immediately invited by the Reverend to participate in the burial ceremony, including the reading of a passage of scripture. Crane accepted the offer graciously, requesting the preacher not to let it be known that he would be participating in the service, his reason being "because I do not want it to take on any political significance."

The church and the church yard were full of town and county folk seeking a last look at the "victim of the ambush," a victim unknown to many of them, but a participant in an incident which many saw as holding possibilities for present and future excitement. Brude, anticipating the possibility of trouble, had moved quickly to employ two new deputies, one being the son of former Sheriff Tate, who had recently returned home from service in the U.S. Army. Pete, seeing victory right around the corner, was already operating like a sheriff. Reluctant to accept directions from Brude, and feeling the strength of his growing popularity in the community, among his friends he spoke with the authority of the principal lawman.

෴

The burial sermon presented by Reverend Bindle was one embodying hope and hostility, love and fear. Looking down from the pulpit at the face of the dead man in the open coffin, Reverend Bindle described the deceased as "a Christian, a man who had dedicated his young life to the service of law and order in the land," and who in carrying out his responsibilities was "so cruelly cut down by the dark hands of murderers." He assured his audience that "Brother Bole" had carved a place for himself "in the mansions up yonder," by his goodness, faith, and devotion to the people he served in the county. He described those responsible for the death of Bole Miles as "the servants of the black hands of Satan" who from the days of Eden, "been trying to destroy them who serve and love the Lawd."

This short sermon was followed by eulogies from the two candidates for the state senate, as well as the mayor of Mudville. The mayor's statement was brief. He described Bole as "a boy who was so dedicated to his work, that he won a place in the hearts of every true citizen of Mudville."

Crane, who was appointed to read a passage of scripture, was determined to make whatever political mileage he could from the opportunity. His text was taken from the words of the Apostle Paul of having "fought a good fight and kept the faith." He assured his audience that Brother Bole had fought a good fight, had kept the faith and therefore there was laid up for him "a crown of glory up yonder." Closing the Bible, Crane warned his audience that there were troubled times ahead. "The issue being decided," he assured, "is whether or not white people, men, women, and children, can live in safety and follow their Lawd-given destiny without having to face the tragic end of Brother Bole. As your representative in the senate, I declare my commitment and I dedicate my life to you, to assure that you and your children will be able to live in peace and free from fear. When you look at Brother Bole lyin' there in this coffin, keep in mind," he reminded them, "that it could've been you, or it could've been me."

Crane looked over to where the mayor sat, not far from Bilbo. "I see others here with positions of leadership in the community, the mayor, I see Mr. Bilbo, who as you all know is seeking to enter a political career. I appeal to the mayor and to all others to join hands with me in a dedication to see to it that this kind of murder will never happen again."

Crane had turned his Bible reading into a political address and had so far stolen some of the thunder created by Bilbo, who now, suppressing his annoyance with his competitor, rose to make his eulogy. He too praised the "sterling and pristine" qualities of the "departed hero." He reminded his audience that he and Bole had "much in common." "We are both ordinary folk without wealth and power in our background. Both of us, our parents were poor folk who struggled all their lives just to put food on the table for their children, and we both have dedication to service for the community."

"Bole is a hero who has fallen in action," he declared, "but the battle ain't over yet." Then looking down steadfastly on the face of Bole lying there in the open coffin, and placing his right hand on his heart, he declared, "I promise you, Brother Bole, that those responsible for your death will receive their just reward. I promise you"—his voice quivered—"I will see to it that your life was not in vain." Then he announced, "Tonight in the town square at six-thirty, there will be a gathering of people. We will discuss some of what we will do in memory of Brother Bole."

⌢ ⌢ ⌢

Bole Miles, inconspicuous and unknown to both political contestants and to the vast majority of people now gathered in and around the church, had in the space of a day assumed the proportions of a hero, a martyr, and a saint. Mrs. Lizzie Miles, Bole's "little woman," sat in the center front pew directly across from the coffin. She listened to the praises and accolades being heaped upon the head of her departed husband of three years, and could hardly believe her ears. "This ain't my Bole they is talking 'bout," she mused. "After all the whiskey drinkin' an' chasin' of no-good women he done! After all, he had gotten worse since he became deputy an' started keepin company with Pete. He gamble his money, an' gave it away to bad women, an' all I had to do was open ma mouth an' he would let me have it up side ma head."

The tooth missing from Lizzie's lower jaw had been a bad tooth, but it was nonetheless knocked out by Bole during one of his drunken episodes when his wife sought to get some money from him to buy groceries. So much had she been abused by Bole that when Lizzie realized that he was gone forever, she had actually breathed a sigh of relief.

"But what is this happening now?" she was saying to herself. "Jus' listen to them words dey is sayln' about my Bole! I sure ain't never seen that good side of him, even when he use' to come acourtin', befo' we was married! He ain't ne'er been to church but once since we bin married! An' the cussin' an' swearin' he use' to do could frighten even the devil. But dem people who is sayin' all this good about Bole—the mayor, Mr. Crane, Mr. Bilbo, the Parson—them is edjacated people! Them is right respectable folk. I didn't knowed that Bole knowed all them uppity people! But listen to them! All them wonderful words they is sayin' about my Bole! Maybe Bole after all was a good man! Maybe he was really all dey is sayin' 'bout him! Maybe is me who is so stupid an' ignorant, that I ain't never recognize Bole's goodness, an' what a great man I really had. Now is too late, he done gone!" She whispered the last words and broke down and wept bitterly.

⌢ ⌢ ⌢

Joshua Wright was laid to rest in the cemetery behind the Baptist church in Wrightsville, only three graves away from where Mother Brown slept. The funeral was quiet and subdued. Mabel, Billy, and Sharon sat in the front pew. All were weeping bitterly. Mabel was being comforted by a deaconess while she in turn tried to comfort her children. She had tried desperately to hold back her tears, but still they flowed freely. Hardly listening to the sermon being preached by Parson Jones, Mabel thought how only one day earlier, she had seen her boy happily whistling as he worked beside the house. It was then that Mabel had suggested that he go to meet his sister, whom Mabel knew would be on her way home. She had watched him as he left the yard, and had seen him as he returned holding up his sister who had been abused by the two deputies. Now here he lay, dead. And Samandra, just yesterday morning, she had heard the child so happily talking about her plans to go off to school in September the following year to study to be a teacher.

"I'm excited about going away to school," she had been saying, "but to tell you the truth, Maw, I love this place on the Yazoo so much I don't know if I can ever leave it."

"It won't be for good," Mabel had replied, "an' when you finish studyin', if you don't meet an' marry some lucky man up there, you will be coming back to Mudville County. There is much you can do to help with the school." Mabel's tears fell faster as she remembered how Samandra's eyes would light up as she spoke about the future. A sweet, innocent child. Now just one day later, she was behind the bars of the county prison, not for a crime she had committed but the result of being the victim of so vicious an attack by two lawmen.

"How cruel and inhuman can life be?" Mabel pondered. "After all the pain and agony the child had suffered while yet an infant, the adult burden she was forced by fate to bear as a child. Just when it appeared that the flowing waters of the river of time had healed the wounds, more pain, more sorrow, more agony."

Samandra wanted so much to be at the funeral of her brother who had given his life in defending her. She wanted to be there to say good-bye, to kiss his forehead, to lay a few rose petals and drops of tears on his grave, to let her heart pour out its agony over him, to cry aloud his name, and let him know the depth of her sorrow, how she wished that it was she rather than he lying dead in the coffin.

But last evening Sheriff Brude had visited her home and almost apologetically told Mabel that Samandra was in grave danger. There was talk among members of the League of attacking the house, taking her by force, and lynching her. Brude told Mabel what Pete was saying with regards to how Bole met his death.

"I can swear before Lawd Almighty that it never happened that way. Parson Jones' wife will testify that she and Samandra were in Mudville, the post mistress Mrs. Prunedish, can also testify to that. Parson Jones' wife can further testify that Samandra had just returned with her from Mudville an' was walking home alone."

"You don't have to prove anything to me," Brude assured Mabel. "I believe that the girl is innocent. I believe that she was the victim of attack. Just the same," he explained to her, "a charge, a serious charge of murder, has been made by the deputy. Two persons are dead. There is got to be a trial. The news and rumors are already spreading across the county and everyone including politicians is becoming involved. Personally, I would prefer to leave her here until tomorrow so she could attend her brother's funeral, but if I did, by tomorrow she too may be dead, and other members of the family could also be in mortal danger." It was thus his duty, for her safety if for no other reason, to take her into custody.

Sheriff Brude assured Mabel that the girl would be perfectly safe. "No one will put a finger on her, and the deputy in question won't get near her at all." He had promised. It was with such promises and assurances that Brude and Hennessee had taken the girl away late the previous evening.

These thoughts and memories flowed through Mabel's mind as she sat there before the coffin that cradled the body of Joshua. As her mind returned to the church, Parson Jones was in the middle of his sermon. "His life has been one of a model 'mong us, young and old," he was saying. "At an early age he had already acquired the seriousness of a man. Joshua is gawn to heaven, cut down by the cruel, inhuman hands of injustice. He's gawn to heaven, but we of the Wrightsville church and community will always hear his clear voice, as it has sung in the youth choir, and the Wright quartet, as long as we shall live. To his loved ones left behind—and that includes all of us—let his life be an example, when we face danger, fear, or persecution; when it is necessary to stand for the right though the heavens may fall—let us remember the courage and fortitude of Joshua Wright.

"Let us all take comfort by the awareness that Joshua is gawn to a home in the sky, yes Lawd! I say, he had fought a good fight, yes Lawd! Joshua Wright has kept the faith. Henceforth, there is laid up a crown of righteousness in heaven for Joshua Wright, a crown which Gawd Almighty will put on his head."

∧∧∧

The death of Bole Miles and the shooting of Joshua Wright were the variables that shifted into high gear the election campaign across the county. With the burial of Bole, competition between the two candidates, Crane and Bilbo, intensified. All stops were opened as the two men blasted away at each other, struggling for the hearts and minds of the people, and the seat in the legislature. The League was now clearly split, with one group led by Tyson supporting Bilbo, and the other faction working for Crane.

Following Miles' funeral, Bilbo held a massive meeting at the square in Mudville. At the meeting he once again repeated his commitment to the people. Once more he called for the trial and immediate punishment of all those involved in the plot to kill the lawmen.

"There is more to this than meets the eye, I tell you. One of the attackers is dead, another is in prison, but the rest of them is right now out there free. Maybe," he suggested, "maybe even now as I is talking to y'all, the resta them is plottin' to carry out more attacks against white people. I ask you, who will be the next victim? You, your wife, your chillen? We want to know who they is an' we want them all tried for murder and hanged, so all can see them as a lesson and a warning to others."

After the meeting which lasted some two hours, Sheriff Brude requested a few words with Jason Bilbo. Both men drew aside from the crowd.

"I am not a politician," Brude confessed to Bilbo, "and I don't fully understand the ways of politics. My job as I see it is to keep law and order in the county. It isn't an easy job in normal times, much less with the death of Deputy Miles, the elections, and everything else. A lot of men here tonight are very riled up. All they need is some whiskey and some encouragement and I can assure you that a lot of innocent black folk will be either killed or burned out. I have two deputies, and I plan to get one more on a temporary basis, till all this is over.

"I have a woman here in jail," the Sheriff continued. "With people out here already talking about taking justice into their own hands, there is no telling what can happen.

"Now this morning and again this evening representatives of the Farmers Association came to me. They are worried over tension and fear being generated in the county, by the election as well as the recent killing, and there is great concern that it will drive blacks off the farms and cause economic disaster. They are saying that if black people start leaving, there will be no one to reap the cotton."

Bilbo listened attentively as Brude continued. "They are already blaming Crane, saying that he is riling up the League and he will be responsible for any unlawful action that takes place."

Jason Bilbo assured the Sheriff that he had no intentions of encouraging unlawful behavior or violence in the community, and would do all in his power to control the situation. As soon as the Sheriff departed, Bilbo walked over to Tyson who was surrounded by a group of his followers. He pulled Tyson aside. "Spread the news," he ordered. "Let it be known that there is to be no attacks against niggers for the present. Don't matter how angry people is. Let the process of law work. If an attack starts, the niggers will head north, the cotton will be left in the field, and the farmers will start blaming us and we could lose in the elections. Jeb, I am depending on you to keep things in control."

Tyson, under the euphoria of recognition of his influence with the people, assured Bilbo that he would 'keep the lid on things.' He then moved back over to his men who stood waiting for him.

^ ^ ^

Crane not to be outdone had planned his own political rally to be held at Crossroads on Monday evening. He would have preferred it on Sunday but knew well that desecrating the Lord's day would indeed not put him in good standing in the eyes of the religious faithful in the area. On Sunday, therefore, with his beautiful wife from New Orleans, Mrs. Florence Crane, he attended service at Reverend Bindle's Baptist Church in Mudville.

Bindle preached a sermon on the book of Revelation from the Bible, warning his members that the "end of all things is at hand."

"What we seen here in these last few days is a clear sign of the end of all things. It is the beginning of the rising of the powers of darkness across the land. Armageddon is a comin'!"

As the sermon started, Bilbo walked in and tiptoed up toward the front pew, where he sat not far from Mr. and Mrs. Crane. Neither man was known for his godliness or church going propensities in normal times. But these times were indeed abnormal. It was election time, a time when serious aspirants to political positions usually became church attendees.

After the service, Brude requested a meeting with Crane. Quietly he repeated to him much of what he had said to Bilbo the previous evening, including the complaint from the Farmers Association.

"As a farmer myself, I understand the problems of the farmers, and the concern of the association. After all," Crane said, "if there are no niggers around, my fields will also suffer. As a government official, I am of course for rule and order, and will use whatever power I have to encourage such."

Brude breathed a sigh of relief as he walked back to his office.

^ ^ ^

Samandra Wright had been in jail for two days. The charge laid against her was that of murder, chief witness being Deputy Pete Drake who had already produced a written statement describing how

Samandra had lured himself and Bole into the woods, how they had been subsequently attacked and Bole killed.

Though imprisoned, Samandra found it difficult to take the charge seriously, so ridiculous it seemed to her. "After all," she thought, "who in their right mind would believe such a claim?" It was the first time, the very first time in thirteen years, that Samandra Wright found herself sleeping away from home.

The jailhouse was not intended to accommodate women, yet Brude did as much as was possible to make life tolerable for Samandra. Mabel brought her food and comfort each day. Parson Jones visited her in prison on Saturday and after Church service on Sunday. He read the Bible to her, and preached an entire sermonette for her before leaving. Parson Jones assured Samandra that the case would bring all the facts to light and that she would be set free.

"Justice will be done," he declared. Yet even as the Parson spoke these words, deep within his heart, he questioned the grounds for his own optimism.

In spite of efforts to comfort and reassure her, Samandra remained in a partial state of shock during her first days of imprisonment. It was not the experience of being in jail, but the occurrences surrounding her imprisonment, so rapid, in such quick succession they occurred. Equal to the agony of the death of her brother was her inability to attend the funeral. These experiences had propelled her into an entirely new dimension of experiences for which no previous experience had even partially prepared her. The allegations directed against her by Pete were the least of her concerns at this time. How swiftly had the happiness of home, the contentment, the optimism of future plans, seemed to vanish. Now she could understand some of the things that her mother, Mabel, had been telling her over the years. How a black woman had to be morally and spiritually strong to survive, how she must be ready to bear great burdens. Now she could understand.

By Sunday night, Samandra began to feel a source of spiritual strength rising within her, and as it grew stronger, some of her stress and anxiety began to dissipate.

"Yes, my brother has died to save me," she mused. "What he did for me, I can never forget. I shall always love and cherish thoughts of him. I know that if there is a place called heaven, he will be there. If he has shown me anything, he has shown his love for me. He has shown me how to be strong, even unto death. I must now be strong. I must never weaken. I must behave so that all my family, my friends, the people, will be proud of me regardless of the outcome of this experience."

Thus, Samandra began to accept her incarceration with a calm dignity, self-confidence, and reconciliation,

Sheriff Brude determined that no harm would come to Samandra Wright while in prison. As part of his caution, he directed that Pete have absolutely nothing to do with the girl. "Don't ever let me catch you even talking to her," he warned him. "Stay clear of her cell." Pete on receiving these directions from the Sheriff, flew into a fit of rage, and would have resigned there and then, but he reasoned that that was exactly what Brude wanted. He therefore contented himself with nursing the wounds of humiliation, and bode his time.

⌃ ⌃ ⌃

Hennessee sat in front of the Sheriff's office on the same bench where one week earlier Pete and Bole had sat and hatched their plans for the attack on Samandra and Sharon. When Brude brought Samandra in, Hennessee had scrutinized her from the light of the lantern. He followed her into the office, and watched as she was booked and locked in the cell. On Saturday, somewhat more sober, he ran errands for Brude as he had done for Tate for several years. Usually Saturday was a time to get drunk and be happy, but now with the tension rising in Mudville and the surrounding area, with the spreading of rumors and ominous predictions about what was "fixin' to happen," he was trying his utmost to remain sober.

On Sunday evening after Parson Jones, Mabel, and Deacon Johnson had departed from the Sheriff's office following their visit to the jail, Brude came on to the verandah and sat beside Hennessee. He looked at the buggy and its passengers, driven by Parson Jones, as it rolled out of town on to the road leading to Wrightsville. Mabel had left her wagon and horse in Wrightsville and had traveled with Parson Jones on the Sunday visit. As the buggy disappeared from his view, Brude looked at Hennessee, who with his hat partly drawn over his face, appeared to be sleeping. Brude sighed heavily, leaned his head against the wall, and closed his eyes.

"I can hear the thunder roaring," he murmured. Then there was silence for several minutes.

Suddenly Hennessee spoke. He spoke without moving, and with the hat still partially covering his face. "Dat there woman ain't no nigger," he said calmly and casually. "She's jus' as white as you an' me."

Brude allowed a few seconds to pass before responding.

"I am not interested in your drunken philosophy," he informed him. "Next thing you will be sayin' is that there ain't no such thing as white and black folks."

Silence followed, and in the silence, Brude could hear the heavy breathing of Hennessee, who had clearly fallen asleep in the middle of the conversation. "Maybe," Brude mused, "the man spoke in a drunken sleep."

⌒⌒⌒

The next day, Monday, Pete was sent by Sheriff Brude on an errand to Four Corners. He was on official business. With Bole, his shadow, no longer around, Pete was glad to accept Hennessee's offer to accompany him on the three-mile run. As they rode, Pete took the opportunity to vent his spleen on the way he was being treated by Brude. Secretly he wished that the old man would take back to the Sheriff what he had to say, but then Pete knew that the old man was neither talkative nor the news carrying kind.

"Just imagine," Pete was saying, "I been workin' in the Sheriff's office goin' on eight years now. There ain't nothing about the office or no job in it that I don't know better than anybody else, or I can't do better than Brude. He wasn't even elected sheriff, he jus' got the job by luck when Tate died. Now he's tellin' me what I should an' shouldn't do. He pushin' me 'round like say I is some kinda nigger. But you wait. Jus' wait an' see! Ha! Jus' watch an' see what's goin' to happen round here. Yesterday he had the gall to tell me, 'have nothin' to do with that murderin' nigger woman in jail. Stay clear of her,' he says. 'I don't want you even talkin' to her.' On Friday he accused me of shooting that nigger who killed Bole, he called me a murderer an' now he is restrictin' who I can talk to! Ha! That bastard is pushin' me. Let him keep it up."

Hennessee listened without interruption. Then he spoke. "That woman what Brude gets in jail, ain't no more nigger than you or me is," he said, ignoring all of Pete's complaints.

Pete, who had thought that the old man was about to comment on his condition and his problems with Brude, was aggravated by Hennessee's change of the topic of conversation.

"I knowed whiskey was goin' to dry out your brains sooner or later," he said. "I is talkin' 'bout how that bastard been pushin' me around, an' you is tellin' me that the woman ain't no nigger. She is got white skin but she is as nigger as the rest of 'em. One o' these days when you ain't drunk, take a train an' go to Soso, Mississippi, it's fulla niggers like that one. The fact is that kinda nigger is worser than the others, since it is difficult to tell what they is. If you been livin' in Mississippi all your days an' you can't recognize a nigger when you see one, you is really in trouble."

Hennessee listened in silence to the deputy, many thoughts flowing through his mind, but he did not verbalize them. He had been suspicious about Pete's story of what had occurred on Friday from the very beginning. His observations at the site of the attack increased his suspicions. Somehow he felt that he knew Pete, perhaps more than the man knew himself. Here was a reckless fellow who would go to any length in pursuit of his interests.

In a way he felt sorry for the man, so weak in character, so eaten up with hostility for Brude and jealousy over his position. "Just as he was with Tate," Hennessee thought, "even playing with the League, hoping to advance hisself. All the same, he is not different from the rest of them—Crane, Bilbo, they are all trying to use the League."

Hennessee looked at Pete as he spoke on the matter of the woman. "You say I is in trouble? Ha!" Hennessee answered. "I ain't in no trouble. You an' Brude is in trouble, 'cause none o' you can recognize a white woman when you see one. I say that there woman ain't no nigger."

"An' I say you is a bigger drunken fool than I thought you was," Pete replied, placing his steed in the gallop, with Hennessee's reluctant mule following.

SIX

THE TRIAL

The trial of Samandra Wright on the charge of participating in the murder of Deputy Bole Miles was to have started on Monday, a week and three days following the incident. It was, however, delayed until Friday due to the absence of Judge Marcus Killjoy who was to preside over the case.

With the killing of Joshua and the arrest of Samandra, Mabel, overwhelmed by the trauma of the double tragedy, had also to struggle with the task of obtaining a lawyer to defend her daughter. But who could she get? The way things were in Mudville County, which white lawyer—and they all were white—would jeopardize his profession and possibly his life to defend her child?

As friends and church members visited her to express sympathy and lend support, many gave suggestions as to which lawyer might be ready to defend the girl. During a visit by Parson Jones and a few church members, the question of a lawyer for Samandra came up. Trying to be helpful, Deacon Johnson gave an opinion on the issue. "If I was you, Mabel, I would try to get Samandra a lawyer from up North. I hear say, you can trust them mo', even if they is all white."

"Oh, no! No!" Parson Jones responded. "A Yankee lawyer? That would be the worst thing you can ever do. You bring a Yankee lawyer down here to defend the child, seeing how white folk in the South hate Yankees, and that child will be done tried and convicted befo' the trial begin in court. The best lawyer that you can get to defend her," he added, "is Lawyer McDougal, the school teacher from Sandy Mountain who eight years back ran for politics and tried hard to convince the ordinary white people that whites an' blacks should work together. In him you will have a reliable defender of Samandra's innocence." That very day, efforts were initiated to obtain the services of McDougal.

Samandra's trial took place in the Mudville courthouse. It was a pre-Civil War structure constructed by slaves, under a builder, himself a slave on the Crane's farm. It was a white two-story building of colonial design, supported in the front by four tall white columns. Old man Crane, the grandfather of the present legislator, had trained some of his slaves in the technology of masonry, carpentry, building, and engineering, and had developed a lucrative trade of hiring them out to the city, county, or whomever was ready to pay for their services.

The week before the trial, contact was made with Attorney McDougal, who had already heard about the case. He decided to accept the challenge. He visited Mabel's home where he spoke to the mother at length. He visited the prison and had several sessions of discussions with Samandra, going over the details of her story of what had occurred. McDougal visited the scene of the attack, spoke to Sheriff Brude, Hennessee, and Pete, as well as the prosecuting attorney. The information gathered from these sources was to form the basis for his defense of Samandra.

⌃ ⌃ ⌃

The prosecuting attorney whom the defense lawyer McDougal would be facing in court, was a man part preacher part lawyer seasoned in the art of southern legal processes, and a psychologist of no mean stature. His name was Bacchus Ebenezer Pierce, a name he carried with pride, claiming that the first Pierce, Ebenezer by name, was among the original settlers of the Virginia colony. Pierce never explained what fate had brought him to the town of Mudville.

Pierce was known as a speaker who could rile his listeners up to any level of frenzy he desired. He boasted on one occasion that not even the Baptist preacher got as many "Amens" on Sundays as he did in court "when I put myself to it."

Pierce was also a man of political aspirations. Secretly he aspired to the highest political position of the state, and had laid long-range plans for its achievement. First, he would enter the legislature, and use that position as a springboard to the governor's mansion. To Pierce, the trial of this case, with all of its implications, was exactly the opportunity he sought.

Judge Marcus Killjoy was to preside over the court. He and Pierce had operated in the same court for several years. Though amiable friends, there were some hidden agendas between them. Secretly Killjoy envied Pierce, not for his position as attorney, but for his talents and sagacity before the bar. The man was so cogent and valuable a speaker, he had the ability to overwhelm his listeners. On occasion Killjoy had seen him cause members of the jury to burst into tears. He had seen him take cases which in terms of existing evidence seemed impossible to win, and turn the evidence around. He had seen him on one occasion make an accused acknowledge his guilt, when it was clear to the judge and the jury that the man was innocent. There were times when as Pierce presented his closing arguments even Killjoy had to contain himself from saying "Amen."

Now as the town attorney, Pierce had become even more flamboyant in his presentations. Killjoy's compensation was in the authority he wielded in the courtroom. There he drove home to Pierce whenever it was necessary that he was in charge. He was a man of small stature, frail body, and sharp forehead, with intelligent penetrating eyes. Though occasionally given to flair, he usually behaved with the dignity of his office.

Judge Killjoy had no political ambitions. He was quite contented with the power he carried in the community, and had been heard to mention at least on one occasion his preference for being "a large fish in a small lake, than a sprat in the ocean." All he desired, so he claimed, was to be able to maintain his course "with sails untrimmed," and woe betide anyone who should endeavor or even give the impression of endeavoring to trim his sails in the court by challenging his authority.

Lawyers who had handled cases in Killjoy's court knew, often from personal experience, that the best way to lose a case or end up in jail was to challenge Killjoy's authority. Two years earlier, when the son of a wealthy farmer was being tried for stealing an expensive racehorse from a neighboring farm and selling it out of state, his daddy hired a lawyer from Jackson. The man, well known in the capital city, came to Mudville and thought, with big city experience, "to show the country folk how to handle a case." He ran smack into Judge Killjoy. During the first ten minutes of the case, the attorney made a statement which appeared to Killjoy as a challenge to his authority.

"Are you questioning my authority?" Killjoy inquired of the lawyer, in a voice of fearsome humility.

Sticking his thumbs into his vest pockets and rocking back on his heels, the man had replied, "I am not questioning your authority, your honor, I am questioning the wisdom and legality of your decision."

As the court listened, enjoying the exchange between the two men, Killjoy ordered the lawyer jailed for twenty-four hours, during which period the case was postponed. Next day the lawyer returned to court, apologized to the judge for his "precipitous response," and proceeded to win the case.

The attitude of blacks in the county to Judge Killjoy was ambivalent. Some who had stood before him in court claimed that he usually tried to be fair, "but God help you if the charges 'gainst you involve a white woman." Others called Killjoy "the hanging judge," a name he brought with him from another county where he had worked previously. Legend had it that Killjoy had "sent to the rope" more black men than any other judge "this side of the Yazoo" when he worked in Bigham County. Yet an objective evaluation of Killjoy's history showed no such propensity. In fact, it appeared that the judge had been equally hard on the necks of whites and blacks through the years.

In any case, such legends are hard to die, and in times of stress and anxiety such as now were faced by the black community, their credibility tended to increase, so that many people were saying, "Samandra Wright don't have a ghost of a chance before Killjoy."

Killjoy himself was the son of a farmer, who though not wealthy had a comfortable living. The old man had had enough slaves to work his plantation. As a child Marcus had grown up with blacks around him, and had been for a while even breastfed by a black maid. While yet a young man, he had drawn from his own empirical observations that the black folk on the plantation were just as innately intelligent as white people. This he had verbalized to his father on more than one occasion, and as an issue, it had become a point of contention between them. In spite of his insight, Marcus was keenly aware of the traditions, folkways, and mores of the south, and showed no propensity as a judge to challenge or alter them.

In preparing his case, Attorney Pierce had visited Samandra in jail, and offered to be lenient if she would reveal the others who were involved in the plot that ended in the murder of Bole Miles. Samandra's response was the assurance that there was no plot, rather she was attacked by the deputies.

"You don't really expect the court to believe that, do you, chile?" he asked.

"Whether they believe it or not, that's the truth," Samandra replied.

Pierce directed Brude to question Sharon and Billy with regards to their whereabouts at the time of the attack. This he did and passed the information on to the attorney.

Efforts on the part of Pierce to tie Sharon and Billy to the "Friday Incident" created further terror in the heart of Mabel Wright. She related to Parson Jones what had transpired, as well as the fear that such efforts to connect her two children with the incident could only increase the danger to their safety. The parson agreed with her and suggested that it would be wise to keep them "out of sight" for the time being. If Pierce insisted on trying to tie the children to the attack, then their lives could be in real danger.

Already alarmed by this new development, Mabel called Sharon and Billy together. Without going into all the details of the situation as she perceived it, she suggested that they go up North for a few weeks until the situation became more settled.

"How can you suggest this, Ma?" they inquired. "We want to stay here and be near Samandra during the trial. We want to be with you, and we are ready to stand in court and testify for Samandra if we have to."

By Tuesday evening, threats were being made openly against the children. After sunset a group of men with torches appeared on River Trail in front of Mabel's house. "Send your boy and your girl out," they demanded. "We wants to talk to them."

Mabel's response was to fire a blast from her gun into the air.

"You can't hide them forever," the voices called out from the darkness. "We know they is part of the plot what killed Bole and we aim to get them sooner or later." Mabel remained awake all night. The next morning she reported the incident to Sheriff Brude. Brude immediately went over to Tyson's place and warned him not to take matters in his hands. Tyson himself had warned his men to do nothing on the issue without his directions, but in the aftermath of a political rally, and the search for excitement, a few had taken it upon themselves to move against Mabel's children.

The following day during her visit to Samandra, Mabel related to her what had occurred.

"Ma, it's dangerous for them to stay here," Samandra replied. "Joshua is dead. And I am being tried for murder. That is enough for you to bear. Please send them somewhere out of the county. Their staying will make no difference in the case; on the other hand during the next few days I may be safer in prison than they will be at home."

Sharon and Billy resisted, but under the urging of Samandra and the pleading of their mother, they finally agreed. It was thus decided that they should travel to Chicago, and remain with an aunt, the sister of Mabel, until after the case. The very next day Sharon and Billy kissed their sister, weeping on her shoulders as they said "Good-bye" and boarded the train for Chicago. They would never see Samandra again.

That evening as her children waited outside the Sheriff's office, Mabel informed Brude that because of her concern for the safety of the children, she had decided to send them up north, until after the case. "Their life is being threatened, and I can't keep them in the house all day, or guard them with a gun. If you tell me 'don't take them out of town' I will keep them here, otherwise I am sendin' them away."

"As far as I am concerned," Brude replied, "no charge has been made against them. You are therefore free to do with them as you will."

⌒ ⌒ ⌒

There was a state of expectation in and around the courthouse. Long before eight in the morning when the court would begin, a crowd had already gathered outside on the road before the courthouse and on the steps leading up to the building.

The first recognizable groups were competing factions of the League. Those supporting Bilbo were the first to gather, followed by the supporters of Crane. Each group had placards calling for justice and demanding that the murderers be hanged.

By the time the wheels of justice began to turn inside, the court was filled to capacity, with an even larger crowd of mostly men in front of the building and jamming the road, making it difficult for coaches and carriages to pass. Aside from the hiring of the son of Sheriff Tate, Brude had employed on a temporary basis two other deputies, thus making, along with himself, a total of five persons, excluding Hennessee who was available for duty during the trial. Hennessee sober as a judge was given the non-paying position of Associate Deputy, and was assigned to keep an eye on the office where there was now another prisoner awaiting trial.

Today the four deputies were to be on duty. Brude would be in the courthouse with Pete. He preferred this arrangement, rather than having Pete outside with the unpredictable crowd. Young Tate and two other deputies would patrol the crowd outside the courtroom, while Brude would circulate as the occasion necessitated.

Towards the front of the courtroom, sitting behind two small tables, one in the center and the other towards the far right, were the two attorneys, Pierce and McDougal. On a row of chairs immediately behind McDougal were Mabel Wright, and beside her sat Parson and Mrs. Jones. Behind them were rows of white spectators, with their black counterparts seated towards the rear.

McDougal sat alone, quietly shifting through paper in a folder on the table.

Pierce who also sat alone had risen and walked over to the wall where Pete stood, and spoken to him briefly.

On the left side of the courthouse, seated on two rows of chairs were the jurors, all male and all white. A low murmur filled the courtroom.

In due time, Judge Killjoy appeared through a door which led from his chambers to the right front of the courtroom, a short distance from his bench. His entrance was something to see and enjoy by those who came for excitement, and to engender awe in others. As the door creaked open and the judge appeared, instant silence prevailed. Before the bailiff could say "All rise," people were already standing. With formal proclamation of the opening of court made by the bailiff, the court was turned over to Judge Killjoy, who from his moment of entrance had acted as if he alone were in the court, totally ignoring the expectant crowd. The jury sat unsmiling and waiting.

Shortly the attention of all turned to a side door at the left of the building, for through it had entered Sheriff Brude leading Samandra Wright. She wore a light cream dress with lace around her neck; her hair, slightly ruffled, fell over her shoulders. Her face was rather pale from her incarceration. She seemed remarkably confident and tranquil as she walked over to McDougal's table. The attorney stood as she approached, and remained standing until she sat on the chair beside him.

Killjoy looked down at the two men seated behind the lawyers' tables in front of the room. He observed that Pierce, generally dressed in informal attire, today wore a black suit, with white shirt and a vest. It was clear to him that Pierce considered this a special occasion and a special case. He could expect some of the courtroom pulpiteering for which Pierce was well known.

Killjoy cleared his throat. "Now before we proceed with the deliberations for this case, I want to remind all that this ain't no church, it ain't no revival. I therefore don't want to hear no "Amens" or see no falling out, or catching no spirit. And I don't want nobody," Killjoy paused, looked at Pierce and then at McDougal, "not nobody to forget who is the final authority here. This is a court of law. This we will not forget."

"Now," he continued, "I recognize that sometimes in court people forget themselves, and become louder than they're supposed to be. But when I strike this here gavel on this desk, I am going to strike it once and if any party or parties, white or colored, persist in disturbance, I'll have them cleared from the court." Killjoy who usually spoke as correctly as an English grammar school master, occasionally would recourse to a form of local dialect if he desired to get a point home in court.

Pierce took much of what the judge had said as particularly directed at him. It was a sort of pre-trial slap, and a ceremonial assertion of the judge's authority. Though he realized the town was in his corner, he would have to be careful not to annoy the judge during the trial.

Pierce began with an introductory statement to the court. Looking directly at the jury he informed them that the task before them would be an easy one "because this case is cut an' dried. It is the case of a cruel and devilish plot developed in the dark minds of heathens, to kill, to murder, a man who was simply doing his job—often a thankless one—of upholding the law. Today, that man lies in a cold, silent grave, below the sod. His companion who miraculously escaped with his life is here, and will testify before you.

"When you have heard the evidence presented against Samandra Wright in this case, there is only one verdict that you, the sober, Christian citizens of this county and this sovereign state of Mississippi will give—guilty."

When Pierce sat down Judge Killjoy looked at McDougal and nodded. McDougal rose and moved a few feet away from his table. "Your honor and members of the jury," he began, "today you will be listening to the story of a woman before you, who is being accused of murder. By the time all the evidence shall have been presented, I know that you will conclude, as I already have due to the evidence before me, that this woman is innocent of murder and in fact was the victim of cruel aggression.

"Members of the jury, I know that you will be sitting in judgment in a county, in a town, which today and during this trial will be full of tension and perhaps full of hate, but I have faith and confidence in you, my fellow citizens, that you will listen and judge this case on the merit of the facts presented, and will not be distracted by those who are trying through emotional appeals to persuade you in the absence of objective evidence. I thank you."

⌢ ⌢ ⌢

The first witness to be called to the chair was Snake-eyed Pete. At the direction of the bailiff, Pete raised his right hand, placing the other on the Bible.

"Do you swear to tell the whole truth and nothing but der truth?"

"Ah do!" Pete replied.

Pierce proceeded to question him. "How long have you been a law enforcement officer in this town, Deputy Peter Drake?"

"Eight years an' some months."

"Do you have a wife and family?"

"No, sir."

"Do you recognize yourself to be a Christian?"

"Yes, sir. I go to church."

"Very good." Pierce nodded his head. "These questions I have raised, so that the court may get an overall picture of the man who is about to testify under oath." Pierce was looking at Pete as he made the comment, but it was intended for the jury.

"Deputy Drake, I would like you to tell this court in your own way, what happened on the afternoon of Friday, the twentieth of September, that led to the death of Deputy Bole Miles and the injury of yourself."

"Well," Drake began, clearing his throat and rubbing the back of his hand nervously across his mouth. "Me an' Deputy Bole Miles was riding on River Trail on that afternoon. We was goin' down to Yazoo. We was, I reckon, two and a half miles from Mudville when we came round a bend on the trail, and we seen this colored woman. She was jus' standin' there lookin' up an' down the road, like say she was lookin' for somebody. Soon as we gets near to her she says, `scuse me, Mr. Sheriff, can you help me with my mule, he's done went an' got his foot caught in a hole, an' I can't get it out. I reckon it must broke.'

"Well, me an' Bole get off our horse an' we follow the woman into the woods, thinkin' she was leadin' us to the mule. I was walkin' behind the girl when all of a sudden I hear a sound like a club hitting on something. When I look round I seen Bole fallin' an' this nigger with a club raised over my head, and befo' I could reach for my gun, he let me have it up side ma head. An' that was the last thing I knowed till I come to."

"What happened when you came to?" Pierce inquired.

"When I came to, first I didn't know where I was. Then I remembered what happened. I looked over a few feet away and I seen Bole. He was lyin' there real quiet. I figure he was knocked out jus' like I was. So I creeps over to where he was, I was still too weak to stand up— an' I shook him. I says, Bole? Hey, buddy! Bole? It is then I notice blurd was comin' from his nose and mouth an' he was dead."

"What did you do after that?"

"I got on the horse and rode back to Mudville where I reported what happened to Sheriff Brude."

"Do you see that woman who told you the story of the mule's foot caught in a hole, and who led you into the woods to the ambush?"

"Yes, sir. I sure does. That is she over there." Pete pointed to Samandra Wright. Pete looked at the woman momentarily. As his eyes caught hers he turned his head towards the jury.

"Let the court note," Pierce cried, "that the deputy is pointing at Samandra Wright."

Pierce paced two steps in the direction of the jury, then turned again towards the deputy. "Did you recognize the other party, the nigger who delivered the blow that killed Deputy Bole and also attacked you?"

"Yes, sir, I sure did. When I looked round I seen his face. He had the fiercest and cruelest look I ever seen. It was the brother of the woman. I seen them both together in Mudville befo'."

"Did you see that boy subsequently?"

"Did I see what?" Pete asked.

"Did you see him after the attack?"

"Yes, I did. Me an' Sheriff Brude an' Mr. Hennessee was on our way to the scene of the ambush to recover Bole's body. We ran into the nigger an' when he seen us, he headed for the woods. I took a shot at him 'cause I meant to stop him, an' he got himself killed."

"I may want to question Deputy Pete further at another point in the trial. For the moment, no further questions." Respectfully, he looked at the judge then the jury before returning to his seat behind the table.

Judge Killjoy looked over at McDougal, and nodded slightly. "Attorney for the defense?" he said quietly.

McDougal rose and took a last look at the brown paper folder open on the table before him. He approached the deputy, still seated on the witness chair.

"Deputy Drake, you said that you and your assistant, Deputy Bole Miles, were on your way to the Yazoo when the incident occurred on Friday the twentieth of September. Were you both fishing?"

"No sir. We was jus' goin' down to see the Yazoo. Bole said he ain't seen the river for a long time, he jus' wanted to go down there an' look 'round."

"The closest point of Yazoo to the town of Mudville was about half mile back along the trail. There is a dirt path leading from River Trail to the Yazoo. Why did you not take that road rather than go half a mile further down the trail?"

"We was jus' ridin' an' talking; an' we jus' didn't give no thought that we could get to Yazoo quicker."

"You said you were following the girl into the woods when you heard a noise and looked back. Then you saw that black man with a stick. Are you trying to tell this court that a boy, a teenager with a piece of stick, attacks two deputies each armed with a gun, just jumps them and overcomes both, before even one could draw his weapon?"

"I is only sayin' what happen as I recall it."

"Are you trying to get this court to believe that a young man and his sister, neither ever having problems with the law, plotted to carry out an attack against the officers with only a piece of stick?" McDougal turned and looked at the jury, then back to Drake.

"Tell me, Deputy Drake," McDougal continued, "prior to this incident, when last were you in that section of the county?"

"I reckon about two months back I passed in that area."

"So you do not go into that area on a regular basis?"

"Nope."

"Then how come they knew you an' Bole Miles were going to be at that point so that they could plot and set up an ambush for you? You told the court that you and Bole just decided to go down there. You did not plan in advance. You did not announce that you were to be in the area. How did they know you were going to be there to set up an ambush?"

"You'll have to ask them that," Pete replied, pointing at Samandra. "I don't know, but that's exactly what they done."

"This is all for now," McDougal said, looking into the eyes of the witness, "but I will be questioning the deputy again later."

As McDougal walked back to his table, Pierce was saying, "I have no questions for the moment." Pete rose and walked back to the left side of the courtroom where he had been standing on duty.

The next witness called to the stand by Pierce was Sheriff Billy Brude. Brude went into great details describing to the court the events of that Friday afternoon some two weeks earlier. Pete stumbled into the office on the Friday afternoon, a big lump on the side of his head, and announced that Bole Miles had been killed. Along with Pete Drake and Hennessee, he set out for the site of the attack. On their way as they traveled on River Trail, they encountered a wagon carrying three black women. The cart had stopped on the trail and a black boy was running across the field after a straw hat that was being blown by the wind. Peter Drake took a shot at the boy, killing him instantly. Pierce ignored the information on the shooting of the boy.

"When you arrived at the scene of the ambush, what was the situation there?"

"Well, there was Deputy Bole Miles lying on his back on the ground; he was obviously dead."

"What do you mean, obviously dead?"

"His eyes were partly open, staring cold. His mouth was full of blood and he was dead."

"Go on," Pierce urged.

"We picked him up and placed his body across his horse and took him back to town. Later on, I went back into the area and took custody of a black woman who Deputy Drake had identified as the one involved in the attack."

"Is there anything else that you would like to add?" Pierce inquired.

"Not unless you have specific questions you want to ask."

"No further questions," Pierce said, returning to his seat.

McDougal was on his feet before Pierce was fully seated. He commenced to address the sheriff even as he moved from his table towards the witness chair.

"Sheriff Brude," he said, an element of deference in his voice, "I would like to go over with you parts of the account you have just given to this court with regards to the occurrences of Friday evening of September twentieth of this year. Was there anything particular about the body on the scene of the accident that has not been mentioned?"

"Yes, sir." When Brude said, "Yes, sir," Pierce stiffened his back and leaned forward attentively.

"Could you describe them to the court?"

"I found a pair of woman's shoes."

"Are the shoes in court?"

"No, sir, but I'll get them. They are still in my office."

"Did you not consider that to be important evidence?" McDougal asked.

"In my written report of the incident, I mentioned all that I saw. Both you and the attorney for the defense have read my report. It is my responsibility to present a particular article in the court if one of you asks for it."

"Have you determined who was the owner of that pair of shoes?"

"Samandra Wright claimed the shoes as hers," Brude explained.

"Did she give any explanation as to how the shoes got there?"

"She said that the shoes came off her feet when she was being attacked by Deputies Drake and Miles."

"From your report, you stated that Deputy Miles' trousers were unbuttoned. Could you explain this further to the court?"

"There ain't nothing else to explain," Brude said. "His trousers were unbuttoned."

"To what extent?" McDougal asked.

"The entire front was open and his belt was unbuckled."

The court, which had fallen into dead silence as the issue of the unbuttoned trousers arose, now broke into a confused murmur. Killjoy struck the desk with his gavel. "Silence!"

"Would you have any idea or opinion as to how his pants became unbuttoned?" McDougal pressed the sheriff.

Pierce sprang to his feet. "I object. I object," he cried. "The sheriff ain't supposed to express opinions, only facts."

"Objection sustained," Killjoy ruled.

McDougal turned and walked towards his table, then turned around. "I have no further questions for the sheriff at this moment, but later on there are some issues I plan to explore with him."

Pierce rose from his chair but did not move from behind the table. "Sheriff Brude, there ain't no way you can tell how those pants became unbuttoned, can you?"

"The woman, I mean Samandra Wright, told me—"

"I am not asking you what nobody told you. I am referring to facts that you know. His pants could have been done like that by someone after he was dead, couldn't it?"

"As you said, sir, I just don't know and ain't supposed to express opinions," Brude said.

Pierce sat down. Brude rose and returned to his post by the front entrance of the courtroom.

Pierce could call the accused to the stand, but the prosecuting attorney's plan of action called for no such thing. From here onward Pierce would lie back, let McDougal call witnesses, and demolish them. Pierce turned to the Judge. "I have no further witnesses, your honor." Then sitting back, he looked over at McDougal.

"I call Samandra Wright to the stand," McDougal said. Courteously, he moved back the chair to assist her as she stood. Samandra looked stunningly beautiful as she stood before the witness chair, swearing to speak the whole truth and nothing but the truth. McDougal's voice was soft and reassuring as he spoke to the woman. "Are you Samandra Wright?"

"Yes, sir."

"Miss Wright, do you understand the charges that are being brought against you?"

"Yes, sir, I do."

"Samandra, I want you to tell the court exactly what happened on Friday afternoon the twentieth of September."

"Well," the girl began, "My mother had given me a dress that she made to take to Miss Prichard in Mudville. I was to take it after school. So after school was out in Wrightsville, I rode to Mudville with Mrs. Jones in her coach. I delivered the dress and rode back to Wrightsville with Mrs. Jones. I was going to walk from Wrightsville to River Trail where we live, but Mr. Brown, who lives between Wrightsville and River Trail, gave me a ride on his cart from Wrightsville to his house which is about half way to River Trail. From Mr. Brown's place, I walked the rest of the way."

"Go on," the attorney encouraged her.

"I just got on River Trail, about five minutes earlier, and had turned right on the trail. I was not more than ten minutes from home when I came around a bend on the road, and there not far up 'head of me was a white man. I recognized him as one of the men who worked in the sheriff's office."

"Do you see that man in court today?" McDougal inquired.

"Yes sir, there he is," she said, pointing to Snake-eyed Pete who stood against the wall, his hands behind his back and legs slightly spread apart.

"Go on," McDougal said once more.

"When I got near to him, it looked as if he was talking to somebody. He was looking towards the woods and talking. Then I heard him say, 'Can't imagine whose gray mule that is. It went an' got its leg stuck in a hole. Seems to me that leg is broke.' Then he looks at me and says, 'Would you know who this gray mule belongs to? It caught his leg in a hole an' it looks broke to me! Why not come an' see if it's your mule?' So I followed him into the woods. We walked a little bit away from the road, then I saw the other man, the other deputy. He jus' came out from behind some trees. Then I say: 'Where is the mule?' An' this one," she pointed at Pete, "who was walkin' ahead of me turn around an' say, 'There ain't no mule. We jus' brung you here cause we wanted to have a good time with you." She paused for a while. One could hear a pin drop in the court, and the sound of the old clock ticking away on the wall. It appeared that her voice would break, but she continued.

"I tried to fight them off, but they threw me on the ground. When I screamed, he put his hands over my mouth and threatened to kill me. The one that was rapin' me had told the other one, 'Don't forget I won the toss, so I was to get her first.'"

"Which of the two men was holding your mouth and hands, and which one was rapin' you?"

"That man standing by the wall," she pointed at Pete, "was the one holding my mouth after I screamed, an' the one that died is the one that tore up my clothes an' raped me."

"Then what happened?" McDougal inquired.

"As they were in the middle of attackin' me," Samandra continued, "my brother Joshua came up. He said later that he heard me scream. He came up and attacked both of the men with a piece of stick. First he hit one—the one that was rapin' me, then he hits the other one—him over there. He was goin' to strike them more, but I says, 'no Joshua, you will kill them,' and he stopped. Joshua took me home, an' my mother with my sister, me, and Joshua, was on the way to Mudville to complain to the sheriff when we met the sheriff and his deputies on River Trail and they shot my brother."

"Samandra, did you know the men before they attacked you?"

"I never talked to them before, but I seen them many times."

"When last did you see them before that incident?"

"I seen them the same day. When I rode by with Mrs. Jones, they were in front of the sheriff's office."

"No further questions."

There was a strange uneasy quiet as McDougal returned to his seat. Pierce himself seemed to have been taken aback by the clarity of the story related by the girl. He cleared his throat as he rose from his chair, and walked over to the witness chair.

"Tell me, girl, do you really expect this court to believe that stupid story you—"

"It's not a stupid story, it's the God's truth," she replied before Pierce could finish his statement.

"Who else aside from you and your brother were involved in the attack against the two lawmen?" the prosecuting attorney asked.

"We didn't do no attacking. They are the ones who attacked us."

"But you just said your brother attacked the two deputies."

"He was just trying to defend me."

"Was the plot against the deputies the idea of you and your brother, or some of your friends in Niggerville?"

"I already said there was no plot," the girl insisted.

"I understand that you teach at the school in Niggerville," he pressed her.

"I help Mrs. Jones with the Baptist church school in Wrightsville," she repeated.

"I see you use the term 'Wrightsville.' Are you one of those white-hating, militant coloreds who claim that the name is Wrightsville?"

McDougal stood to his feet. "I object to that line of questioning, your honor. The name of that town has nothing to do with this case."

Killjoy turned to Pierce, but before he could respond Pierce spoke. "It has all to do with the case, your honor."

"Would you explain to the court how it is related," Killjoy invited.

"If you will allow me to continue my line of questioning, it will all be revealed, your honor."

"I'll do no such thing." Killjoy bellowed. "If you can't give a satisfactory answer I'll accept the objection."

"Your honor, I am trying to show the jury—and the court," Pierce said, trying not to display his annoyance, "the kind of mental attitude of this woman, the anti-white hatred, and the militancy of which she was a part and which was at the base of the attack on the lawman."

"In that case, I shall overrule the objection," Killjoy concluded.

"Now, Samandra," Pierce continued, "are you one of those who worked to try to change the name of Niggerville?"

"No, sir, I wasn't one but I sure supported it. The real name of the town was always Wrightsvllle. It was only certain white folks that called it Niggerville."

"Are you one of those who believe that niggers are equal to whites?"

McDougal was on his feet again. "Your honor, I object to this line of questioning and to the use of the term 'nigger' by the prosecuting attorney."

"Your honor," Pierce countered, pretending to be surprised at the objection, "there ain't nothing wrong with the term 'nigger.' Colored folk use the term themselves when they talk to each other, and as I said earlier, I am trying to explore the mentality or the frame of mind that would allow a woman like this to participate in an attack against two lawmen."

"Carry on," Judge Killjoy directed.

"Do you feel colored people to be equal to white folk?" Pierce asked again.

"As far as I am concerned," the girl replied, "God made all people equal. The Bible say so and I believe in the Bible. Furthermore, the American Constitution also say all Americans suppose' to be equal."

"Would you be ready to kill to support that view?" Pierce pressed her.

"I don't believe in killin'," Samandra replied. "The Bible says, 'Thou shalt not kill."

"But you and your brother killed a man!"

"My brother didn't mean to kill nobody. He just was mad when he seen what the two men were doin' to me and was trying to defend me."

"Do you know what perjury is?"

"No, sir."

"It means lying before a court after you swear to tell the truth."

"I ain't lyin'. It happened just like I say it did."

"Why did you and your brother want to have the two deputies dead?"

"We didn't have no plans."

"You mean you just wanted to kill them for no reason?"

"We didn't want to kill nobody, even though they attacked and raped me. I didn't want them killed."

"If you didn't want them killed, why did you lure them into the woods?"

"I didn't lure them into the woods. They is the one who got me into the woods by lyin' an' sayin' that a gray mule was stuck in a hole."

In spite of pressure from Pierce, Samandra had stuck to her story. Pierce walked and shook his head slowly. "I've been lawyer for years, but I never seen one lie before the court with such a look of sincerity."

McDougal was on his feet. "Your honor, I object to the statement. The defendant has not been proven to be lying. Such a statement can only prejudice the jury."

While he yet spoke, Pierce was saying, "I have no further questions," and walked to his chair.

"Objection sustained." cried Killjoy. "I direct the jury to ignore the last statement made by the prosecuting attorney."

⌒ ⌒ ⌒

The next witness McDougal called was Mrs. Prichard, the sister of the postmistress. Mrs. Prichard, a godly lady and outstanding contributor to the poor fund in the white Baptist church in Mudville, testified that Samandra had indeed brought her the dress that afternoon. "It was just past two o'clock," she recalled, "when she knocked at the back door." She testified that she had known Samandra for years as "a nice, respectful colored chile." When McDougal was finished with Mrs. Prichard, Pierce had little to ask her. He stood but never moved from behind the table.

"Mrs. Prichard, are you aware of the fact that many who grow up and become law breakers or killers were once nice, respectful children?"

"I guess so," she answered.

"No further questions."

Next came Mrs. Jones to the stand. She testified that she and Samandra had traveled to Mudville together that afternoon after school, and by three o'clock they had returned to Wrightsville. She also testified about the Christian character of the girl. Pierce selected not to question her.

The next witness called to the stand was Samandra's mother, Mabel Wright. She told the court how she had made a dress for Mrs. Prichard. She had an order for two dresses, but only one was finished and Samandra was to take the dress to Mrs. Prichard after school, apologize for the other dress being late, and inform the lady that it would be brought to her on Saturday evening. Samandra's sister, Sharon, was to have gone with her but she was sick in bed most of the day. It was about three thirty when Joshua came up from the river and she asked him to go up the road to meet his sister, who she figured should be on her way home by now. "I been little worried," she explained, "with all the talk by the League, an' dem politicians creatin' racial tension with their talk. I is always worried when dem chillen ain't home. That is why I sent my boy to meet Samandra."

"Shortly after, Joshua is coming home an' Samandra is cryin'. I ran outside an' sure nuf there was the child. Her clothes all torn up, her hair all rumpled, and she didn't have her shoes. When I ask her what happen, she told me that she been attacked by them two men. She say she recognize them as the sheriff's deputies."

"What did you do then?" McDougal asked.

"I decided that the best thing to do was to take the girl to the sheriff's office an' let her tell him in her own words what they done to her. I didn't want to leave none of the chillen home so I brung them with me. We was travelin' on River Trail when the wind blows my hat from my head. My boy Joshua went after it as the wind was blowin' it across the field. Just then the sheriff came up with two men, an' one of them shot and killed my boy."

"Was he actually running away, as Deputy Drake testified earlier today?"

"No sir! He was jus' goin' to fetch my hat. He didn't have no reason to run nowhere. He was jus' defendin' his sister. Further, we didn't know then that the man was dead."

"Mrs. Wright," McDougal said, "you have heard the testimony of Pete Drake, who claims that he and Bole Miles were ambushed by your son and daughter. What do you have to say about that?"

"It ain't nothin' but lies, sir. My chillen will never do nothin' like that. My boy was only gone twenty minutes befo' he come back with Samandra. They done kilt my boy an' rape my daughter, now they is tryin' to do more hurt to her."

"No further questions." McDougal returned to his seat.

Pierce rose and began questioning the woman even before he moved from the table. "How would you explain the hate and hostility your children have for white folk, that they will plot and murder a deputy and attempt to murder another?"

"My chillen ain't murder no one," she emphasized, raising her voice in the quiet courtroom. "They don't hate white people. They don't hate no one for I done teach them not to hate. There ain't no person in this court white or colored who knows me over the years who can say I or my chillen hate white folk, or ever done anything to suggest that we hate white folk."

"Didn't you fire a shotgun at some white men a few days ago?"

"These men come into my yard in the black of night an' threaten me an' my chillen. I fire the gun in the air an' drive them off."

"How do you account for the murder of a deputy and the injury of another by your two children?"

"That warn't no murder. That was self-defense. My boy was tryin' to defend his sister. Are you tryin' to say that if your sister was bein' raped by two men, you won't try to defend her?" she asked Pierce defiantly.

With this question, the court broke into commotion. Some were saying, "The nerve of that nigger!" All across the room, people were conversing. Killjoy gaveled the court to order, and Pierce, whose declaration of "No further questions," had been drowned in the commotion, marched back to his chair.

"This is a good moment to adjourn the court," the judge observed. "The weekend will give us all time to quiet down. This court is adjourned till Monday morning at nine o'clock."

⌃ ⌃ ⌃

Throughout the week, Bilbo and Crane, both campaigning for the same seat in the state legislature, had been stomping the county declaring a state of crisis. Each sought to outdo the other in their claim of the rising threat of blacks in the county, using "the situation in Mudville" as an example. This process continued over the weekend, with each candidate demanding what the result of the trial of Samandra Wright must be. On Thursday night at a rally supported by hundreds of lighted torches, Bilbo addressed the crowd at Four Corners.

"This here case," he declared, "this case in which a group of niggers—we don't know yet how many—ambushed two white deputies, killed one and left the other for dead. This here case is a test case. It will prove if those who claim to be in charge in this county is really in charge. It will prove whether or not white folk will have to take the law into their own hands. In the meantime, I will encourage the people of Mudville County to be calm an' wait. Let us see how they will treat this case. As the Good Book says, 'Them that kill by the sword must die by the sword.' That deputy, Deputy Bole Miles, was a good boy. He was doin' his duty an' he was murdered in cold blood. The people of this county demand that whoever is found to be responsible must hang. We expect that everything will be done legally, but let it be known that we won't sit back no how an' see that murderin' nigger woman set free."

The crowd exploded in a frenzy. "Kill the nigger! Kill all niggers! Hang! Kill!"

Bilbo looked around and noted that many of the farmers at the meeting, standing directly in front of him, had not joined in the uproarious response. Some stood coldly observing the frenzy around them. When the noise abated, he continued, "Now, there are some who would say, all niggers is no good, and ought to be drove out of the county. But I can't agree with that, for you know an' I know, especially those of you who are farmers, that there is good niggers an' bad niggers. There is niggers who is 'umble, obedient, respectful. They do what they are told, and are happy for the opportunity to work. They accept the way how Gawd Almighty in His infinite wisdom created things an' placed the white man in charge. There are good niggers. Without them, many of our farmers could not survive. But there is them others. They are bold an' brazen, they reject their traditional place in society, they don't want to pick no cotton. They want to live like white folk. They want to be equal to white folk. They want to change the system and are ready to commit murder to do it. Them is the dangerous ones we have to watch carefully. The fact is that good niggers play an important part in the local economy, but bad niggers must be rooted out."

He paused, looking at the mass of red faces around him. "Much of the problems in this county is because of inaction on the part of those who claim to represent you in Jackson. All they been doin' is spendin' government money and enjoyin' themself while you back home face the danger."

Before the night was out, Crane had been given a full account of what had transpired at Four Corners, what was said and how the people responded. Wherever Bilbo held meetings, Crane made sure to have spies in the crowd to keep him abreast with the progress of his opponent and to provide him with ammunition for the future. Much of the data he obtained from his meeting at Four Corners would be used by Crane against his opponent at the next political rally he planned to hold on Saturday evening.

Friday evening, Mabel spent long hours with Samandra in her cell. Mabel tried her best to comfort the child, to help her endure the severe experience to which she was being exposed. Mabel herself had had little time to weep for Joshua, for no sooner was he placed to rest, than saving the lives of her remaining children had become her prime concern.

"It is hard to believe that after all they done to you, they now accuse you of murder and the real criminal remains free. It seems to me the evidence is clear what happen on that evening. There ain't no way the judge or the jury will believe that story being told by Pete Drake.

"Yet, he is a lawman" she continued, "an' he ain't never befo' been accused of rapin' a woman. Furthermore, he is white. You put all that together, with the present efforts of the politicians to paint black people as being dangerous, an' consider what they all sayin' about this case, an' you come to the conclusion that the outcome may have nothing to do with wrong or right, guilty or not guilty. They may simply do what racial an' political pressures want done."

"I realize what you sayin', Ma," Samandra said, "an' that is why I have little faith in the law. It is suppose' to be fair to all, but I don't see how it can be with all that's goin' on."

Mabel remained silent for a moment. She sat on the small rough bed beside her daughter, holding her hands tenderly in hers. She looked steadfastly at the gray wall across the cell as if seeking to decipher some invisible inscription.

"Samandra, I been thinking," Mabel finally said, "maybe it will give you a little better chance. It will make it easier for them to believe you, if they know that you is white. The way politics an' the League is playin' this thing up as a plot by black folk against the white system, I frankly don't see how you can get justice. What do you think?"

Mabel looked into Samandra's eyes, studying her face, waiting for her to reply. Samandra, who had been resting her back against the wall as her mother spoke, straightened up, and seemed to grow tense. "Ma," she said, looking away from her mother's gaze onto the floor of her cell, "that must never happen. Please, don't ever suggest or even think about it again. I am not going to be tried as a white woman, no way. I have thought about it, but the very thought is as humiliating as what they done to me out there in the wood. You are my mother, Joshua is my brother, Billy an' Sharon are my brother and sister. I will be a traitor not only to my family, but to all those who have cared for me and loved me since I came to the county as a parentless chile, an' most of all I will be a traitor to myself. The books say that this is America, the land of liberty an' justice. There is suppose' to be one justice, not one for black folk an' one for white. I will be sayin' that I accept their double standards an' I can never do that. If they set me free just because I am white, my life will be meaningless, an' I will be even more lost than when you found me twelve years back."

She paused for a while, her face as pale as the glow of a full moon on a stalk of yellow delta corn. She looked and saw that there were tears in Mabel's eyes, they were running down her face and falling gently on Samandra's hands.

"I say to them, try me as a woman," she continued, "try me as a human being, try me as an American. I will never say to them, 'try me in a special way, cause am white." Samandra paused again. "'Sides, only my skin is white. All the rest of me is like you. If I am to live or die, that's how I want to be."

Mabel shook her head and managed a tired smile amid her tears. "I knew you woulda said that, chile. I is so proud of you. But I want you to live. There been so much pain an' sufferin' in my life an' in yours. It jus' ain't fair." She was still shaking her head from side to side. "We have to jus' pray a bit more, and let the Almighty have His hand. He knows I can't take much more."

∧∧∧

On Saturday evening, Julius Crane held a political rally in the small town of Raymonsville, at the foot of Sand Mountains. The meeting place was strategically located. It enabled whites from both the hill country and the flatlands to attend. Old man Crane now seventy-three, having just had a birthday a few weeks earlier, accompanied his son. As an old racehorse accustomed to the track that he no longer ran, he could share the excitement of the occasion and reminisce on old times.

League members were present in large numbers. Some of them on Thursday evening had been at the meeting at Cross Roads and had heard Bilbo's presentation. Crane was determined to outdo his opponent.

He assured his listeners that he would "do whatever got to be done" to see to it that the murderer or murderers of Deputy Bole Miles be punished. 'I am surprised and angered," he declared, "that at a time like this, when white people, a lawman at that, is bein' attacked an' killed by niggers, that my opponent Jason Bilbo would go around telling people to be sure they is able to recognize a good nigger from a bad one. What he is sayin' is that if you are attacked by a nigger, be sure to find out if he's a good or bad one before you defend yourself." There was laughter in the crowd, but most took it seriously.

"That is the most stupid piece of advice I ever heard. How can a man who will expose you to that kind of danger want to represent you in Jackson? I will never know.

"If you listen to that kind of advice, you will not only be exposing your wives an' children to danger, you will be exposing the entire county to the threat of being overrun by the forces of evil. I hope that many of you will be at the courthouse in Mudville on Monday, not to cause trouble or to be rowdy, but to show your support for law and order in the county. I say nothing short of hanging will be a just punishment for the murder of that deputy.

"I want you to know," Crane continued, "that decisions are being made in this county today which will influence your future for years to come. It will determine whether or not you and your children are to have the land, the political power, the opportunities that you are entitled to as white people and the true owners of this county and this sovereign state of Mississippi. If we allow ourselves to be scared by a few criminals or misled by blind politicians, we are finished."

That evening as Crane and his father rode their carriage back to the farm, the old man was reticent and pensive. He had listened to the comments of his son who seemed almost possessed with concern over what Jason Bilbo was saying and doing.

They arrived home after nightfall. The cattle which had been milked by black farm hands were grazing peacefully in the field bordering the road, their heads riveted to the ground. In a smaller pasture nearby, a prized bull grazed alone. The old man ate a light supper, and invited his son to share with him a glass of wine in his office. This was the old man's way of saying "I want to talk to you alone," and the younger man, anxious to know what was on his father's mind, withdrew to the study in response to the invitation.

After they had each drunk a glass of vintage wine, the sprightly old man walked over to the small bar to refill his glass. As he reached the bar, with his back turned to his son, he introduced the topic that had been disturbing his thoughts.

"Tell me, boy," he said, "don't you think that perhaps you using this—er, this nigger thing too much?"

The son was clearly taken aback by the question. "What do you mean, Pa? Why, I have seen you use the same approach over and over since I was a boy!"

"Yes," the old man said, turning around to face his son and nodding his head. "I certainly did, but not the way you are doing it. I would make a statement here or there, and it would bring me some extra votes, but I must confess that it sends chills of fear up my spine, as I listened to you this evening. It appears to me that you and Bilbo are unwittingly helping to awaken a sleeping giant that could be the undoing of all of us." He paused, and with glass in hand, walked towards the window across the room by which stood his son.

"Who would you say is the greatest threat to us here in Mississippi?" he asked, slowly measuring each word as he looked out on the falling night.

"The niggers, of course," his son replied. "They are the ones who would like to change the system, including the pattern of economic relationship between whites and blacks in the South."

"It is clear that niggers don't want to go back into slavery," the old man commented, "and I do not blame them. It is also clear that they would like to be equal to white people, and I don't believe it will ever happen in this economic system, at least not in my or your lifetime. But let me tell you something, boy," the old man continued. "The greatest threat that we face is not the nigger, it is that white trash out there that you were talking to this evening, and on whose votes you will rely to remain in office! The poor white man in Mudville County, as well as in this state and this country, is frustrated and hostile. His numbers are increasing like rabbits each year, as those idiots in Washington who ain't got nuf sense to come in out of the rain, allow millions of the worse trash from Europe—the poor, the ignorant, the landless—to flood into this country."

The old man raised his aged voice, still looking through the window into the deepening darkness as he spoke. "They have one thing on their mind—land, property, power, wealth. Niggers have none of what they want. We are the ones that have it. Fortunately, we have been able to direct the hostility and frustration of the poor whites in the South against niggers. But who do you think will be the final objects of their demands? Those who own the land, those who have wealth and power, and that means us." He pointed his right index finger at himself.

"What the poor white wants in this county and across the nation, he cannot get from niggers. Don't you forget that!" The old man was emphatic. "When people are frustrated and hostile, they strike out at anybody, and when they are ignorant, it is easy to channel their hostility in a desired direction.

"From this point of view, the nigger has been a God-send for the white political and economic aristocracy. For if we continue to manipulate it carefully, we can keep the attention of the white trash focused on niggers indefinitely. As long as he has the nigger to look at, he won't pay any attention to us."

"Take it from me, son," the old man said seriously, "you get that white scum out there—the ignorant, the landless—you get them too politically aware, you keep raising questions before them about who owns the lands and who are the rightful inheritors to the country, and you mark my words, one day their eyes will open, and they will understand what's going on, and we will be finished.

"Don't forget," the old man continued, "a few years back, John Walton, the cousin of that attorney who is defending that black woman charged with murder, ran for the office you now occupy, and his main argument to the people out there was that we, and not niggers, were their greatest enemy. We've just been lucky, but if we keep pushing our luck, this whole thing will blow up in our face one of these days."

Young Crane was standing with his back to the window overlooking the field as he listened to his father. "Dad," he said, "you know better than I, how these people think and the motivations that prod them to action. If I could not use this 'nigger thing' successfully as a political tool, I probably never would have gotten in the senate in the first place. The reason Bilbo lost in the last two elections was because he has never been able to use this issue successfully."

"Ah, yes!" the old man agreed, "but not this time. As you know, he is pushing it just as hard as you, if what I have been hearing is true. And in your efforts to outdo each other, both are making the League into what it ought not to be. Can't you see it, boy?" The old man looked into the dark, intelligent eyes of his only son. "The League is becoming more and more powerful, thanks to both of you. If they get all the poor whites organized under their brand of leadership, once they get the taste of power, there's no telling where it will all end.

"First they are going to drive away the niggers, because we would have convinced them that niggers are a threat to them, and when there are no more niggers to hold their attention, they are going to turn on us." He shook his finger at his son. "I see it happening as clearly as I see you standing here before me.

"I am not saying to drop the use of the nigger issue. Use it, but understand what you are doing and make sure the League don't get out of control. Otherwise you are going to find that rather than the dog wagging the tail, the tail will become the wagger in this county."

⌃ ⌃ ⌃

News spread around Wrightsville and the surrounding countryside that a special meeting was to be held in the town on Sunday afternoon following church service. The site selected for the meeting was a one-acre lot of grassland off North Street and next to the home of Irene Smith.

The one who had called for the meeting was a stranger to many, a man named Leroy Battles. Leroy for the past eleven years had lived in New York City and Philadelphia. His father had been a sharecropper in the county and was well known among the older folks, due to nothing else but the method by which he left Mudville County. Old Jacob Battles had been a sharecropper since 1865. Like others of his breed, he had become entangled in the economic web of the plantation system so cunningly devised by his boss, Jeremy Benbow. Each year they found themselves hopelessly in debt to the plantation store, each year sinking deeper into the quagmire in spite of their work to extricate themselves. When his wife died of malaria, the spirit of the old man was broken. No longer did the twenty acres and mule which Mr. Benbow had promised to sell him when he "gits out of owin' the store" seem attractive. He decided to run away with his five children, three boys and two girls. Leroy was the youngest of the boys. The old man placed his children on a mule cart as he usually did on Sunday to go to church. Under some straw on the cart, he hid an old suitcase and a bundle of their belongings. Rather than going to church that Sunday, he rode to a town twenty miles away where he sold the mule and cart to a pre-arranged buyer, and with a few other dollars he had saved by selling some young pigs that were his own, he took the train north and was never heard from again.

Whatever became of the old man and the other children was unclear. It was obvious, however, that Leroy had done quite well up

North. He sported two huge gold rings on a finger. He wore an expensive looking suit, with white suede shoes, and a classy white hat, and he smoked expensive cigars and occasionally he checked the time on a gold watch which hung from his pocket by a golden chain.

For several days since Leroy's appearance in Wrightsville, he had strutted around the region seeing family, contacting old friends, and making new ones especially among the youth. Finally, Leroy announced the meeting for Sunday afternoon. It was about four o'clock when the crowd began to gather. Some came directly from church, others from their homes, some from the surrounding county. By four-thirty, there were at least two hundred present, including Reverend Jones who, not to be left out, came with two of his deacons to hear what Leroy Battles had to say. In the sky overhead, a flock of wild pigeons flew in wide circles over the field.

When Leroy climbed onto the old table, a makeshift platform, the crowd became silent. He looked over the crowd of expectant faces and then he began to speak.

"Brothers and sisters of Wrightsville and Mudville County, I have come down to you from Philadelphia because I have heard of the evil days that have befallen black people in this here county, and because I have an idea of what is coming in the future of this section of the nation. I want you to know," he said, "that what is happening here in Mudville County—the murder of Joshua Wright, the raping of his sister, and now the humiliating trial of the victim—is only part of a wider program of persecution sweeping not only across Mississippi, but across the entire Southland of these New Nited States of America. In the last five years, hundreds of innocent black folk have been murdered and lynched. Hundreds of black mothers have been raped in a brutal system which refuses to recognize the murder of a black person or a rape of one of our women as a crime if it is committed by a white man. In cases where the police is not involved, they turn their back and pretend that they cannot see. They did it in Atlanta, they did it in Birmingham, they have done it in many other areas of the nation."

"I want you to know," Leroy continued, "that what is creeping into this county is part of a wider plan to return us to the old form of slavery. I say the old, because in some ways we are still slaves. My daddy was being held in a new form of slavery, and as some of you all know, he took his chillen an' escaped up north."

There was a loud "Amen" amid some laughter, for many of the older folk knew how Leroy's father had departed.

"Nearly every state in the South has passed laws so that today, in most cases, black folk can no longer vote and many of the jobs that our fathers did, the trades they had—carpentry, building, masonry, and others—are now declared as white jobs. All of this is part of a plan to keep black folk in the cotton field by unfair laws, by violence, brute force, and fear."

"Brothers and sisters," he continued, "my message to you is that the storm of brutality and injustice which presently engulfs most of the Southland is about to break upon this county. I call upon you to rise, pack up, and leave the South. Leave as Israel left the bondage under Pharaoh.

"The only way you can save yourself, your children, your wives, from what is about to befall this place, is to leave now. I say to you, let the white man pick his own cotton, let him plant and reap his own crops, let him clean his own kitchen, let him work for a change. As long as you stay down here in this God-forsaken place, your daughters and your wives will be exposed to rape and humiliation and will be open to cruelty and murder."

He paused and gazed at the faces beneath him. "I represent an organization called 'Jobs Incorporated' which can get you all the jobs you want in Philadelphia and New York City. We will get you a job. We will help you get settled, get some place to live when you arrive there. All you will have to pay is two dollars to cover the processing of each person. I am asking you to come up North. I am not offering you a place in heaven, for there are problems up North also, but at least you will be able to leave this section of hell called Dixie, and add greater happiness to and control of your lives. Why, in New York, we is got a place called Harlem. There are more colored folk in Harlem than you ever seen in all your born days. They ain't rich, but many of them are comfortable, they have jobs, and they know how to defend themselves. There are schools you can go to and send your children, there are trades you can learn, and you can even start your own business."

"Now is the time to leave, before the clouds burst," he urged them solemnly. "The League and other groups are getting together with the help of the politicians. They all have one goal in common—destroy the will of black folk. Take it from me, brothers and sisters;"—his eyes searched the crowd—"the southern white man is all the same, they ain't no good. As long as you try to resist them, they will not rest until they destroy you. They are the children of the devil, and they will do his work. The po' white trash is the greatest threat to the life and freedom of black folk—and the majority of whites in the South fall in that category."

Once more he paused and looked at the upturned faces. He could tell from their serious countenance that they were pondering what he had said. "I am leaving for up North in a few days," he continued. "I will take the names of all who want to leave and in a few weeks we can arrange everything."

When Leroy had finished speaking, several questions were thrown at him by members of the crowd. "How much will it cost to get there?" "What will happen when we gets there?" "How much do jobs pay in Philadelphia and New York?" "Is it true the white man up there is just like the white man in Mississippi?" To all questions, Leroy had good answers. The crowd broke into small groups, discussing what they had heard. Some agreed that perhaps it would be a good thing to clear out, while others disagreed strongly. "I is jus' as entitled to live in Mississippi as the white man, an' perhaps even mo'. Ain't nobody gonna drive me out," an old man was loudly protesting as he did a war dance.

As all of this was happening, Parson Jones who was off to the side with two of his deacons moved towards the front of the crowd and requested of Leroy, who had called the meeting, that he be allowed to address the people.

"Anyone who wants to speak may speak," Leroy informed him.

Parson Jones climbed onto the table that was the makeshift podium. As he did so, silence moved like a wave across the crowd as all faces turned to hear the parson.

"It is not my intention, my children," he began, "to challenge what Brother Battles has said, but as the pastor and spiritual shepherd of this town I must say a few words which I hope will clarify some of the ideas already expressed."

"I have been a part of the South all my life," he informed all his listeners. "I have shared her joys, but mostly her sorrows. I have watched the South and listened to her heartbeat. Over the many years, I have studied the white man of the Southland closely. I have examined him and I have seen the best and the worst of him. I know that what I am going to say," he told the crowd, shaking a finger at them, "may sound to many of you like heresy or the words of a crazy man, but let me tell you this." As he paused, the crowd pressed closer so as not to miss a word.

"Of all the white folk of the Southland, those that are commonly called po' white trash are in fact the purest of heart among the white population." There was a murmur of disapproval from the crowd. "Believe it or not, brothers and sisters," the parson continued, "they are the simplest, the most trustworthy, the most easily deceived, the most illiterate because of their ignorance, and the most exploited of the white race. They are exploited by the wealthy class of their own race who see them as a threat because of their vast numbers, who see them as well as colored folk as fodder, material to be used and exploited for personal benefit.

"Who do you think invented the terms 'white trash' and 'nigger'?" Parson Jones asked rhetorically. "It was the rich, the upper level white man. For the past three hundred years, they have exploited the ignorance of their white brothers as well as blacks. They are the ones who benefited from the system that enslaved both blacks and poor whites. The fact that they gave the poor white man his freedom first was not due to love, any more than it was love that caused the emancipation of blacks from slavery. They did it because they couldn't help it."

"Yes," he continued, "whenever there is an attack against black folk, it's usually the poor white man that you see, but if you look behind him long enough, and far back enough, you will discover that it's the better-off whites, the rich—some of their writers and even religious leaders—an entire class who, in order to maintain their leadership, have provided the support, the rationale, and the religious justification for the dehumanization of black folks. They are the ones that have been and are still the main obstacles to racial harmony in the South."

"Look at what is happening in Mudville," he urged them. "Is it not the politicians who are stirring up racial hatred today? Yes! When you look, you see the League, but look behind the League and you'll see who the culprits are. So my brothers, do not hate the poor white man. Pity him. Be sorry for him, for he is being exploited just like you. And while he will be held accountable for his own behavior, the Almighty God will bring his greatest vengeance on those who have deceived, exploited, and used him as a tool and weapon against black folk."

The parson turned to the other issue raised by Leroy. "On the question of going North, I shall not support the idea one way or the other. But this I know. I shall remain here with my flock in this little town of ours. I shall bear with my people whatever they bear—the joys and the sorrows, the pain and the trials—and God in His own good time will transform this land, open the eyes of the oppressor, and depose the forces of evil."

Some said "Amen!" but others maintained a confused silence, still thinking about what Leroy had said.

As Parson Jones finished speaking, the crowd broke into excited discussions. "I say it's a good opportunity and the right time to get the hell out of here," one man said.

"They is tryin' to chase us out so they can get our land," another suggested.

Thus some were talking about accepting Leroy's offer to go north, while others were expressing doubts about the scheme. It was as these activities were occurring that Babs Jacobs, who with a crowd around him had been heatedly debating the issues, climbed on the bench that stood near to the table on which Parson Jones and Leroy Battles both had spoken. His ascent to the bench was to assure that members of the crowd beyond his immediate vision could see him and hear what he had to say. He gesticulated wildly with his hands as he spoke.

"Git on the table and talk loud so we can hear you," yelled one from the back of the crowd.

Babs complied. "My wife Mildred been tellin' me fer a long time that I talks too much," he started, as he climbed onto the table.

"She is a sure nuf wise woman," a man from the crowd called, to the laughter from those around him.

Babs ignored the man. "But when I got something to say, I just got to say it, and sho' can't keep me mouth shut after what I done heard this evening."

"Leroy Battles," he said, pointing to the man standing nearby, "offer you the opportunity to go up North, get a job, and live in the big city, an' I is sho' that some of you gonna accept the offer. Even if Leroy didn't come down here, with all what is happenin' in this county—the violence 'gainst black people, the murder of brother Joshua Wright, the rape of his sister an' her trial for what she ain't done—some of you will decide to leave anyway."

"In fact, seein' how things is gettin' more uncertain in this county, is easy to see how some will see up north as a heaven. I can read," he informed his listeners, "an' I been readin' for a long time now, an' I know that even up north, in Chicago, in Detroit, in many northern cities, black folk is bein' kilt, bein' taken advantage of, an' bein' pushed around jus' as dey is bein' done here in the south. There's been riots up there in big cities by whites 'gainst black folk. We is bein' brutalized all over these New Nited States by the white man.

"I agree with Parson Jones that all white folks ain't devils, but dem what is devils is spread all over America. As I see it"—he was he still gesticulating with both hands—"is a choice of whether you is ready to stand an' fight fer rights. I don't know 'bout the rest of you, but this here county is my home like it is the white man's home. His folk come from overseas an' my folk come from overseas. This land belonged to the Indians, the Choctaws, the Chickasaws, the Ibitoupa, the Chokechiuma, the Troy, the Tunica, the Korea, and the Guge—this county and this state was theirs. The white man took it from them by force. My parents fought and died on the land jus' like his. The only difference is that he fought the Indians, while we had to fight him an' is still fightin' him. My daddy lost a leg fighting in Lincoln's army, and his brother, my uncle Phillip, died fightin' on the side of the Confederates. Some of you who feel that hell is South and heaven is North, I say to you, you wrong. Hell is all over America. Don't you know that if the President of this nation want to stop the persecution of black folk, he can stop it in the South or in the North? I say to you people, don't listen to those who will encourage you to leave your home and your land for a strange place. This here Southland is our home. Our fathers cut the first trees, cleared the first land, we build the first roads, an' didn't receive no pay aside from the whip; we built the houses as slaves, we did all the hard work for more than three hundred years, we done it in chains, but we done it. This land is fertilized with the bones of our forefathers who died by the millions building the South."

Babs had his audience spellbound as they pressed closer to hear him.

"They say that the South makes its livin' off of cotton," he continued, bending forward, his eyes flashing as he drove home his points. "They say that cotton is king in Dixie. I ask you, who made cotton king? Who put him on his throne, eh? We! We the black people! We done it, even though we was in the chains of slavery. If it was not for us an' our fathers who were slaves, this land would have been still unplanted, its roads uncut, an' its towns and cities unbuilt. Mudville County and Wrightsville is my home. I gonna stay here, an' if I have to fight to stay alive, I will fight, but here in my home, not in a foreign place in some far off city. If I is gonna die, I will die defending my property, my town, an' my family!"

As he spoke, Babs became so riled up that the spittle gathered on the sides of his mouth. He wiped his mouth with the back of his hand. "Dat's all I have to say." There was a roar of approval from areas of the crowd, while others seemed yet uncertain as to what course they would follow.

⌃ ⌃ ⌃

Monday morning the sun eased out of a gray cloudbank and quickly dispelled an early mist which lay like a blanket over the town of Mudville. Long before the opening of the doors of the courthouse, crowds of men had already gathered. There were members of both factions of the League, each group standing around its leader, talking, laughing, awaiting the opening of the doors of the courthouse. Black people stood by themselves close to the door. As the door opened, they trooped inside onto the back benches of the courtroom. Shortly, the room was full. The overflow stood outside. Black people stood apart under a large oak tree at the side of the building, while the League and the white overflow occupied the walk and lawn in front of the building, all under the watchful eyes of the two deputies.

The carriage with Judge Killjoy arrived. The judge stepped out and the black driver guided the horse and carriage through the crowd and disappeared around the corner. The judge, holding a folder under his arm, moved toward the front door of the building. Spectators melted before him as he moved up the steps, seemingly oblivious to the people crowded around.

Tyson, who had closed his shop for the day, moved among his men, giving directions. A few were sent into the court with the publicly expressed intent of "keepin' an eye on the jury to make sure that justice is done." One of Tyson's men came out the front door to inform him that the court proceedings had started.

"What did he say?" someone asked.

"He says that the court is now in session."

As time passed, the crowd outside was becoming tense with expectation.

"When is dey bringin' in that murderin' nigger woman?" Tyson asked the informant who had just come from inside.

"The sheriff done took her in through the back door."

"Dammit," Tyson said angrily. "I was hopin' to catch a glimpse of that hell cat."

⌒ ⌒ ⌒

Deputy Pete Drake was the first witness recalled to the stand by Attorney McDougal the defense attorney. There was some talk as to whether he should be sworn in again.

"I done swore to tell the truth already," Pete protested angrily. "Furthermore, ain't no one in this court can say dey ever caught me lyin'."

"Because you never been caught, that does not mean that you don't lie," McDougal reminded him.

"Cut that bickering out and let the trial go on," Killjoy thundered, pounding the gavel on the table.

There was silence for a few moments. Then McDougal spoke. "Deputy Drake, I want you to go back to part of your earlier testimony before the court. You said that when you came to in the woods after being hit on the head by a black man, you found that Deputy Bole was already dead. You then got on your horse and rode to Mudville to report the incident to Sheriff Brude."

"That's right."

"Did you miss anything from your pocket?"

- 340 -

"I can't say I did."

"Did you have any money on your person?"

"Yes, sir. I had over ten dollars in my pocket."

"Was any of it stolen?"

"No."

"Was anything at all taken from you?"

"No, nothing."

"What about your gun?"

"My gun wasn't gone."

"So you want this court to believe that you were attacked by that young woman and her brother, without any weapons aside from a club, that they attacked two gun-carrying deputies, knocked them out, then just walked away. Is it not strange that even though they thought that both you and Bole were dead, they did not touch your money, they did not take your guns? In fact, they took nothing! Isn't that strange?"

"You is askin' the wrong man," Pete informed him.

"What about the pair of women's shoes, that Sheriff Brude removed from the scene of the attack? Did you see them?"

"Not when I came to. Only when I returned with Sheriff Brude."

"Did you notice that Bole's pants was open at the front when you examined him to see if he was alive?"

"They weren't open when I left him."

"I suppose that they opened miraculously and the pair of shoes also appeared there miraculously?"

"You can suppose whatever you want. I'd say they came back and put them there to frame us."

"And opened his pants also?" McDougal raised his voice reflecting his anger with what to him were blatant lies being told by the deputy.

"That ain't impossible," Pete snarled. "Niggers would do anything to save dey skin."

"You said that the girl stopped you on the trail and you and Bole followed her into the woods."

"Dat's correct."

"Where did you both leave your horses?"

"By the side of the road."

"But you said that when you came to, you climbed on your horse and headed for Mudville."

"Sure I climbed on my horse, but fuss' I had to walk to where the horse was."

"Sheriff Brude said in his report that when he came to the body of Bole Miles, his horse was standing nearby."

"He musta got loose and walked to where Bole was lyin'," Pete replied.

"You heard on Friday afternoon the evidence of Mrs. Jones and Mrs. Prichard. Mrs. Prichard testified that Samandra Wright was at their place that very afternoon, roughly one and a half hours before the incident on River Trail. Mrs. Jones testified that she took Samandra Wright to Mudville and back to Wrightsville. The girl left Wrightsville for her home roughly half an hour before the incident on River Trail. Both Mrs. Jones and the girl testified that they saw you in front of the sheriff's office when they passed on their way back to Wrightsville. Yet you are trying to tell the court that when you got to River Trail, the girl was there with her brother lyin' in wait for you and your companion.

"How did the girl know that you and Bole Miles would be on the trail? Is it not far more plausible that you are the one who would have known that the girl would be passing there on her way home?"

One could feel the air of tension rising as McDougal grilled the deputy, seeking to expose the holes in his testimony.

"I ain't no jury, I ain't no judge, I don't read niggers' minds. If you want to find out why the niggers done what they done, ask them. Furthermore," Pete added angrily, "I been deputy in this here town for most of eight years, an' I never befo' been accused of lyin' to this court or attackin' no nigger, so you go ahead tryin' to turn this case 'round and make it look like I is the one bein' tried."

"I am not tryin' to turn anything around. I am seeking the truth!" McDougal injected.

"As far as I can see, it's whether you is ready to take my word or the word of a nigger," Pete added.

"And what about that boy you murdered? He should have been here to testify today."

"Murdered?" Pete sprang to his feet, fire flashing from his eyes. At the same moment, Attorney Pierce was on his feet.

"I object, Your Honor, to the deputy being called a murderer."

"Sit down, Pierce, the deputy can handle himself," Killjoy was saying. "Sit down, Deputy Drake, you don't have to stand up to make your point."

Pete sat down as he continued speaking. "I didn't murder nothin'. I shot at a nigger who moments earlier had kilt my associate, Deputy Bole Miles, and tried to kill me, an' was now tryin' to escape."

"Sheriff Brude indicated that the young man was running after a hat, not tryin' to escape."

"I ain't concerned with what Sheriff Brude say," Pete said scornfully, "'cause I ain't shure if he is interested in upholding the law in the county, or protectin' niggers."

Brude jumped to his feet; the court broke into pandemonium. Pete had finally said in the open what some of the League members were saying in private.

Judge Killjoy was pounding the table with his gavel. "Sit down," he bellowed, "everybody silence, or I'll clear the court."

"But your honor—"

"You'll have your opportunity, Brude. Sit down." Then he turned to the jury. "I am going to ask the jury to ignore that statement made by Deputy Drake. Everyone in this town," he stared at the crowded court, "including me, knows that Sheriff Brude is a man who upholds the law."

"No further questions," McDougal said.

Pierce declined to cross-examine.

⌒ ⌒ ⌒

McDougal called Sheriff Brude back to the stand. But the sheriff had little to add to the testimony he had given on Friday. Once more McDougal asked him, "Sheriff Brude, from the evidence you have seen and heard, and from your personal experience with this case, can you say that you believe the version of what transpired as given by your deputy?"

Pierce sprang to his feet before Brude could respond, calling for objections. "The opinion of the sheriff has no part in this case," he protested. "It will only serve to unduly influence or prejudice the jury. The sheriff's job is to present evidence, not to give opinion."

Killjoy concurred and sustained the objection.

McDougal next recalled Samandra Wright to the stand. Once more she was made to go over in great detail each step of the evidence she had given to the court the week before. She stuck to her story. As she went over the details of how she was attacked by the two men and the subsequent killing of her brother, there were tears in the eyes of some of the black people sitting at the back of the courtroom, but Samandra herself remained calm, stoically looking at the court and jury as she spoke.

Finally McDougal asked, "Samandra, what you have told the court today, is it all the truth?"

"Sir, I swear befo' Gawd Almighty that it is nothin' but the truth."

"No further questions," McDougal said, returning to his table.

Pierce had declined to cross examine any of those recalled by McDougal. This behavior had intrigued Killjoy, who now awaited the closing arguments of both men.

McDougal was the first to present his closing remarks at the invitation of Killjoy. "Your honor, members of the jury," he began, "you have heard the charges brought against my client, Samandra Wright, and you have heard all the testimonies presented. I am sure the evidence is loud and clear to you as it is to me. Here we have an example of a young lady who has been raped and abused, and on top of it all, has faced a trumped up charge of murder. What are the facts that we have seen in the face of this malicious attempt to cover up a criminal act? You have heard the testimony of Mrs. Prichard that Samandra Wright was at her place only some two hours before the incident on River Trail. You heard the testimony by Samandra Wright and Mrs. Jones that when they passed the sheriff's office, both deputies were seated outside. It was impossible for Samandra or her brother to know that these deputies, who claim they made a last minute decision to visit the Yazoo, would be in the area. It was absolutely impossible for these two children—for children they are—to have known in advance of the spur-of-the-moment plans to visit the Yazoo.

"On the other hand, it was the deputies who, having observed the girl in Mudville and realizing that she would be going home on Friday evening, could have laid wait for her. In fact, members of the jury, that is actually what happened. They guessed that she would ride to Wrightsville and walk the rest of the way home. They set a trap for her on the road, but things did not go as planned. While they were in the process of committing their beastly act upon this young lady, her brother, having heard her scream, came to her rescue. The end result was a dead deputy, and the boy, whose only crime is that he sought to rescue his sister from a bestial attack, was murdered."

"Consider the scene of the attack," McDougal walked over to the jury, placing his hands on the rail that separated them from the rest of the court. "A pair of ladies' shoes, the dead man with his pants open and questionable parts of his body exposed. The failure to rob, to take money or weapons from the men, both left for dead! A girl and a boy, for no apparent reason, attacking two armed deputies, using only a piece of stick."

"When the girl's mother heard what had occurred, she loaded them on her cart and was heading for Mudville to the sheriff's office. This black family we are talking about has been one of the most respected in Mudville County. These children have never been anything but gentle and respectful to everyone. When all the facts are viewed, it is clear that it is in fact Deputy Pete Drake who should have been on trial for rape and subsequent murder.

"Fellow citizens, this is not a racial issue. It is not an issue of white versus black, as the politicians are trying to make it. It is the simple issue of criminal behavior on the part of two deputies employed by the County Sheriff's office—men who swore to uphold the law. It just happens that the victim was a black woman. It could have been anyone, even a member of your own family!"

"Members of the jury, I appeal to you in the name of justice, and the Christian values which I know you cherish, that you let justice prevail and set Samandra free. I thank you."

Judge Killjoy gave a deep sigh as McDougal solemnly walked back to his table. The court remained in dead silence. Killjoy turned, looked at Pierce and nodded. Pierce rose slowly. Leaving all his notes on the table, he walked to the middle of the floor, and then slowly approached the jury until he stood directly before them. Turning sideways, he looked at the judge.

"Your honor," he turned to the jury, "noble citizens, members of the jury," his voice had already taken on the tone of a preacher introducing a sermon on the end of the world. "It is in your hands," he continued, "and in others like yours, that has been placed the responsibility of protecting a system and a way of life that is sacred and God-given to all of us. Were it not for the nobility and determination of people like you to stand up"—he raised his voice then let it drop again—"and resist the forces of evil whether it comes from the north or from among us, we would be finished, and our wives, our children would be doomed. And our land, our dear land"—he shook his head, lowering his voice—"would be possessed by heathens and others who would like to destroy us."

He paused, and in the stillness, one could hear the old clock ticking on the wall as its dull brass pendulum swung back and forth.

"Members of the jury, what we have here is not an ordinary case." He placed his two hands on the rail and bent forward, lowering his voice. "It is a case involving an incident which on the surface may appear to be cut and dried, but in fact it's just the tip of an iceberg. The attack against the two deputies was just a trial run. If it had been successful, then two lawmen, white lawmen, would just have mysteriously disappeared, and we would have seen the beginning of a campaign of terror worse than John Brown and Nat Turner.

"You have listened to the testimony of an officer of the law. A man with eight years of service to the community. I believe every word he said," Pierce emphasized each word separately. "The attorney for the defense attacked white political leaders, accusing them of stirring up racial trouble, but it is they—our political leaders—who throughout the history of Mississippi have sounded the clarion call when danger was near.

"What happened to Deputy Bole Miles could have happened to you. For this was to be the beginning of a terror campaign against white people. As of now, we have not yet even determined how many were really involved in the plot. You are dealing with a dedicated murderess, who is just one of many out there. The fact that her skin is fair made her even more cunning. That's why she was used to trap the two lawmen into goin' into the wood where they were attacked.

"If you do not find this woman guilty," he warned, "and see that she pay the price for her crime, I am sorry for all of us." He threw both his hands in the air. "We will be signing our own death warrant. You have the opportunity to stand aside and see a reign of black terror let loose in this county, or to make this county free and safe, for yourself, your wives and daughters, your children. It's in your hands. Outside, there are large numbers of your friends who depend upon you to protect them and save our system of democracy. If you do not find that woman guilty and recommend the death penalty, you will be playing into the hands of the forces of darkness, and your blood, the blood of your wives, your daughters, and your sons will be on your own heads."

He struck his hands forcefully on the rail, raising his voice to a crescendo. "We have to show the dark forces of evil that we will not stand still while they destroy us. We have to set a severe example here, that others who have ideas about attacking and killing white folk in this county will know what to expect, if they rise against us.

"Members of the jury, I ask you, Mudville County asks you, and hundreds of your friends and relatives standing outside ask you, to do your duty. I thank you."

Pierce started back to his table. The jury remained spellbound, till their attention was demanded by Judge Killjoy.

"You have heard the evidence," he informed them. "Your job is to determine whether in the light of the evidence, if the accused is guilty. If she is innocent, she must be set free. If found guilty, she will have to pay the awful price equaled to that of the crime."

The jury rose, and single filed stone-faced through a door which opened in the wall next to the jury benches. A few people left the courtroom, but most sat and waited. There was a look of hopelessness on the faces of many blacks in the back of the courtroom. Mabel sat next to Samandra, holding her hand to offer comfort and assurance. Her lips were moving in silence. She was praying.

The news spread outside that the jury was out. The sound of excited talking which had gone on all morning from the opening of the court, decreased and was replaced by a tense silence, as the crowd waited on the verdict. Tyson and some one hundred of his followers crowded across the street from the courthouse. One man carried a placard which read, "Jury, We Watching and Hearing." Further up the street, a group of Crane's supporters gathered around him. Jason Bilbo, who had just appeared on the scene, was shaking hands and greeting people as he walked down towards the courthouse.

Scarcely half an hour had gone into deliberations when there was a slight commotion at the front door of the courthouse. Some people were hurrying, pushing to get into the building.

"The jury is returning. The jury is returning!" The word spread among the crowd, who instantly began pressing closer to the front door of the court.

Inside the courtroom, Judge Killjoy had returned to his bench and this had led to the spreading of the news about the jury's return. Shortly, led by its foreman, the jury marched back into the courtroom, and took its seat on the two long wooden benches. All was silence. Killjoy cleared his throat, a sure indication that he was about to say something.

"Has the jury reached a verdict?" All faces turned to the jury. Only Killjoy was scrutinizing some papers before him. A ruddy, stone-faced man in his late fifties now the spokesman for the jury rose to his feet. "We has, your honor." The man had a piece of white paper in his hands on which the verdict was written. Killjoy called to the clerk, who walked over to the jury, took the note, handed it to the judge, and returned to his seat.

Killjoy examined the note closely. He moved it further away from his face to facilitate his reading. Killjoy looked at the jury in silence. He pursed his mouth thoughtfully. Then he called upon the clerk to take the note and read the verdict.

The man took the note, and holding it far away from his eyes he read: "We the jury find the accused, Samandra Wright, guilty of murder."

"Is this your verdict?" Killjoy inquired sternly.

"Yeh," was the chorus reply.

"So say one, so say all?"

"Yeh."

There was a murmur throughout the court, some people sobbing in the back section of the court. Mabel was shaking her head back and forth, and whispering inaudibly. She was weeping silently, but Samandra, the condemned, sat, a look of quiet resignation on her face.

All eyes now turned to the judge, who waited for the court to return to silence. Silence. Killjoy looked over the court as if reluctant to speak. Then, "Samandra Wright," he said in a low, unhurried voice, "stand and come forward to be sentenced."

Samandra stood without help. She walked forward and stood directly before the judge. The judge looked down on her. "Do you have anything to say, child, before sentence is passed upon you?"

"I have nothing to say that ain't been said befo', your honor. Since what is goin' to happen is goin' to happen, it ain't necessary for me to say nothing 'bout the charges against me. I will say, though, that I am right sorry for the jury that found me guilty, and for your honor, who have to condemn me. This is a sad day for me an' my people, but it is a sadder day for this county and America. I hope God Almighty will forgive you all."

There was a murmur of voices from the white section of the audience. Killjoy raised his gavel, but it was not necessary to strike. Silence fell. "Samandra Wright," his voice was solemn as he spoke, "you have been duly tried by a jury of your peers according to the laws of the land, and found guilty of murder of Deputy Bole Miles. It is therefore the decision of this court that you, at an appointed time, be taken to a place of execution and hanged by the neck until you are dead. May God have mercy on your soul." He raised his gavel, but even before it struck the table the court broke into pandemonium.

"Justice been done," some were saying.

Many blacks, particularly women, were crying. "There ain't no justice in this county for black folk," a voice protested.

"Clear the courtroom! Clear the courtroom!" the bailiff was calling.

News of the verdict reached the people outside. There was cheering and an air of festivity among the two groups of League members; blacks observed in silent anger. Tyson was telling his followers, "If we didn't show up an' act up, I bet they woulda set that murderin' nigger free."

Inside the court, Mabel embraced her daughter, crying. Brude stood nearby, waiting to take the condemned prisoner away. The crowd was now leaving the courtroom. One white man, holding the arm of his wife as he moved to the door, shook his head sadly. "That girl ain't no mo' guilty than I is," he whispered to his wife. "Dem no-good—"

Judge Killjoy had already disappeared into his chambers. Pierce was being congratulated by a group of men. "We need a man like you to represent us in Jackson," one was saying. The jurors were cheered by some whites outside as they left the court. Some men were shouting, "Long live the League!"

⌃ ⌃ ⌃

Friday was the day set for the hanging of Samandra Wright. The time was to be nine o'clock in the morning. It was not clear what formula was used to determine the day and time, nevertheless, it was the time appointed by the court. The authorities in Mudville had the responsibility of preparing the basic equipment for the hanging, the platform, the rope, and other items essential.

The political climate and the demand for vengeance called for a public execution. Some of the viler elements of the county had already been worked up into a fit of frenzy. To them the trial. the judgment. was just the first part of the drama. The rest had to be carried out in public view. No one dared raise the issue of change of venue. Everyone with an ax to grind, was taking responsibility for the outcome of the trial. Tyson pointed out to anyone who would listen, the goal of the League in keeping the "fat of the authorities in the fire." Bilbo was quick to suggest that his public declarations and warnings had helped keep the trial on track, while Crane declared his "public and private warnings" as being a prime factor.

The news had already spread far beyond the county that the "nigger woman accused of murderin' a lawman was to be hanged in Mudville on Friday. "The hangin' is got to be done here!" Tyson emphasized to his followers. "If they takes her out of the county or out of the jeridiction of the county, next thing you knows, some smart, fas' talkin' lawyer may get her free."

Some white folks who had followed the details of the case were worried and somewhat distressed by the verdict, but with the growing crescendo of voices supporting the verdict, conventional wisdom recommended silence.

The one who would actually carry out the hanging was a professional hangman by the ironic name of Boaz Blind. Blind, like his old man, had taken up hanging as a profession. Now with his father deceased—actually accidentally hanging himself when experimenting with a new hanging device—Boaz traveled from place to place throughout the year, from one county to another in Mississippi as well as in other states, in the service of the grim reaper. In any case, Blind was to arrive soon in Mudville to test the equipment and was to depart by Friday evening for a double-hanging appointment in Arkansas.

⌃ ⌃ ⌃

Sheriff Brude from the beginning was unconvinced about the guilt of the woman to be hanged. This conviction, however, could not be transformed into any effective action during the trial, since only circumstantial evidence existed and in the trial environment, any such was ignored. Now Brude set about to try to have the sentence reprieved or changed to something less severe. It was clear to him that the four vital persons whose intervention could have an impact were the Mayor of Mudville, Judge Killjoy, Jason Bilbo, and Julius Crane. If he could get them privately to recommend clemency to the governor, the girl's life could be saved.

The mayor's office was just one block up the street from the sheriff's in the courthouse building, the same building in which Samandra Wright had been tried and condemned to die. The Mayor, Charles Simpson, saw through the open door the sheriff coming up the hallway, and rising from his desk, walked to the door to meet him. Sticking out his hand, he shook that of the sheriff warmly. His other hand he placed on Brude's shoulder, as he urged him to come in and chat for a while.

Simpson had been Mayor of Mudville for fifteen years. Though challenged more than once, he had never been beaten for the job. Now at fifty-five years of age, he bore a respectable paunch. Somewhat shorter than Brude, he was very much like the former Sheriff Tate. His head, touched with specks of gray, rested on a massive neck, which like his arms and back of his hands were covered by a forest of reddish hair. He had hazel eyes with heavy eyebrows, which carried a look of cunning; yet he was a mild-mannered man, skilled in the art of political survival and getting along with all men, agreeing with both sides of political issues as much as was possible.

The mayor greeted Brude, "Come set down here and rest your legs awhile. Try a cigar," the mayor offered, but Brude, who smoked only cigarettes, declined.

"Brude, I was thinking 'bout you since yesterday, and I was fixin' to call on you," the mayor began. "You are to be congratulated for the way you organized and kept things under control so far. It all is pretty touchy business, but I guess as officials we have to deal with it and move along." He leaned back in his chair which creaked loudly, and smiled emptily as he studied the sheriff's face.

"It is the trial I came to discuss with you, Mayor," Brude said, "and particularly its results. I am convinced that it will be a cruel tragedy if that black woman is hanged, not just because she is a woman, but because I am convinced that she is innocent."

The mayor looked startled. The smile on his face had vanished. He looked around the room as if to be sure that no one else was listening or had heard what Brude had just stated. Rising slowly from his seat, he went and closed the door which had been left ajar when Brude arrived. Walking back to his desk he responded to Brude.

"Do you have any idea what will happen if what you just said gets out in the community, much less to whom you said it?"

"Well, I know that there are folks out there who figure that because the woman is black that makes her guilty," Brude responded.

"Be it so or not, Sheriff Brude," the mayor said, as if suddenly endeavoring to be formal, "I am sure you know that you are dealing with dynamite. You're dealing with something that is bigger than you. It is bigger than me. It is more powerful than both of us independently or together. To follow up now what you just said, is like trying—me and you—to stop the Yazoo from flowing in the spring, when it's all riled up and overflowing its banks. The hard fact is, Brude," the mayor was somber, "there ain't nothing you or me can do to change the course of what is done and what will be done."

"All I am suggesting, Mr. Mayor," Brude pleaded, "is that someone with political influence like yourself can easily telegraph the governor of the state, explain the situation to him, and request clemency for the woman. Request that her sentence be changed from death to—maybe—life in prison."

The mayor placed the unlit cigar he held in the side of his mouth on the glass tray, his fingers slightly trembling. For brief moments, he covered his face with both hands, resting his elbows on the desk. He raised his head and looked at Brude.

"Listen, son," he said, an almost fatherly sound in his voice, but with an element of concern, "as far as I am concerned, you ain't never raised this issue with me, or said what you said. Yes, there are questions in my mind and in those of some folk I know, about what really happened down there by the Yazoo. But I tell you this," he paused briefly, "if you are hoping to find somebody of meaning who will say this out loud, you're wasting your time. If the League or other noisemakers around here even hear that I asked the governor for clemency for the nigger woman, do you know what will happen in the present political climate? Why, they will tar and feather me and run me out of the county, and leading the pack will be Crane and Jason Bilbo.

"Yes," he continued soberly, "I got some questions too, but I don't have no answers, and dere ain't no one, including you," he pointed his finger at the sheriff, "who can find answers for me."

"Therefore," he continued, "all I can do, and all you can do, is to let the process of law work. It's not perfect, but it's all we got."

He paused, and Brude was silent, pondering, his eyes fixed on the dark corner of the room. "I have been mayor of this town for fifteen years," Simpson sounded as one protesting.

Brude looked at him as he spoke, and momentarily he was surprised at how pudgy the man's face looked, how suddenly old. Or maybe he had never really looked at him so closely before. From where he sat, Brude could see the tiny distended red blood vessels on the mayor's face.

"They been fifteen good years," the mayor was saying. "Yes, there was ups and downs, but I learned how to live with them. I reckon I'm going to have one more term and call it quits. I don't particularly like how things are turning."

$\frown \frown \frown$

Tuesday evening. Mabel left the prison cell where her daughter was being held awaiting execution. Brude watched her leave. She was trying desperately to hold back the tears. After she had departed, Brude entered the prison area to Samandra's cell. He inquired regarding her health, and tried to encourage her with the thought that it might be possible to obtain clemency from the governor of the state. He assured her that he, as well as others in the white community, believed that she was innocent and was trying to help her. To these assurances, Samandra remained sullenly silent.

It was just after sundown. Judge Killjoy, having completed his supper, had settled into his favorite covered easy chair to read a new book on Homer he had recently received by mail. Behind him on the wall, a reproduction of the Madonna and Child looked down on the room. A black male servant opened the large oaken front door when someone knocked, and informed the judge that Sheriff Brude wished to see him.

Killjoy greeted the sheriff inside the front portal and invited him into his office while Brude apologized for calling on the judge at such a late hour.

"Think nothing of it," Judge Killjoy responded. "I have not had much of an opportunity to converse with you outside the confines of the courthouse." He seated the sheriff on the sofa under the window and turned his easy chair so that from where he sat, he faced the sheriff.

"Well, what brings you out here this time of the evening?" he asked, an element of genuine interest in his voice. "Don't tell me your prisoner has escaped!"

Brude was not sure whether the latter statement was meant to be humorous or serious, but he assured the judge that was not the case.

"Actually, I came to talk to you, your honor, about Samandra Wright." There was an element of formality and deference in his voice. "She is condemned to die for a crime I believe she did not commit. I am convinced that she is innocent."

Judge Killjoy looked up at the sheriff and frowned slightly as Brude continued. "I am convinced that she was the victim of a crime rather than the criminal."

"Are you saying, Sheriff Brude, that the court has been derelict in its duty of meting out justice?" Killjoy asked in a stern, quiet voice.

"No, your honor, not at all. The court is made up of human beings, and as human beings, members of the jury operating particularly in such a charged atmosphere as has existed in Mudville these past weeks, could make mistakes in judgment."

"Do you have any added information, germane data that can be defined as new evidence, to suggest the need for a retrial?"

"No, your honor, it is just a gut feeling and a strong conviction based on the circumstantial evidence presented by the defense attorney at the trial. Frankly, I do not believe a word of Drake's testimony of either why he and Bole were down on River Trail, or what occurred there."

"Why did you not express such opinions during the trial?" Killjoy asked.

"When the question was placed to me by the defense attorney, Pierce objected and you supported his objection."

"Yes, yes, you are correct," Killjoy acceded, nodding his head. "Of course, let me tell you right here, Sheriff," he continued. "There is nothing I can do at this point to reopen the case or postpone the hanging, short of new evidence. The only person who can do anything at this point, as you well know, is the Governor of Mississippi, and I as judge am in no position to request such of him.

"If a request is to be made, it should be by the mayor, a senator, a citizen committee or some such group. And, of course, you know as much as I do the kind of atmosphere in which we are operating. Frankly, I doubt whether you will find any person of substance, single or jointly, who will assume such a responsibility at this time."

Before Brude could respond, the judge continued, "It seems strange to hear a sheriff of a Mississippi county talking the language that you are talking."

"I am trying to be fair, your Honor," Brude responded. "It's just not right, it's not fair to have this woman hanged for something she has not done."

"Can you swear for sure that she is innocent?" Killjoy asked.

"I cannot swear, since I have no other evidence than what has already been presented in court, but I know that she is innocent. I believe that the jury responded to fear of the League, and just downright racial prejudice that blinded their sense of justice. It's neither fair nor right to hang that woman."

The serious expression on the judge's face led Brude to believe that Killjoy had taken umbrage to his statement, but the judge closed the book which he had held open on his lap. He looked at the sheriff and a calm, confident smile escaped his lips.

"I have heard you use the terms `fair' and 'right' twice this evening, Sheriff Brude," Killjoy said, thoughtfully. "But tell me, what does it mean to be right? What does it mean to be fair?" he asked rhetorically, his alert penetrating eyes studying the sheriff's expression. "What kind of definitions do you give to these terms?" he insisted. "Was it fair for the white man to take this land away from the Indians, and place the remnants that he has not destroyed on reservations? Was it fair to have brought poor whites from Europe, and blacks from Africa and use them as slaves to enhance the welfare of a fortunate class? Was it fair to free the poor white and to keep the black man in slavery for another two hundred years? Was it fair to emancipate him and yet exclude him from the democratic process of the nation as almost every state including Mississippi has done over the past few years? Is it fair for this land of democracy and plenty to be dominated both north and south by a small gentry class while the many millions scrounge off of nothing?"

"Is it fair or right," Killjoy persisted, "to try a black woman by an all-white jury, when in fact the law stipulates that you must be tried by a jury of your peers?" He paused, but Brude did not respond.

"When we use the terms 'fair' and `right'," the judge persisted, "they are both relative, to say the least, for they change in meaning from time to time. Much of what we call right today was defined as wrong yesterday. In fact, the criteria of what is right or fair are determined by consensus of those that wield power and are thus in a position to make laws and set standards. It was all right a few years back to have slaves. It was supported by law. Today, the law says it's wrong. Whether you and I like it or not, that is how the scheme of things is, and how it will remain, until the consensus is broad enough to support change.

"Going back to the main issue of discussion," Killjoy said, "we have had a jury trial and a decision was arrived at by the jury. Now if you feel that it ought to be changed, only the governor has that power.

Talk to the politicians," he suggested. "Much of the consensus of today is the product of their influence."

Early next day, Wednesday, Brude rode east of Mudville some five miles into the county to the spreading farm which was the home of Julius Crane. The beautiful white pillared, colonial mansion stood on a bluff, surrounded by well-manicured lawns, trees, and garden shrubs carefully cared for by a brigade of black servants, some of them having resided on the Crane's place since the days of slavery.

Crane listened to the sheriff's appeal and request that he, Crane, intercede with the governor of the state on behalf of the condemned woman.

"I can't believe that you, of all persons, would make a request of this nature," Crane said, a look of concern on his face. "Have you discussed this matter with Jason Bilbo?"

"Not as yet, but I intend to," Brude assured the senator. "I am convinced, however, that if you, who come from an influential family, are the local representative to the state government, and know the governor personally, can intercede, the best chance will be provided for getting a positive response from the governor."

"But the jury found her guilty, and the judge has sentenced her. Who am I to challenge the sentence?" Crane asked. "Can you imagine what my political competitors and opponents will say? With the present state of mind in this county, it would be tantamount to committing political and possibly physical suicide, were I to ask clemency for that black woman. Why, I'll be handing the election to my opponent on a golden platter." He held out his hands as if bearing the platter.

"If you, who are the most politically powerful man in the community, can do nothing on behalf of this condemned woman, then no one will try," Brude said. "I can't believe that this town will sit and watch that woman hanged for a crime she did not commit!"

"If you have new evidence," Crane advised, "turn it over to Judge Killjoy."

"I have none, aside from what was presented in court," Brude responded.

"Well," Crane said, turning his back to the sheriff and walking slowly towards the winding staircase that led to the second floor, "I do not want to get involved in details of the trial. I want to believe that the judge and the jury knew more about the case than I do."

"But I'll tell you this," he said, turning to face Brude once more. "If you can get Jason to sign such an appeal as you have requested of me, I will also sign, and send it to the governor. In that case, neither of us will be able to use it against the other in this election. This is as far as I can go, Sheriff Brude, and maintain my position in the community."

The logical person for Sheriff Brude to approach now was Jason Bilbo. This he did immediately upon his return to Mudville. Jason was a slim man, with slightly stooped shoulders. He had searching eyes that fell back deep in their sockets. When he spoke, he revealed a powerful, persuasive voice. Jason made no effort to challenge, neither did he seem surprised at what Brude was saying of his convictions of the innocence of the girl. He allowed Brude to finish all he had to say, along with his request for communication with the state governor on the girl's behalf.

"Do you realize what you are asking me, Brude?" he said calmly. "You are asking me to throw in the towel right now in this election, and let Crane walk away with it, the way he done for the past eight years."

"If I did such a thing," Jason continued, "I would be branded 'the biggest nigger lover' this county has ever seen, and I wouldn't be able to win a hog calling contest, much less a seat in the state government. The main political issues in this state during any election revolve around niggers—rightfully and wrongfully. Now," Bilbo was speaking a bit louder and becoming more intense as he spoke, "for over eight years I have held back on this issue 'cause I felt that there are so many important problems that need addressing in this state. But that's zactly why I never won." He irascibly stabbed a finger toward the sheriff. "That's why!"

"Do you know why Crane won in the last election? 'Cause he out-niggered me, that's why! Do you know why he won the one before that? 'Cause he out-niggered me!" As he spoke, his anger brimmed.

"But I tell you this, Brude," he said, shaking his finger at the sheriff, "that bastard ain't never goin' to out-nigger me no more. No, sirree! I'll see to that. I got my possum tail burnt twice and I sure aim to keep it out the fire this time."

"What do you mean, 'out-niggered' you?" Brude asked.

"Why, using that nigger scare to get votes from white folk. That's what I mean. Now," as he paused, he seemed to calm down, breathing less rapidly. "Now, I ain't no legislator as of now. He, Crane, is the one with all the power and contact. Let him contact the Governor. But as for me," looking Brude dead in the eyes, "I ain't getting' involved in any way, manner, or form in this case. Anyone who fools with it is done fer in this county. Anyone!" he emphasized.

"It took me years to learn how to fight an election here in Mudville County. I learned from bitter experiences. An' I ain't never goin' to ferget." His voice was growing excited again. "That rascal is running scared now, and I intend to keep it that way till the election is over," he shouted, pounding the table with his fists, to emphasize his point.

Having said his piece, Jason walked towards the wall of the room and for several moments studied the picture of his father, Abraham Jason Bilbo, hanging thereon. Brude got to up to leave, and as he rose, Jason turned around to face him.

"It's a pity, I'll say," his voice low and meditative. "It's a real pity that that nigger woman got herself in this fix at this time. Now if it was a few months later, after the elections, maybe. There is a lot of things that could have been done—behind the scenes, of course—to save her. But the way it is now, it's hopeless." He shook his head, looking at the sheriff's boots. "Any politician who touches her, even with a long pole, is just as good as finished."

⌃ ⌃ ⌃

Among black folks in Wrightsville and other areas of the county, there was a sense of despair. During the trial, some of the more optimistic, including Parson Jones, felt assured that "right will prevail" and that "Gawd would intervene," while others, analyzing the situation in the county in the light of the upcoming elections, even before the trial felt that Samandra did not have a chance. Now with the trial ended and the girl actually condemned to die, disbelief prevailed. How could such a thing happen? That Samandra Wright, such a lovely, respectful, and innocent young lady, could be condemned to die for a crime they all knew she had not committed. The entire series of episodes—the killing of Joshua, the attack on Samandra, her trial and death sentence—had come in such quick succession, that many were still in a state of shock and incredulity.

In times of such crisis and impending human tragedy, when all mortal efforts to alter the course of events seem to be expended in vain, then many—the religious as well as others who in normal times are oblivious to the existence of the supernatural—begin to search for a miracle, and proceed to look to the stars and other natural phenomena for wonders and signs. Some of the older folk and the more religious took to speculating and prophesying. Deacon Johnson declared the morning after the trial that, "This is a sure nuf sign of the end. The Good Book says that the last happenings will be rapid ones, jus' as we seen in the last few days."

Some prophesied, "Jus' as de angel of Gawd opened de gate of de prison for Peter an' Paul, broke de chains an' put the prison guards to sleep, jus' so they will do for po' dear Samandra, so she can escape an' save her life."

Others said, "Jus' wait an' see, some miracle gonna be worked this very week."

But while such predictions were being made, others were making plans to leave the county and head up north. Leroy Battles had collected a number of names of people who wanted to go to Philadelphia and New York City.

On Monday night after the trial, many black people from Wrightsville and the surrounding area drifted spontaneously to the only place where solace and comfort could be sought—the church. News had spread that evening that Parson Jones would be holding a special prayer meeting for Samandra Wright, but others seeking the church knew nothing of plans for a meeting and just followed the impulse to seek relief there.

At the meeting, Reverend Jones announced that each night during that week a prayer meeting would be held for Samandra. "This is gonna be a week of prayer an' supplication befo' the Lawd," he announced. "If it be His will, He will save Samandra. He had the power to open up the Red Sea in the days of old so the chillen' of Israel could walk on dry lan', He had the power to stay the hand of Sennacherib, the king of Assyria, when his people was in trouble, an' I feel that He can do the same for that chile."

SEVEN:

THE HANGING

Thursday evening. Rumors, encouraged by Snake-eyed Pete, had spread around Mudville that efforts were being made by Brude and other unidentified persons to save the life of Samandra.

As the rumor traveled, it altered its form and shape, as rumors are wont to do during times of crisis. A few men, all members of the League, determined to see to it that "justice be carried out," sat around all day in front of Tyson's store. Some sat through the night to raise the alarm should any suspicious acts be observed. They paid close attention to the comings and goings at the jailhouse.

All day, work on the hanging place had proceeded slowly. By sundown, the platform was constructed, and the gallows installed. The men lingering around Tyson's place gathered around the platform to talk about the upcoming event. By four-thirty, the men had drifted back to Tyson's shop, and a few children from the town played near the platform.

Shortly, the attention of the men was drawn to a stranger approaching from the direction of the courthouse. He was dressed in a dark suit, black shoes, and a black top hat. With his attire, he looked more like a mortician than a preacher. As the stranger drew nearer, the men got a better look at him. He bore a long, hard visage, with inward drawn cheeks that were rough and marked with scars of chicken pox; his eyes were dark hazel and carried an expression of morose sadness.

There was silence from the men by Tyson's as the stranger approached. The children playing near the gallows saw him coming and ran. The stranger passed the men without as much as looking in their direction, as if those looking at him in silence did not exist. He walked down the middle of the road directly towards the platform on which the gallows was built. The stranger stood and gazed at the structure in silence. He climbed on to the platform and examined closely the structure and the hanging mechanism. He pulled on the wooden handle projecting from the side of the gallows, and carefully observed the response of the mechanism. Then he repeated the action again. Satisfied that it performed properly, he descended the platform and headed back in the direction of the courthouse, once more completely ignoring the men gathered in front of Tyson's place.

Brude had given up all hope of saving the life of Samandra. In a last desperate act, he had wired the Governor of the state appealing for clemency for the girl. There was no reply. Ominously, irrevocably, the minutes were passing, bringing ever closer the moment of execution. There was not a single person of political substance or influence in the town to whom he had not appealed for assistance. All in vain.

From his office, Brude could hear the echoes of the sound of hammers as nails were driven into the hanging platform by men putting the finishing touches to the job. Samandra, too, could hear the rhythmic sounds of hammer beat and could see the structure standing there in the open field.

Brude, a hard and sturdy man, struggled to keep himself from being overcome by a state of depression and despair which like an uninvited guest, stood by the door waiting to enter.

Brude walked into the prison area behind the office. Samandra, using the light of the cell, was writing a letter. Brude looked through the bars at the woman seated there. He wondered if she fully understood the dreadful fate which awaited her in a matter of hours. She, he thought, like an innocent lamb, was to be sacrificed on the altar of racial bigotry and political avarice.

"How do you feel this evening?" Brude inquired.

"As well as can be expected," she answered. "I have just finished writing a letter to my sister and brother who have gone to Chicago. I have never had to write them before because we were always in the same house. This is the first and last letter they will get from me." There was a sound of resignation in her voice.

"Don't give up hope," Brude urged. "I can't say I have been too successful in my efforts to get community leaders to intercede with the governor on your behalf. As a last resort, I wired the governor myself and now we can only wait." Brude sighed deeply. He watched Samandra as she folded the letters and placed them under her pillow.

"If you were a white woman, you never would have been in jail this evening," he said remorsefully, shaking his head and looking down at the floor of the cell. "It is those who accused you who would have been tried and jailed. It's really unbelievable what a few drops of colored blood in a person's veins could do here in Mississippi," Brude continued. "There is so much hostility, irrational fear, hatred, and ignorance, literally generated or encouraged by the politics of this state, that even normally decent, sane, and Christian folk become hamstrung and helpless."

Samandra stood and walked over towards the cell door, so that now only the bars separated her from the sheriff. "Why do I have to be a white woman to find justice in Mississippi?" she asked. "Seems to me that justice shouldn't have no color or race. Justice should be just justice. Like the sun shines and the rain falls on everybody, it should be for all the same. God ain't never said, 'I ain't goin' to let my sun shine on white folk, or on colored, or on Indians, 'cause their color is different.' Seems to me justice ought to be the same. As I see it, it ain't possible to have justice for white folk if the same laws ain't gonna give justice to them what ain't white." She was looking directly into Brude's eyes. "If the jury know that I is innocent, an' the judge know that I is innocent, an' if all dem people crowded outside the court know that I is innocent, an' they still condemn me or support my condemnation, then they is doin' far more harm to themselves as white folk than they doin' to me, for in hangin' me they may destroy my body, but at the same time they is destroyin' their souls, an' that of their children."

Brude pondered on what the girl had said. In the ensuing silence, he seemed reaching into his soul in search of an answer.

"You are a brave woman, Samandra Wright," Brude finally said, holding onto the bars as he spoke, "a very brave woman. In the face of death and humiliation, to talk the way you are talking. Whatever source your strength come from, it must be very deep! Do all black women feel the way you do?" he inquired.

"Black women is jus' as different from each other as white women is," she responded. "There is strong an' there is weak ones. If I am strong, I am strong 'cause I had to be since I was a chile in order to survive, an' because my mother when I was a child, an' my adopted mother, Mabel, taught me how to be strong."

"As a black woman," Samandra continued, "you got to be strong, real strong, in order to survive in a white world an' keep your self respect an' don't go crazy. You got to have strength to live and you got to be even stronger to die for something you ain't guilty of."

As Brude spoke to the girl and listened to her responses, as he looked at her through the iron bars and saw the quiet resignation on her face, feelings of unfathomable grief and sorrow like a rising tide surged into his soul. Glimpses of his own past, subliminal flashes, rushed across the screen of his mind, and mingled painfully with the present, so that for a moment, for a brief moment, he sensed a feeling of unity with the condemned woman. It was as if part of his own soul was behind those iron bars, condemned to die. As the disquieting emotions swelled within him, rays of the evening sun flickered through the bars of the small window behind the cell. He yearned to reach, to reach through the bars and merge his troubled spirit with that of the suffering woman in mutual agony. Cognizance of his feeling brought an ephemeral sense of guilt, that such sentiments were being so profoundly shared with a black woman, he a white sheriff in a Mississippi town.

Presently, it seemed to the sheriff that he, not Samandra Wright, was behind those bars condemned to die. Now, stronger than the transitory feeling of guilt and shame, was an intense yearning to expose, to spill his soul before the black woman, let it pour forth like a gushing stream from the heart of a mountain after the rain. Perhaps it would bring some peace to him and comfort her, to let her know that he too was a child of sorrow.

But how could one comfort an innocent condemned to ignoble death? In the confusion of his soul, he questioned himself. "How can a white man feel this way towards a black woman? Is this love? Is this pity?"

Strangely, this reaching out of his soul was similar to the feeling that surged in him when first he encountered Samandra some four years earlier, when with Sheriff Tate, his predecessor, he had visited Mabel's place by the Yazoo, in search of the black man who had attacked Tyson in his shop and left him for dead. Brude recalled how he had seen Samandra with her sister standing on the porch of their house. For moments, he had stood there gazing at the girl while ambivalent feelings rose within him. The girl had recoiled at his gaze, and with her sister had withdrawn into the house, closing the door loudly behind them.

Samandra, now as she looked and listened to the sheriff, sensed the agony of his spirit and was sorry for him. All along, she had viewed him as a lawman. Now she perceived his humanity.

⌒⌒⌒

It was that time of the evening in Mudville when most businesses closed for the day. Mayor Simpson was in the process of putting his desk in order before departing, when Sheriff Brude walked in. He walked with a rapid pace as a man in a great hurry. The mayor paused from what he was doing to greet the sheriff, who had entered the open door without knocking.

"Well, Brude, how are things looking?"

Brude did not reply. Taking the sheriff's star that had decorated the front of his_shirt, he slammed it down onto the mayor's desk. "I resign as of now. Find someone else to officiate over that murder that this county will commit tomorrow," he said. "I'll have no part in it." Brude turned and headed for the open door.

"Jus' wait here a minute. Brude," the mayor said. "Jus a minute, son," his voice was strangely sad and almost fatherly.

Brude paused, and in that moment of hesitation, the mayor walked over and closed the door. "Come sit down here just a minute," he urged. Brude walked to the desk and sat on one of the two cane chairs.

"Now you know jus' as much as I do," the mayor said, "that there is already rumors around that efforts will be made to keep the judgment of the court from being carried out. There is a lot of drinking going on this evening, and there are some who would like to take that woman out tonight and lynch her. You are the only one in this here town that can offer any protection for that girl tonight," the mayor pointed out.

"Everyone is so paralyzed by the present atmosphere in the county. I can't see a soul—except myself perhaps—who would raise a finger if people decide to take the law into their own hands. If you leave," the mayor continued, "Snake-eyed Pete will be in charge, and that will be like putting the League in charge of the sheriff's office and the jail. If that woman is going to die—whether it be just or unjust—it should be how the law calls for it and not the lynch mob."

A feeling of defeat and despair had fallen over the sheriff. The flesh on the sides of his face and jaw seemed to hang lifeless. Brude pondered what the mayor had said. The mayor had spoken the truth. Indeed, Pete had for the past few days settled in the shadow, sulking, waiting for something to happen. This would be playing into his hands. Presently, his thoughts returned to the condemned woman.

"I am feeling the agony and frustration that that black woman is feeling over there in the jailhouse," he said. "Because I know what it means to suffer for something you never done." His voice was low, reflecting an element of morbid resignation. "I know what it is to be thrown in jail, called a criminal, when in fact you ain't guilty of no crime. You know that you are innocent, yet there you are, locked up. . . . I know how it feels 'cause that's exactly what happened to me some years back!"

He looked at the mayor. There was an element of surprise on the mayor's face.

"Yes, I was in jail for two years," Brude assured him, "yet I was innocent. It was in New York City. I was just walking down the road, minding my own business in a place called Harlem. I just happened to pass where some poor whites and coloreds were protesting and marching. The authorities called it a riot. The next thing I knew, the police had me before this Irish judge. Once the judge heard my Mississippi accent, I didn't have a chance. He gave me two years in jail with hard labor. I'll tell you this," he continued, "if it weren't for the help I got from niggers in the jail, I'd still be there, and probably dead today. I had three months left to go, and the warden, one of the meanest

Irishmen you ever seen, let it be known that he was going to fix it so I'd never leave."

As he spoke, it seemed as if he had returned to his prison experience, a distant look appearing in his eyes. It was as if his body was with the mayor but his spirit was at another place. "Well, they took me out on a road gang. Some niggers got into a fight to divert the attention of the guards, and I took off. I changed my name and came back south."

Brude paused. He seemed struggling to go further. He opened his mouth but no words came forth. He wiped his lips with the back of his hand, his eyes reflected immeasurable sadness.

"I always figured there was something strange 'bout you, Brude," the mayor said. "Something kind of distant that I could not understand. Now I know."

"Do you?" Brude asked, raising his eyes and staring at the mayor.

As if unable to bear the agony reflected in the gaze, the mayor shifted his eyes away from the sheriff. "I always wondered why your thoughts seemed so far away," he said.

"There is much reason for my thoughts being far away," Brude responded. "You see, I escaped from jail, but in many ways I am still a prisoner. For what happened to me was worse than being killed. Yes," he said, as the mayor looked at him troubled and perplexed. "I had the loveliest wife and two children this side of heaven," Brude said, his voice weighted with emotion. "We lived on a small farm about seventy-five miles west of here at a place called Rocky Bottom, in Bolton County. My name was not Brude then. It was McBride, Billy McBride.

"That summer, I went to New York to make some quick money in order to do some work on my house and expand my herd of cattle. They kept me in jail for two years from my family. When I escaped, I headed directly for Rocky Bottom and my family, but when I got there, the house was empty. There was a grave with a wooden cross with my wife's name written on it. A stranger, calling himself the children's uncle, had sold all our possessions and even tried to sell the land. Worst of all, he took my children away.

"His name was Enoch Drude. I tracked him down for more than six years, from state to state all across the west. I was always a few days or weeks behind him. Finally, I caught up with what was left of him in a small town in Wyoming. He had been shot and killed two weeks earlier over a game of poker. They buried him in a shallow grave overlooking the town. All I found was a crude wooden cross, with his name, date, and cause of death."

"Some folks I spoke to along the road said he claimed to have had two children, living someplace with relatives. One woman told me she understood that the children were somewhere in Missouri. A man in Fargo, North Dakota, told me he heard the man say his two children, a boy and a girl, had died from swamp fever. Those could have been my children. There are so many unanswered questions. How did my wife die? Did he kill her? What had he done with my children? Are they dead? Are they still living? For a while, I accepted that perhaps my children were dead. But since this incident with this black woman, everything has returned. Night after night, I have dreamt about my children. I hear them calling me. I see them reaching out for me. I am convinced once more that they are alive. This case—the cruel injustice of it all, the helplessness—has brought it all back to me. It is as if some mysterious force is seeking to lead me to my children." He paused, as the mayor listened in stunned silence.

"I did not plan to stay in Mudville when first I came to this town," Brude continued. "I was on my way back out west. That tornado, four years back and the tragedy it caused, got me involved. I tried to help and became involved with the fate of this county. Now, four years later, I am sheriff with all this happening around me."

"This yearning, this calling, I hope it will lead me to my children. Looking at the woman in jail has brought back a sense of emptiness to me. I know it sounds insane," he said, shaking his head in sadness, "but that black woman over there in that jail, she somehow reminds me of my wife. She has the same kind of face and body—only she is black and my wife was white. The same eyes, the same lips—I shall leave tomorrow evening," he said. "I must find my children if they are alive. I shall go back over the trail. Somewhere, hopefully, I'll run into something. Until then, I shall keep the sheriff's badge."

"Now I think I finally understand you," the mayor said. "You have answered a lot of questions for me. I am dreadfully sorry 'bout what has happened to you, Brude, and I hope that somehow you will find answers to all your questions and be reunited with your children. I am grateful that you have decided to stay on until tomorrow."

~ ~ ~

The setting of the sun on Thursday evening in late October was an awesome sight. It provided food for new myths and legends, and for those who during periods of stress and extreme crisis see signs and wonders in the heavens and in the behavior of natural phenomena. Just before sundown, the whole of the western sky was drenched in crimson. It was as if the very heart of the sun had broken, spilling blood across the heavens. The softening rays of falling evening light spread the crimson glow over the entire delta. It persisted long after the sun had departed behind a dark crimson cloudbank which rimmed the western sky. The men seated by the front door of Tyson's store observed the spectacle in silence.

On his small farm, directly south of Wrightsville, Jim Brown paused from feeding his hogs to observe the autumn sky. "There is blood in dem clouds," he muttered. "It don't look too good at all for poor Samandra."

Gently, the light of evening faded. A deceptive calm settled over the town of Wrightsville. The gallows stood grotesquely against the skyline. The men in front of Tyson's place were now faint shadows and voices.

⌒ ⌒ ⌒

Shortly after seven o'clock, the sound of a galloping horse caught the attention of the men seated in the darkness before Tyson's store. It was clearly a single rider coming at great speed from the direction of Wrightsville. Some of the men arose and walked to the middle of the road, all looking in the direction from which the horse was approaching. As the horse drew near, its rider could be recognized in the darkness. It was Snake-eyed Pete. Pete sprang from the horse in a single motion and the men crowded around him. Hastily he exchanged words with the men, who suddenly scattered like a flock of sheep having spotted a wolf. Some dashed into Tyson's shop. Others headed pell-mell down the road past the sheriff's office. Brude, who had been standing by the door of the office brooding in darkness, observed all that had transpired. He had seen the behavior of the men and immediately ordered his deputies, along with Hennessee, to arm themselves—part of a pre-planned arrangement to be executed in case of trouble during the night.

Pete, whom Brude had not seen all evening, rushed towards the door of the sheriff's office, and while Brude was demanding to know what was the cause of alarm, blurted out as he passed the sheriff, "The niggers is comin' to break in the jail an' free that woman. There is hundreds of them armed to the teeth. Look like everyone who can handle a gun in Niggerville is headin' this way."

"Are you sure about that?" Brude asked skeptically.

"Jus' as I is sure they kilt Bole Miles, jus' so I is sure they comin'. I seen them with my own eyes." Pete walked to the rack, pulled a rifle and proceeded to load it. "I done alerted all the white folks along the road," he said hastily. "I suggested that they all come to Mudville for protection."

This development had taken Brude by complete surprise. He was still skeptical of the report. As he tried to pull further details from Pete, a gathering din of voices could be heard outside. Brude opened the door and stepped onto the porch. The men gathered before the office were all armed. There were fifteen outside already and the number was increasing. Shortly, a horse-drawn carriage came galloping into town. It carried a white farmer, his wife, and three children. In a short space of time, four other carriages arrived, leaving only one white family on the road unaccounted for.

"Where is the Stephen family?" Pete inquired of the last arrival.

"Dat damn fool said he ain't runnin' from no niggers," the man said. "Said he been workin' and livin' near niggers all his life. Said a nigger done learnt him how to lay bricks, an' he don't have no quarrel wid them. An' that fool wife of his agree with him."

"Seen anything?" Pete asked another.

"Yeh, I seen them," the man replied. "They is marchin' from Niggerville. The whole road is black with them. I reckon they woulda wiped me an' the missus out if Pete here didn't warn us that dey was comin'."

Pete was acting more like sheriff than deputy, and the men were looking to him for leadership.

"I say we set an ambush for them along the road an' cut dem down, rather than wait for dem to attack us." There was a murmur of assent from the crowd of men now gathered before the sheriff's office.

"There isn't going to be no ambush," Brude informed him,

"So what do ya expect us to do? Sit here an' wait for dem to attack?" Pete asked heatedly.

"I expect you to keep your mouth shut and await orders from me. I've done told you before, I am the sheriff in this county." Brude was obviously angry as he spoke. Here was a clear effort on the part of Pete to usurp the authority of his office.

"Seems to me that whenever niggers is involved, there is reluctance to take action," Pete said, looking at the man. "Like how long it took to arrest that woman after she done kilt Bole Miles. These people here is got wives an' children in this town. They don't want them to be exposed to no danger from niggers or nobody else." Pete surveyed the faces of the men to gauge the support he was receiving from them. The flickering torches showed a grim crowd of red faces. They were ready and seemed eager for action.

Had Pete not been looking at the men from whom he sought support, he would have observed that Brude had drawn his gun from its holster and had it pointed straight at the deputy's head. This was a coup in the making and Brude aimed to stop it and avert a disaster if possible.

"Your gun and your badge." His voice was soft and cold. Pete turned and was looking right into the muzzle of the Colt 45. Startled by the sudden change of affairs, Pete hesitated. In the meantime, Brude calmly took the rifle from his hands, passing it to young Deputy Tate standing nearby. "That gun and holster is county property. Let's have it."

Pete looked at the sheriff. There was a cold stare, the kind which Pete knew, too well, meant business. A finger clutched the trigger. Quietly, he unbuckled the holster and handed it to Brude.

"This ain't the end of this, you know," he said, backing away.

"You are no longer a deputy in this county, and I am telling you right now. Between tonight and tomorrow evening, don't let me catch you carrying a gun in public and don't start any ruckus, for you'll be the first one to catch a bullet."

"Now," Brude continued, "you can get off the road or sleep in jail. Make up your mind."

Pete turned, pushed his way through the men and walked off into the darkness.

Brude turned to the men. They were sullen and silent. "Men," he said, "it seems as if we may have some trouble tonight. I am going to be in need of some deputies. Which of you are ready to be deputized?"

One hand went up, another, and another, till all thirty of the men gathered outside had their hands in the air.

"Do you all swear to represent the law and follow my orders?"

"Yeah," was the response.

Brude looked over the men hurriedly. "Tyson, I want you to take these ten men and line them up behind those carriages." He pointed to the five carriages not more than half a block up the road. "Put one of the carriages right across the road," he ordered, "and don't do anything until you get orders from me."

"Come on boys, let's go to it," Tyson called excitedly. The other men, Brude placed under his two deputies. He deployed one group behind the prison and the other on both sides of the road leading to the sheriff's office. Brude, along with Hennessee, stood before the office. The men with guns at ready, were now all in place waiting in the darkness.

All was now motionless in the autumn night, save in the silent dome above, where a myriad of stars nervously trembled around a pale, sickle moon. The eyes of the armed men were fixed in the direction of the dirt road leading westward. Shortly, a star fell from the sky over Wrightsville. An eerie trail of fire marked its path as it hurtled earthward and vanished.

⌃ ⌃ ⌃

A single light appeared on the Wrightsville road. "They is comin'! The niggers is comin'!" someone called from the darkness. Brude walked away from the door of the sheriff's office onto the road.

Hennessee, completely sober, walked by his side. The light had appeared where the road curved about one thousand feet away. As the light drew nearer, its rhythmic movement in the darkness revealed that it was being borne by one on horseback. Now it approached that part of the road which ran athwart the field where the gallows stood. Nearer and nearer it came. Now the tramping of a hundred feet could be heard, as the yet unseen crowd, following the horseback rider, approached the town of Mudville on the dusty dirt road. They were coming directly towards the corner where stood the sheriff's office. As they drew near, Brude recognized that the lantern carrier on horseback was Reverend Jones himself. Behind him was a crowd of at least two hundred persons on foot. Old men and women, young people, children. A few feet from the corner of the sheriff's office, the procession stopped.

Parson Jones dismounted and placed the lantern on the ground. Some thirty feet away were the prison walls, with the small iron grated window marking the cell that held Samandra. The people formed a semi-circle around the lamp by which stood the preacher. As they formed, one of the old deacons started to sing and immediately the entire group joined in:

"Amazin' grace, how sweet da sound.
Dat saved a wretch like me;
Ah once woz loss an' now ahm found,
Woz blind but now I see."

The old deacon, with pathos in his voice, cried out the remaining words of the song, line by line, as the people sang:

"Twas grace that taught ma heart to fear,
An' grace ma fears relieve'
How pre-shus did that grace appear,
The hour I furs believe.

Through many dangers, toils, and sneers,
I been already come;
Tis grace that brung me safe thus far,
An' grace will lead me home."

As they sang, the armed men guarding the approaches to the town left their posts and crowded the road behind the sheriff. They observed with surprise the unrealism of what was transpiring as contrasted with their expectations.

Having completed the words of the song, the people took to humming the tune. As they hummed, Parson Jones began to speak and gradually the humming died away.

"We are gathered here tonight as one family, people from across the county," the parson began. "We come here in the name of Jesus to bring courage and strength to the heart of one of us held behind these here prison walls. One who has been condemned to die for a crime of which we believe she is innocent. All week, we been having prayer meetings beseeching the Almighty to intercede and set Samandra free. We believe that the Almighty moves in His own ways, His wonders to perform. He plants His footsteps on the sea and rides upon the storm. Sometimes, he does not answer us 'zactly as we wants, but this we know, that He always answer the pleadin' of his children. He came to Daniel while he was in the den of lions. He came to Israel while they was in bondage.

"He came to the three Hebrew boys in the fiery furnace of Nebuchadnezzer. An' we believe that He can come an' save Samandra. Jus' as He worked on the heart of Pharaoh to let Israel go, so He can work on the heart of the governor of Mississippi to set Samandra free.

"Some of us know Samandra since she was a little chile. We seen her through sickness an' health. I remember years back when she was sick to the point of death an' we prayed an' Gawd came an' healed her. We believe! Yes, we believe, that that same Gawd, can save her now."

"Oh Samandra, we want you to know that we loves you, chile. Our hearts is full of pain an' anguish in that prison with you. Yes, I is an old man. I have lived my life. I is ready to take your place an' die for you if they will let me."

His sermon was interspersed with "Amens" and "Yes, Lawd," from the people.

"Oh Samandra, we says to you as Abraham said to his son Isaac when he was laid out on the altar, the will of Gawd must be glorified. If He sees it fit, he will set you free." There were tears in his eyes which ran down his cheeks, and his voice broke as he spoke. Samandra, standing on the bunk bed, was looking through and holding onto the bars of the small window. She too was crying. So were many people in the group outside, including Mabel Wright who stood in the front line of the crowd.

Parson Jones continued his sermon. "If it be the Almighty's will, He will set you free, an' if it is not His will, you must, my dear chile, be able to say as Job said, 'Though they slays me, yet will I serve him.' Be strong, Samandra, be strong. We will be pleading to God for you through the night and tomorrow. If you be called to lay down your young and precious life tomorrow, know that our prayers, our tears, will follow you all the way to paradise. Oh, so much injustice, so much inhumanity. What a wonderful world it would be if we could only show love for one another.

"I say to you, dear chile, what I say to all of us here tonight. Let us all declare, The Lord is my shepherd, I shall not want. He maketh me to lie down in green pastures, He leadeth me beside still waters, He restoreth my soul." Samandra was repeating the words of the text of scripture as were the people. 'Yeah, though I walk through the valley of the shadow of death, I shall fear no evil, for thou art with me, thy rod and thy staff they comfort me.' So goodbye we say to you tonight, dear chile, until we meet again—on earth or in heaven—Gawd be with you."

When Parson Jones finished, there was not a dry eye among his followers. There was a death-like silence among the armed men. The parson led his people in prayer. This was followed by the further singing of songs. As they sang, Mabel, accompanied by Parson Jones, was allowed to enter the prison for a last meeting with Samandra. Parson Jones prayed with Samandra, kissed her on the cheek and then left her alone with her mother. Mother and child cried in each other's arms. They kissed and said goodbye.

Having achieved the purpose of the visit, Parson Jones once more climbed onto his horse. Taking the lantern, solemnly as in a funeral procession he turned his face towards Wrightsville. As they moved away from the town, the people were led in singing by an old deacon.

> Gawd be wid you till we meet again,
> By His counsel guide, uphold you,
> With his arms securely fold you,
> Gawd be wid you till we meet again.
>
> Gawd be wid you till we meet again,
> When life's perils thick confound you,
> Put His arms enfolding 'round you,
> Gawd be wid you till we meet again.
>
> Till we meet, till we meet,
> Till we meet at Jesus' feet,
> Till we meet, till we meet,
> Gawd be with you till we meet again.

Soon the night had swallowed up the preacher and his followers. There were now only voices and a light glimmering ever dimmer in the distance. The voices of the women wailing and mourning could be heard among the singing. Now the light was gone and only the wailing and singing remained, the voices rising and falling in the distant darkness, like gushing wind among the weeping willows. Gradually, the wailing and the singing died away.

⌃ ⌃ ⌃

Long before the sun had risen, when the first gray of early dawn still made it difficult to distinguish an inanimate object from a man a few feet away, the first of the spectators began to arrive in the town of Mudville. They came from Limestone Hills, from across the Yazoo, from the farming country beyond Four Corners, and from across the county line. They had one aim in mind—"to see the nigger woman hang." Some of them had seen hangings before and as they traveled to Mudville, they talked among themselves, giving lurid details often exaggerated, of earlier hangings of "niggers" they had witnessed. Samandra's hanging was set for nine in the morning.

By the time the sun edged over the horizon, the men gathered into small groups were stretched out between the sheriff's office and the platform on which the gallows was built. Some moved from one group to another, listening to the various conversations and stories being told.

Rumors had it that the black woman might not hang after all, that certain people had sent telegrams to the governor, asking for clemency for the girl. Some had it that the girl had already been secretly removed during the night. These rumors only heightened the expectations among the gathering on the street. Rumors also had it that "niggers is planning an attack to free the woman before she is hanged." Some of the early arrivals brought whiskey with them and were already drunk.

The various groups into which the men had formed themselves moved restlessly from one point of interest to another. Now they stood across from the sheriff's office, now they moved to the hanging place, scrutinizing the gallows, speculating as to how it would operate. Now they drifted back in the direction of the prison, looking at the window behind which the prisoner was supposed to be held.

"I is willin' to bet that there ain't nobody in that there jail. She been done took out an' carried out o' the county," one man said.

"I hear say Brude is soft on her. Won't be s'prised if she ain't done give him a piece in jail an' he helped her escape," another said. "There he goes now, the sheriff. Wonder where he's headin'? He goin' back in the office!"

"Maybe we ought to send one or two men inside to look round an' see what's goin' on," another suggested.

"Yes, yes," others agreed.

Two men approached the office and requested entrance. An armed deputy stood behind the door.

"What do you all want?"

"We want to come an' talk to the sheriff."

"What do you want to talk to him fer?"

The men hesitated.

"The sheriff is busy," the deputy said.

The men walked back to the group waiting across the road. "Won't even let us in," they complained. Another group of men further down the road drew near to learn what had transpired.

As the seconds and minutes ticked away, bringing ever nearer the hour of hanging, the small groups of men shifting back and forth between the sheriff's office and the hanging place were gradually merging into one and assuming the characteristics of a pack.

A large number of canine gathered at the same place and time cannot be called a pack. To be a pack, there must be the element of commonalty of interest along with the variable of propinquity. The pack emerges from a process which draws canines together and imbues them with certain primeval urges and drives related to the hunt. They become forged into a single unit with characteristics separate from those of individual members.

The cur, the stray, the product of mating in the cotton field of an ownerless bitch nurtured on hardship, scowling balefully and fearful of her own shadow; the mongrel that whimpers and scampers at the drop of a hat, or yelps in response to a passerby who bends down not to throw a stone but to scratch his ankle; the mutt, discarded in his youth and adopted by some kind farmer, who repays his master by eating much and sleeping while the fox and the wolf attack the livestock, all acquire now a sense of fortitude and power when drawn together in the pack. They sniff at the wind restlessly, ready to test their new found strength against any foe!

The well-trained house dog becomes part of the pack, the obedient coon dog, the disciplined German shepherd, and the gentle poodle—each merges with the less fortunate of their land, drawn by urges out of their distant past. Once together, they are no longer themselves, and become a force to be reckoned with. In vain their masters call! Now they ignore their voices, following rather a voice from their primeval ancestors.

So it was with the men gathered from across the county and beyond, to witness the hanging of Samandra Wright. Without regard for background, economic or social standing; without regard for past attitudes or feelings towards each other. The political adherents of both Crane and Bilbo mingled together as part of the pack. Responsible town folk as well as some farmers who under normal times were constrained by their upbringing or religious orientation towards moderation, now as part of the pack were caught in a whirl of uncontrolled anticipation. A profound libidinal drive, primitive animal instinct, normally submerged under layers of culture and socialization, was forcing its way to the surface in response to a primeval tribal call.

Jeb Tyson momentarily assumed leadership of the pack. His eyes were bloodshot and glaring, one side of his face twitching with excitement. "All hell is goin' to break loose in this here town today," he declared, "an' there is gonna be mo' than one hangin' if nine o'clock come an' that nigger woman ain't brought out."

"Yeh," the men responded.

"If that nigger woman ain't brought out come nine, Brude is goin' to be up shit creek without a paddle," a little man added.

"We ought to find out now if or not Brude mean to carry out the rulin' of the court an' hang the nigger," another said.

"There you is!" another responded.

"I say we go over now and demand to see the prisoner," Tyson suggested.

"Let's go! Let's go!" The pack, now by the hanging platform, headed toward the sheriff's office.

"Bring out that nigger woman! We want to see her wid our own eyes," a drunk fellow bellowed. There was a roar of approval.

"Brude! Come out! We want to talk to you!" another demanded.

"I say we break down the damn' door!" the little man bellowed. He was normally faceless and quiet, pusillanimous, subdued by years of existence with a massive, rambunctious wife three times his size, who often "wupped" him if he dared spend a penny at the gambling table. Many a night she would lock him out of his own house, forcing him to beg on his knees to be let in. Yet here he was, intrepid, a sense of consummate power surging through his veins.

The door slowly opened and Brude stood there, rifle in hand.

"Bring out the nigger woman!" the little man demanded.

Brude looked at the men. "If I ever seen a group hungry for blood, this one is," he thought. "It is as if some satanic force has gained control of them." Aloud he said, "The order of the court will be carried out. I will also see to it that nobody takes the law into their own hands, even if I have to shoot some of you. Now, just quiet down and control yourselves." Unhurriedly, Brude withdrew into the office, shutting the door behind him.

"Jus' as I said earlier!" a man yelled triumphantly, "Dey done played a trick on us. Done took the nigger away!"

"Let's get the mayor," the little man yelled, "force him to go in the jail, an' let's go in behind him."

"Yeh! Yeh!" the pack cried, and as one man, it turned and headed down Main Street towards the mayor's office. Suddenly the men at the front of the pack stopped dead in their tracks. From the direction of the courthouse a tall man dressed in black, a black top hat on his head, a black valise in his left hand, was approaching. He walked slowly, deliberately, and solemnly down the center of the road.

"The hengman! The hengman!" Tyson announced.

The words like an echo passed from lip to lip. The sight of the man approaching in measured steps infused awe. There was something about him that resembled the messenger of death. His appearance had diverted the interest of the pack from the mayor. Here was the hangman indeed. He would not be walking in the direction of the gallows were there not someone to hang.

As the man approached the tightly knit pack, he continued his pace and direction as if no one stood before him. A path through the men opened as he walked. Those nearest to him drew back as if fearful to touch him. It was the little man, quiet and faceless, who now possessed with self-confidence and a sense of fortitude swelling through his being boldly addressed the stranger. "Is you the hengman?" he demanded.

"I am an execution engineer," the man responded unsmiling and without turning to face the questioner. The little man following persisted.

"Oh! That there nigger woman you is goin' to heng, she is a terrible one! She done—"

The stranger turned to the little man and raised his hand, signaling him to cease. Two heavy gold rings on his fingers sparkled in the morning sun. "I am not interested in such information—her race or her crime," he said. His hazel eyes seemed to pierce into the very soul of the little man.

The stranger turned and continued his measured steps toward the place of hanging.

"Well, I'll be damned!" the little man said, turning to his companions. "Ain't never seen the likes o' him befo'. He's as ugly as a mud fence."

The stranger turned and entered the sheriff's office. The pack waited outside. Minutes later, he emerged and turned in the direction of the gallows and the hanging place. The pack followed behind, leaving a respectable distance between themselves and the stranger. The stranger reached the platform and climbed on the deck. The pack pressed in on all sides.

⌒ ⌒ ⌒

When Parson Jones and his followers returned from the farewell service for Samandra on Thursday night, they went directly to the church. It had already been announced that there would be an all-night prayer service. The "prayer and supplication" was to continue all through the night until nine the following morning, the time when the hanging was to take place. Parson Jones had sent a call throughout the county to black folks and white Christians to pray for Samandra.

By the time Parson Jones and his group returned from Mudville, there were already a sizable number of people in and outside the church. Many of the people had fasted all day in response to the call for "prayer an' fastin'. All night long, the singing, the praying, the weeping and waiting continued before their God. Many who had not attended church in years were there, some who usually attended only funerals and weddings were there.

Brentwood, the white farmer for whom Jim Brown worked, came in at midnight with his wife and stayed to add his prayers until the hour of execution. Sister Ebenezer, just turned eighty years, was there. She had fasted all day except for a glass of milk and had walked with the group to Mudville and was now in her seat in the church. Some stood and gave "testimonies," some "caught the spirit" during the singing and the preaching.

Parson Jones himself, in a short sermon after midnight, had "caught the spirit" and had spoken in "tongues" for several minutes. The parson called upon his members to put their differences aside, to confess, to discard animosities, and "join in one voice before the Lawd." This they did. Some who had long held grievances against one another made up, confessed, and cried on each other's shoulders.

All night long they prayed. All night long they called upon God, agonizing before Him. Now the first light of day had broken, but still they prayed and louder they called. "If it be Thy will, save her, oh Lawd."

Her heart pounding with fear and anxiety as time ticked away, Mabel had prayed and wept all night. Her hair seemed to have grown grayer over the past two weeks by the deep agony she had been made to suffer. The old clock on the church wall struck eight. The church fell to silence and listened. Each stroke seemed louder, ominous, doleful, like funeral bells. "One more hour," she thought. "If God is gonna make a miracle, it's got to be soon."

Fear and terror had gripped her heart, smothering what simple faith she had had during the night. Here was a woman whose entire life had been one of pain and struggle. She had lost her man to another woman, she had lost two of her own children to death. God, it seemed, had sent her Billy and Samandra. She had lost her boy Joshua, murdered before her eyes, and now Samandra? Only one more year and the children would have gone to school. Just when it had begun to appear that the storm would pass away, a tornado had struck her life.

Now, one hour before the time of hanging, Mabel and fellow believers and friends were still in church praying and hoping. Parson Jones was once more in the midst of a prayer.

"Lawd, you know," he was saying, "that there ain't nothing mo' we can do but call on you. Save the life of that poor chile, we plead. You know she ain't done nothin' wrong. The sheriff hisself said to me las' night, he says, 'I know that woman ain't guilty but my hands is tied.' Lawd, yours ain't tied an' dat's why we is callin' on you dis mawnin'. The sheriff told me, Lawd," he continued "that if that chile Samandra was a white woman, she never woulda been condemned to die, an' even if she was guilty—which she ain't—as a white woman dey never woulda hanged her. Lawd, You know she's innocent, an' You the only 'just and true' we is prayin' to."

Mabel Wright jumped to her feet. She rushed out the door of the church to where her horse and wagon stood.

"Sister Mabel, what is happenin'? Where is you goin'?" Deacon Johnson asked. She neither heard nor answered him. She climbed on the wagon, tugged on the rein and headed the horse at a galloping pace along the road leading to her place on the banks of the Yazoo. When she reached her home, the horse was frothing at the mouth. She jumped from the wagon and hurried inside. The horse walked below the tree and proceeded to drink from the trough.

Inside, Mabel frantically searched through the bottom drawer of her bedroom closet. In it was an old wooden box; from within she withdrew what appeared to be a framed picture. Sticking it in her bosom, she dashed back into the yard, climbed on the wagon, and uncharacteristically lashing away at the horse, headed in the direction of the town of Mudville.

The "execution engineer" went about his preparation for the hanging methodically, completely oblivious to the growing crowd around him. Others were joining by the moment. They pressed around the platform, observing his every move. Carefully he checked the rope mechanism. He went through the process of pulling the lever and observing its performance.

The hangman took a small jar from the black case he carried. Taking some of its contents with a finger, he carefully daubed it over the rope around the noose and up through the knot. All of this the people observed with keen interest.

About fifteen minutes before nine, the mayor of Mudville arrived, accompanied by a number of men. They stood silently beyond the circle of the crowd. On the periphery stood deputies armed and watching. There were now seven deputies in all, four having been employed for temporary duty the night before.

Earlier, the people had been loud and rambunctious. Now as the time of hanging approached, the voices became subdued, tense with expectation—like the calm before a storm.

When the hangman stiffened his body as if called to attention by some superior power and set his face in the direction of the sheriff's office, the entire mass of people turned their heads towards Main Street where stood the sheriff's office and the jail.

From the front door of the sheriff's office had stepped Sheriff Brude. Beside him walked a woman. She was dressed in a white silk gown. Her hands were unshackled, and at both sides a few feet behind, walked deputies armed with rifles. They walked in silence, unhurriedly. The woman's head was upright, her hair rested softly on her shoulders. A look of serenity was on her face. She seemed even more beautiful than during the trial.

The silence lasted only moments. As the sheriff with the prisoner approached, a mass murmur rose from the all white crowd. Then a drunk man yelled, "hang de nigger!" Another voice and another. Soon the voices of the people rose in a crescendo, each in his own way declaring some obsession. "Dey have the gall to dress her in white?" said the little man, wildly shaking his fist in the air. "Seems t'me she should be dressed in black for who she is an' what she done."

Some were laughing scurrilously, while others stared unbelieving at the serenity of the woman about to be hanged.

"Jus' look at her," Tyson said to the men around him as the woman escorted by Brude approached. "Look how quiet she is walkin' to her death! Jus' as if it don't bother her none! She ain't crying, she ain't beggin' . . . jus' like that nigger we wupped by the Yazoo. She's a dangerous nigger!"

"Send the nigger to glory," a voice advised.

"She ain't goin' to no glory," another cried. "She is headin' fer Lucifer."

"Fess up, nigger!" the little man said, "fess up an' tell us who was the others that kilt po' Deputy Bole."

As they reached the crowd, other deputies joined the procession. Using their rifles as shields, they moved to clear a path to the hanging place, but it was unnecessary. The crowd itself opened a path through its body, and as the procession entered, closed behind it like an amoeba. Now they reached the platform. Brude went up first, followed by Samandra. Two deputies behind stood at the foot of the steps. The few women in the crowd were behaving just like their men folk. Some had brought children, now held high on their shoulders to observe the spectacle.

Samandra stood there. She looked at the faces of people around her, jostling with each other to get closer to the stand.

Calmly and alone, with an element of gentleness, the hangman went about his task. Taking a piece of purple silken cord from his case, he gently tied Samandra's hands behind her back. "Is it too tight?" he inquired. Samandra shook her head.

Brude turned his back to the gallows, facing the crowds. He did not wish to witness the end. The mayor, who had followed the procession towards the platform, had stood farther away, but the pressure of the crowd pushed him ever forward. Now he stood right before the step. Almost unknowingly, he climbed onto the last step. There was a look of surprise on his visage as he viewed the sea of hostile faces, heard their primeval screams, and saw the thirst in their eyes. A lot of these people were members of his community. Some he knew well, but now in a fit of frenzy they were oblivious of his presence. Never in his life had he seen such behavior from people he knew. "Lawd, have mercy," the mayor whispered, "have mercy on us."

Here was a classic example of a human aggregate out of itself, controlled by forces so entrenched that neither the observed nor the observer fully understood their dimensions. Here was a creature, conceived in the womb of the politics of the county—the fear, hate, hostility, sparsely mingled with religious fervor and buttressed by primeval tribal bonds. There was a madness of desire. It mattered not—the element of guilt. Here was a black woman, a nigger—a symbol of all that their leaders had warned them was a threat to their existence. The hanging would be symbolic destruction of the "enemy."

Having tied her hands, the hangman once more turned to his valise. From it, he took a black facemask which he usually used to cover

- 379 -

the head of the condemned. As he unfolded the mask, he approached Samandra. She spoke. It was the first time since leaving the cell.

"Please do not cover my face," she pleaded. "I want to be able to see when I die." The man had to place his ear close to her lips to hear what was said. He dropped the mask back into the open case.

Holding her by the arm, he moved her to the square elevation below part of which stood the trap door—a box-like contraption standing some three feet above the platform.

The hangman placed the noose around the neck of the girl. Carefully he adjusted it so that the rope hung from the back of her neck. All was now complete save for the hanging. Moving his face close to the woman's ear, the hangman asked her a procedural question, one he had asked many before her.

"Lady, are you guilty of what they say you done?"

Samandra looked at her executioner. Even those fearsome eyes seemed to hold an element of tenderness. "Sir, I am innocent, but I am ready to die."

"Is there anything you want to say before you cross over to eternity?"

"No, sir."

The hangman paused for a moment. Over the hanging place, a hawk was surveying the scenc with wings outspread. It floated leisurely in wide circles, in a soft and almost cloudless sky.

"Would you like me to repeat with you the shepherd's psalm?"

Without answering, Samandra began: "The Lord is my Shepherd," the hangman joined in with her. "I shall not want..."

The din of maddened voices rising from the sea of angry faces was growing to a crescendo. "He maketh me to lie down in green pastures. He leadeth me beside the still waters—"

"What the hell is you waitin' fer?"

"He restoreth my soul,"

"Hang the nigger for Chris' sake." "Send her to Hell!"

"Yea, though I walk through the valley of the shadow of death—" tears were streaming down Samandra's face onto her white dress.

"Fer Chris' sake, hang the bitch!"

"I shall fear no evil for Thou art with me, Thy rod and Thy staff they comfort me." Samandra's eyes were beyond the crowd, looking towards the sky. Not a cloud was there. "Surely goodness and mercy shall follow me all the days of my life and I shall dwell in the house of the Lord forever."

The hangman pulled the lever.

To most of the crowd, this was a moment of bizarre ecstasy. Her dying body struggling, jerking fit-like in the spasm of death, as the rope clutched around the neck. Her eyes, yet tearstained, bulged, and froth gathered on both sides of her mouth. As the body struggled, an orgasmic sound rose from the crowd.

A few people close to the stage clutched at their throats, as if vicariously experiencing the hanging. There was garrulous laughter, shrieking, and howling. The pack was breaking, the deed having been committed.

⌃ ⌃ ⌃

Now the body, its life having departed, ceased to struggle. Now it swung back and forth on the rope, gently turning counterclockwise, then in the opposite direction. The noise from the crowd had by now largely subsided. Then from across the field, south of the hanging place, a black woman emerged from among the trees. She was running towards the crowd, waving her hands and screaming. The woman had started her journey on a horse-drawn wagon; the horse, weary from running, had stumbled to his knees, forcing the woman to come the rest of the way on foot.

The crowd turned around to observe the approaching black woman. As she neared the place of hanging, they could hear her pleading voice. "Please don't hang her. Please for Gawd sake don't kill my baby. I beg you in the name of Jesus, take her down, don't let her die." She pressed through the crowd which opened to let her pass. Reaching the platform, she struggled breathlessly up the steps.

Brude stood before her. "She's already dead, ma'am."

Mabel pushed past him towards her daughter. Folding her arms around her daughter's legs, she fell to her knees, embracing her feet and crying with a loud voice. Some in the crowd were laughing, others were silent.

"They murdered you, they murdered you, my poor baby," she was crying, swaying back and forth. "How could they do this to you?" she cried. "First they kill Joshua, now they kill you also."

She looked at the hostile crowd. An air of cold defiance swelled in her tired bloodshot eyes. "Murderers!" she yelled, "bloody murderers! The curse of Almighty Gawd on you all!"

A wave of restless agitation began to stir the crowd. "Hang her, too," someone said.

"Murderers!" she screamed hysterically as she clutched the body hanging from the rope. "You murdered my innocent chile, you kilt a white woman! That's what you done. An innocent white woman!"

A man in front of the crowd lunged towards the steps, but a deputy interposed between the crowd and the steps, forced him back. "Kill dat nigger," he yelled. "Hang the black bitch." The pack was beginning to frenzy again.

Sheriff Brude, sensing the growing danger from the maddened crowd, bent over Mabel in an effort to quiet her. He had heard her hysterical cry about "killing a white woman." As he bent over her, Mabel reached into her bosom, her heavy, heaving bosom; from it she drew a small, framed picture. She pushed the picture towards the face of the sheriff. It was the picture which Billy and his sister Samandra had brought with them twelve years earlier, the morning when Mabel, working in her garden, looked up and saw a horse-drawn wagon with two white children sleeping. She had kept it through the years, and now had fetched it with the desperate hope that it would save Samandra's life.

Brude looked at the picture and straightened up from his bending position. He drew the picture closer to his eyes. It showed a man and woman seated. The man had a baby on his lap. A little boy stood beside them. On the lower left side of the picture was written in partly faded letters, "Rebecca, Billy, Billy Junior, and Sandra McBride, Bolton, 1880."

Brude's eyes shifted from the picture to the body of the woman hanging above the platform. His hands began to tremble like the pillars of a building troubled by an earthquake. His mouth fell partly open. His face began to quiver, his eyes narrowed as one about to have an epileptic fit.

The crowd was dumbfounded by this new development. Its attention had now shifted from the dead body and the sobbing black woman to the sheriff. Tears were streaming down his ruddy face. "What had he seen?" They wondered as they looked on, now in strange silence.

In the ensuing stillness, they could hear the sobbing of the black woman. Then from the lips, from the contorted face and trembling lips of the sheriff, came a sound—a cry such as the crowd had never heard. It was one of agony, of sorrow, of anger, of grief. It came from a single mortal, from the depths of a human soul, but it was as the sound of an entire people, the excruciating agony of a nation, experiencing the pain of self-immolation. Now weeping uncontrollably, Brude embraced the body of his daughter. Now he could see it clearly—the visage of his wife, regenerated in his child.

"Oh my daughter, my lost child, what have I done? The child I have searched for all these years. I sought you all over the country, all through the west, and you were right here under my eyes. Oh, God! What have I done?"

Suddenly the mayor realized what had happened, as he heard the words the sheriff had spoken. "Dat's the sheriff's long lost daughter we just done hanged! We hanged an innocent white woman!" he said, shaking his head. The words went from lip to lip among the crowd. "It's a white woman we just done hanged. She was the sheriff's daughter that he been lookin' fer fer years. Lordy Gawd! Lordy Gawd! What we done done!"

The hangman, with the help of deputies, removed the rope from Samandra's neck, lowering the body to the platform. Mabel, enfolding the girl's head in her arms, mumbled between her tears: "She an' her brother came to me twelve years back. They was white, but they had no one to help them. I took them in and cared for them as my own, my own babies. I love them. They are my chillen."

A stranger sight had Mississippi never beheld. A black woman and a white sheriff kneeling over the body of a dead girl—weeping.

Yes, Sheriff. Yes, black woman. Weep! Weep to your heart's content. Let your tears flow. Give vent to the pain, the agony, the heart-rending sorrow that wrenches the depth of your soul. Remember as you weep, that you weep not just for yourself or for the innocent child lying in cruel, merciless death before you. No! You weep for the soul of a nation, for a people caught in the throes of self-immolation, rent by hate, ignorance, and greed, yet searching for light in the darkness.

⌃ ⌃ ⌃

The crowd began to disperse in silence, some heading for Mudville, some heading out along the county roads on which they had traveled hours before. In small groups they went. Others walked alone. All unbelieving of what they had seen and heard.

The place of hanging was now deserted save for the sheriff and the black woman, kneeling and weeping over the dead. From somewhere southwest across the Yazoo, rumblings of thunder rose and fell with pale streaks of lightning barely visible beyond the trees.

Some distance away, between the place of hanging and the entrance to Mudville, the deputies and the mayor stood in a small group, looking incredulously at the scene on the gallows platform. A few yards away from them, Hennessee was standing by himself. He had declined to be deputized that morning. He took a small bottle of whiskey from his pocket and placed it to his mouth, emptying its contents.

"I is a damn fool, dat's what I is," he was saying. "I don't know nothin', only a stupid drunk. 'It ain't you talkin',' dey always say, 'is the whiskey in your brain.' Ha! Was it whiskey talkin' when I said dat dat woman was a white woman? You tell me—none o' dem will listen. Dey know she was innocent. Damn dem all! I been most o' ma life among niggers. I was growed up by a nigger. After ma mammy—"

Made in the USA
Columbia, SC
14 April 2019